THE HUNT BEGINS

QUINN LOFTIS

PROLOGUE

"Life itself was never a sure thing. For as long as I can remember, I was never certain from one day to the next where I might end up or who I might end up with, or whether those people might do me harm. Until Nick. I didn't know how much I needed him until he was actually there. His steady presence became a beacon of light I could turn to any time the darkness of my past threatened to consume me. Now that light is gone. And I am surrounded by evil I thought only existed in the lower depths of hell. But now I know hell has moved topside. I know because I'm living in it." ~Kara

Kara picked up the closest thing to her—a vase, opulent and probably the most expensive thing she'd ever held in her hands. She screamed and hurled it across the room. It shattered when it hit the wall. The act wasn't nearly as satisfying as she'd hoped. The broken pieces fell and joined the graveyard of busted objects that had suffered the same fate.

Her feet began moving as they often did after one of her outbursts. Kara's body could never be still. In the past two weeks, she'd paced so much she was surprised there wasn't a path worn in the carpet. After her ritualistic marching, she walked over to the door and slammed her palm against it. "I will never choose you!" she screamed. Her hand beat the door repeatedly. Finally, her energy spent, she stopped pounding the door and leaned against it. "I'd rather burn in hell," Kara muttered.

Her body was strong, but Kara was exhausted. At first, she'd tried to refuse to eat anything. Then she realized how foolish that was. If she wanted to fight back, she couldn't let herself get weak. And the food they brought her made her hunger strike all the more difficult. It was some of the most delicious fare she'd ever seen or smelled. The meals looked as if they had been plucked from a seven-course spread served at a fancy country club and brought directly to her. On silver platters, she was presented daily with turkey, lamb, and every garnish and side dish imaginable. And the desserts ... those she did actually feel guilty about eating because, really, did she need chocolate cake to survive? No. But the temptation was too much. Everything tasted amazing, and she cursed the elf king the whole time she ate, which somewhat tempered the guilt she felt for giving in to the confectionary seductions. Kara recognized the meals for what they were—bribes from Ludcarab. Offerings, gifts of courtship. It was as if with every meal he was saying, "Look, Kara, these are things I can offer you if you would only quit being stubborn and choose me." She hadn't even begun to be stubborn. She'd eat the damn food, but she would never choose him.

Despite the meals that provided nourishment to her physical body, Kara felt as if she was fading away. She missed her mate—Nick. She'd heard from other pack members that being separated from your true mate could be painful. Whoever had explained that little tidbit should be given an award for understatement of the year. They should have said that being separated from your mate was like having a hot poker shoved into your heart, while at the same time feeling like your soul was being ripped from your body. So, even though she wanted to fight back, and despite the sustenance the food provided, Kara felt weak.

There were times when Kara couldn't breathe from the pain of being away from Nick. Her lungs would attempt to take in air, but she felt as if bricks sat on her chest, preventing even the smallest breath. Her lungs wouldn't expand, and she'd sit there gasping, praying she would pass out. Most times, she did. And that wasn't a bad thing.

Nick appeared when she was unconscious. Real or imagined, she wasn't sure, and she didn't care. The only thing that mattered was that he was there.

She closed her eyes, attempting to conjure his face in her mind's eye. Kara's brow drew low as she thought about him as hard as she could. But all she could picture was a vague image of a man dressed in biker clothes. His face was blurry, like she suddenly needed glasses to see him properly. "Nick," Kara whispered. She stumbled blindly across the room, her feet attempting to drag her toward a vision in her head, one that wasn't even clear. Why couldn't she see him? Why couldn't she remember what he looked like?

Panic rushed through her like a river. Somewhere within her, a dam broke, and a torrent of fear cascaded over her, filling Kara until she was sure she would drown.

Why can't I see him?

She clenched her fists and stomped around the room, her energy suddenly boosted by a surge of adrenaline coursing through her bloodstream.

When did I stop being able to see him?

That was probably the better question. Kara tried to remember the last time that she'd truly been able to picture all of her mate. His shaved head, his piercing gaze, the stubble on his face that was never unruly but always seemed to need just a bit of cleaning up. Even now, as she thought of those things, things she knew to be true of him, Kara could no longer picture them in her head. It was like smoke slipping through her hands.

She gasped. "That damn liquid!" Her teeth gnashed as she realized it had to be the potion she'd been drinking. What else could possibly cause her to lose the vivid memories of her mate?

Kara tried again to close her eyes and think of Nick's smell, his taste, the way his arms felt around her. But there were only hazy memories. Now, even her soul, which had always reached so strongly, so longingly, for her mate, seemed to question the authenticity of the memories. She looked around the beautiful room, taking in what was left of the things she hadn't thrown at the door. A roar forming low in Kara's gut rose until she opened her mouth and bellowed. She ran at the first thing her eyes landed on. The drapes, thick and no doubt worth a small fortune. They hung from the top of the wall, staring down at Kara as if lording their richness over her. She grabbed a fistful of fabric and yanked. One sharp pull was all it took. The curtain rod ripped from the wall and fell with a thud. Light streamed into the room. Kara didn't spare a glance for the acres of meticulously manicured grounds that rolled outward from Ludcarab's castle. She had no idea if she was in the elfin or human realm, and he never answered when she asked. It did appear, however, that she was imprisoned in a real-life castle. Under any other circumstances, her accommodations would have been cool as hell. Instead, they simply *were* hell ... without all the coolness.

Kara's heart squeezed tightly, and tears filled her eyes. "NICK!" Her chest rose and fell, forcing heavy air into her lungs. Kara turned her attention to the bed. She grabbed the comforter and, with a snap of her wrists, tore it away. The sheets were next, but she didn't merely pull them off. Instead, Kara grabbed one end of the sheets with her teeth and held the other with her hand. It shouldn't have been possible, but Kara gave a sharp yank of her head, and the fabric tore with a loud ripping sound. And she kept ripping until nothing but shreds remained. Kara forced herself to pause. Again, she tried to picture her male. Again, there was simply a figure with blurred features. The more she tried to remember, the more unfocused the image became.

"Why?" she breathed out, her voice hoarse from shouting. "Why?" Although she didn't expect an answer, it still pissed her off that there wasn't one. It was as if gasoline had been poured on the fire of her rage. The lamp beside the bed was her next victim. She slammed it into the wall. Then she picked up a large, pewter tray that sat on the bedside table and smashed it into the mirror that hung over the dresser. She continued to use the heavy tray to hit the ever-loving-shit out of every object that could be broken, dented, scratched, or damaged in any way. "AHHH!" She wailed and turned in a circle, flinging the tray away. The corner hit the wall and bounced off, clattering to the ground and leaving a large hole in the wall. All Kara could see was darkness within. She paused, momentarily stunned by the damage. She stared, open-mouthed, at the gaping hole. Just as quickly as the fight had come, it whooshed out of her. She realized her soul was like that wall. There was a gaping hole where Nick should be. In his stead, there was simply a black, empty void. The pulse of her heartbeat was loud in her ears as Kara continued to stare at the hole. Surely this was not going to be her life. After eighteen years of never being able to trust anyone, of never being able to count on anyone, she finally had true friends. And she had Nick, her soul mate. Her life was full, complete. Was it all really going to be ripped away? Was she now going to be left with an empty shell of life, a half-life of misery, where her only comfort came from the memories of her brief time spent with Nick? Could she live like this? "No," she whispered, shaking her head, unable to let that question linger for more than a couple seconds. "No, I can't think like that."

She knew without a doubt that Nick searched for her. He would scour the earth and every adjacent realm until he found her. But the smugness of the elf king made Kara afraid that her mate would never find her. Ludcarab always seemed to know something she didn't. It terrified Kara that she might lose hope, especially after only two weeks. She'd spent much more than two weeks in all manner of horrible situations. At least they had seemed horrible at the time. But Kara had only thought she'd been miserable. What was verbal, physical, or even sexual abuse compared to being separated from her true mate? During her orphanage and foster care days, she hadn't even known her soul was missing its other half. Now, that other half had been ripped out of her. How could she survive that?

Kara stumbled to the wall across the room from her cemetery of broken decorations and slid to the floor. She leaned her head back and closed her eyes. She willed sleep to take her. Kara remembered how Jewel had seen Dalton in her dreams when she'd been unconscious and how she'd said she hadn't wanted to wake up for fear that he wasn't real. Every time Kara woke up, she found herself feeling the same thing. But was Nick real? She found herself questioning his presence more and more, considering she couldn't remember what he looked like at times. Was Nick simply a figment of her imagination? Merely an unconscious hallucination she'd created in order to cope with her hopeless situation?

"No," she growled out loud. "He's real. He's mine. And he's looking for me." These were words she repeated to herself every day, sometimes a hundred times a day.

"Are you so sure about that?" Ludcarab's voice came from the doorway as he entered the room.

Kara didn't get up. But she did open her eyes so she could glare at the elf king. He glanced around the room, his lips turning up in a smirk as if the destruction was exactly what he had wanted her to do. He never got upset with her when he found the room destroyed. He simply had the broken things replaced with new, equally opulent items. His patience was maddening. Kara would have preferred it if he would get upset, if he would rail at her, even hit her if it revealed to her that Ludcarab understood how futile his plan was. She needed him to understand he was failing, that he would never have her, no matter how much luxury he surrounded her with. Yet his cool facade never wavered.

Once he'd taken in his fill of the space, he turned his gaze back on her. He was handsome, true, but he was evil.

"Are you sure about that as well? Are you quite sure I'm failing?"

What? Had she said that out loud?

"You often speak out loud when you're distressed," he said, as if reading her mind. "Your mind is simply coming to terms with reality. It's destroying the imaginary world you've built inside your head," he explained. It was the same crap he fed her daily. "I won't lie and say the way you ended up in my care wasn't less than savory, but I did rescue you, Kara. You were an orphan. Alone. And now I will take care of you, always."

But that wasn't true. Yes, she *had* been an orphan, but that was *before* Perizada and the others found her. She'd been rescued all right. But it was by Peri, not by him. And then she had a family. Anna, Heather, Stella, and Jewel were her sisters. Their mates were her pack, and Nick was her true mate. Ludcarab hadn't saved her from anything. He'd taken her away from the best things she'd ever had in her life.

"I will never believe the lies you're feeding me," she said, her voice flat despite the disgust she felt when she looked at him.

His smile widened. "That's the beautiful thing about the supernatural world. There are no true absolutes. There are exceptions to every rule. Anything, absolutely anything, is possible."

"Not this."

He shrugged. "I have nothing but time, love. I can be patient when I need to be, and you're worth waiting for." He pulled a vial from his pocket and strode over to her. Ludcarab squatted down in front of her. His masculine scent, unfortunately not unpleasant, flowed over her. It was becoming familiar. Yet another thing that pissed her off. "You know the drill." He held out the vial to her.

Kara didn't want to take it. Everything inside of her screamed at her to knock it from his hand and tell him to jump off the highest mountain. But, way down deep, in a tiny dark place, there was a miniscule amount of hope. She wondered. Maybe … just maybe … that potion, whatever it was, could make her fertile again. If it did, and Nick found her, then perhaps they would be able to have children together. Could there be anything on earth better than bearing Nick's child?

She was a fool. Kara knew it, and yet she watched as her hand reached out for the vial, uncorked it, and then held it to her lips. In one quick motion, she tilted her head back, letting the smooth liquid slide down her throat. There was a tingling sensation, as always, and then her stomach warmed. The warmth continued to move lower until she felt it deep in her gut. She hated that her mind always pictured something similar to what her own magic could do when knitting bone and marrow back together. It was as if she could actually see the potion healing whatever it was inside of her that prevented her from getting pregnant. The idea fed her delusion, and she hated herself for it.

After a minute of simply staring at her, the elf king took the vial and then rose. He turned and walked out of the room without another word just like he did every day. Only this time, he spoke over his shoulder, "Don't worry about the room, lovely Kara. I'll have it taken care of. Again."

"I'm sorry, Nick," she whispered into the empty room as tears ran down her cheeks. She felt like she was betraying him by drinking the potion Ludcarab offered. "I should be stronger." She slammed the back of her head against the wall. Then she gripped her hair with her hands. "I should be so much stronger than this."

"I've spent my life waiting to love you. My arms have waited to hold you. My lips have longed to taste you. And, finally, you were in my grasp ... but for a breath. Now, you're gone. I will search for you. I will search until I find you, until my body gives out, or until my life is snuffed out by my enemy." ~Nick

Nick knew he and his wolf needed sleep. Though he understood his body needed rest in order to function, resting felt like such a waste of time when his true mate was being held captive by the Order. He did not know what was happening to her. His mind kept conjuring the worst. But he really had no idea what the worst was. The reality could actually be even more horrible than whatever he could imagine.

He stared up at the night sky, the hot air from his lungs letting out puffs of smoke as Nick breathed into the frosty night air. From the grounds of the Colorado compound, the stars lit up the darkness like city lights. Nick had been offered a bed inside, just like everyone else, but being inside felt stifling. His wolf didn't want to be enclosed behind walls. It wanted to be out in the open, where he could see his enemy coming. *If* they were coming. Unfortunately, he'd seen neither hide nor hair of the Order's members. Nick would give anything for an all-out battle right now, if only to distract himself from thoughts of his missing mate.

He forced his heavy lids to stay open and let his mind think about the past two weeks, searching for any mistake they might have made or clue they might have missed. The first night of the hunt, they'd gone directly to the Order's destroyed compound. It was well after midnight, and all the human authorities, reporters, and curious on-lookers had mostly gone. Elle and Adam had masked their presence, so the straggler humans hadn't seen them. The horror of what Nick had seen was still fresh in his mind as he drifted back to that night.

"Bloody hell." Drayden stared down at the massive crater in the ground where several large warehouses had once stood.

"Peri did this?" The horror in Decebel's voice mirrored Nick's own feelings.

"Is there any chance Kara could have been here?" Nick asked through a constricted throat. He wasn't sure if he really wanted to know the answer. No one replied for several seconds.

Then Fane finally spoke up. "I don't think so. Your bond may not be complete, but the connection is still there, enough that you would know if she was gone."

Then why can't I feel her? Hear her? Sense her presence somehow? Nick wanted to snap at the alpha, but he knew that would bring him no closer to his Kara.

"Did you two know Peri was this powerful?" Dillon asked Elle and Adam as he pointed to the devastation.

Adam snorted, though no humor filled his eyes. "All those times she warned you about her power, and you ask us that?"

"With Peri, it was hard to know how much was smoke and mirrors," the Colorado alpha answered.

"Well, now you know," Elle replied softly.

"The wolves will phase." Fane's eyes glowed brightly with his wolf. "Smell everything within a ten-mile radius of this area. Thalion, Cyn, Elle, and Adam"—he looked at the elf prince and the three fae— "if you could check the actual site." He motioned down the hill. "You all can detect magic better than us. It's likely Peri's spell obliterated the magical signatures of anyone else who might have been present. Still, check and see if you can sense anyone or anything."

An hour later, Nick heard his alpha's howl—a signal call. He bolted toward Drayden who was three miles away. He reached the alpha within minutes. When Nick was within fifty feet, he smelled her. *His mate.*

"She was here," he said the moment he phased. Nick walked back and forth, trying to determine how much area Kara's scent covered. It led in one direction for a hundred yards or so, but then returned to the original spot where Drayden had first smelled her.

"Alston was here," Adam said as he and Elle appeared next to them. "I can feel his magic. He was definitely with her."

Nick snarled, cursed, and clenched his fists. It took everything in him, and a command from Drayden, to calm his wolf. The beast wanted to fly to their mate, it just didn't know which way to go.

"And he isn't the only thing I smell," Fane said. "There's an elf..."

"Ludcarab most likely," Adam said.

"...and a vampire," continued Fane.

"Cain." Decebel spat out the word.

The sound coming from Nick, though being formed by a man's mouth, wasn't anything human vocal cords could have produced. It sounded like a growl, whimper, and howl all rolled into one. Drayden gripped his shoulder, letting his claws sink in slightly. He looked directly into Nick's eyes. "We *will* find her."

Nick quieted somewhat, and his eyes went to the ground.

"Their scents mingle here, then disappear," Fane said.

"Well, Alston certainly wouldn't be traveling by foot," Elle scanned the ground around them. "He flashed them all somewhere, I'm sure."

"I wish we had a way of tracking them." Fane looked around and saw nothing but blank faces staring back at him. "Let's think about this logically. You've just kidnapped a healer. You've returned to find your compound completely and utterly destroyed. What is the first thing you would do?"

"Find a new hideout?" Decebel tilted his head.

"Exactly," Fane confirmed. "But where?"

"After seeing this"—Adam gestured to the ruined compound—"as far away as I could possibly get."

Everyone in the group nodded. "That doesn't exactly narrow it down," Decebel said.

"She could be anywhere." Nick fell to his knees and picked up a handful of dirt, putting it to his nose and inhaling the smell. He needed his mate's scent in his nostrils. The smell was more precious than the air that came in with it. But it was tainted. With his Kara's scent came the smell of others, those who'd stolen her. They'd touched her. They'd put their filthy hands on her. He would make them pay for that. He would get his mate back and destroy those who'd taken her. But where was she? Where? Where? Where?

Where indeed. Now, two weeks into the hunt, they were still no closer to finding his Kara. Nick whispered the word to himself over and over. *Where?*

"If you're going to sleep outside, you could at least do it in your fur." Drayden sat beside Nick, pulling him from his compulsive thoughts.

"I like the way the cold air feels on my skin." Nick didn't wear a jacket, only a short sleeve T-shirt, pants, and his boots. He didn't want to feel any comfort, not until he had his Kara back. Nick had no idea what sort of conditions his mate was living in. He couldn't bear the thought of being comfortable when she might be being mistreated or even— he shuddered to think about it—tortured.

"She's a healer, Nick," his alpha said, seeming to understand Nick's self-punishment. "She's valuable to them."

"That didn't stop them from hurting Sally," he bit out through clenched teeth. Fane had shared with him the things that had happened to the Romanian pack healer. At one particular point in the story, Nick had rushed outside to vomit. He couldn't fathom how Costin endured what his mate went through.

Drayden sighed and leaned back against a tree, his legs stretched out in front of him. "I wish Fane had waited to tell you Costin and Sally's story until after we found Kara."

"It wouldn't matter when or if he told me. The Order is not known for their mercy. They will use any means necessary to get Kara to cooperate with them."

"And that's what scares you, isn't it? She will never cooperate with them."

Nick finally let his eyes close, and her face immediately filled his mind. His strong, stubborn mate who'd seen too much in her short life. "I don't think she will. And I fear they will kill her when she doesn't. But I also fear she might cooperate, perhaps only to buy time until I can reach her. And that choice will break her."

"You should give her more credit than that," Drayden said, his voice admonishing. "She may be young, but she's a fighter."

"Fighters don't always survive." Nick's wolf snapped inside his mind at the harsh thought. His beast refused to even entertain the idea that they wouldn't get their mate back. But Nick understood what the wolf didn't. They weren't bonded. If it came down to it, and Kara was faced with the tough decision of sacrificing herself instead of hurting someone else, he knew what she would do. Perhaps it was better that they weren't yet bonded. If she died, he would live on. If Kara had his life to think about as well, then it might make her hesitate. And innocent people could die as a result.

They were quiet for a time, Nick thinking about everything he could and should have done differently to prevent his Kara from being taken. He knew it didn't do any good to think about the past. His wolf continually reminded him of that. But that didn't make it any easier to block out all the "could have" and "should have" thoughts assaulting his mind. He growled at himself. He was having a major-ass pity party, and it served no purpose.

Nick pushed himself up until he was sitting, his legs bent and his arms wrapped around his knees. "We've searched every lead," he said. They'd come across dozens of vampires that all knew nothing. For some reason, the bloodsuckers were out of control and seemed to be wandering around leaderless. After questioning them and finding out nothing concerning Kara's whereabouts, the wolves dispatched the vamps and burned the bodies. Nick wished he could resurrect them and kill them all over again, just to have an outlet for his frustration.

They'd returned to the Colorado pack to regroup. Since then, they'd taken to watching the news to see what the humans were making of the string of murders that were occurring along the western portion of the United States. Speculation of multiple serial killers, alien invasions, and, yes, even vampires had become the prevailing theories. Every eyewitness seemed to have seen something different, each more unbelievable than the last. The human law enforcement authorities were at a loss and stretched thin. Dillon mentioned that if things continued to deteriorate, the military might get involved. Nick had a feeling things could get messy fast if that happened. Backing a desperate animal into a corner never ends well. And both sides, the Order and the humans, appeared to be very desperate.

"It's frustrating, I know," Drayden said, "but we will find something. Someone, somewhere, knows something. We just have to find them." He reached over and patted Nick's shoulder. "We're hunters, Nick. It's what we do, and we do it well."

"Damn straight we do." Adam stepped out of the darkness.

"You're not a wolf," Sorin said dryly, stepping up beside him.

One by one, wolves padded out of the woods surrounding Nick. Fane, Decebel, Dillon, Ciro, Gustavo, and Crina, all in their fur.

"We're pack." Fane's voice filled his mind, the power of being the alpha of alphas. *"We fight as one, we rejoice as one, and we struggle as one. You're not alone."*

The wolves surrounded him, and each laid down so that some part of them was pressed up against him. *This* was what pack did. Nick had separated himself from them and hadn't even realized how badly he needed them.

"Those of us who aren't wolfy," Adam said, "aren't into cuddle piles."

Nick snorted. "You're missing out."

"I've experienced it once. That was enough until my next major life crisis," the fae responded.

Elle appeared out of nowhere. "We're still pack. Our way of contributing is to offer a different kind of protection than your wolf brothers and sisters. Cyn, Adam, and I have put a ward around this area. It will alert us if another supernatural being comes within a five-mile radius."

Drayden bowed his head to the two fae. "Thank you."

"Thalion said to tell you all to get some rest," Elle said. "He and his warriors will keep watch."

"Elle and I will be sleeping on this cold, hard ground, for obvious reasons." Adam huffed and stared at his mate in her wolf form. There was a teasing glint in his eyes that Nick was jealous of. He wanted Kara there with him so he could tease her. He wished he could hear her smart retort.

Crina's wolf bared her teeth at Adam. She closed her eyes and laid her head down as if dismissing her mate. Adam simply grinned.

"He's such a diva." Elle sat and leaned her back against a tree.

"Let's get some sleep," Drayden said and then phased to his wolf.

Nick looked around at the pile of wolves and felt a tiny

semblance of peace. He phased and let his beast take over as he pressed in tightly to the warmth surrounding him. For now, he'd let his wolf have control so his human emotions could take a break. *"We will find her,"* his wolf promised. They would, Nick agreed. He couldn't live with any other outcome.

CHAPTER

TWO

"I knew there was a reason I never wanted close friends. Not only do they take up too much time, energy, and emotion, it also sucks big draheim balls when they suddenly up and die." ~Myanin

"**W**ho the hell does she think she is?" Myanin stomped back and forth across the floor of the training room within the warlock mountain. The Romanian pack had delivered the news to Queen Lilly that the Order compound had been reduced to ash. The announcement should have been good news. But not for Myanin. Not when she knew her friend was trapped inside when the buildings were obliterated. And the djinn knew of only one way to handle loss—to fight. She'd beaten the crap out of anyone willing to spar with her. Even without her power, she had no problem putting the warlock warriors on their asses. "I mean, did she think I let her become my friend because I *wanted* to worry about her?" Myanin let her hand fly at her current opponent, catching the female warlock in the solar plexus, knocking her back several feet. "Where the hell am I supposed to get cotton candy now? Did she even consider that before she went and let herself get blown up?"

"Uhh," Lilly began, but it was clear she didn't know how to respond. Myanin's mind raced as fast as her fists and feet. And her mouth followed suit.

"We bonded, dammit." Myanin dropped her body, sweeping out a leg. The warlock female she faced hit the ground on her backside with a hard thud. "I don't go around bonding with just any rando that happens to walk by." Myanin flung her hands in the air. "There is only a certain kind of rando that I will even consider as worthy of becoming my friend. And I haven't had a friend in a *very* long time because there are some seriously weird-ass supernaturals out there but very few that are the right kind of weird."

"You don't say?" The warlock female climbed to her feet. Myanin took a step toward her, but the woman held up her hand. "I'm done."

Gerick stepped into the sparring circle and held up his own hands, which were attached to punching pads. Myanin took the invitation, happily letting out her anger and frustration on them. Her mate didn't even budge as she punched and kicked the pads with enough force to drop a water buffalo. Sweat dripped down her forehead and into her eyes, blurring her vision, but the djinn just kept going.

"She should have called." Myanin grunted with another punch. "If she'd told us what was happening, we could have helped. What the hell was she thinking?"

"She didn't know what was coming, love." Gerick shifted so Myanin had to move with him in order to continue to hit her targets.

She narrowed her eyes. "Tenia knew how twisted and insane Alston is. I should have suspected something when that bastard said he wanted to see her. I should have gone back with her." Myanin's punches increased in speed, and she felt her knuckles split beneath the protective tape wrappings. With every punch, she growled in frustration. "Did she even consider what *I* wanted?" It was a completely irrational question, but that didn't keep Myanin from asking it.

"I'm going to go out on a limb here and guess"—Lilly stood off to the side, watching the djinn's tirade—"that perhaps she had no idea she was about to die? And, therefore, it didn't even cross her mind to call and tell you of her imminent demise."

Myanin whipped around and pointed her finger at the warlock queen. "She's *not* dead."

"Myanin." Gerick sounded stern and gentle all at once. "Lilly is not the enemy."

"I know that," she growled. She closed her eyes and then looked back at the queen. "I apologize, Lilly. I shouldn't take my frustrations out on you."

"But you're right," Lilly said. "We don't know for certain that she is dead. I will be more considerate with my words."

Myanin's eyes focused on the floor. She knew there was no way in hell Tenia could have survived the cold fire of a high fae. No one could. But her mind refused to accept the fact that Tenia was gone. *She isn't. She just can't be, dammit!* The djinn appeared to deflate like a balloon. "But how could she have survived?" Myanin almost whispered. "How?"

Lilly sighed, drawing Myanin's attention. The djinn folded her arms in front of her and turned to look at the warlock queen. "Is it possible? Do you think she could have somehow lived through it?" Myanin asked. "Because I'm a hell of a lot older than you, and I've never heard of anyone surviving cold fire."

Lilly frowned, and then her eyes widened. "Thadrick."

"Dillon," Myanin shot back.

Lilly rolled her eyes.

"What?" Myanin asked. "I thought we were just shouting out past unrequited loves." She glanced at Gerick. "You got one you want to add?" She paused and then shook her head. "Never mind. You better not say anyone's name lest I decide to hunt her down and act like a jealous girlfriend. I've never wanted to be that girl. But I've done a lot of things lately I thought I'd never do. Becoming a clingy, psycho girlfriend might be next on the list."

Lilly coughed, and Myanin narrowed her eyes at the warlock queen's hand, which was trying to cover a smile.

"*Again*," Myanin amended. "I never want to be that girl *again*." She waved her hand at Lilly. "Now, go on. Why did you mention Thadrick?"

"He's the history keeper," Lilly said, her excitement returning. "I'm sure he probably has a record of all prior uses of cold fire stored away in that supernatural, cavernous brain. Wouldn't he be able to tell us if anyone has ever survived?"

Myanin considered patting the female on the head to ease the crushing blow she was about to deliver. "You forget, Queen, that Thadrick's history keeping is a tad jacked up because of yours truly." If there was ever a time in her life when Myanin wished she could go back and make different choices, it was right then. Because of Myanin's choices, she had completely messed up Thadrick's mind. She didn't know if it would ever return to normal, but she was sure of one thing: he wouldn't be able to tell them about cold fire.

"Are all the historical records in his head messed up?" Lilly asked. "Or just the stuff since you had your little tantrum with it?"

Myanin might have laughed if her soul didn't feel like it was withering away inside of her. "Little tantrum" was a kind way to describe the ridiculous stunt she'd pulled.

"Perhaps," Gerick spoke up, "instead of speculating, we should simply call the djinn."

Myanin met his eyes and tried to see if she could detect any anger there. They'd not known each other long enough for her to be able to discern his expressions with any accuracy, but that didn't stop her from trying to read something into every wrinkle on his face. Regardless of all the kind things he'd said to her, she still had moments of insecurity. Myanin wasn't sure she'd ever truly believe herself deserving of love after what she'd done.

Lilly nodded. "I think that's a good idea."

"Wait. What?" Myanin sputtered, realizing they were both serious. She didn't have feelings for Thadrick, not anymore. And yes, the Great Luna had shown a massive amount of grace in how she'd dealt with Myanin's transgressions. But that didn't mean she wanted to talk to her prior flame, especially while she was in such a vulnerable place. Her emotions were volatile, to put it mildly. If he wasn't able to help them, there was a high probability she might stab him out of simple frustration.

"Everything will be okay with Thadrick," Gerick said as if he could see into her mind. She'd found that he tended to do that a lot. Even though she had difficulty reading him, Gerick seemed to know what she was thinking without her even saying a single word. To say it made Myanin unsettled was an understatement. In her mind, it was the equivalent of being naked with nothing, not even a conveniently placed houseplant, to hide behind. Maybe it was an intimacy she should welcome. Perhaps she could find peace in someone who seemed to know her, and accept her, so completely. But after all the sins she'd committed, Myanin didn't know if she could ever open her heart to such exposure.

She took several deep breaths and reminded herself that she wasn't the person she'd once been. Despite the stain she still felt on her soul, the Great Luna had wiped the slate clean. She was a new person. Even though she must deal with the consequences of her actions, Myanin was no longer a slave to the sins she had committed. She could stand before anyone and know that, in truth, they were no better than her. Everyone had skeletons in their closets. Some were simply more visible than others.

"Fine," she conceded. Myanin shifted on her feet and slipped her hands into her pockets. "When are we doing this?" At the same time the words left her mouth, Lilly's phone rang.

The warlock queen pulled the phone from her back pocket and glanced at her screen. Her brow rose as she looked to Myanin and then Gerick.

"Speak of the devil," Lilly said as she answered the phone.

Myanin turned her back away from the queen. She walked toward the workout equipment, heading for the punching bag that had endured so much of her abuse the past couple of weeks. But before she could reach it, Gerick wrapped an arm around her waist and pulled her back to his chest.

She was tall, but he was even taller, which she loved. Myanin rarely felt feminine, but the few times he'd held her, he'd always managed to make her feel like a lady.

"Talk to me," he said gently, his warm breath ghosting across her ear. She forced herself not to shiver or to turn in his arms and bury her face in his chest the way she wanted to. What was the point? No amount of comfort he could offer would bring back her friend.

Myanin's shoulders fell as the air whooshed out of her. For the most part, as long as she was sparring with someone, she could keep her feelings locked away. But when everything was still, when there was nothing to distract her, then the lock would break and all the pain would come surging out. This was one of those moments, but she wasn't about to let that happen.

Myanin bit her lips so hard that she tasted the sharp metallic tang of blood.

"Hey," Gerick said more sharply. He released her waist and took her arms in his hands, turning her until she faced him. Then he reached up with one hand and raised her chin until she was forced to either stare at his neck or grow a pair and look into his eyes.

Myanin knew what he would see because she'd seen it many times in the mirror.

"There is nothing set in stone yet," he said, his hand still under her chin. "Until we know for sure that Tenia is no longer with us, then we will continue to have hope."

"What if that's a waste of time? A waste of my emotions?" Myanin asked, unable to quell her natural instinct to be a pessimist. Tenia would have pointed it out to her and probably made fun of her. Bloody hell, she missed that. "What if there is no point in any of this? Talking to Thadrick is probably a waste of time, too. What if I just need to accept Tenia's gone and move on?"

"Is that what you want to do?" He took a step back as if he understood that she needed some breathing room.

"Yes," she blurted out and then pinched the bridge of her nose. "No. Seven hells, Gerick, I don't know what I want. I mean, I want her to have kept her ass out of the damn compound. I want to have gotten Torion out sooner. We shouldn't have waited. We bargained her child's life, and for what?"

"There was no way for you to know that," he pointed out. "The leaders of the Order are ruthless and unpredictable."

"Apparently it wasn't them we needed to be worried about," Myanin said. She could hear the bitterness in her voice. "We should have paid more attention to a certain unhinged high fae with a vigilante issue."

She could hear the soft murmur of Lilly's voice behind them, though without her supernatural abilities, she couldn't make out anything being said.

"Perizada is old. She's endured much, and I think that even the most powerful supernaturals have their breaking point," Gerick offered. "I've known her a long time, and I don't think she would have made such a decision lightly."

"Myanin?" Lilly's voice interrupted their conversation. She turned to find the queen holding out the phone to her.

Myanin stared at the device for a moment, unsure if she really wanted to touch it. Lilly kind of shook it at her and raised her brow as if to say "take the damn thing," or maybe that's simply what Myanin would have said in her shoes.

Finally, she reached out and took the phone, looked at it

in her hand, and then put it to her ear.

"Hello?" Her voice cracked, and she wanted to kick her own ass for it.

"Myanin." Thadrick's deep voice filled the line. "I am very sorry for what you have been going through." Myanin had known the male djinn for a very long time, and she could tell he was sincere. Even with his weird sense of humor, entitled attitude, and, at times, downright asshole tendencies, Thadrick cared deeply.

"Do you know anything?" she asked, getting straight to the point. Idle chitchat would serve no purpose. Myanin had things she needed to get done. Namely finding her hopefully-not-dead BFF and then beating the ever-loving crap out of her, because nothing says I love you like a beating from your BFF.

"I wish I could give you something," he said, sounding much too defeated for her liking. "Things are still so chaotic. I do remember a high fae using the cold fire a very long time ago, but there was nothing left standing, much like the Order compound. There's just not a lot we know about the cold fire."

Myanin tapped her foot as she considered his words. "You may not know for sure. Even though you've held the memories of things that have passed, that doesn't mean you possess all of the secrets, right?"

"True," he said, the word sounding more like a question.

"But the high fae council knows everything about the fae. And weren't they super pissed about those of their people who had died in the battle of the Keep?" Myanin's mind was taking off at a run with this new line of thought. Why hadn't she considered it before? Maybe because the fae have always kept to themselves. They've never concerned themselves with those outside of their own realm unless directed by the Great Luna. If there was ever a time for them to turn over a new leaf, it was now. "Okay, thank you, Thadrick," she said quickly. "I've got to go. Keep in touch and all that stuff." Pleasantries still weren't her strong suit.

"Myanin, maybe—" he began but she ended the call before she could hear whatever he had been going to say, no doubt a warning of some kind that she would ignore anyway.

"Let's go see the high fae." Myanin tossed Lilly back her phone. "They said they were going to join in this fight. It's time they held up their end of the deal."

Lilly glanced at Gerick. Myanin couldn't see his face, but she assumed her mate would support her. *Her mate?* The thought almost came naturally to her now, but if she hesitated and truly considered the implications of the word, then the whole concept would become unreal to her again. She shook her head. No time for that now. Gotta see some fae about a cold fire.

"They *are* on our side," Gerick said, raising his eyebrows. "I don't think there would be any harm in speaking with them. Though perhaps giving them some notice would be respectful."

Myanin held her hand out to Lilly. "Let me see your phone again."

"What happened to your phone?" A leery expression passed Lilly's face as she held out the phone to the djinn. Myanin plucked it from the queen's hand. "Who should I call in order to get in touch with the fae?"

Lilly arched a brow at her. "I could make the call."

"You could. But I need to do something. Who do I call?" Myanin stared at the phone, unable to look at the queen.

She'd been one of the warriors that stood at the veil of her people for centuries. It was a job that required patience. Apparently her patience ended when she'd lost her friend.

After several beats of silence, Lilly finally spoke. "Click on the contacts, then search for Wadim. He's the pack historian. If anyone will have that information it will be him."

Myanin did what Lilly told her, found his name, and clicked it. After three rings, Wadim answered.

"What's up, warlock queen?" he asked. Clearly, Lilly's contact information was programmed into his phone.

"Not the queen," Myanin said dryly. "This is Myanin. If that means nothing to you then know that I am an ally, and I will protect Lilly with my life. Now, I need to get in touch with the high fae."

"I've heard of you. More importantly than who you are is why do you have Lilly's phone?" Wadim asked, sounding a little more tense and alert than he had been when he'd first answered.

"She's telling the truth, Wadim," Lilly said loud enough that she would no doubt be heard through the phone. "I'm fine. She's here at my invitation."

Myanin's jaw clenched. She ignored Lilly's declaration as she answered, "Because I'm at her mountain, and we are trying to figure out what happened at the Order's compound."

"Well, that's no mystery. It's been incinerated, courtesy of the lovely Perizada." Wadim's voice was clipped, and he sounded pissed.

"Thank you for that enlightening revelation, wolf. But how about something like 'is there any possibility that anyone survived'?" She snapped before she could tell her mouth to stay shut.

"You do realize I'm a historian, and facts are sort of my thing, right?" Wadim asked dryly. "Cold fire isn't something anyone survives."

"And you do realize that you're a flawed person who doesn't always know everything despite what your beast ego wants you to believe, right?" she shot back.

"Myanin," Lilly said, her voice stern. "It's best not to be a jerk when asking for a favor."

Myanin closed her eyes and took a calming breath. Not the enemy, she reminded herself. "Sorry," she told Wadim. "I'm just a little tense."

"It's understandable." Wadim sighed. "I'm sorry I was—"

"An ass." Myanin heard a female voice through the phone.

"Yes, Z," Wadim said, his voice much gentler. "I'm sorry I was an ass. What was it you needed?"

"We need to talk to the high fae," Myanin repeated, though she tried to sound a little less demanding.

"I'll text you Disir and Nissa's numbers," he responded. "Can I inquire as to why you need to speak with them?"

"We want to learn more about the cold fire that took out the Order, or at least most of it," she amended. "We've heard about the healer that has gone missing, which means some of the leaders must still be alive and well."

"I've been researching it myself, and I can't find jack."

Myanin frowned. "Who is Jack, and what does he have to do with cold fire?"

She heard Lilly and Gerick chuckle. Dammit! Where was Tenia when she needed her to explain the human expressions? Oh, that's right, she was busy getting her fae butt set on blue fire.

"It just means I can't find any information," Wadim

explained. To his credit, he didn't laugh at her lack of understanding. "I'd been planning on contacting the fae myself, but things have been a little intense around here with Fane's mate injured, Lucian being caged, and sprites gone missing," he said. "I could go on, but then we'll have to get some alcohol to go with our pity party."

"The alpha's mate is hurt?" Myanin asked, her brow furrowed as she turned to face Lilly.

The warlock queen's eyes widened and then in a blink, she plucked the phone from the djinn's hand.

"What's wrong with Jacque?" Lilly asked, her voice brisk. "I told her to stay put."

Myanin watched as Lilly listened to whatever the historian said. She tried to decipher the queen's facial expressions, but Lilly was doing a great job at keeping her emotions closed down.

"I'll be there as soon as we're done speaking with the fae," Lilly said and then ended the call.

"Is she all right?" Gerick asked, his hand resting on his sword as if he could somehow slay whatever it was that had hurt his queen's offspring.

Lilly visibly swallowed hard and her jaw clenched. Myanin was impressed by her ability to not lose her cool even though whatever Wadim had told her must have been terrible.

Finally, she answered. "Jacque was hurt during the rogue challenges. There was a full-on attack against the mansion after Fane fought and defeated many of the individual attackers. One of the rogues"—she paused and took a shuddering breath—"pierced Jacque's heart with his claws. She's alive but injured. They took her to the sprite realm for healing, but..." She paused again and took another deep breath. "There aren't enough sprites to do the job.

Apparently some of the sprites they need to perform the magic have been captured by the Order."

Myanin forced herself to remain quiet. She wanted to throw out a few expletives, but that wouldn't help the situation. Nor did she mention that those same sprites could very well have been at the compound when it was reduced to ash. *Fricking, frick, frack, fruck!* Her hands fisted at her sides, itching for a blade. Someone needed to die. Someone needed to suffer. Someone needed to pay for all the pain the Order had caused. They might not have been responsible for Lilly's daughter getting hurt, but they were definitely responsible for the fact that she couldn't be helped.

For several minutes, the room was simply quiet. What could be said? Platitudes would not fix anything. Perhaps, like Myanin, Gerick and Lilly felt that a moment of silence was necessary to allow each of them to gather their emotions back up, shove them into a mental box labeled "drag back out when it's time to stab someone," and refocus on what they *could* do.

Lilly began tapping on her phone and then placed it to her ear. "Nissa," she said after a few seconds. "Could I have a moment of your time?"

Less than three heartbeats later, the high fae was standing in their midst.

"I can take you to your daughter," Nissa said immediately.

Lilly tucked her phone in her back pocket and nodded. "I would appreciate that. But before we go, can I ask you—"

"We," Myanin interrupted. "Can *we* ask you?"

Lilly raised a brow at her but then shrugged. "Okay, can *we* ask you some questions about the cold fire?"

Nissa pursed her lips, and her shoulders seemed to slump as the air deflated out of her. "We have been searching our own archives for anything concerning the cold fire," she said. "Honestly, there is little known about the spell other than it is only used as a last resort because of the destruction it causes. One thing does intrigue us about Peri's use of the cold fire, but I hesitate to mention it, lest it proves meaningless and ends up providing false hope."

"What?" Myanin said through clenched teeth, her tone making it clear Nissa wasn't getting out of there without voicing her thought.

Nissa turned her gaze to the djinn. "Well, no fae who has ever used the spell in the past has been bonded to a *Canis lupus.*"

"How does that change things?" Myanin asked.

The fae shrugged. "Who can say? The true mate bond is powerful. Even between wolves, it is mysterious in many ways. But between two separate species? The fae wolf pairs can attest that the mate bond has altered their magic in ways they don't understand. We have no idea how the bond can affect different aspects of their individual magic."

"Exception to every rule," Myanin murmured as she considered the high fae's words.

"Perhaps it would be better to continue this conversation with the other leaders," Lilly offered. "I'm assuming they're all at the sprite stronghold?"

Nissa nodded. "Most of them. Some have gone out on a hunt for the Canadian beta's mate."

Lilly turned to Gerick. "Put your second in charge of the mountain while we're gone. I won't ask you to be separated from Myanin right now."

Gerick nodded, pulled out his phone, and tapped out a text. "Done."

Nissa held out her arms, and each of them placed a hand on her. They flashed and a moment later reappeared in a room filled with chairs that created a barrier around a bed. Each chair was occupied by a different female. Their heads turned in unison and their eyes blinked.

"That's a bit creepy," Myanin said to the group.

There was a soft laugh from the bed, and Myanin saw Jacque with a grin, albeit a pained one, on her face.

"Being together for two weeks straight has turned them into a hive-mind collective," Jacque said. Though the dark circles under her eyes and pale skin made it apparent the alpha was anything but well, her voice was still strong.

Lilly walked over, and several girls stood and shifted their chairs out of the way so the queen could get to her daughter. "I didn't *see* this." She brushed Jacque's hair back from her face.

"You aren't omniscient, Mom," Jacque chastised. "This isn't your fault."

"Regardless, it doesn't make it any less frustrating that I have a gift that doesn't allow me to help." Lilly stood up straight, and Myanin watched as her demeanor went from that of a concerned mother to a pissed-off supernatural ruler. "We will figure out a way to fix this."

Jacque nodded with a confident smile. "We always do."

"So," a blonde girl with bright blue eyes said as she rubbed her hands together, "I see that you brought the murdering djinn with you. Does that mean we're going on a killing spree while the men are away?"

"Absolutely," Myanin said. In unison several other voices called out, "No!" Gerick's included.

"Damn," Myanin and the blonde female said together which made Myanin inwardly smirk. She was going to like this female. That irritated her because liking someone meant caring for them. She refused to care for anyone else.

"We have much to discuss," Lilly said. "Nissa, could you

please ask the sprite queen, and anyone else she feels might be useful, to join us?"

The high fae nodded and then flashed from the room.

Myanin glanced around and then back at Lilly. "Could we make some introductions so I can stop thinking of them as 'the blonde chick,' 'the lost-in-space-looking chick,' 'the greenish-hue chick,' and so forth?"

"Please tell me that you called this one"—the blonde chick pointed to a female who also had blonde hair—"the 'lost-in-space-looking chick.'"

"I would think that was obvious," Myanin said. "She looks about as with it as a drunk pixie."

The first blonde cackled.

Lost-in-space-girl didn't seem offended in the least. "I'm Heather. I'm blind, and I often allow myself to get lost in thought because otherwise my brain cells begin dying. Which, I should warn you, is a consequence of hanging out with the blonde chick for longer than a minute, tops."

Myanin waited to see if the blonde would react, but she simply waved Heather off. "Pull up a chair, CT. Let's get to know one another."

Myanin's head tilted as she asked, "CT?"

There was a combined groan from the entire room, including Lilly.

"Cutthroat," the blonde answered. "It's your road name."

"Ignore her," Jacque said. "She's been watching a motorcycle club drama on her phone and has decided we all need road names. Whatever the crap that is."

Myanin blew out a breath and then took the offered chair. "Well, at least it's not going to be boring while we figure out who to kill and when."

"That's my girl." The blonde grinned. "CT in the house.

At first, I didn't like you because, you know, the whole murdering an innocent chick and all. But now, I think you might be good people."

"Jen," Jacque said as she pinched the bridge of her nose. "Shut it."

"Yep," Myanin muttered. "Not boring."

CHAPTER

THREE

"I don't think people have any idea how difficult it is to take over the world. Not just one world, but multiple worlds, or realms, as they're more appropriately called. It's not like there's a takeover checklist full of items that can be marked off one by one.
Kill off my main enemies. Check.
Force other supernaturals to do your bidding. Check.
Pretend you will allow others to share your power.
Check, check, and double check.
If it was that easy I'd be sipping fae wine and resting my feet on the back of a human slave by now. Alas. Instead, I'm attempting to reorganize the disheveled remnants of the Order after the pesky high fae's little stunt, while also trying to make sure our enemy has not discovered just how badly a blow they've delivered us. Sometimes being an evil genius is very exhausting." ~Alston

"Is she pregnant yet?" Alston asked. The fae paced the throne room of Ludcarab's castle, staring at the stone floor. It wasn't the castle that Ludcarab had inhabited when he'd still been the king of the elves. Once he'd left the elf realm to join the headquarters of the Order, Ludcarab's son had gained control of the former elf king's seat of power. The castle he now used was also in the elf realm, but it was a long-forgotten fortress that his ancestors had lived in before the new one was built. Alston had suggested using it as their main headquarters now that the compound had been obliterated—curse that damn fae—but quickly discarded the idea because having so many different types of magic in the elf realm would draw attention. Instead, he was still attempting to find a suitable replacement while also trying to figure out if any of his other race leaders had been absent from the compound when it had gone down.

"That's a very personal question," the elf king answered. He poured himself a glass of wine and asked, "Would you like a schedule of when I attempt to mate with her?"

"Don't be ridiculous."

Ludcarab turned to face him, his eyes narrowed. "Then don't be disrespectful regarding my future queen."

Alston felt his ire rise. He paused to meet the elf king's stare. "Have you forgotten that she is a means to an end?"

"I have forgotten nothing," Ludcarab snapped. "But you need to remember we're playing the long game here. The more positive Kara's experience here, the weaker her bond with her mate—what little is left of it—will become. Tenia's magic will be more effective as well." He took a sip from his glass and then said, "Speaking of the fae female, have you heard from her?"

It was a question Alston had hoped the elf king would not ask. He had not seen or heard from Tenia since the last time she'd been in his office discussing her offspring's gift. She wasn't supposed to be at the compound after that meeting, so he'd been sure she hadn't been killed by Perizada's attack. But after radio silence from the fae, Alston was beginning to question his assumption. "I have not," he admitted.

"What about the djinn?" the elf king asked. The smirk on his face only served to infuriate Alston more.

"I have not heard from her either." A thought had been forming in the back of Alston's mind. One that he loathed to consider but could no longer ignore. What if the fae and djinn hadn't been as loyal to the Order as they had made out? He didn't want to believe the two females had taken him for a fool. But considering he hadn't heard from them and neither was supposed to have been at the compound at the time it was attacked, he was beginning to wonder if their loyalties actually lay elsewhere. *Where the hell are those damn women?*

"The djinn was supposed to be with the warlock queen," Ludcarab said, swirling the liquid around in his glass. "If she was truly loyal to the Order, one would think that she'd have been in contact by now. Especially since she'd been in enemy territory while this all took place."

Alston ground his teeth together. "I am well aware of what it looks like, but—"

"Really?" Ludcarab interrupted. "You're *well aware* that it is highly probable that two of our members—key members, mind you, who know quite a lot about our operations—are more than likely spies for our enemy? Because, if that's what you're well aware of, it seems to me like that should be where you are spending your energy, not here in my home worried about whether my future mate's menstrual cycle is late."

Alston opened his mouth to snap back at the elf king, but the pompous ass just kept going.

"Have you found us a new headquarters yet? Have you heard from Cain? What about the other council members? Do we know how many, if any, survived?"

Alston closed his eyes briefly and forced himself to calm down. Killing the elf king now would not be beneficial to regaining the upper hand against the Romanian pack and their allies. For now, he needed Ludcarab. One day though... One day he would take great pleasure in watching the life fade from the smug face of the elf king, and Alston would be the one to snuff it out.

"You worry about your task"—Alston finally spoke when he knew his voice would remain calm—"and I will worry about mine. I simply wanted to see how things were progressing."

Ludcarab chuckled. "It's so nice of you to check on me. I assure you that everything is under control."

Alston nodded. "Good. Every part of the plan is crucial, even yours." He waited for the elf to respond to the jab, but Ludcarab just gazed at him with a heavy expression. "I will be in touch as soon as I have everything worked out."

"This will only work if we stay united, Alston," Ludcarab said, his voice no longer sarcastic but serious as his intense gaze met the fae's. "We cannot allow our petty differences to get in the way, no matter how much we dislike one another."

"Agreed," Alston said and then flashed. There was no point staying any longer. Though he hated to admit it,

Ludcarab was right. Alston needed to get things done, and quickly. "First things first," he muttered as he reappeared in a remote mountain range in Wyoming. Alston had been doing research on a location and decided, instead of a city, it might be wise to "get off the grid," as the humans called it. He'd found that the Black Hills mountain range appealed to him, as it was very isolated. He'd also decided it would be better to utilize the mountains themselves as shelters instead of erecting human buildings. It would make it harder for them to be detected. His own magic would be magnified by the nature around him. With Peri gone, Alston should be able to create a spell that would hide them from anyone who got near them, supernatural and human alike.

He stood at the base of a large mountain and closed his eyes. Alston held out his hands and began to speak in his native language, pushing his power into the earth and toward the towering structure. He pictured in his mind what he wanted his magic to do, and when he heard the rocks groan and creak, he opened his eyes. His lips turned up in a small smile as the face of the mountain began to shift and move. "You thought you could snuff us out, Perizada," he said as he continued to shape the rock into the form of an entrance into the mountain. "All you succeeded in doing was removing yourself from my path. Burn me down, and I will rise from the ashes."

"I'M NOT LEAVING until you talk to me." Lucian didn't acknowledge Heather's words. She'd been visiting him every day for the past week, and it was becoming harder and harder to ignore her.

"I know you're beating yourself up over what

happened, Lucian," Heather continued. "It was an accident. You're just like every male in these packs. You would never purposely hurt a female. And I'm fine. No harm, no foul." Lucian was surprised Kale had even let her come. Lucian wouldn't want his mate near a male who'd attacked his female, and he was shocked that Kale hadn't physically restrained Heather to keep her away from his cell. But Lucian was learning the blind healer was stubborn. So, here she sat on the floor in a futile effort to get him to forgive himself. And her large Irish wolf stood behind her, silent, his eyes boring a hole through Lucian.

Kale snorted derisively.

Lucian heard a grunt and imagined that the little female had retaliated at her mate's interruption. Lucian didn't blame Kale. Her mate was right. Heather *wasn't* fine. She'd been attacked and injured by someone who should be one of her protectors. It was the job of all the males to keep the females safe, especially the healers because they didn't have the strength of a *Canis lupus* female. Though some of the healers were far from defenseless, as they had their own dark magic now that they could use to cause serious damage. Still, they shouldn't have to worry about being attacked by one of their own pack members. Lucian had done that. He'd attacked her, marred her with his claws, and he would never forgive himself for it.

"Well, if you won't talk, I will," she said. It was the same every day. She asked him to talk. He didn't respond. Then she proceeded to tell him all about what was happening on the floors above his cell. "The warlock queen is here with Myanin, the djinn who was originally loyal to the Order after she killed one of her elders. They're having a meeting with all the alphas and leaders of the other races."

Lucian heard her shift, but he kept his eyes closed.

"Lilly, Myanin, and Wadim are trying to discover more about the cold fire." Heather sighed. "Sometimes, I just don't understand how there can be all these ancient archives of knowledge that don't have the information we need." Exasperation laced her voice, and he heard a pebble hit the ground. She often picked up rocks and tossed them at the wall. Lucian was surprised she hadn't thrown any at him. He wished she would. He would welcome the sting caused by a flying rock.

"So much depends upon the survival of those at the compound," she said. "Though I don't see how anyone could have lived through that destruction." She paused for a moment. "I have heard all of the stories of those in the Romanian pack who have died and then been brought back to life. I think everyone up there is secretly hoping that will happen again.

"I know it's got to be painful to hear, but Peri is the key to all of this. I don't see how she could be dead and you still be sane."

Lucian bit his tongue to keep from growling. The blind healer had no idea what was going on inside of his head. She didn't know that half of the time he wasn't lucid. He was back in the Dark Forest, and he welcomed the delusion. He'd stay there forever if he could. But for some reason, he kept periodically returning to his right mind. Every time it happened, he wished there was a way he could end it all. What did he have left to live for? His mate was gone, and he couldn't trust himself not to lose control. His wolf was standing precariously on the edge of going feral. Perhaps he should release the rein he held on his beast and let the wolf do what it will. That would force one of the other males to put him down, and his misery would be over. But Lucian knew the responsibility would fall to Fane, and that stayed his hand. Lucian couldn't force his own nephew to have to kill his uncle, the brother of his father who he'd only recently lost. Lucian might be on the verge of going feral, but he wasn't so far gone that he would put his own nephew through something so cruel.

Lucian suddenly felt sprinkles of dirt hit him, and his wolf forced his eyes open. He knew they were glowing because his beast was too close to the surface.

"Dammit," Heather practically growled. She threw a second handful of dirt and rocks at him. "Are you even listening to me?"

"Heather," Kale said from behind his mate. He reached down and attempted to pull her up, but she slapped his hands away. Lucian watched as she crawled forward, her hands feeling carefully out in front of her. She tilted her head, and he realized she was listening. She continued along, periodically raising her hand to feel for the bars. When she finally reached them, she clasped both hands around them and leaned forward until her forehead was pressed against the metal.

Lucian's eyes rose to look at the angry male that stood over his mate. Kale looked ready to kill. Lucian's wolf perked up slightly and narrowed his eyes on the male. His beast didn't like the challenge that the Irish beta was throwing down. Though neither of them ever wanted to hurt a female, Lucian's wolf was dominant enough that he wouldn't be able to help but respond to a challenge issued by another male.

"I can feel the testosterone level rising in here," Heather said. "Which means, Lucian, you must actually be paying attention to our presence, finally. Kale, whatever you're doing, stop, please."

"Then back away from the cell," he told her.

"Not happening," she bit out. "He's not going to hurt me."

"Two weeks ago, I would have believed you." Kale's teeth snapped together as he continued to glare at Lucian.

"Ugh," the blind healer groaned. "At some point, you're going to have to let it go."

"No, I'm not," her mate said coolly. "I can hold onto it for as long as I like."

"Fine." She waved flippantly at him. "Be a bitter, fur butt who can't forgive. But remember there will come a day when you want someone's forgiveness because *you've* made a mistake in the heat of the moment. I want you to think about this moment when that day comes."

Kale's eyes dropped to look down at his mate who resolutely stared straight at Lucian, despite the fact that she couldn't see him. Her ability to hone in on where people were in a room was uncanny. Lucian felt his wolf's admiration for the healer. Some might think she was helpless because of her lack of sight, but she obviously did not see herself that way. Good for her.

"All right, now that I apparently have your attention"—she leaned her body closer to the bars—"just listen. You don't have to talk. Well, one day you will. I'm not one to give up so easily. But that's for another day. For now, just listen." She paused, perhaps to see if he would actually respond. He didn't. "Your mate's not dead, Lucian. I don't care what anyone says. She's not dead. If she was, you would have already gone feral and let Fane kill you. And yes, I'm intelligent enough to know that it would be your nephew who would be the one to deal with you. But the fact that you're able to keep yourself from losing it because you don't want your brother's son to have to kill you speaks volumes. And the loudest thing it says is that your mate bond, no matter what it feels like, is still intact." Her breathing had increased with every word she spoke. "Only the influence of your mate's light could keep you in that kind of control."

The passion and belief in her voice were so intense that Lucian wanted to believe her. He wanted to hope. But hope couldn't change reality. It didn't make something true that wasn't.

He stared at Heather a moment longer before closing his eyes again. The hope that had started to build inside of him made him want to retreat. He looked for the familiar path in his mind that would take him to the memories of his time in the Dark Forest, and then he was there. He knew it wasn't real, but he didn't care. It felt real. He could smell the musky earth, feel the despair that permeated the air, and feel the ground beneath his feet. When he'd been trapped there, it had been a massive prison, but now it was an escape.

He found a path that was worn from all the walking he'd done and began to follow it. He knew it didn't lead anywhere. Eventually, he would end up back at the place he started. That was one of the many enchantments of the forest, roaming in circles, walking and walking, and yet never getting anywhere. When he'd been here before, he'd been desperate to get out. Now, he wished he couldn't.

The ground was cold beneath his bare feet, and dead leaves crackled as he walked. He took a deep breath. A scent on the wind caused him to stumble. Then he froze and held his breath, afraid to take any more of the surrounding air into his nose. It was ... *her* scent. The smell filled him. But it wasn't possible. Peri wasn't here. Even if she was alive, why would Peri be in the Dark Forest? His head swung around as he searched through the trees. There was nothing, just dead trees, darkness, and emptiness. Slowly, he let out his breath and then hesitantly took another one. The scent was gone, as he knew it would be. It had only been a ghost memory of his former mate. Part of him mourned the fact that this time when he sniffed there was only the smell of the surrounding forest. But the other part was relieved. He didn't want Peri's scent in his nostrils. The smell would only drive him over the edge even faster.

"She's alive," his wolf said in his mind as he continued to search the woods around them.

"No."

"I know she's not lost to us."

"You can't possibly know that," Lucian responded. He didn't want to hear what his wolf had been trying to tell him since Heather had begun visiting him. He didn't want to think for even a moment that his mate, his female, was still present in this life. Because if he entertained that idea for even a second, and then found out it wasn't true, he would be destroyed all over again. Only this time, he didn't think he would be able to control what that devastation would do to him.

"We will wait," his wolf said. *"We waited for her here before, in this very forest, and she came to us. So, we will wait again."*

It amazed him that just the scent of their mate had calmed his wolf to a level that he was willing to simply stay put instead of actively seeking her out as he'd wanted to do before.

"I was wrong. Pursuing her would chase her away. We must let her return to us on her own. She must choose us," said the wolf.

Lucian refrained from pointing out that she'd already specifically *not* chosen them. There was no point in arguing with his beast. He was as stubborn as the human, and more discussion would only serve to frustrate him. Instead, Lucian found a large tree and sat down at the base. He leaned back and stretched his legs out in front of him. His hands rested in his lap, and his head laid back so that it was pressed against the trunk. Then Lucian closed his eyes, and for the first time since the mountaintop, he allowed himself to remember. He thought back to the beginning of their mating when she was so adamant that she wouldn't accept him as her other half.

"I have asked you politely to stay out of my head," Peri spoke into the dark room they shared.

Lucian chuckled, letting his voice whisper through her mind. "So telling me to get a damn life and leave you the hell alone is your version of polite?" he asked.

"I didn't throw anything at you, and I didn't stab you. So yes, that is my version of polite," she snapped.

"I don't know why you are fighting this, Perizada. You are my true mate. You have the other half of my soul, and I have yours."

"You can keep it. I've gotten along fine without it for all this time."

"I could help you with the nightmares," he murmured into her mind.

"I don't think my nightmares are afraid of the big bad wolf —sorry to disappoint."

"You underestimate the healing power of love. Love mends many things. It could mend the brokenness inside of you."

"Bloody hell! Did you get that from a Hallmark card?"

Lucian smiled to himself at the memory. She'd fought their bond valiantly, but she'd lost. The mate bond was not something that could be ignored so easily, not even by the great Perizada. There had been a few times that he'd honestly been afraid she would be successful and walk away from him, but ultimately, she'd given in. She'd realized the blessing of having someone to share your burdens with. Peri had decided that being alone, having the so-called freedom she vehemently argued for, wasn't all it was cracked up to be. He'd been patient with her. Lucian had given her space. He'd given her time to come to terms with the changes she was facing. He wondered now if he had ended up enabling her to believe her own lies. The Great Luna had even visited him to help him understand.

A soothing voice came from behind him. "You are acclimating well to this environment." He turned and knelt all in one motion, bowing his head to his Creator.

"Great Luna," he rumbled.

"But for all your acclimation, you hesitate at the door of your true mate. Why?"

Lucian didn't miss the reprimand in the Great Luna's voice and fought the urge to cringe at the picture she painted. He, a dominant male, and an Alpha in his own right, stood like a scared pup outside the door of his mate instead of claiming what was his.

"She doesn't fully understand the bond, and I won't push her before she is ready," he explained, and though it made sense to him, it sounded like an excuse as he said it out loud.

"Perhaps you aren't giving her enough credit. Peri is a strong female, which is why I picked her for you. She has shouldered many burdens and dealt with much evil in her time. I have a feeling she is plenty up to the challenge of an Alpha male werewolf. Stand, Lucian," she commanded gently.

Lucian rose from his position on the ground and looked at the Great Luna. His eyes met hers briefly but then dropped in humility. He decided to voice what he knew his Creator already knew. "What if she doesn't want me? What if she doesn't want the mate bond?"

He felt her hand on his shoulder and her warmth, love, and comfort from that simple touch.

"You aren't asking the right questions. What you should be asking is what if she does?" She tilted his chin up so that he had to look at her. "I know you were in the dark for a very long time and that has affected the wolf you are, but do not let it affect the man I created you to be. The struggles that you endure in your life can either chip away at the goodness inside of you, or they can cause you to grow stronger, fortifying your character. Don't let that time in the Dark Forest ruin the good things I have in store for you. Don't allow yourself to be robbed of joy because of fears that might never come to fruition. I made you, wolf. I have a purpose for you, but I cannot fulfill it. That is something only you can do. I gave you a true mate, and now you must claim her. Love her as she needs, be the servant male that she has never known, and watch the walls that she has built up around herself come crashing down only for you."

"It *has* come to fruition," Lucian said as the emptiness of the Dark Forest crept into his soul. He didn't blame the Great Luna for what happened. It wasn't the goddess's fault that Peri exercised her free will. He didn't want Peri's love if it was forced. He couldn't imagine anyone wanting a person to love them without choosing to.

He heard Heather's voice again, but Lucian pushed it away and allowed himself to drift deeper into his mind, letting more memories keep him from having to deal with his current reality.

FOUR

"There is something beautiful about the dark. I know it sounds crazy, but without darkness, there can be no light. There can be no golden glow to shine into the black void and reveal the things that have been hidden. Evil is not the only thing that darkness conceals. More often than not, it is the lovely things of the world that darkness seeks to hide. It is our job to bring the light into those places that need to be illuminated so that we can show the hope waiting to be seized." ~Jacque

"Is she going to die?" Lilly asked.

"Wow." Jen breathed out. "Just going straight to the depressing stuff, huh?"

Jacque watched as her mother, Lilly, ignored Jen's statement and stared directly at the sprite queen. Andora's expression didn't change in response to Lilly's question. Jacque felt the weight of her mom's fear on her chest. She could see the warlock queen holding her breath, waiting for the answer.

Jacque glanced around the room, her eyes taking in those who'd gathered to discuss the events that had taken place a couple of weeks prior. Jen had even managed to coax Sally and Costin from their room, no doubt somehow guilting their best friend into the action. Jacque didn't care how'd she'd gotten the couple to come. She was just glad to see them.

Only a few were missing. The males who'd gone on the hunt for Kara and some lower members of the Romanian pack. The Poland and Hungary pack alphas were also absent. They tended to keep to themselves, though Fane had been in touch with them during the mourning period. The alphas of the other packs had opted to leave their other wolves in their territories. They wanted to protect the humans that lived close to each of their packs. They suspected the Order would begin to attack humans in a bid to get the packs to engage them in all-out war. They'd even called in the Coldspring and Springfield pack alphas, even though they hadn't had any sign of the Order anywhere near their territories.

Cindy Morgan and her husband Chris were also present, and neither looked like they were coping very well. Cindy's eyes kept jumping to Sally, but she seemed at a loss as to how to help her daughter. Jacque hurt to see the woman looking so helpless. Chris looked even worse as he wrapped an arm around his wife as if that could somehow keep her from falling apart. All in all, it was a room filled with somber supernaturals who were unsure how to move forward in a battle that was unlike one they'd ever faced.

"If you're asking me to tell you if the seer sprites have seen anything concerning your daughter's life, you know I cannot, nor can Cindy," Andora said. Her voice was unwavering, revealing not even a hint of remorse over the fact that she couldn't offer the information that Lilly wanted. Jacque glanced at Sally's mom and saw defeat in her eyes. Jacque wondered if Cindy had seen anything and perhaps that was what weighed so heavily on her.

"Wait," Stella spoke up. "These seer sprites can see the future?"

"Hence the name: *seer* sprites," Jen said dryly.

"You better be happy I like you." Stella glanced at Jen. "Otherwise I'd have Jewel put a hex on you."

"Dude, I'm so jealous of your witchy powers." Jen sighed as she looked longingly at Jewel.

"I'm not asking you to break any rules, nor would I ask that of Cindy," Lilly said, once again ignoring the others in the room. "I'm asking you your opinion as one with healing powers."

"The only thing I can tell you is that I will do everything in my power to make sure Jacque pulls through." Andora's eyes softened briefly, though her voice was hard as steel.

Jacque's mom gave a sharp nod of her head, seeming to accept that it was the best answer she was going to get.

"Regardless of what I can and cannot reveal," Cindy said, "I haven't been able to see anything, even when I attempt it." She looked at Jacque, her lips turning up in a sad smile. "I wish I could."

Jacque shook her head. "Sometimes not knowing is better because our actions aren't dictated by something we think we can't change. Nothing is set in stone, remember? No matter what you or anyone else sees."

"Not to be insensitive in regards to the alpha female's predicament," Myanin said, "but can we discuss the cold fire explosion? And whether or not Peri could have survived it?"

"Heather is convinced that she did," Zara said. "So am I."

"Why?" Myanin narrowed her eyes on Wadim's mate.

The Romanian pack historian pulled his mate closer to him. Since Kara's abduction and the battle at the Romanian pack mansion, the males had gone from merely protective to overbearing and ridiculous.

"I've got a—" Wadim began but his words were cut off by a flash of light. And then the high fae in question suddenly stood in their midst. Jacque shot up in her bed, the shock of Peri's appearance giving her strength she hadn't had since before her attack. There was a collective gasp, and everyone seemed frozen as if they were afraid the slightest movement might make Peri disappear again.

The high fae opened her hand, and five fae stones floated into the air. "They go where they are needed most," Peri said. The fae's voice sounded strained to Jacque's ears as if the mere act of speaking was somehow an effort. "The power of the stones is a mystery. They heal, and they reveal. And so they've brought me here. I bid you listen and do not speak. Now is not the time for questions.

"The prodigal is returning, and a new son will join your ranks. Evil will think it has prevailed, but hope will be born from the supposed triumph." Her eyes roamed over the room, and Jacque saw what looked like a thunderstorm of emotions behind the fae's eyes. Finally they stopped on Jacque. "I am sorry." A thousand responses ran through Jacque's mind. *Where the hell have you been? Why the hell did you try and take down the Order without us? How could you do that to all those innocents?* But Jacque couldn't seem to force her lips to form any words.

Then Peri looked at Sally, and her eyes softened even more. "So, so sorry." And before anyone in the room could make a sound, the fae disappeared. The stones dropped to the floor with a clatter. At the same time, the door to the room flew open, crashing against the wall so hard the stone cracked where it hit.

Lucian looked around frantically, his chest rising and falling as he turned in a circle. "Where is she?" he snarled. "I felt her. Where the hell is my mate?"

Heather and Kale rushed into the room a few seconds later. The healer bent over, huffing and puffing, resting her hands on her knees. "I. Need. To..." She breathed out the words in between gasps. "Work out more."

"Where is my mate?" Lucian snarled again.

"I told you she was alive." Zara folded her arms across her chest.

Heather jerked to an upright position. Her unseeing eyes widened. "I knew it." She beat a fist in the air.

"She was here," Jacque spoke up, hoping to calm Lucian down. "But only for a few seconds. She dropped the fae stones and vanished before any of us could stop her."

Lucian looked at Nissa and Disir, the two high fae. "Can you trace her?"

"I can try." Disir walked over to the wolf. He held out his arm. And before anyone could stop them, they flashed from the room.

"How in the world did he get out of that cell?" Sally asked.

Heather sheepishly raised her hand. "I might have had something to do with it."

"How?" Andora asked.

"Well, you see..." Heather began. "People always under-estimate blind chicks. Supernaturals, in particular, I've noticed, seem to view me as weak. And for some reason, they even think my lack of sight also means I have a lack of intelligence."

Jewel huffed. "Get to the point, Helen."

"I stole the key to the cell from one of your guards," Heather said. "You really should remind them that those who are underestimated are often the biggest threat."

"Every day, I love her more." Jen grinned.

Jacque rolled her eyes at her best friend. The more devious a person, the more the blonde approved. Jen's mind was truly a scary place.

"Okay, the mystery of Peri's crazy mate's escape has been solved." Myanin stepped forward. "We have bigger things to figure out. Like the cryptic message Peri delivered." She knelt and stared at the fae stones. Jacque had forgotten they were there.

"Does anyone even remember what she said?" Cindy Morgan asked as Nissa walked over to where Myanin knelt. She gathered the stones and held them close, staring down at them while a deep V marred her brow.

Wadim raised his arm. He held a small pad of paper. "While the rest of you were staring with your mouths hanging open, I was doing my job."

"We'll give you a cookie later, history boy," Jen told him. "Please continue to dazzle us with your competence."

Myanin pinched the bridge of her nose. "How is it possible you all have managed to save the world *one* time, let alone on multiple occasions?"

Jacque understood the djinn's frustration. "Believe it or not, we pull it together when it counts."

Wadim cleared his throat and then began to read what he'd written as Peri was speaking. When he'd finished, the room was quiet. Now that Jacque was over the surprise of Peri's visit, the pain and exhaustion returned. She gave a stifled groan and leaned back in the bed.

"That's clear as mud," Cindy muttered.

"Let's start with what we know." Jacque motioned to the stones in Nissa's hands. "She said they go where they are needed most, which we already knew about the stones. She said they heal but also reveal. Throw out some ideas. Nissa"—Jacque's eyes rose to hers—"do you have any insight?"

"The fae stones have many powers," Nissa said. "More than likely, we don't know all they're capable of. What we do know is that they can amplify the power of other supernaturals, if the intentions of that power are used for good."

"She said they can heal," Zara said. "If you're saying they magnify power, then could they magnify all the gypsy chicks' powers?" She motioned toward Jacque. "Maybe that's the answer to healing our female alpha."

"Team history boy is up two cookies." Jen pointed to each of the healers. "Let's see if you gals can catch up by working your mojo and save my girl."

"Might I suggest adding the healer sprites as well?" Andora asked.

"There goes another cookie," Jen gave the queen a thumbs-up.

"She doesn't really have any cookies, does she?" Heather asked.

"No," Jacque and Sally answered at the same time Jen said, "You're down negative one cookie. Don't think I will have mercy on you just because your eyeballs are broken."

Kale growled, but Heather placed a hand on his chest and smiled. "If you did show me mercy because my eyes are broken, I'd kick your seeing ass."

Jen made a heart with her hands and fluttered her eyelashes. "My girl crush just got deeper."

"If you two are quite done, could we please work on saving my daughter?" Lilly asked, exasperation filling her voice.

Jacque placed a hand over her mother's hand where it rested on the bed next to her. She squeezed, hoping to reassure Lilly that she wasn't as weak as she looked.

"I'm feeling all sorts of emotions coming from you, Luna." Fane's voice filled her mind. Jacque was surprised it had taken him so long to contact her. She'd attempted to tamp down the bond, but she didn't have the strength it took to keep him out. *"Peri was there?"* He no doubt picked the image of the high fae from her memories. *"She's alive?"*

"Briefly and apparently so," Jacque answered. *"She was here long enough to show us she is alive and give us an obscure riddle. We're working through that right now."* She explained to him about the fae stones and what was about to happen. A moment later, he stood next to her with Adam at his side. From the corner of her eye, Jacque noticed several people startle and a few more cuss under their breath. She didn't think any of them would ever get used to people just popping in and out unannounced.

"Nissa," Fane said, his eyes on Jacque. "Is this going to work?"

"I don't know."

"That's pretty much the going answer for any question asked," Heather offered.

"But it's worth a try," Nissa said.

"What's the worst that could happen?" Anna asked.

"That's a question we *never* ask," Jen told her. "It's like poking a bear while it hibernates, thinking it won't wake up."

"Noted," Anna said.

One by one, the healers laid their hands on Jacque. The healer sprites had entered the room while Fane had been getting an answer, or non-answer as it were, and each laid a hand on the healers gathered around Jacque's bed, Cindy included. Nissa also walked over and placed her hand on Jacque's head.

"Wait," Nissa said quickly then flashed. A minute later, she returned with Rachel.

"Good call." Jen nodded.

Rachel joined the group as Sally quickly filled her in on what was taking place. Rachel pursed her lips and took and released a deep breath. "Let's do this."

Sally began speaking in the language that Jacque had heard many times when her friend had used her healing magic. One by one, the other healers joined in, and soon the room was filled with the sound of their chanting. Warmth flowed over Jacque's head and began to move down her body. It felt like warm liquid, though not water. This was something thicker. It flowed downward, filling her chest, which had been chilled to the bone, with a soothing warmth. Her stomach felt as if she'd drank hot chocolate, then her legs felt as if a warm blanket had been laid over her. All the way to the bottom of her feet, Jacque felt cocooned in the warmth. She started to relax for the first time in two weeks.

Jacque let out a contented sigh. She wanted to stay wrapped in the coziness, but just as she had the thought, the warmth began to increase in temperature. Slowly, steadily, she became hotter and hotter until the sensation was no longer pleasant. In a matter of several breaths, her body began to feel as if a fire had been lit inside her veins, and she was burning from the inside out. She tried to scream, but nothing would come out of her throat. Her body tensed, and then she felt her back arch.

"What the hell is happening?" Jacque heard Jen's voice bark.

"I have no idea," Nissa answered.

"Take your hands off of her," Lilly said, her voice frantic.

"I can't," Sally cried.

"I can't either," Stella said. The other healers made sounds of agreement.

"Luna!" Fane's voice reached out to her through their bond, but it sounded far away. Why was he so far away?

This is why they never asked what's the worst that could happen. Apparently, the worst that could happen was Jacque burning to ash internally.

"She's alive. She's alive. The words were a mantra in my mind as my wolf howled inside of me. She's alive, and come hell or high water, I will have her back at my side no matter what she thinks she wants. She *needs* me every bit as much as I need her." ~Lucian

"Where are we?" Lucian asked Disir as he glanced around the forest surrounding them. The beauty of their environment was a stark contrast to the Dark Forest where Lucian had been mentally sequestering himself. This one was full of life and light. He heard the sounds of birds chirping and wind rustling through the leaves of the trees. Light from the sun filtered down through the branches, illuminating the place where they stood.

The high fae stepped toward two large trees that stood several feet apart. About ten feet from the ground, leafy vines grew together, bridging the trees and forming an archway. "The veil to the draheim realm," Disir answered. He lifted his hand and held it up to the space between the two trees. The air rippled as if still water had been disturbed. "I can feel her power," Disir said, "but it's weak."

Lucian stepped closer to the veil, and for a brief second, he felt her. His wolf instinctively reached for her through the bond, but there was nothing attached to the end of it. The cord that had once attached them was cut and frayed at the end. It felt the same as earlier when he'd been in the sprite stronghold. He'd sensed her presence enough that he'd *known* she'd been there, but the feeling had only lasted long enough for him to make his way to the room where the group had been gathered. By the time he'd arrived, she was gone, along with her magic. "She's in the draheim realm?"

"Looks that way," Disir said.

"Why?" Lucian couldn't imagine a reason his mate might have traveled to the realm of the great beasts. If she'd been able to come to the sprite realm, then she wasn't the draheim's prisoner. They would have kept her from flashing. She must be hiding in the realm, and they hadn't been alerted to her presence. A second, more disturbing, thought occurred to Lucian. Perhaps the beasts knew of Peri's presence and were tolerating her for some reason. He fought back a shudder.

"It's not the first time the draheim realm has been used for a fugitive to hide," Disir pointed out. "Not only that, but at least two of the draheim worked with Volcan."

Lucian thought back to Volcan, the high fae turned traitor, and how he had hidden in this very realm to keep from being found by the Romanian pack and its allies. Peri wasn't a traitor. Why would she hide?

Lucian lifted his hand and pressed against the invisible

veil. He snarled and jumped back when his hand was stung with unfamiliar power. He glared at Disir. "Why didn't it zap *you*?"

The high fae appeared as baffled as Lucian felt. "It always surprises me when other supernaturals think that we high fae know the answer to every question."

"Gee, I wonder if that's because the high fae always act like the biggest know-it-alls on the planet. Hiding your-selves away in your realm as if you're too good to join the rest of us trying to deal with the evil of the world?" Lucian clenched his smarting hand and glanced down when he opened it. There was a dark, charred spot in the middle of his palm.

"We should have gotten involved sooner," Disir replied, surprising Lucian. "I can admit that it was wrong to expect the other supernaturals of the world to have to fight against enemies that, had they won, would have affected all of us."

Lucian supposed he should have said thank you for the man's admission, but his hand was burning, his mate was just out of his reach, and graciousness was not an emotion he was able to muster at the moment. "Can you get through?" He motioned to the veil.

Disir didn't answer. Instead, he pushed his hand against the space between the trees, but his hand didn't disappear through the veil. "Doesn't appear so."

Lucian cursed under his breath. He walked over to a tree and pressed his back against it, then slid down until he sat on the warm ground. The smell of the air filled his lungs, and Lucian was reminded again just how different this place was from the Dark Forest. The air in his former prison was not refreshing or cleansing. It seemed to fuel the dark-ness inside of him. Only hours ago, he had wanted to stay in that darkness forever. A split second could change everything. Instead of sitting in the Dark Forest hoping for his mate to return to him, he sat by the draheim veil and hoped for the same thing.

"You're just going to sit there?" Disir asked.

Lucian's wolf growled in his mind. "You got a better idea?"

Disir took a seat across from him, sighing and resting his head against the trunk of his own tree. "I feel like my answer should be yes, but honestly, the magic of the draheim is a mystery that few know the secret to. Getting into their realm is one of those mysteries."

Lucian ran through ideas in his mind, dismissing each one until something finally piqued his wolf's interest. "What about the djinn?" The race was even more elusive than the fae, though as of late they'd stepped out of their own realm and began to involve themselves in what was happening in the human world. And they were powerful.

Disir pulled his legs up until his feet rested on the ground and then draped his arms across them. His head tilted to the side as his eyes roamed around the forest. He seemed to be considering Lucian's suggestion. After several minutes, the fae shrugged. "No harm in asking I guess. If anyone could help, it would more than likely be them."

"You go," Lucian said. "I'm staying here. My wolf isn't going to let me leave this spot even if I wanted to. We're too close to her. Closer than we've been in a long time."

Disir nodded. Without a word, he flashed from the forest.

Lucian's eyes moved from where the high fae had just been and then stopped on the spot between the trees. To a human, the trees would simply appear as if the foliage of the forest had grown into a unique bow of trees and vines. They'd probably stand beneath it and take their picture—a selfie, Lucian had learned it was called—and be completely oblivious to the fact that the spot was a gateway to a world filled with dragons.

His gaze bore into the space as if he would be able to see into the other side if he stared hard enough. Of course, he wasn't able to. His jaw clenched, and Lucian tried to keep the tiny flame of hope burning inside of him. He thought it had been extinguished, but all it took was a second of feeling his mate's power, and the spark reignited.

"Why?" he asked through clenched teeth. He could feel emotion closing his throat and his eyes glazing over with moisture. "Why won't you come back to me? Why won't you choose me?"

~

"He looks really sad," Torion said.

Peri glanced down at the fae child and then back at Lucian who sat just on the other side of the veil to the draheim realm. She'd felt her mate the instant he'd arrived. It had been instinctual to go to him, but she'd stopped herself just in front of the veil, not crossing over into the human realm. The fae boy had been pulling on her robe at the same time she'd flashed, and so he'd traveled with her.

"Do you know him?"

Peri sighed. "Why do you ask so many questions, child?"

"Why do you refuse to call me by my name? I've told it to you like—"

"A hundred times." Peri wasn't exaggerating.

Torion huffed and stepped closer to the veil. "Do you know *his* name? And why can we see him but not hear him? Who was the other man? I mean, he's obviously a fae, but I don't know who he is. Do they work for the Order? Are they—"

"Do you want me to answer any of your questions, or do you plan to just keep going until I get so annoyed with you that I freeze your vocal cords?" Peri was only half-joking. Okay, so she wasn't joking at all. She would totally freeze the runt's vocal cords.

"You haven't answered any of my questions yet. So, I figured it's pointless to wait to see if you answer. Plus, if I keep going, you might get annoyed enough that you will finally answer one just to get me to shut up." He turned to look up at her, a mischievous grin on his small face.

"You remind me of another annoying boy I know," Peri told him and then looked back at Lucian. He sat motionless; his eyes locked onto the veil. She knew he couldn't see her, but it still felt as if he was looking straight at her, peering into her soul.

"Titus?" Torion asked.

Peri's eyes snapped back to him. "How do you know Titus?"

"The angel took me to see him," he answered as if the practice of the Great Luna whisking supernatural children around the world for playdates was a common occurrence. Then again, it did seem that the goddess held a special place in her heart for children.

"Of course she did," Peri muttered. She narrowed her eyes on Torion. "When did this happen?"

"While I was asleep. Before I woke up and saw you in the cave."

"Did the angel say anything to you?" she asked.

Torion nodded.

"You're not going to tell me what it was?"

He shook his head.

Peri sighed and pinched the bridge of her nose. "Why?"

"I think it was just for me and Titus to know." He looked proud of himself for keeping the secret.

"Why do you think that?" Peri was getting tired of playing twenty questions, although it was a welcome change for her to be the one doing the interrogating.

Torion rolled his eyes at her. "Because if she wanted you to know, she would have brought you with us."

It annoyed her when children made sense.

"Does it have anything to do with that necklace around your neck?" Peri asked, motioning to the pendent.

He shrugged. "Are we going to talk to him?" Torion pointed at Lucian.

"No," Peri said quickly.

"You look at him the way my mom looked at Skender." Torion's voice was soft as if the words were painful for him to admit.

"And how is that?" she asked, her eyes still on her mate.

"Like you love him."

Peri snorted, the sound full of derision. "What do you know about love, kid?"

"Not a lot. But I know that it seems like grown-ups have a very hard time talking about it. And then when that person they love is gone, they regret they didn't tell them. My mom told me all the time that she loved me."

"She never told Skender?"

"I'm not sure. I never heard it."

Peri wasn't about to tell the kid that the reason his mom probably hadn't told Skender was because she might have found out about his checkered past. Not that she was judging. Okay, she *was* totally judging. Apparently, it made her feel a teeny bit better about her own shit choices.

"But I think if they'd known what was going to happen

to them, they would have said it a lot more," Torion continued. "Now, all he can do is tell her and hope she hears him." His voice softened as his shoulders fell forward. "All I can do is hope that she hears me, too."

Peri closed her eyes. She didn't want to think about the last words she'd said to her mate. She didn't want to remember the cruelty in them. Unable to look at Lucian any longer, she took Torion's hand and flashed them back to the cliffside cave where they'd taken refuge in the draheim realm.

Torion immediately hurried over to his mother's side. Skender sat on the other side of Tenia, ever her sentinel, only leaving her if he had to. He reached across and placed a hand on Torion's head. "Where did you go?"

"To stare at a man Peri loves," Torion said. "But she won't tell him. She's afraid."

Skender glanced at Peri and a world of understanding filled his eyes. "Love is a scary thing, Torion."

The boy looked at Skender, his jaw set. "It's also rare. This kind of love." He pointed to his mom and then to Skender. "I may be young, but even I know that this isn't the kind of love you should fear. My mom told me when you love someone, you hold on tightly like she holds onto me."

Peri watched as Torion placed a small hand on her cheek and then pressed his forehead to hers. "I love you, Mom. I'm holding on tight, and so is Skender."

Peri looked at Skender and then the unconscious woman. There'd been no change in her condition since they'd been brought to the realm. Tenia remained still as stone, except for a slight rise and fall of her chest as she breathed. And Torion spoke the truth—he and Skender had been holding on tight.

Peri turned away from the emotional scene and walked to the mouth of the cave. She sat down, her feet dangling off the edge and her eyes roaming over the landscape. This had been their refuge since Peri had set part of the world on fire. She watched as several draheim flew in the clear blue sky. Some merely glided, while others dived toward a huge lake where she knew they liked to bathe and hunt for food. They seemed so carefree. No worries, no heartache, no regrets weighing them down. Peri couldn't remember a time in her long life that she felt that way. In fact, in all of her time alive, this was the worst she'd ever felt. Experiencing the great purge, the werewolf wars, Desdemona, Reyaz, her sister, Volcan... None of it compared to what she endured now. Perhaps obliterating the Order compound had been about more than just defeating their enemy.

As she sat there opening the mental box she'd shoved her emotions into, she couldn't deny the fact that there had been a sliver of peace that had taken root in her from knowing that her time on earth would be over. Over three thousand years of life. She'd watched the rise and fall of nations. The birth of new civilizations. Armies conquering others in the name of religion, greed, and overinflated egos. Peri had seen the earth endure the chaos of nature and all the awesome power the human Creator had given it. She had experienced some joy—moments of fleeting happiness that were gone in the blink of an eye. But the pain she'd experienced over the past months completely obliterated every ounce of happiness she'd ever felt.

A tear rolled down her cheek, and she didn't bother to wipe it away. She was tired of not allowing herself to grieve. It was time to give in to her desolation. Peri was so weary of being strong—if that's what she could call her recent actions. She felt as if she'd been holding her breath since she'd watched Alina's heart being ripped from her chest. "Shit." Peri gasped as the images that would never leave her mind played again like a movie, one she'd wished she'd never watched. Alina's determined stare, her set jaw, the sheer defiance written across her face as she met her attacker's gaze and held it. There'd been no fear, only resolve.

Peri kept trying to remember if she'd attempted to move the second she realized what happened or if she'd been frozen out of shock. If there had been any hesitation, had it been the seconds needed that could have saved the alpha female? It was a question she hadn't allowed herself to fully express for fear of the answer. But the truth was, Peri didn't know. There were times that the battle was a crisp, clear memory in her mind, and other times, it was a blur. She preferred the blur because seeing the faces of those she had lost twisted her stomach until she was sure she'd never be able to eat again. Food was ash in her mouth. Air was like poison to her lungs because she honestly was sick of breathing it. Water, so necessary to life, had become a curse. Three things designed to keep her on this earth, and she wanted no part of them.

Peri swallowed down the agony and forced herself to stop thinking about Alina. Instead, she was taken back to the moment when she'd contemplated attacking the Order compound. The minute she'd made the decision, peace had filled her. She snorted. "Right, peace. Just keep telling yourself that, Peri," she muttered. She needed to be honest with herself, but at the moment, she'd rather not. But perhaps it was time to not only be honest but to face reality as well. Peace was not the right word. How in the world could she find peace in killing innocents? Torion's face flashed through her thoughts as she remembered the minute he'd arrived while she'd been in the middle of destroying the compound with the cold fire. Her eyes had met those of the young boy, and along with him, she'd seen Titus, Thia, Slate, and Hope. Innocent children caught in the chaos of her vengeance. Though it had only been Torion present, she'd felt as if the other's lives were also in her hands.

She was damned if she did, but also equally as damned if she didn't. If she left the Order intact, they might get their hands on the children again. And if she destroyed them, as she had, she took innocent lives down with the guilty. But not Torion. He hadn't died. No thanks to her. By the grace of the Great Luna, the draheim Ludcarab captured had rescued them. The only supernatural beings impervious to cold fire—a fact she'd forgotten in the heat of the moment.

Peri remembered wrapping herself around Torion, hoping to minimize the pain he might feel from the cold fire. She'd begged the Great Luna to intervene, to keep Peri's own choice from taking the life of one so young. The answer had come with the sound of huge beating wings. Peri hadn't seen the draheim. She'd only felt his large talons wrap around her and Torion. Before the dragon could take off, she'd yelled at him and pointed in Tenia's direction. Peri had not known if the fae woman was alive, but she refused to leave her body to burn. The large beast had gently scooped up Tenia's body in his other talon and flown them away from the falling compound. Peri remembered looking down to find a sea of cold fire quenching its thirst with everything in its path. The sight of all the desolation her power caused still sickened her.

Without thinking about her sudden choice, Peri flashed. Maybe she needed to see what the final result had been, or maybe she wanted to punish herself.

A second later, she stood on blackened land of the

former Order compound, surrounded by craters and ashes. She turned in a slow circle, her eyes soaking in the emptiness around her. There was nothing left to indicate that a compound full of supernaturals had occupied the space around her. She took a deep breath, and the smell of her magic pushed her to her knees. "What did I do?" she gasped. She laid her hands on top of the ashes. She couldn't have stopped the tears even if she'd wanted to. They ran down her face, dropping onto the damaged ground. Peri let her hands glide reverently over the remains and wondered who had spent their last moments in this very spot. Did they die quickly, or had the agony ripped through every nerve, lasting until there were no buildings left standing? Was it someone the Order had blackmailed into service? Or was it a loyal Order member who deserved Peri's retribution? Did it matter? They'd been a living being. This hadn't been an attack by the enemy. She hadn't been caught up in the heat of battle, fighting for her life. "But I might have been one day," she said to her unspoken thoughts.

As she pushed her hands further into the earth, the ashes covered them until they could no longer be seen. If her heart hadn't been broken before, it was shattered now, seeing firsthand what she was capable of when she let her pain and anger rule. She'd abandoned reason. She'd abandoned her obedience to the Great Luna and taken matters into her own hands. Judge, jury, and executioner.

She wanted to say she was sorry, but her lips wouldn't move. She didn't know if it would be true. "What kind of person does that make me?" A sob tore through her as she leaned forward until her forehead pressed against the ashes. Her body shook as she completely released the final reins she'd held on her emotions. "AHHHH," Peri yelled into the ground until there was no air left in her lungs. Every muscle in her body grew rigid. She attempted to keep herself from splaying out on the ground and begging it to swallow her into the earth. Her hands fisted the remains of all that she'd destroyed. "I should have been with you," she said. "My ashes should be mingled with all of yours." But she'd survived. She felt her power growing inside of her, rising with her tumultuous emotions, and she knew she had to get out of there before she did even more damage, if that was possible. "I'm sorry," she whispered, gripping the remains tighter in her hands. "I'm so sorry." And she found as the words left her mouth, that she did indeed mean them.

Peri flashed again, but she didn't return to her spot on the ledge. Instead, she appeared on a high mountain back in the draheim across a valley from where Torion and his unconscious mother lay. She couldn't return to him. How could she sit mere feet from them when Peri was the cause of the woman's condition? Tenia's child clung to his mother every night, begging for her to wake up. That was Peri's fault. "Damn." She looked down at her hands which still clutched the ashes from the graveyard that had once been the Order compound. Her stomach rolled, and vomit rose up in her throat. Tenia could have been these ashes. She would have died much too soon because of Peri's need to destroy that which had destroyed her.

"Why did you let me live this long?" she asked the empty space around her, forcing her voice to remain soft. But what she really wanted to do was scream. "If you knew this was going to happen, why did you allow me to live?" Peri opened her hands and watched as the contents blew away out over the forest of the draheim realm until there was nothing left. "If you knew I was going to make this terrible choice, why did you allow air to continue to flow through my lungs?" Her questions were for the goddess who created her. The one who held life in her hands. She didn't know if the Great Luna would answer, but she asked anyway.

How on earth could one person go on living with all the pain, guilt, rage, and dread that was strangling her? It was too much.

Peri grabbed the neck of her robe and pulled, ripping the fabric away from her throat, hoping it would make breathing easier. But still, she gasped for air. She raked her nails across her neck and fell to the ground. Her legs seemed to be useless to her for the past few hours. Her knees struck the earth with a jarring pain. But the pain was a release.

"WHY!" she wailed and pounded her fists into the dirt. With every smack of the ground, her power radiated through the mountain, shaking the bedrock beneath her. The trees around Peri snapped like toothpicks, and birds squawked as they jumped from the falling trunks and limbs. Over and over, she slammed fist and magic, her voice rising to the heavens, carrying every ounce of misery she felt.

Exhaustion slowed her movements as she knelt, panting, her palms flat against the earth. The skin of her knuckles split, and blood dripped from them. The bright red liquid—a reminder that she still lived while many no longer did. All because of her. "How is it fair?" She asked the question out loud. Her voice was hoarse from her screams. "How many lives will I get to live? How many transgressions must I commit before you will cut me down?"

Peri pushed up from the ground until she rested on the heels of her feet. She could feel the breeze on her skin where she'd torn her robes. The air burned the scratches she'd left on her neck. And her knees ached from hitting the ground. She welcomed every bit of the physical pain. Physical pain was sufferable. The cut of a blade, the scorch from magic, or the claws of a beast were more acceptable than this. "Is this my punishment? Is death too merciful for all that I've done?" The space around her remained quiet. No answers came.

"What could you do from the grave?" A small voice spoke from behind her. Peri turned her head to see Torion standing a few feet away. His face was streaked with tears, his eyes red from crying. "How could you help if there's no life in you to do what you must?"

Peri pressed her lips together and turned away from the child, ducking her head until her chin touched her chest. She bit the inside of her cheek, not allowing the words she wanted to snap at the boy to come out. Damn his ability to flash. She didn't want to have a child question her, especially not if his questions made her probe too deeply into her own consciousness.

She heard his feet on the ground approach. "Who needs you in the next life more than we do here?"

"There's more than enough people to step in and take my place," Peri answered.

"That's not true." Torion sat down next to her, so close that Peri could feel the heat from his body. "Did the creator make another just like you? Skender has told me stories about you. All the incredible things you've done. What if you had not been there to do them?"

"Someone else would have." She shifted away from him.

"You don't know that." Torion shook his head. "Nobody stepped up to help my mom until Skender came. He says that he has done terrible things. But despite those terrible things, he's protected me and my mom. If he'd not been there, who would have done it?"

Peri didn't have an answer for him. Skender was Tenia's mate. There wasn't anything he wouldn't do for her, no matter his transgressions, past or present. So, no, someone else wouldn't have done what he has. "That's different," she said. "Skender is the other half of your mom's soul. He couldn't keep from helping her, or you for that matter."

"He wouldn't have been able to if he was dead."

Bloody hell, the kid wasn't pulling any punches. Peri's gut clenched at the boy's words. She thought back to the many times when she'd used her magic, or a blade, to fight evil. She thought about the lives she'd protected and been willing to sacrifice for. Would someone else have been willing to do those things? She shook her head. "I'm no one special, Torion. And for me to think so would be hubris."

He sighed. "Skender said you were stubborn."

Peri almost smiled at the weariness in the boy's voice, as if he were the adult and she an errant child who refused to obey.

"Do you honestly believe that you weren't created specifically to be you? The creator said she has a specific purpose for my life. Does that mean she doesn't have a specific purpose for you, too?" He turned so he was facing her and scooted forward until his small knees touched hers. "Do you think she created you and then said 'oops'? Because I'm pretty sure the creator of our races doesn't make 'oopses.'"

"That's not a word," Peri said dryly. She knew he made a good point, but she didn't want to allow his words to affect her.

"Yes, it is. Get a dictionary and look it up."

She glanced up at him and lifted a brow.

He shrugged. "What? My mom tells me that all the time."

"Are you done?" Peri knew what Torion's answer would be, but she was hoping he'd surprise her.

"No."

Nope. No surprise.

"I'm not leaving you while you're like this, Peri." Her hands rested on her legs, and Torion reached out and wrapped one of his smaller ones around hers.

She swallowed hard. "Like what?"

"Alone."

The word reverberated through her mind, deep into the marrow of her bones and straight to her soul. Alone. It's what she'd been for so long. After everything, she'd begun to believe that it was what was best for her.

"Sometimes, I want to be alone," Torion continued. He turned his body so he was once again sitting beside her. Peri looked at his face while he stared out over the destruction she'd caused by throwing her little tantrum. "Every once in a while it just feels good to be alone. But my mom says being *too* alone is never a good thing." He reached down and picked up a blade of grass and began to pull it apart. "She says that being too alone can fill the empty places inside with dark things."

Peri bit her lip, but it didn't stop her from asking. "What dark things?"

Torion kept staring at the area around them. "She said we fill them with doubt. Lies that we tell ourselves, lies that we've heard others say about us, and anger that we refuse to release."

"Does your mom always speak to you as if you're grown?" Peri was deflecting, but what else was she supposed to do? Pour her heart out to a six-year-old fae child?

Torion tossed the mutilated piece of grass to the ground. "She talks to me like I have a brain in my head. Just because I'm young doesn't mean I don't understand things."

Peri's lips turned up slightly. "You really do remind me of Titus."

"He knows things, too." Torion grinned.

"He knows too much." Peri snorted. "That's his uncle Gavril's fault. And his aunt Jen's."

"He told me about his aunt Jen. I don't think I want to meet her." He shivered as if the thought was enough to cause him discomfort.

"Nobody does, kid." She took a deep breath and slipped down to the ground so she could fold her legs in front of her. "You need to get back to the cave. Skender will be worried about you."

He titled his head and pursed his lips. "Is that your way of telling me to get lost?"

"Pretty much."

"Are you going to keep destroying the mountain?"

Peri glanced around. It wasn't the first time she'd leveled a forest. Probably wouldn't be the last. "I'll try to refrain. For now. But I refuse to make promises that I won't be able to keep." She could practically feel the disapproval rolling off of him as he stood and brushed off his pants.

"I suppose that will have to be enough for now. Please, come back." His voice cracked on the last word. She didn't look up at him. Her emotions were still not entirely under control, and Peri was afraid she might completely lose it if she met his gaze.

"I'm not going anywhere, not while your mom is

vulnerable, and not until I know what Skender's plan is." Peri was still trying to come to terms with the fact that Skender was Tenia's mate and that she couldn't kill him. At least not yet.

Torion placed his hand on her shoulder and gave it a pat, then he was gone. And she was alone again.

"Why do you insist on destroying our land?"

"Dammit," Peri growled. "What does a high fae have to do to get some peace and quiet in this place?" Peri glanced over at the female draheim who'd landed next to her. For a beast so large, the dragon had hardly made a sound.

"You can have peace and quiet when you stop causing chaos," Serapha replied.

If humans ever found out about supernatural beings, Peri had a feeling talking dragons might be the one race that their mortal minds simply wouldn't accept. "Your offspring should have left me in that compound to die, then I wouldn't be here to cause chaos."

Serapha shifted her massive form and settled onto her haunches. "Your actions freed him from the elf king's clutches. He was indebted to you, just as I am."

"I'm releasing you of your debt." Peri waved a hand at the beast. "You've provided sanctuary for me and my charges in your realm. That is enough."

The draheim was quiet for a few minutes. Peri could feel the dragon's gaze, which was nearly as hot as the fire it could breathe.

"What?" Peri finally snapped. "I've already had a fae child put me in my place. You might as well continue the theme."

"The Great Luna visited my son while he was held captive," Serapha said.

Peri's head snapped around to look at her. The

draheim's scales shimmered a pale, iridescent white in the afternoon sun. Her large eyes glowed a bright blue, nearly matching the sky above. "When?"

"The night before you arrived at the Order," she answered.

"And what did the Great Luna say?" Good grief, was she going to have to pull every bit of information out of Serapha's big snout?

"She told my son that the time had come for his purpose to be fulfilled. She said that his capture by Ludcarab allowed him to be where she needed him to be. The goddess wanted him at the Order compound so he could help you and the others he rescued."

Peri's mouth dropped open. She jumped to her feet and glared at the draheim, even though it wasn't Serapha she was angry with. "You're telling me your juvenile son had to be held captive by a mad man so I could live?"

Serapha's eyes softened, and she lowered her head so her eyes were level with Peri's. "No. I'm telling you your creator, my creator, and my son's creator, knew in eternity past that this day would come. That his life would serve a greater purpose than flying through the air and diving into our sea for fish. He saved a fae child. He saved a mom. He saved a mate. And, yes, he saved you. It is not the first time your life has been saved by one of mine, though your mind doesn't remember."

Shock radiated through Peri as the draheim's words penetrated the fog of bitterness. She'd been saved by a draheim? When? Peri wanted to stomp her foot, but she'd done enough damage to the draheim realm. She began to pace as Serapha's words rattled around in her head. How long ago had that been? And why didn't she remember something so monumental?

"There is evil in every realm, Perizada." Serapha said, completely moving past the fact that she'd just laid a doozy of a revelation on her. Maybe it was for the best that Peri just let the news marinate. Her mind could only take so much, and it was at its breaking point. She set the information aside and focused back on Serapha. "You've seen the evil of my kind. You've seen the evil of the likes of Ludcarab and those who have come before him. You have also seen those who have stood against them."

Peri had heard the words before, from a different voice, but with every bit the same conviction. "But why?" she gritted out through clenched teeth. "Why must anyone sacrifice? Why does the Great Luna allow evil? Why did something so horrible have to happen to your son for Tenia's son to live? What's the point of any of this if people we love are just going to keep sacrificing themselves while evil continues to roam the earth?" Three thousand years and Peri had never questioned the goddess. She'd followed faithfully. She'd obeyed even when she didn't understand. But now, she had doubts. She had fear.

"Have you ever considered that evil isn't a 'thing'? It's not a being like you and me. Instead, it is the absence of good. Evil is not roaming the earth. It is simply present where there is a lack of virtue, morality, and righteousness. And since we know our creator is all of those things, she is not the author of evil. She doesn't make evil. It is our choices that make evil exist. It is the gift of free will that allows us to have the world we do. And though that world contains evil, it holds many amazing and wonderful things as well." Serapha looked over the landscape. "Our choices, every day, big and small, help bring more good into our realms, where before there was an absence of it. That is your purpose. That is why sacrifices must happen."

Peri swallowed hard. The words rang true, and she knew the draheim was right. But under the weight of her heartache, she found it hard to have faith in what she knew to be true.

The large, white draheim shifted, causing the ground to tremble. She seemed to be settling in as she curled her front legs beneath her and lowered her body. The dragon didn't speak. She didn't answer any of Peri's questions.

"What are you doing?" Peri asked.

"I'm being still," Serapha answered. "Just as you need to be still. Come, sit." The beast motioned with her head for Peri to sit next to her.

Peri's hands fisted at her sides. "I don't want to be still. I want to understand. What did you mean that it wasn't the first time I'd been saved by one of yours?"

Serapha shook her head. "It is not time for that answer. For now, you will have to accept that it is not your decision when your life is over. For now, it is time to let go, just for a while, and be still."

Peri sighed. What else did she have to do? She walked over and sat down beside the huge draheim. Serapha leaned her big head down and nudged Peri with her snout, pulling her closer until the fae was pressed against her chest just in front of her front leg. The draheim's body heat warmed Peri immediately. Her stiff body relaxed, and Peri found herself leaning back until her head rested against Serapha as well.

"We're just going to sit here?"

Serapha's large head rested on the ground, and the breath that came out of her nose rustled the grass. "We're just going to sit here. Close your eyes, Perizada of the fae. Ask your questions in your mind. Humble yourself before your creator. Open your heart, bare your soul to your creator, though she already knows you inside and out. Bare your soul because you want to be in communion with the Great Luna. And then be ready and willing to receive those answers."

Peri had no fight left in her. She had no idea what she was supposed to do. So, she did as the draheim said and closed her eyes.

CHAPTER
SIX

"Evil comes in many forms. It masquerades as something beautiful, desirable, and even necessary. It makes me wonder: If evil can trick us, can goodness do the same? Can those things that look evil actually be good? Perhaps something sinister can be transformed into something of value, something helpful? Or is it as I've feared? Are we who've given ourselves over to evil forever forced to wear the scars from the corruption that has infected us? Can we ever be beautiful again?
~Skender

Tenia's lifeless hand was cold, though Skender could still hear his mate's heart beating. The sound was faint, but it meant life. Skender didn't dare stop touching her for longer than a few minutes for fear she would slip away, and he wouldn't be connected to her when it happened. And when it did happen, he knew he and Torion would be without her. He wished that they'd already performed the Blood Rites. Then he could make that trek with her. Skender shook his head. *No.* That's a selfish thought. If he was gone, Torion would be unprotected. He wouldn't leave the boy ... ever. Selfishness had caused him to make some very poor decisions in that past. Decisions he was going to have to live with. But those days were over. Skender didn't know how long he had left, but he would spend the time watching over Tenia for as long as he could. Then, if it was his destiny that she leave this life, Skender would watch over her son for as long as either of them drew breath.

"Will you tell me more of the story?" Torion sat down across from Skender on the other side of Tenia. Three days had passed since Peri had left them. Three days since Torion had returned with tears in his eyes because the boy did not know how to help the high fae. Torion wouldn't say why, but he was absolutely determined the fae had to stay alive.

Skender ran a finger across Tenia's forehead and down the bridge of her nose. He loved touching her. His wolf craved it. He wanted to wrap himself around her and never let her go. It was a liberty he didn't deserve, but he still ached for. Skender took a deep breath and steeled himself for the words that needed to be said, the story that Torion needed to hear. Skender could not bear to allow this child —the son he'd claimed as his own—to believe lies about him. Torion believed Skender was a hero. He'd told Skender he wanted to be a warrior just like him. The wolf quickly learned that there were few pains as great as having to tell your child you're not the unblemished paragon of virtue they've built you up to be. Painful was an understatement. Skewering himself with a hot poker in the heart would be more bearable than seeing the adoration fade from Torion's eyes. It had to be done, and the information needed to come from him.

But Skender wasn't yet ready to face his demons. Up until now, he'd been telling Torion the story as if the events had occurred to someone else. Skender was merely the narrator, rather than the hero ... or villain, to put it more accurately. He was working up toward the reveal that would forever change the way Torion looked at him.

"I will tell you more," Skender finally answered. "Where were we?"

"The boy's parents had just died, killed by rogue were-wolves," Torion reminded him.

Skender nodded. "That's right. The Order informed the boy that his parents had been attacked by rogue wolves, but that he wasn't safe with them. The boy needed the protection of a strong pack, a powerful alpha. But the alpha couldn't know that the boy's family had been a part of the Order or he might not accept the orphan into his pack. It had to be a secret."

"Because the Order was bad?" Torion asked, his lips drawn tight across his face and his hands clenched into little fists.

Skender let out a heavy sigh. "The boy's parents didn't think so, and the boy believed and trusted his parents. When he was told to keep his membership in the Order a secret at all costs, the boy took the words to heart and never spoke of that part of his life again." Skender's mind rewound to that day—the day he'd been dropped off a couple of miles from the Romanian pack mansion. He'd been terrified that he would somehow give himself away, and they would kill him. The Order had told him that the Romanian pack alpha was ruthless, showing no mercy to his enemies. But they'd also said he was powerful, perhaps the most powerful of all alphas, and would keep Skender safe from the rogues. The child didn't understand why his safety was so important to the Order. Who was he? Just a werewolf orphan. But he'd been told by the leaders of the Order that they would have a task for him one day. When that day came, he would need to be ready. His task would be very important, and when the time came, he would know what that task was. If he'd known then what he knew now, he would have run far, far away from the Order *and* the Romanian pack. He would have refused to bring such evil anywhere near Vasile's pack—the pack that had accepted, welcomed, and loved him.

"What happened when the boy got to the Romanian pack? Did they know he was from the Order? Did they kill him?"

Skender smirked. "The boy was terrified. He was left on the steps of a giant mansion, all alone, and too afraid even to cry out. But he was soon surprised by the alpha pair. Instead of attacking the child, they welcomed him with open arms. The boy had been expecting the alpha to be the monster that the Order had described, but that wasn't the case at all."

To this day, Skender remembered the way Alina had looked at him with such compassion.

After several long minutes of standing, his knees quaking almost to the point of buckling, Skender gathered the courage to knock on the wooden door to the large stone house. His entire body began to tremble, and he fought the urge to turn and bolt for the woods. But the forest surrounding him was dark. He had no idea how he had gotten there or where he would go. He couldn't have made it back to find the Order if he wanted to. So, with tears in his eyes, he waited. The entire house, even the surrounding forest, seemed to be holding its breath, and Skender along with them. What would happen? If this alpha was as fierce as Skender had been told, he might just transform into a wolf and gobble him up on sight. Or they might carry him out into the forest and leave him. The night was cold, and he knew he wouldn't be able to survive on his own.

The seconds Skender waited seemed to go on forever. Finally, just when Skender was about to knock again, or perhaps cry out, one of the huge, oaken double doors creaked open. Standing in the doorway was the most beautiful woman he'd ever seen. Instantly, Skender understood that this woman's beauty wasn't merely skin deep. Somehow, he sensed that she was a mother, perhaps not to a child of her own, but to an entire pack. To any who might be helpless, who might need the love and tender compassion that only a mother could provide. At that time, however, he wouldn't have been able to put any of that into words. He only knew he felt peace—a peace he hadn't felt since his parents had been killed.

The woman was looking over him as she'd obviously been expecting the visitor to be an adult. Then she lowered her head, and her gaze settled on Skender. Her face softened, and her eyes filled with a compassion he'd seen in his own mother's eyes many times when she'd looked at him.

"My name is Alina. What has happened to you child?" Skender knew he looked rough, but as he couldn't really see himself without a mirror, he had no idea how rough. His clothes were filthy, and his face and hands were covered in dirt. The leader of the Order had told Skender that he had to look the part of a child in need, and so they'd made sure to dress him up as if he'd been through a terrible ordeal and had wandered on his own.

"My parents were killed by rogues," Skender told her. "I've been looking for a pack. I didn't know what else to do." His voice shook, and that part wasn't an act. Despite the peace and

compassion he felt coming from this woman, he was still terri-fied. The stories told by the Order of the great and terrible Vasile still stuck in his mind. But more than that, he missed his family. He missed all that was familiar to him. Above all, he wanted his mother.

A large man walked up to stand next to Alina. His face was stern, his gaze assessing as he stared down at Skender. For a moment, he said nothing. The longer they looked at one another in silence, the more Skender's previous fears intensified. His shaking legs, which had stilled under the compassionate gaze of Alina, began to tremble again. It felt like forever until the man finally spoke.

"I am Vasile, alpha of the Romanian pack, and you have met my mate." He motioned to Alina and wrapped an arm around her, settling his hand on her waist. "Come in, young one, and get out of the cold." Vasile and his mate stepped aside at the same time as if they were one body sharing the same mind. His parents had moved that way. True mates. A bond that was unlike anything else between supernaturals. His parents had often told him the story of true mates and how one day he would meet his own.

Skender lifted his leg to take a step and paused awkwardly before finally stepping inside. His fate was now in their hands. There was no longer a chance to run. No possibility of escape. For better or worse, his life from here on out was tied to the Romanians.

"What were they like?" Torion asked, his voice pulling Skender from the decades-old memory. The fae boy leaned closer, his eyes wide, waiting for Skender to continue.

"They were kind," Skender answered. "For a long time, the boy didn't trust their kindness. He thought it was an act, a facade. It's hard to know what to believe when someone you trust has told you something about someone else you *don't* know. The child's natural inclination was to believe the Order because they were the only thing he knew." Skender paused and ran his fingers through Tenia's hair and took a deep breath. Her scent washed over him, and his wolf rumbled in contentment. "Over time, the boy realized the kindness of the alpha pair was genuine. Vasile and Alina loved their pack. They looked out for the well-being of those under their care, including the boy. It wasn't something he'd ever seen in the Order. As the boy grew up, his memories of the Order began to fade. Eventually, all he knew was that he was a part of the Romanian pack, and he always had been and always would be."

Torion frowned. "How could he just lose his memories like that? What about the memory of his parents? Did he lose those as well?"

It was a question Skender had asked himself many times. Why did he forget, and why had he suddenly remembered? It was the reason he'd left the Romanian pack and told Vasile he needed to look for his mate. That part had been true. He'd felt the pull of his mate. But the rest of the memories he didn't share with his alpha. Partly because he was ashamed that he'd ever been a part of the Order. But another part of him felt a strong need to keep it a secret. There was a part of him that he hadn't known existed that was loyal to the Order because his parents had been loyal.

"I don't know," Skender admitted.

"It sounds like a spell of some kind," Torion said absently. He reached for his mother's hand and held it tightly in his own. "It would have had to have been cast by someone powerful. A fae or a djinn." Torion paused. "Or a witch. Were there still witches around back then?"

Skender's eyes snapped to Torion's face, but the boy was looking at Tenia. Torion didn't see the surprise that

Skender knew must have been in his eyes. He'd never considered that he might have had magic used on him. But what else would explain the memory loss and then the sudden return of them a century or more later? His mind jumped back to a time he'd rather not remember, but one that was forever burned into his mind. Alston had captured the healer, Sally, and performed a memory spell on her. At the time, Skender felt uneasy about what they were doing because he knew Sally was the true mate of his packmate, Costin. But Skender did nothing to stop the Order. There was something inside of him pushing him to do whatever was necessary to see the Order succeed. He'd been convinced that the supernaturals of the world shouldn't have to live in secret. "I was such a fool," he murmured as he threaded his fingers through Tenia's hand. He felt tears welling up in his eyes, tears he didn't deserve to cry because the pain he felt had been of his own making. No one had held a gun to his head and made him cooperate with the Order.

"You can tell me more later," Torion said gently.

"I would be interested to hear more of this story as well," Peri's voice said from the entrance of the cave.

Skender glanced over at her. The high fae's face held an expression of interest, but her eyes were narrowed dangerously. He wondered if she would have already killed him if Tenia wasn't his true mate. Yes, of course, she would have, and with a smile on her face while she did it.

He gave her a knowing look, then bowed his head, acknowledging her request. Then she flashed and was gone again, leaving him and Torion to watch and wait for Tenia to wake up.

∾

*W*E SHOULDN'T BE ALLOWED *to exist.* Tenia had come to the conclusion over the past few weeks as she sat languishing on a bench in the middle of a lush forest. She knew the bench and the forest weren't real. She knew they only existed in her mind because she could feel her body, but she couldn't move. She could hear her son's voice, and Skender's, but she couldn't respond. Her eyes wouldn't open no matter how many times she commanded them to. She was stuck.

The last thing she remembered was being engulfed by the cold fire. Tenia had been sure her life was over. In her thoughts, she'd told Torion and Skender goodbye. She'd mourned the life she would never have. She had no idea how much time had passed when she found herself awake in the forest. *Awake* wasn't the correct word. She was *aware* but not awake. The forest looked very similar to the one in the fae realm. The colors were more vivid than those in the human realm, and the scents were stronger. But the magic of the realm felt weak, and she wondered why.

In her unconscious-yet-aware state, Tenia had listened to the story Skender had been telling her son. Slowly, the pieces were beginning to fit together. Torion was correct. The only thing that could have affected Skender's memories was magic. And if it made him turn on the people he'd grown to love and trust, it had been extremely dark magic. This was what had convinced her that the world would be better off without supernaturals in it.

After all the atrocities she'd seen the Order commit, Tenia had come to realize the depth of their depravity. If the Order was any example, not only were supernatural beings not superior to humans, but they were far inferior, capable of feats of evil the humans couldn't dream of. The supernatural races had too much power and too many willing to

use it for their own gain, no matter the terrible consequences. Perhaps it would be better for everyone if the
supernatural races no longer were allowed to leave their
own realms. Then their evil could not put humans in
danger.

"I was such a fool." She heard Skender's words and the
pain that filled them.

We are all fools. She wished she could communicate to
him through their bond. She could still feel the tether
connecting them. Yet no matter how many times she tried
to reach out to him, she was unsuccessful.

Tenia pushed up from the bench and began to walk. She
strolled in a large circle around the bench. Not because it
was what she wanted, but because it was all she was
allowed in this place that seemed to be holding her.
Regardless of which direction she tried to go, her body was
forced to turn, pushed by an invisible hand, back toward
the bench. She could see the dense forest beyond the small
field surrounding the bench, but it was out of reach. Her
imprisonment began as an irritation, but it was quickly
becoming maddening.

Her thoughts veered toward Myanin, and Tenia
wondered how her unlikely friend was doing. If she knew
Myanin at all, she would guess the djinn was probably
ticked off she'd lost her primary source of cotton candy. The
thought made her smile, but it also brought pain to her
heart. Would she ever see Myanin again? How long would
she be in this stasis? Tenia felt fingers run across her cheek
and knew it was Skender touching her. She felt her hand
being squeezed by a much smaller one and pictured the
worried face of her son. Her stomach clenched as tears ran
down her face. Tenia wondered, not for the first time, if
death, real death, would be better than being so close to the

two males she loved deeply but being unable to reciprocate their affections.

Perhaps this was her punishment for the part she'd played in assisting the Order: to forever hear and feel her son and mate but never be able to reach out to them.

"*Patience.*" The Great Luna's voice filled her mind. "*It is one of the greatest disciplines a person can learn, and yet it is also one of the most difficult to practice.*"

"Why?" Tenia asked. "Why must I be patient? What purpose do I serve simply existing without being able to help others?"

"*Sometimes, the answer is simply 'because I said so',*" the goddess answered. "*You are the created, Tenia. I am your creator, and I love you in a way that your finite mind cannot begin to comprehend. It is not for you to know my plans. Simply trust that I always have your best interest at heart.*"

Faith, Tenia thought. Her creator was asking for Tenia to exercise faith *and* patience. Faith required her to simply believe despite not being able to see the outcome. And patience was only possible if she set her own desires aside and waited for something to happen that was beyond her control. Could she do it? Tenia sighed. "What other choice do I have?" she asked the empty forest around her. There was no response from the Great Luna, though there was a measure of peace that filled her as she accepted her circumstances.

Tenia resumed her place on the bench and focused on the voices outside of her body. Voices that were precious to her. For now, simply hearing them would have to be enough.

CHAPTER

SEVEN

"So many good things in life start with pain. The birth of a child, getting out of an abusive relationship, going through treatment to recover from an illness, even death. I have experienced so many things that felt like I wouldn't survive ... yet I did. I have learned through the trials that the resulting joy is so much deeper because of the anguish. I must keep reminding myself of this—and those I love—so that we will stay strong through the pain." ~Jacque

If this is what hell is like, Jacque thought as her body continued to burn, *then count me out.* She could still hear the voices around her, but she couldn't see anyone.

Jen was pissed as ever. "What is the point of you being a historian if you don't know a lick of history?"

"He's doing the best he can, Jen." Zara's voice was calm

yet sharp. "I don't think your griping is going to make him discover a solution any faster."

Jacque heard Jen sigh. "I know. It's just so hard to see her in pain. She's stopped screaming, but her body is so rigid she looks like she would shatter with even the slightest touch. I just want to do something."

"We all want to help." Myanin's voice broke in. "Sometimes helping is just being present."

Jacque could imagine the look Jen was giving the djinn, but her friend stayed silent. It had been three days, or that was the last number she'd heard someone mention as her friends, pack, and family attempted to heal her injuries and undo ... whatever it was that the werewolf had done to her heart. She was tired, she wanted to hold her son, and she wanted to stare into the blue eyes of her mate. As she thought of those things, she knew the torment she was enduring would eventually pass. And all of her sufferings would be worth the blessings experienced on the other side.

"You will do those things, Luna." Fane's voice filled her mind. He'd kept their bond open wide and attempted to take some of her pain away, pulling it into his own body, but Jacque didn't want him to weaken himself in any way. *"Stop worrying about me,"* he chastised. An open bond meant no privacy. *"The Great Luna will provide the strength I need. You and our son are always my first responsibility, no matter what."*

Jacque wasn't about to argue with him. She knew it would be pointless. And she didn't have the strength to anyway. So she focused inward on the healers' power she felt streaming into her body. The harder she focused, the more she could see their light, their magic. It moved through her body, healing everything it came in contact with, from the smallest muscle strain to the grisly damage done to her heart. Jacque took a deep breath and realized the burning was beginning to abate.

"Fane, it's working," she told him as the flames began to subside, and the sensation of heat weakened until she was once again in a state of blissful warmth.

"Open your eyes, Jacquelyn," he commanded.

"Pipe down, wolf-man. Give a girl a moment to get her bearings." Jacque experimented with telling her limbs to move. She felt her feet flex and then her fingers tap on the bed she laid on. Then she took another deep breath and let it out slowly. The room fell silent, but that didn't last long.

"She's moving," Jen said, her voice sounding strangled as if she was trying to keep from crying. "Open your eyes, Red, or so help me, I will pry them open and use toothpicks to keep them that way."

"Wow, and I thought I had anger issues," Myanin said.

Jacque ignored the rest of the voices as chatter broke out around her. She focused on her body. She was almost afraid to move too much, for fear the pain would return. After what felt like several minutes with her heart pounding in her throat, she began to move her eyes, then slowly opened them. With a pathetic yelp, she immediately slammed her eyelids shut.

"The lights," Fane said. He'd felt her pain through the bond at the brightness of the lights. She heard a click and then sensed darkness behind her closed lids. "Try again, Luna."

Jacque opened her eyes slowly, squinting to make sure she wouldn't be blinded again. When she was certain the room was comfortably dim, she opened them the rest of the way. The first thing she saw was her mate's face, which was hovering a few inches above her own. His hands framed her cheeks, and he leaned down until his forehead rested against hers. Fane took a deep breath, and Jacque felt his wolf settle as her scent filled his body.

"Never again, mate," he whispered, his lips brushing against hers. "I would hide you and Slate away far from all of this if I didn't know that you would never forgive me. I love you." Jacque didn't have time to respond because his lips were suddenly pressed firmly against hers. It wasn't a gentle kiss. Despite her recent injuries, he wasn't treating her as if she was a porcelain doll. It was a kiss to remind them both that they were okay, that they would make it through this. His tongue brushed against her lips, and Jacque opened her mouth, giving him what he wanted. Her body filled with a different kind of heat, this time pleasant. Very pleasant.

The bed beside her dipped, and she felt Fane settle his chest against her. One of his hands threaded his fingers through her hair. She shamelessly moaned when he gave a gentle tug, forcing her head back and her mouth higher for him to deepen the kiss. Her arms lifted, and Jacque wrapped her hands around his arms and slowly ran them up and over his firm biceps to his strong shoulders until they cupped his neck. His skin was hot, and she could feel the pulse of his heart in the artery beneath her hand.

"It beats for you," he said through their bond as his mouth continued to work its magic. She felt as if his lips were assaulting hers, and she was all too happy to let him continue.

"I prefer to think of it as devouring, not assaulting," he said, having picked up on her thoughts through their bond.

Jacque smiled. *"Whatever it is, I don't want you to stop."*

She felt his wolf rumble, and his body press harder against her. *"Wasn't planning on it."*

Jacque sighed, sinking into the mattress as she tried to pull him further onto the bed. She wanted more. His taste was driving her crazy. She mentally urged him on. His hand moved from her face to her neck, then began to slide down her collarbone. Her skin tingled in its wake, and the slightest movement from him made her shiver.

"Unless you two want to show us how to make a baby, you might want to hit the pause button on this, admittedly, very hot make-out session." Jen's voice sounded as if it was coming from far away.

"Make her go away," Jacque said into his mind as she began to pull at his shirt.

Fane pulled his mouth back long enough to growl, "Everyone out." Then his lips were right back on hers.

"What the hell is going on?" A deep voice rumbled. Jacque couldn't place who it was and frankly didn't care.

"What? What am I missing?" She recognized that voice as Heather's.

"I can lead you over there and let you feel what's going on," Jen said. "It's getting really interesting. The shirt is about to come off."

There was a loud sigh. "Jacque, unless you want Jen to get to see your man naked, you might want to stop."

Sally's words penetrated her lust-fogged brain. *"Fane, we have an audience."* she reminded him. She released him and then grabbed his roaming hand, even though she was quite okay with the road trip it was on. Her mate didn't seem inclined to stop, even as Jacque tried to pull her face from his. Jacque snapped her face to the side, and his mouth simply moved to her cheek, heading toward her neck. Then Jacque met the eyes of her mother, who was still sitting in the same place she had been when they'd all started their attempt at healing. "Wow, this is awkward," she muttered before shoving at Fane's shoulder. "Nissa—" Jacque gasped as her mate bit gently on her mate mark. She recovered and continued. "Since Peri isn't here to do the honors, could you please zap my mate?"

The high fae stepped into Jacque's line of sight, and her lips turned up into a small smile. "Everyone might want to back up," she told the room as she laid her hand on Fane's back. There was a flash of light and then Fane snarled. He jumped to his feet and swung around to look at the room. Jacque noticed he made sure that she was behind him.

Jacque leaned to the side and saw that Nissa had her hands up. "I meant no harm, Alpha," she said, her voice calm. "But your mate wanted to get your attention. And I've never been one to ignore an alpha female in distress."

"She was not in distress," he ground out. "Far from it." His breathing began to slow, and he straightened from the fighting crouch he'd taken, though he continued to give Nissa a death glare.

The high fae only raised her eyebrows and shrugged.

"Fane," Jacque said, reaching out to grab his hand. She gave it a squeeze.

He looked over his shoulder at her, and his face softened. "This is not over."

She laughed as the rest of the room groaned.

"Noted," she said, and then glanced around at all of the women who had helped heal her. She met each of their eyes, and tears filled her own. "Thank you," Jacque said. "You all must be exhausted. Thank you for being willing to fight for me."

"That's what pack does." Sally reached over and patted her hand.

Jacque's eyes widened. She tried to sit up as she turned her hand to grip Sally's. "Your baby?"

Sally smiled. "Is just fine."

"You shouldn't have taken that risk. And I was so selfish not to think of it before." She would never forgive herself if something happened to Sally's child because Sally had overexerted herself trying to heal her.

"You're my best friend, Jacque."

"I'm right here, you know?" Jen interrupted.

"Yes." Sally rolled her eyes. "We always know where you are, Jen, because you can't keep your trap shut."

There was a pause and then Jen said, "Fair enough. Carry on."

"Do you think Costin would have let me do this if he thought for a second that it would hurt me or our child?" Sally asked.

The man in question stepped up beside her and smiled a dimpled grin at Jacque. "Glad to see you're better, Alpha. And you know the answer to that question. But you also know that you females generally do whatever you damn well please. Our job is mainly to try and lessen the damage."

Jacque blinked, and she made sure her face remained blank of all emotion. "I have no idea what you're talking about."

Fane finally relaxed and sat back down on the bed, though closer now to the foot as if he was attempting to resist temptation. He chuckled. "Sure you don't. You're also a terrible liar."

The tension in the room was beginning to evaporate, and Jacque pulled her legs up, folding them, and resting her arms on her knees. She glanced around the room. "I've been out of it for three days, correct? That's what I heard someone say while I was unconscious."

"That's correct," Lilly said. "And speaking of you being

out of it, what was happening that caused you so much pain?"

"I felt like I was being burned from the inside out," she said and then waved her hand at her mom. Lilly's mouth opened and her eyebrows raised so high they nearly touch her hair line. "But that's not important." Jacque turned her head to her mate. "You need to get back to the hunt with Nick and the others." Then she looked at Jen. "Will you bring me Slate?"

"On it." Jen nodded. "He's been with Bethany and Drake. He's getting a crash course on how to take care of more than one child and keep them alive."

Jacque's eyes widened. "That's not encouraging."

Jen simply waved over her shoulder as she exited.

Jacque looked around the room until her eyes found Myanin. "I believe, before I became a human barbeque, we were working on figuring out Peri's little riddle. Have you made any progress?"

Myanin blinked several times before she answered. "Did you forget the part where you were burning like a barbecue? There hasn't been a whole lot going on other than making sure the healers were taken care of while they worked on you. And keeping that blonde psycho from stabbing everyone for, well, any reason she could come up with."

Jacque bit her lip and then sighed. "Jen can be a little overbearing."

"She's psycho," Myanin said dryly.

"I'm going to have to agree with her." Heather pointed at Myanin. Though she couldn't see the djinn, the healer was extremely adroit at knowing where people were based on the sounds they made. "Although I do adore her. It's hard not to love her crazy just a bit. It's something to aspire to, ya know?"

Jacque couldn't help but laugh as everyone said in unison, "No!"

"All right, we've wasted enough time," Jacque said, pulling herself together. "Let's get to work on this riddle."

Fane shifted, causing her attention to fall back on him. "Why are you still here? Nick needs you."

"And I will go help him after you are taken care of."

Jacque started to speak but snapped her mouth shut when he gave her a stern look.

"You need a shower, you need to eat, and you need to spend some time with Slate. The others can work on the riddle while you do those things. And I need just a little more time with my mate after the three days you've endured." He looked over at the sprite queen. "Do you have a place where I can see to my mate?"

Andora nodded. "I'll show you to your room. We've assigned everyone a place to stay."

"Thank you, Andora," Fane said, sincerity evident in his voice. "Your hospitality will not be forgotten."

The alpha stood and scooped Jacque into his arms. "She will be back in a little while," he told them. Andora headed for the door and Fane followed.

Jacque glanced over his shoulder, looking at each of the women who had helped her. "Thank you, again."

They'd just stepped out of the entrance to the room when Jen came around the corner with Slate in her arms. "Are you two sure you're going to give the crumb catcher your full attention and not start clawing each other's clothes off?"

Jacque held her arms out for Slate. He clapped and grinned and then reached for her. "I think we can restrain ourselves." Jacque nuzzled against her son's cheek and breathed in his precious scent. She'd missed him fiercely.

Jen's eyes softened, and she placed a hand on Jacque's cheek. "I'm in agreement with your mate, Red. Never do that again. You're my ride-or-die chick."

Jacque's eyes filled with tears as she patted Jen's hand. "Ditto."

Jen dropped her hand and stepped aside so Fane could walk past. When she looked back at Jen, she saw her friend still staring at them, wiping at the tears streaming down her face. Jen was tough as nails, but she was also fragile, and sometimes it was easy to forget that she needed to know how much she was loved. Jacque held her blonde best friend's stare until Fane turned a corner and she could no longer see her.

Slate's babbling grabbed her attention. His smile was contagious, and when she was focused on him and the hope and joy that he instilled in her, everything else faded away. "Missed you, little man," she said and rubbed his nose with hers.

Slate patted her cheek and said, "Dada."

Fane's chest shook with his laughter.

"He only says it because 'd's are easier than 'm's."

"Whatever you need to tell yourself, Luna." He pressed a kiss first to her head and then to Slate's and continued to follow Andora, who must have waited on them while they'd been talking to Jen.

When they reached their assigned room, Andora stood in the doorway but didn't step inside. "I will have food brought up. They will knock and then leave it outside of the door. There are clothes in the closet, and, yes, they will fit. Please, Jacque," she said, her bright eyes imploring, "take all the time you need. You've been through a lot."

Memories of the past few years flashed through Jacque's mind as she looked at the sprite queen. "It's no more than I've endured before. And as my mate said, your hospitality will not be forgotten."

Andora bowed her head and then closed the door behind her.

Fane set her down on her feet and took Slate from her arms. "You shower. I'll get you clothes. Then I'll feed you and Slate. You will let me hold you until my wolf is calm enough to leave you."

Jacque felt his worry through the bond and knew he was being bossy because he had felt helpless to take care of her. One of his strongest instincts was always to take care of his mate. She would give him this, even though she felt the need to make sure everyone else was taken care of as well.

"That is the gift of a female alpha, beloved," Fane said softly. "You love all of those under your care. You will give of yourself until there's nothing left."

"And what is the gift of the male alpha?" Jacque asked.

"When I return from the hunt with Nick and his mate, I will show you."

Jacque threw her head back and laughed, which in turn made Slate laugh.

"It always comes back to that, doesn't it?"

She felt the brush of his hand down her back, even though he was across the room. "It always comes back to me loving you and showing you that love in every way that I can."

JEN PULLED herself together and marched to the medical room where Jacque had been fighting for her life for the past two weeks. Jen took a breath and stepped inside and saw that everyone was still present. "Can we take this meeting back into the great hall?" All eyes turned to her. "I need a change of scenery, and staring at that bed where my best friend suffered is not going to inspire any brilliant idea about this freaking riddle."

"Agreed." Sally stood up.

Jen looked over at Nissa. The high fae had not only helped with Jacque, but she'd also magicked clean clothes on to the healers and sprites as they'd kept their vigil next to their alpha. "I apologize for treating you like a clothing store, but would you mind?" Jen motioned around the room. "The rest of us can take showers later. But clean clothes would be great."

"I'm happy to help," Nissa said in her gentle way. She spoke in the language that Jen had heard Peri use many times in the past. A few seconds later, everyone in the room was dressed in clean clothes: simple jeans and T-shirts. Jen was fine with that. Saving the world didn't need to be done in a dress, no matter how badass she would look.

"And maybe make sure we smell decent," Heather said. "I don't know about supernaturals, but we humans can get some serious B.O."

"Two words, blind chick," Jen said. "Wet dog."

"You do remember that *you* have a wolf form, too, right?" Costin took Sally's hand and began to lead her toward the door. "So the wet dog smell applies to you as well."

"Not the point." Jen stepped aside as everyone filed out.

Jeff, of the Coldspring pack, was the last to exit. He paused next to her. "What *is* the point?"

"Annoyance." Jen smiled, and she knew her face showed the smile that Decebel described as her wicked grin. "It annoys the crap out of the males of our pack to be compared to dogs. Annoying *Canis lupus* males is sort of a hobby for me."

To Jen's surprise, Jeff shook his head with a sly smile as he started walking again. "It's too bad that you're taken. I bet there's never a dull moment with you around."

Jen's eyes widened. She tried to slam the bond shut before her mate could pick the alpha's words from her mind.

"Please pass on my condolences to the Coldspring pack," Decebel's voice rumbled in her mind.

"Dammit." She groaned out loud.

"And let them know we will assist them in finding a new alpha if none of their males are dominant enough for the task."

Jen shook her head and followed after the group. *"He wasn't hitting on me, B. Put away your claws and fangs. He was just making an observation. A very astute observation, I might add."* Jen started down the hall and felt her mate's irritation through bond. She also felt his longing for her and his need to see their daughter.

"He can observe something else, like an unmated female."

"I'll pass that along," she assured him.

"No you won't. You will not talk to him. I love you." His voice softened, and she felt his hand run across her cheek.

"I love you back. Any progress?"

His sigh came through as loud and clear as if he was standing right beside her. *"Aside from keeping Nick from attempting to kill every supernatural he comes across while he shakes them down for any scrap of information they might have about his mate or the Order, we got nothing."*

Killing something sounded pretty cathartic to Jen at the moment. *"Considering Kara has been taken, we can assume some members of the Order survived the cold fire. I'd lay even money that Alston made it through and that he is behind our healer's disappearance."* Jen stepped into the great hall and saw everyone sitting around a large round table filled with food. Her stomach rumbled at the sight.

"I think that is a pretty good assumption."

Jen could feel his frustration and wished there was something she could do to help. *"We need to speak with Peri."*

"Does Lucian know she showed up?" he asked.

Jen frowned when she realized how little they had communicated over the past few days. She'd been so focused on Jacque and taking care of Thia that she'd done little more than make sure he was okay and tell him she loved him. *"He does. He came in here, realized she'd already vanished without so much as a 'Hey, big boy, where've you been all my life?' and then took off with Disir, the high fae. Disir said he could follow Peri's magical signature. We haven't heard from either of them since."*

"Fantastic," her mate growled. *"Just what we need. An unstable male, possibly on the verge of going feral, out chasing his equally unstable mate."*

"Unstable is putting it mildly. Peri has proven that she has surpassed me in the insane department. She is off-the-charts unhinged." Jen didn't want to believe the high fae who'd become so dear to her had gone completely crazy, but it was difficult to argue with the evidence.

"Perhaps we shouldn't count her out just yet. If she came to you all and gave you some sort of warning or message, then maybe she is not as lost to us as we first thought."

Jen hoped that was true. She wanted to believe that everyone was redeemable, though she wasn't always great at giving grace. Perhaps this was an opportunity for her to work on that flaw. *Ugh.* Working on flaws was not her strong suit. Beheading things, that was more her jam.

"Please attempt to refrain from beheading anything or anyone while I am not around. Working on the grace thing seems much less dangerous." Decebel's voice was stern, but she detected a bit of humor underneath.

"I'll do my best. I love you. Now, do what you do, and help Nick save his chick."

"Yes, ma'am."

"Oh, I like the sound of that." Jen grinned. She took a seat at the table and reached for an empty plate.

"Promise to keep your clothes on and don't kill anyone, and I'll say it to you under different circumstances." She felt his lips on her forehead.

"I'll try, but I can't make any promises."

"Give Thia a kiss for me," he replied.

"Will do. Love you, B."

"And I you."

Jen focused her attention back on the group. She began adding food to her plate and looked at Wadim as she remembered something he'd said before Jacque's ordeal started. "Wadim, prior to Peri popping in and blowing our circuits, you started to tell us about finding out ... *something.* We got a tad sidetracked. Can you share with us what you know?"

He nodded, swallowing a mouthful of water, and then wiped his mouth with a napkin. The historian grabbed a pad of paper sitting next to his plate. "Before all of that excitement, I *had* been able to get some research done. The sprites allowed me to dig into their archives. Considering many of the supernaturals are a bit touchy about letting others into their business, there's much we don't know about the past. It's very interesting to see—"

"Babe." Zara placed her hand on his forearm and smiled at him. "While I love to see you get excited over your nerdy, history stuff, I think they just want you to get to the point."

Jen was really glad it was his mate that had stepped in because her own words wouldn't have been quite so diplomatic.

Wadim cleared his throat. "Right. So, what I found was that a long, long, like ridiculously long time ago, there was an incident recorded by the sprite historians when cold fire had been used by a high fae."

Nissa sucked in a breath, and all eyes shifted to her.

"Okay, the whole atmosphere of the room just changed," Heather said. She popped a grape in her mouth and then added. "Who's the one attempting not to freak out but is obviously not doing a good job judging by that amazing gasp, not to mention the power that's vibrating out of them like a generator?"

Jen couldn't help but marvel, not for the first time, at what an amazing attitude Heather had in regard to her blindness. She could have been bitter over her sightless life, but instead she took joy in the senses she did have. Not to mention she was funny as hell.

"Nissa looks like she's seen a ghost," Anna offered. "And she's glowing just a bit, like Peri sometimes does."

"You do realize that I've never seen Peri glow, right?" Heather asked.

"You asked where the power was coming from, and I'm giving you an answer. Don't get picky just because you're unable to experience all the weird things in this—"

"I will cut you." Heather tossed a roll, unerringly, at Anna.

"Wow, they're just like you three." Cindy glanced at Jen and Sally.

"Good grief," Myanin muttered. "Nissa, what's your damage?"

Jen nearly laughed at the djinn's use of human slang. Apparently she'd been in their realm a little too long. But Nissa's glowing skin, which was getting brighter, quickly stifled the laughter.

The high fae swallowed and then looked around the table until her gaze landed on Jen. "The time of which your historian speaks... It was thousands of years ago. Perizada was a child. I was a child."

"Whoa," Stella murmured. "It's hard to think of Peri, or you, for that matter, as a child. I've always thought she just came out as an adult fae with a ridiculous amount of power."

"You look like you're about to throw up," Jen told Nissa. "And I've seen that look before. It's the same one Peri got when the memory of the witches returned. You've forgotten something. Actually, it isn't that you've forgotten, it's that you've—"

"Hidden it away."

"Hidden it away?" asked Heather.

"They do that sometimes," said Jen. "Crap that is better left forgotten."

"So, this is really, really bad?" asked Stella.

"Whatever happened must be too painful to even consider. And if I know the fae, they not only considered it, but they allowed it to happen?" Lilly offered. The pain in the warlock queen's eyes made Jen ache. Her appetite was suddenly gone. Jen set down the forkful of vegetables she'd been about to put in her mouth.

"Exactly." Nissa nodded. She looked at Wadim. "Did the archives tell you which fae performed the cold fire? Or why?"

Wadim shook his head. "The record only stated there had been two survivors within the cold fire: two female fae children."

"How?" Heather almost whispered.

"The archive entry stated the children had survived because they'd been protected."

No one spoke for several seconds. Everyone stared wide-eyed at Wadim.

Jen's wolf growled as she waited for him to continue. "What the hell are you waiting on, history-boy? Spit it out!"

"The children were protected by the draheim."

"What?" The expectant look on Lilly's face was replaced with confusion. "I've seen the draheim. They did *not* seem like the type of supernaturals to protect anything but their own. They were quite ... volatile."

Nissa folded her hands and set them on the table in front of her. "Every race has those who choose the wrong path. That does not mean the entirety of them follow in those footsteps."

"So, the draheim can withstand the cold fire..." Jen thought back to her attack on the Order compound, attempting to remember any details she might have noticed. Then her mind slipped even further back, and she remembered the very first battle at the compound. "There was a draheim at the compound," she said quickly as she snapped her fingers. "Ludcarab," she looked at Sally, "remember? He was riding that draheim."

"Holy pixie babies." Sally's eyes widened.

"You think that draheim helped Peri?" Costin asked.

Jen held out her hands. "The proof is in the pudding."

Costin frowned. "Is that some weird American saying? All I needed was a yes."

"Bloody hell. Yes. I think that if that draheim was still

around when Peri went kaboom, and it chose to help her, then that would explain why she survived."

"Okay, that mystery is *possibly* solved." Anna looked back at Nissa. "But I wonder who the two fae children were that were saved long ago."

"Perizada, naturally, and ... Nissa." A male voice spoke from the door of the great hall. It was Disir. Lucian was nowhere to be seen. "Perizada and Nissa were the fae children saved that day."

"Why do I feel like my entire world has just shifted on its axis?" Sally asked. "First the draheim can withstand cold fire, next we remember the Order had a draheim, and now Peri and Nissa are not simply high fae but miracle-baby high fae."

Jen, along with every head at the table, turned to look at Nissa. The high fae reached for her glass of water, her hand shaking as she picked it up and took a quick sip. The skin around her mouth drew tight. Nissa kept her eyes down, avoiding the probing stares of everyone. "The memory of that day," she finally spoke, "is lost to me. It is only now that I realize it happened."

"You and Peri were saved, not for a single reason, but for hundreds if not thousands of reasons," Disir continued. "You and Peri both have your flaws. But so do we all. That day, you were both protected by those who loved you and saved by those who knew that your life, and Peri's life, would serve to protect many others. For whatever reason, Nissa's path has led her here, where she has been able to help in so many ways. She is not in need of rescuing. But Peri needs to be saved again. This time, from herself."

"I'm assuming you've found her considering you're back from your adventure with her mate?" Jen pushed up from the table so fast her chair fell back to the ground.

"She's in the draheim realm." Disir's eyes dropped, and he looked as if he saw something the rest of them could not. "I felt her magic end there, but that wasn't all. Mingled with her magic, there was despair—such hopelessness. I don't..." He paused and swallowed, seemingly trying to hold himself together. "I didn't tell Lucian. Only that I felt her magic there."

"Where is he?" Wadim asked.

"He's at the veil to the draheim realm. We tried to enter, but we couldn't. Something has it blocked. I told him I would see if I could figure out a way in, but he refused to leave."

"Of course he did." Jen's chest tightened, her heart beating hard in her throat.

"So, we need to get into that realm." Myanin spoke up. Gerick took her hand in his and ran his thumb across the top in a soothing gesture.

"This sucks pixie balls." Heather huffed.

"Some of our females were trapped in the pixie realm," Kale said. His hand rested under Heather's hair on her neck, and she leaned into him. "We were eventually able to get through the veil. It was not an easy task, and it required the help of other supernaturals."

"Who helped?" Lilly asked.

"Thadrick, the djinn," Heather answered. "We were in the realm for four months."

"But once Thad took the job, he had them out in no time at all," Elle added.

"This isn't the pixie realm we're talking about," Wadim said. "The draheim are a hell of a lot more powerful than pixies. And if Peri is working with them on keeping the veil closed, it will be even more difficult."

"Son of a troll's ass." Myanin slammed her hand onto the table.

"Don't think that's a thing," Anna muttered, then held up her hands in a placating gesture when the djinn shot her a glare. "Just saying that being the son of anyone's ass would be quite a feat."

Jen shrugged. The healer wasn't wrong. Myanin mumbled something about cotton candy and turned her eyes away from Anna.

"In summary," Heather said, "Kara hasn't been found, Lucian is out of his cell, Peri is off her rocker and hiding out in a realm full of dragons, and the veil to that realm is locked."

"Also," Lilly added softly, "we have no idea how many of the Order leaders survived."

"Add Tenia and Torion, the fae and her son, to that list. We don't know if they survived the cold fire. Maybe if Peri did, then she managed to get them out," Myanin said, her voice strained as if it hurt to talk about the people she mentioned.

Jen pinched the bridge of her nose and took a deep breath. No worries. They had faced impossible odds before and beaten them. "It does suck," Jen agreed, "but then, most things in life do."

"Agreed," Anna, Stella, and Heather said in unison.

"But that simply makes the victories even better." Jen looked around the table. "And we have had many victories."

"Kicking ass is sort of our thing." Jacque's voice came from behind her. Jen turned to see her best friend walking in. She wore black boots, black jeans, and a black shirt and jacket. Her red hair had been tamed into a braid so it was away from her face. She looked ready for battle.

"Damn straight it is." Jen smiled.

Sally stood up and walked over to Jacque. She wrapped her arms around her friend and gave her a quick squeeze then stepped back. "I'm pretty sure we've earned an advanced degree in kicking ass."

"A doctorate in ass kicking even," said Jacque.

"Dr. Ass Kicker. I like the sound of that," added Jen.

"You're on a leave of absence from kicking ass, brown eyes," Costin said from where he still sat. Sally rolled her eyes at him, and he gave her his trademark dimpled smile and winked.

Lilly stood next and smiled at her daughter. "You've been kicking ass since you and Jen had it out in the front yard when you were three. I've no doubt we've got this."

"You kept the locks of hair we ripped out as keepsakes," said Jacque with a smile.

The rest of the group around the table smiled and stood. Each of the fae pulled blades from various places on their person and laid them on the table. Each wolf turned toward Jacque and bared their necks to her. Jewel lifted her hands and lightning began to dance in her palms, jumping from finger to finger. Stella and Anna joined her. Then the two high fae both began to glow, the brightness filling the room like the noonday sun.

"Why do I feel like I'm missing something?" Heather asked. She stood next to her mate, but her hands weren't raised like the other healers.

"Wheeler power," Stella said. "Light it up, Helen."

"Oh, right. This is a knight's round table moment, isn't it?" Heather raised her hands, and her own lightning began to bounce around in her palms.

"I usually go with *The Fellowship of the Ring*," Jen said absently.

"I like it." Heather grinned.

"No," Jacque said, her voice strong as it filled the entire hall. "This is a moment for *us*. For those who need us. For those who have sacrificed for us. This is a moment for the pack."

"FOR THE PACK!" The voices around the table rose as one. Then those who weren't at the table—the pack members, the sprites, and the fae—added their voices to the battle cry.

When the room fell silent again, Jacque looked at Disir. "Now, let's get that veil open and do what Peri has done so many times for us."

CHAPTER

EIGHT

"I don't know his name, and I can't see his face, but at night, when all is still and the darkness takes over the light, I hear his quiet voice. It soothes me. I dread the daylight because then he is gone, and the emptiness is overwhelming." ~Kara

Kara didn't have to turn around to know that Ludcarab had entered her room. The elf king's power was familiar to her now. She'd been his prisoner for a little over a month now, at least that's what the marks she'd made on the wall behind her door indicated. She wasn't entirely sure they were accurate, however, because sometimes she felt as if she'd lost time, like maybe she'd blacked out for some reason. Oftentimes, she would find herself standing in the middle of the room or staring out of a window with no recollection as to how she got there or what she'd been doing.

Though Kara knew he would stand there quietly until

she turned and looked at him, she didn't acknowledge the elf king right away. They were engaged in a not-so-subtle power struggle. When she'd realized his twisted tactic—that he always waited for her to face him before he greeted her—Kara had resolved to beat him at his own game. She tried to wait him out, hoping he'd leave if she didn't do what he wanted. The longest she'd made it had been three hours. She realized then that someone as old as Ludcarab had, no doubt, endless patience. Life wasn't a sprint to him; it wasn't even a marathon. It was a thousand-mile hike across continents. She took a deep breath, hoping to ensure she wouldn't vomit as she finally turned around. Her eyes met Ludcarab's, and the desire in them nearly caused her to double over.

"It has been long enough," Ludcarab's voice broke the silent stand-off. "You've been on the formula for a month. You should be ready."

Kara swallowed the bile that rose in her throat. The conversation Ludcarab and Alston had when they'd brought her here reverberated in her mind like a crashing gong. *"It will do two things: ensure she is able to conceive and help make her mind even more susceptible to Tenia's power."* She had no idea who Tenia was, nor did she particularly care, considering the woman had never shown up. She did, however, care about the fact that she'd continued to drink a liquid that a high fae claimed would make her able to conceive a child. Now, it looked as if the elf king had come to collect.

"You told me that you could give me everything," she said through gritted teeth. "You said you could lay the world at my feet. That I would want for nothing. You said you would protect me like I'd never been protected before." Her jaw clenched as she stared at him. "Is this how you treat someone you claim to be willing to do all those things for? To force yourself on me?"

The king took a deep breath and let out a sigh. He held out his hands in front of him, palms up as if in supplication. "Would I like for you to give yourself to me willingly? Of course. I have shown you kindness. I've provided for you. I've not harmed you. What more must I do in order for you to give yourself to me?"

All of those things were true, except he *had* harmed her. He'd taken her from her home, from *him*, the one she couldn't quite remember, but knew was her heart, her soul. There was an emptiness inside of her that she felt would swallow her whole. Kara fisted her hands at her side and straightened her spine. "There is nothing you could do. I will never willingly give myself to you." Her chin rose as she watched emotions roll over his face. His lips pursed, making it obvious that he was not pleased with her response. His eyes narrowed, honing in on her as if she was his prey. She was pretty sure if she took a step back, he would pursue her.

He dropped his hands and then folded them behind his back. "That is unfortunate. Regardless..." He reached back with one of his hands and snapped his fingers toward the door. "We must move forward." Several female elves walked in, all with their eyes on the floor. "Get her ready. Then bring her to my chambers. She is to be prepared as my queen."

"As you wish," the three women said in unison.

When Kara looked away from the females, she nearly stumbled back. Ludcarab had moved and she hadn't even realized it. He stood so close she could feel his breath on her face when he leaned down. He cupped her cheek in his hand, and his fingers were ice cold. So unlike another hand that she remembered cupping the same cheek, one that had been warm and welcomed.

"This is happening, Kara," he whispered. He made her name sound exotic as his voice took on an accent she didn't recognize. "I promise you, it will be good. I will not hurt you. After tonight, you will be mine." He pressed his lips to her forehead.

Kara felt tears welling up in her eyes but squeezed them tight, not wanting any to fall. When she opened them, a single drop rolled slowly down her cheek. "You might have my body," she said as she took a step away from him and out of his touch, "but I will never be yours."

"I've got nothing but time. And it is amazing what time can change." He turned without another word and strode from the room.

Kara's brain worked overtime. She watched the three women begin to move around the room. One pulled clothing from a closet, and another headed into the bathroom. Kara heard water running in the opulent bathtub. Moments later, a sweet aroma flowed from the bathroom as steam billowed out. Kara stared and wondered if they were going to try to boil her alive. How hot was that water to produce that much steam? And why was she worried about the damn temperature of the water when she'd just been told she'd be sleeping with Ludcarab that very night?

"Shock," she muttered under her breath. "I'm in shock." Kara took a deep breath and let it out slowly. She closed her eyes and tried for the millionth time to see the face of the man she knew meant the world to her but seemed just out of her reach.

"My lady."

One of the three elves. Kara's eyes snapped open, and she looked at the woman.

"My name is Dyna," the she-elf said. Her flowing hair was a deep, rich red. Her eyes held something Kara couldn't identify—kindness or maybe sadness. "This is Coya." Dyna motioned to another female attendant. This one was blessed with hair just as long but sleek black. "And that's Reena." She pointed to the third elf. This one had shorter hair that only reached the middle of her back instead of her waist. It was the same black as Coya's. Both of the females bowed their heads to her but then went about their tasks without a word.

Kara nodded to them and then looked back at Dyna. "This is going to sound rude, but why do you work for him?" She motioned to the door where Ludcarab had walked through. "He's a monster."

Dyna dropped her eyes to the fabric in her hands. She went to the bed and laid out the dress—if you could call the tiny bundle of skimpy, see-through fabric a dress. After a few moments, she snorted. "I could ask you why you're here, Kara."

"I'm a prisoner," Kara bit out, her temper rising at the thought of anyone thinking she would actually choose to be with someone like the elf king.

Dyna's green eyes snapped to hers. "What makes you think we are not?" The elf held out her arm. Kara noticed something she hadn't seen before—tattoo-like bands around the woman's wrists. Kara glanced down at the similar marks that encircled her own wrists. Then she looked over at Reena and Coya. Both women held their arms out for inspection. The same patterns.

Shame filled Kara as she realized that she'd done exactly what she thought Dyna was doing to her. "I'm sorry," Kara whispered. "I shouldn't have assumed."

Dyna waved her off. "We take no offense." She motioned

Kara toward the bathroom. "We all have a story, some uglier than others. But now is not the time to tell them. Right now you have to prepare yourself for your king."

"He is *not* my king," Kara said a little harsher than she meant to.

Dyna's eyes narrowed, though she looked determined, not angry. "If you want to live, you will make him believe he is."

Kara's eyes widened. When the elf didn't elaborate, Kara frowned and marched toward the steam-filled room. "He's not hurt me since I've been here."

Reena made a snorting sound, and Dyna clucked her tongue at the she-elf.

"What?" Reena said softly. "He's been giving her that poison."

"Hush!" Dyna snapped, her eyes like ice as she stared at Reena. "You would do well to remember that the walls have ears." She looked at Coya and then Kara. "You would *all* do well to remember that."

Kara couldn't help but glance around the room. This was something she hadn't considered. Were there cameras? Did they even *have* cameras in this nightmarish fantasy land she found herself? Perhaps they used other creatures. Were invisible pixies hiding on the walls, reporting back to Ludcarab about every move she made? Kara shook her head. She was being ridiculous. But she was also losing her mind, that much she knew. So maybe imagining pixies on the wall wasn't such a stretch.

"Reena," Dyna said, her voice firm. "Begin."

Kara looked at the dark-haired female. The woman began to chant. Her voice was smooth like silk. It ebbed and flowed as words Kara didn't understand filled the room.

Coya joined her. Her voice was a little deeper but harmonized pleasantly with Reena's.

Dyna gently pushed Kara the rest of the way into the bathroom. The room was dim, a collection of randomly placed candles providing the only light. Steam danced hypnotically through the air. Incense burned on the edge of the large, ornate tub. Since she'd been in captivity, she'd only used the shower in the bathroom and paid little attention to the tub. Now that she was looking at it, she saw that it was made from gold and contained etchings of words on the outside. The words were written in a language she didn't know, but she assumed it must be elvish. She saw the words were beginning to glow. Okay, she was sure *that* had never happened before.

Dyna joined the other two in the chant, and Kara felt the hair on the back of her neck stand on end. Goose bumps rippled across her skin as the elves' voices flowed around her. She sensed power rising in the room. It felt similar to the kind of power that Peri had exhibited, except twisted somehow, dark and forbidden. The women began to help her out of her clothes, and Kara was so caught up in the sound of their voices that she didn't even think to be embarrassed about her nakedness in front of the three women.

Reena held her right hand and Dyna held her left, leading her to the tub. They helped her balance as Kara stepped into the water. It was hot against her flesh, so hot that she should have snatched her foot back. But even though she knew the water was too hot, her brain couldn't command her body to do what it wanted. Instead, Kara put the other foot in and then eased herself down until she sat on the tub floor. Kara's mind screamed at the temperature, and anywhere the water touched, her skin turned bright red.

The chanting continued, while Dyna poured small vials of liquids into the water.

"What are those?" Kara asked. Her voice sounded dreamy to her ears. She ran her hand over the top of the water where some of the liquid had landed and settled on the surface as little, shimmering circles.

"Simple oils. Lavender, sandalwood, and clary sage," Dyna replied while Reena and Coya continued to chant. "They will help your desire grow."

This seemed to clear a bit of the fog in Kara's brain. She grunted. "It's going to take a hell of a lot more than a few snake oils for me to even develop a desire for that man, much less for one to *grow*."

The she-elf ignored her. Dyna retrieved a much larger bottle from somewhere Kara couldn't see. She opened it and began to pour it over the top of Kara's head. "Close your eyes," she commanded.

Kara wanted to scream. She wanted to jump out of the tub and snatch up her clothes. She wanted to run, to pound on the door until someone came and rescued her. She wanted to fling herself out the window—anything to escape what was coming. But she couldn't. No matter how hard she tried to do any of those things, she couldn't move. Instead, she obeyed, closing her eyes with a soft sigh.

The warm liquid flowed down Kara's hair, onto her shoulders, and down her back and chest. "This is hyssop, to cleanse and purify you before you join with the king."

Kara shuddered. She tried to keep her mind blank, not wanting to think about what "joining" was to come. She wanted to sink so deep inside of herself that at least her mind wouldn't experience the sensation of the touch of a man she didn't want. He might violate her body, but she was determined he wouldn't reach her soul. The chanting around her combined with the aromas lulled her further into a trance. She searched for something familiar, something that would bring her comfort in this time of utter terror. Kara had been trying to tell herself that she would not let fear rule her, but she'd also thought somehow she'd be free before Ludcarab could follow through with his intentions.

All too soon, Dyna took her hand. "Rise," she instructed softly. Like a robot, Kara's body obeyed. She stood and stepped from the bathtub. Kara felt as if she stood on the outside of her body, observing herself, watching the mechanical motions of the pliant, sandy brown-haired girl while the three elf women dried her wet skin. Coya ran a comb through Kara's thick hair, the oil making it shiny and smooth.

When they'd finished drying her, Reena sprayed Kara's skin with something that made it shimmer. It looked like tiny flecks of glitter, causing the candlelight to make her sparkle as she moved. She raised her head and looked at the girl staring back at her out of the mirror. Kara might have thought herself to be beautiful with her shiny hair and glowing skin flushed from the hot water. But she remembered the reason for the pampering. Instead of feeling beautiful, she felt dirty.

Once again, Dyna took her hand. She led Kara from the bathroom and back into the lavish bedroom. Coya picked up the gown that had been placed on the bed earlier. "Raise your arms, my lady."

Kara did so without arguing. There was no point. The gown slipped over her hands, down her arms, and over her head. As it cascaded down her body, Kara shivered. This was not how she'd imagined the moments leading up to losing her virginity. Her brow drew low on her face, and she tried to remember how or when she'd even thought about what her first time might look like. It wasn't like she'd had a lot of time to think about such things when she'd been in foster care. She'd been too busy trying to survive unscathed. But then something had happened. Kara knew it had; she just couldn't quite remember what it was. Someone, she thought, had come into her life, someone who had made her consider something so special and intimate. The more she tried to remember, the further it slipped from her mind.

"It's time." Dyna's voice sounded sad, much weaker than it had been while she'd chanted.

Kara's eyes met the female's, and she saw tears filling them. She bit the inside of her cheek to keep her own tears from welling up. She would not go before Ludcarab as a weakling. She refused to give that pathetic excuse for a king any more of her tears. Maybe later she would weep for herself, but not now.

"Lead the way." Kara's voice held a steadiness even as her hands shook at her sides. She wasn't entirely sure where she was garnering the strength, but she gritted her teeth and held her chin high.

She followed the three women from the room. Her gaze stayed fixed straight ahead. With every step, her heart pounded harder in her chest. Her lungs didn't want to take in air, but she growled and forced herself to swallow shallow breaths. Kara wondered briefly if her body was attempting to make her pass out so she might avoid, a little longer, what was about to happen. Unfortunately, before her body was successful, they stopped in front of a large, ornate wooden door.

"This is where we leave you," Dyna said gently. She turned to look at Kara. "The Great Luna has not forgotten you, child. Whatever reason you must endure what is to come, there is a purpose beyond what you or I can understand right now. Do not give up hope."

The three women stepped back so that Kara stood before the door by herself. She closed her eyes and took a deep breath. When she was reasonably sure she wouldn't vomit on the king's bedroom floor, she grabbed the handle and pushed the door open.

Her senses were immediately overwhelmed. The room smelled of the same incense that had been present in the bathroom, and a wordless melody filled the room. The windows were draped with black velvet curtains, pushed open so that the night sky could be seen beyond. Flames danced within a huge fireplace, causing shadows to climb across the stone walls. In the center of the room an oversized, round bed hovered a foot from the floor. Black silk flowed around the bed near the ceiling, but nothing appeared to be supporting the fabric. It undulated in time with the music, twisting and swirling.

"You are a vision," Ludcarab's voice came from farther in the room, but Kara couldn't see him.

The door closed behind her with a resounding click. The finality of the sound threatened to overwhelm her with panic.

The elf king stepped around from the other side of the bed, emerging from behind a swirl of the dancing fabric. He was clothed in a black robe, his long, platinum hair draping over his shoulders. The shining locks stood out starkly against the dark material. His green eyes seemed to glow, and the fire that reflected in them made him appear even more sinister than normal. Despite the surrealness of the situation and the wicked vibes emanating from Ludcarab, she couldn't deny the fact that he was very handsome. And she hated herself for even acknowledging it. It felt like a betrayal to someone, but she couldn't think of who.

He walked toward her with slow steps. The satisfied smirk on his face made her want to slap him. Her hand even twitched at her side, but she held it still with sheer willpower. Something inside of her whispered that now wasn't the time. Later. Perhaps not today, tomorrow, or even a year from now, but one day. One day he would get what was coming to him. And it would be a hell of a lot worse than a simple slap.

Ludcarab advanced with a catlike grace. The moments seemed to drag on forever. *Get on with it!* She wanted to scream at him. Finally, he stood in front of her, so close she was inhaling his scent—unfortunately not unpleasant— with every breath. Kara forced herself not to tremble or look away. He reached up and traced her face with a finger. Here, she couldn't stop the involuntary shudder. But neither she nor Ludcarab acknowledged it.

He ran the finger across her forehead, down her cheek, then down to the V of the gown. She knew he could see straight through the fabric. Nothing was hidden from him.

"You are so brave," he whispered as his finger dipped into the gown and tugged it away from her skin. "You stand before me like a warrior. You do not cower. You do not attempt to hide yourself from me. That is how I know you are perfect to stand at my side, to lead with me as we take over both the supernatural and human worlds."

He slipped an arm around her waist and pulled her against him. His other hand tugged at the gown until it tore on one side and hung off her shoulder. Ludcarab leaned down and touched his lips to hers. Kara didn't respond. Her body did not curve into his, and her flesh did not warm as he held her tighter. He chuckled but continued to move his mouth over her skin, kissing her cheek, her jaw, and then on to her ear. "I will enjoy bending you to my will, little Kara." His breath against her skin disgusted her, but still, she did not move.

His hands roamed over her body, but Kara didn't feel any of it. She heard the gown tear again and felt the cold air across her chest and stomach. The sensation almost made her flinch, but she remained as still as a statue. Eventually, Ludcarab picked her up and carried her to the floating bed. She was briefly aware of being laid on the plush surface. Kara felt his body cover hers.

She knew it was now time to go. If she stayed in the moment, she would break. She would be shattered, and there would be no way to put herself back together. There would be nothing left for ... for whom?

Kara threw herself into the world she'd created in her mind. She dove so deep that the pain of what was happening outside of her mind barely registered.

Though her body lay on a bed with an unwanted partner, in her mind's eye, she stood in a forest. The air was cool but not uncomfortable. The forest was lush, but also dark and mysterious within. She looked down and found that she was fully clothed, wearing jeans and a T-shirt—something familiar and comforting.

She turned in a slow circle until her eyes landed on a golden cord—like a thick, shimmering length of yarn—that floated in the air. The end of it hovered a few feet away, but the rest led off into the darkness of the forest. Something about the cord called to her. Kara walked to it and saw that the cord appeared to be two separate lengths of rope, each golden, entwining one another. She placed her hand upon it. She almost gasped when warmth flooded her body. The cord felt like soft silk in her palm. Immediately, she was filled with a sense of peace, of belonging.

But Kara was scared. She was terrified the cord would vanish and she would wake up. She would appear *back there.* She didn't know what was going on *back there,* but she knew it wasn't good. She knew there was a monster there, and he was devouring her. So Kara gripped the cord with everything she had.

She heard a voice in her mind. *"Don't be scared. Come to me."* Somehow Kara knew she was meant to follow the cord to its end. She loosened her grip and began to walk, letting the soft material flow under her hand. The forest passed her by as she walked, but Kara kept her eyes on the shimmering rope. She knew outside the soft glow of light cast by the cord, the forest around her was growing darker. Kara had no idea if she walked for minutes, hours, or days. Time seemed to have both stopped and passed by in a great leap all at once. Suddenly, she reached the end of the rope.

Slowly, Kara raised her head and saw before her a giant black wolf.

The large beast wasn't facing her. Instead, it looked toward the dense trees—his ears erect, his back straight, and his tail held out stiff behind him. He was focused on something she couldn't see. He was beautiful, his dark, black fur looked soft and thick. She itched to run her fingers through it.

Like the cord, the wolf called to her. Kara wanted to get closer. Even though the beast might be dangerous to her, all she could think about was wrapping her hand in his thick coat and holding on for dear life.

She took a step toward it, and the grass beneath her feet crunched. The wolf's head swung around. His glowing eyes were the color of obsidian. His head tilted slightly to the side, and he dropped it a couple of inches. His eyes narrowed even more. After several heartbeats, the wolf stuck his nose in the air, and he took a deep breath.

Kara watched the beast close his eyes. His body tensed. Then the wolf's head snapped down, and his black eyes reopened, focused on her. There was something so familiar about him, something that made her trust him.

"Who are you?" she asked out loud. Did she expect a wolf to answer her? It was her world, her imagination, so why not?

The wolf didn't answer. Instead, it shimmered, and suddenly the wolf was gone, replaced by a tall, handsome man. She should have been shocked. But rather than surprise, she once again felt peace—the same sense of belonging she received when she touched the golden rope. Kara sensed she *knew* this man, just as she knew the wolf.

"Kara?" The man's deep voice reached inside of her, as if it was a hand wrapping around her spine and tugging her toward him. Her feet stood their ground, though everything inside her screamed at her to go to him.

"I'm coming," he said. "Stay alive. Don't you dare give up. I lo—"

His words were cut off, and the man disappeared.

"What...?" Kara made to take a step toward the spot where the man had vanished when she was ripped violently out of the forest. She screamed, but her voice made no sound. Her eyes flew open, and she was once again *back there*. She stared up at a dark ceiling and saw black silk billowing around. Kara felt movement beside her and then smelled something she'd encountered many times before in foster homes where she'd lived, though thankfully never one she'd had to associate with herself—

until now. Her stomach roiled and vomit rose in her throat. She had to swallow hard to keep from puking in the elf king's bed, not that she cared too much about the damn sheets, but she didn't feel like wearing her own vomit. She shifted her body and immediately felt an unfamiliar soreness in a place she'd never been sore before. That was the last straw. She turned her head quickly as the contents from her stomach ejected itself from her mouth. Thankfully, she'd been close enough to the edge of the bed that the majority of her lunch made it onto the floor.

A hand ran down her bare back. The sensation only made her wretch harder. Kara vomited until she dry heaved when there was nothing left in her stomach. She used the sheet to wipe her face. Despite the mess, she stayed on her side of the bed. She didn't want to face the elf king. All she wanted was to crawl back into the steaming, hot bath and scrub his touch from her flesh.

"You will become accustomed to my presence." His voice purred behind her. "I had planned for a longer evening, but you will no doubt want to clean up, and I'm sure you will be hungry now." He sounded so unaffected, so unconcerned, over the fact that he'd just raped her. "I will come for you again later. We must ensure that you carry my heir very soon."

Kara trembled violently. She pushed herself up until she was sitting on the edge of the bed. With a look of disgust, she had no choice but to take the tainted sheet and wrap it around herself. Her feet hit the floor with a jolt from the height of the bed, and she almost collapsed. Kara had forgotten it was hovering above the ground. She didn't wait to see if Ludcarab had anything else to say. Walking quickly to the door, she remembered to hold her head high and keep her shoulders pulled back. She would *not* fold beneath this monster, not even after what he'd done to her.

Somehow, she found her way back to her room. Once inside, she slammed the door behind her and pressed her back against it. Her breathing came in rapid pants as if she'd run a marathon rather than down a few twisty, stone corridors. Her chest tightened, and her body continued to shake. The trembling worsened when she felt the evidence of his disgusting actions trickle down the inside of her thighs.

Without another thought, Kara bolted for the bathroom. She dropped the sheet, practically leaped into the shower, and turned the nozzle for the hot water to the left as far as it would go, not even bothering to add any cold. She wasn't looking for comfort or calmness. She needed to be seared. The sizzling water hit her flesh, and she couldn't stop the scream that erupted from her throat. Despite the pain from the scalding liquid, she welcomed it. The physical pain was so much better than what she felt on the inside. She released the tight rein she'd held over her emotions and let the tears flow freely. Her nails clawed at her skin, and all the while, the scream exploding from her throat continued, as if it might go on forever.

Eventually, the scream morphed into a warble, a sound that alternated between growls, heaving sounds, and then back to ear-piercing screeches. Her eyes landed on a bar of soap. She snatched it up and vigorously scoured herself, attempting to wash away what he'd done to her. But Kara knew no amount of washing could cleanse her. The soap fell from her hands and hit the floor with a thud. Kara's body shuddered, and her hands formed into fists, her nails biting into the palms of her hands. The skin felt tight stretched across her bent knuckles.

Her sandy brown hair fell in wet strings in front of her face. She could see the wall between the strands, but it wasn't the tile she saw. It was his face. Ludcarab and his smug smile. Kara roared. She pulled her arm back and slammed her fist into the mirage. The skin tore, and blood dripped from her knuckles. She ignored it and punched the wall again. Over and over, she bellowed until her voice was hoarse, and she was sure she'd probably broken some bones in both hands.

Exhaustion finally caught up with Kara, and her arms dropped. Her head fell forward, and she watched her blood drip onto the shower floor only to be washed away by the water. Instead of feeling weaker, the healer felt stronger. The monster had taken something from her. And she knew he would take it again and again. And she would most likely lose her shit every single time, but one day... One day it would be her turn. Her time would come, and she would take everything from him. Every ounce of pain he caused her she would return tenfold. "I swear it," she whispered as she stood motionless beneath the burning water. "I will end you."

CHAPTER
NINE

**"I would like to say that if I lost you, I would be strong
enough to carry on, that I would keep your memory
alive for the rest of the world. But this, I cannot do. If
you are gone, then I am gone. If your life is over, then
mine is as well. Without you, I am simply a shadow of
the person I would have been with you at my side.
There is no me without you."**

~Nick

"**W**hy the hell not?" Kara growled at him. "You keep
giving me the same material, Nick. It's time that
you come up with something new. Reruns aren't my
thing."

Nick's wolf clamped the man's mouth shut. No matter how
angry he got, the wolf would not allow him to say anything that
might cause their mate pain. She'd endured enough in her life.

But the man's frustration with her was at an all-time high. She just couldn't leave it alone. "We've been over this, Kara," he said when his wolf finally released its hold on him. "You're not ready."

Kara whirled around so fast he was surprised she didn't give herself whiplash. "Who the hell are you to tell me what I am or am not ready for?" She took a step toward him, her finger pointed. If that finger had been a gun, he thought she just might shoot him. Not to kill, but maybe just to wound him. "I am a grown woman. I am not the seventeen-year-old girl you met over a year ago. I'm eighteen, legally an adult. And not just any eighteen-year-old. I know about the supernatural world, found out I'm a gypsy healer, then added witch to my resume. I've had werewolf males paraded before me like I'm at a weird courting auction. I dealt with a semi-narcissistic high fae who loved to insult people just so she didn't have to show she cared for them. I faced off with another crazy high fae, who was completely off his rocker. I voluntarily gave up my ability to have children. And if all of that is not enough to show that I'm not a child, I willingly entered into a relationship with a bossy, possessive, growly, domineering ass-wipe. A relationship, I will remind you, that is forever. And not like a normal life span forever that humans commit to. We're talking a long-as-hell, normal-people-would-dry-up-into-husks kind of forever. So, in conclusion..." She stepped closer to him until her pointed finger pushed into his chest. He relished the touch, even in anger. "You do not get to determine what I am ready for." Her words were clipped, and every single one was emphasized by a poke of her finger.

"I know all this," Nick said before his beast could intercede.

His mate snarled at him. Okay, so maybe that hadn't been the best thing to say. "Keep your mouth shut, human," his wolf snapped at him.

Kara threw her hands up in the air and turned away from him. It was a motion he was very familiar with considering she did it all of the time when talking to him. That wasn't to say they argued every waking moment. There were times, not as many as he wanted, when she softened to him and let him hold her, kiss her, and cuddle her. And yes, he was man enough to admit he loved to cuddle with his mate. Lately, those times have grown less and less. And it was his fault.

Nick watched her with an intensity that humans would no doubt find a little disturbing. Maybe they wouldn't if it lasted only a moment, but Nick could stare at her, watch her every move, for hours and not grow tired. He loved everything about her, even the passion that drove her to such rage. Rage meant she cared. It meant she felt as strongly for him as he did for her.

She stomped back and forth in front of the windows that revealed the mansion grounds. That land had become her escape from him. At first, he watched her the whole time. But then, as his own temper grew, he found he needed to burn off his emotions. But it wasn't just his anger he needed to exorcise. It was also his desire. He refused to complete the bond with her, but that didn't mean he didn't want her ... badly. He hadn't even allowed himself to bite her because he knew it wouldn't stop there. His beast was ravenous for her. And he didn't understand why Nick was waiting. "She's ours. She's not a child. Her body does all the things that a female's body is supposed to. We can scent her ov—" Nick snarled at his wolf, cutting him off from pointing out something of which Nick was painfully aware. The man didn't need reminding that once a month his desire grew for her because, unlike a human male, Nick and his wolf could smell it. "It's true," his wolf grumbled.

"Why are you snarling at me?" Kara glanced over her shoulder at him. Her back was ramrod straight, her shoulders

pulled back, and her hands rested on her hips. "This is your fault, Nick. You don't get to be pissed at me for wanting what is my right. Isn't that what I hear you males continually spout? That you have a right to your true mate. Does that right only go one way?"

"Dammit, female!" Nick shouted, his irritation getting the best of him. "Can't you see that I'm just protecting you? I will always look out for your best interest. Your health, safety, and happiness will always come before my own."

She turned to face him. Her hands dropped from her waist and fisted at her sides. "Do I look happy to you?" Her eyes glistened with unshed tears, and a piece of him shattered. He hated when he caused her tears.

"Baby," he said softly, taking a step toward her. He needed to touch her, to feel her flesh against his own. His wolf needed the reassurance that, despite their quarreling, she still wanted him, that she wasn't giving up on him.

Kara put up a hand. "Don't," she breathed out at him, sounding defeated. She wiped away a tear she hadn't managed to keep from falling. "I'm done fo—"

"What!" Nick practically roared, causing her to jump.

"Fix this. NOW," his wolf bellowed inside his mind. "If she leaves us, I will destroy everything and everyone near us until our alpha is forced to put us down." Nick ignored his beast's threat. The man didn't bother to argue because he agreed with him. Nick would not want to live if Kara chose to live without him.

"Nick," Kara's voice trembled as she took a step back. She held up both hands as if to keep him away. Like hell, he thought. "You need to calm down. Now."

"You just told me you are done with me, and you expect me to calm down?" He could feel the nails on his hands phasing into the claws of his wolf. He would never, ever, hurt Kara, but his

emotions were out of control, and he was fighting his need to phase. "You are the other half of my soul, and you expect me to live without you. You would choose to live without me?" He knew his eyes glowed, and he felt his teeth sharpening and lengthening. "Just because I won't give you what you want, you would throw us away?" He was too busy trying to keep from tackling her to the ground and tying her up to notice the confusion on her face. "I am your male, and you are my female. I will not give you up. I told you that. You knew that before you came to our pack. That hasn't changed, Kara, and it won't change. I will do anything to keep you."

"Not anything," she said, finally dropping her hands. "Don't lie to me. Ever. And don't interrupt me. It's rude, and it makes you assume things because you weren't smart enough to keep your muzzle shut."

Nick glared at her. He wanted to throw her over his shoulder and carry her to her room and lock her inside so she could never follow through with her words.

"I wasn't saying I was leaving you—"

"You said you were done."

She stomped her foot. And it would have been adorable if she wasn't staring daggers at him. "I just told you not to interrupt me, dammit. I was about to say, I'm done, for now, you overgrown hairball." Kara took a deep breath as she seemed to attempt to calm herself. "By 'for now,' I mean that I am done fighting with you. I'm exhausted mentally. I'm beginning to wonder if I can use my witchy magic on you if only to zap your ass. I don't want to hear your voice for at least a few hours, because if you attempt to tell me, one more time, that I don't know what I need or what I'm ready for, I just might cut out your tongue while you sleep.

Nick didn't move, afraid that if he so much as twitched she might follow through with trying to zap him. "There's no need for name-calling," he said after several moments of silence filled only with their respective glares.

Her brow rose, causing her forehead to wrinkle. "Seriously? You have the nerve to say that to me after you just went apeshit over a conclusion you made because you couldn't just listen to me?"

"Apparently," Nick groused as his teeth and nails phased back to human form.

"I need a drink," Kara huffed.

"N—"

"But because I'm mature, and know that it's not legal for me to have a drink, then I won't have one. But know that it's my choice whether I do or don't. Instead, I will take my mature ass out for a run. Bite me, Nick. I'll talk to you later."

Nick refrained from telling her how badly he wanted to do just that. He didn't want to send mixed signals. He even kept their mental bond minimized so she didn't pick up on his need for her. "You aren't very good at being a mate. Maybe you should let me take over," his wolf pointed out. "And you aren't human. You don't understand that they don't think like you. It's not as simple as claiming and bedding her because she's our true mate," Nick responded. He watched her storm from the room. "From where I'm standing, it is that simple. If it wasn't, our mate would want to be with us instead of always trying to get away from us." Nick didn't respond to his wolf's observation. Maybe his beast was right.

Nick shook his head, pushing away the memory as his feet pounded against the ground. Every day since they'd returned to the pack mansion, Nick had gone out into the field where his mate had run after they'd had their arguments. He jogged the same route, the grass worn where her much smaller feet created a trail. In his mind, he pictured her ponytail swishing back and forth, her arms pumping at her sides, and the determined look in her eyes as she burned through her frustration at him. His mind kept dragging him back to the times when they'd argued, which had ultimately put her in the dangerous situation that had gotten her taken. He rarely allowed himself to think of the good memories. Nick didn't feel he had a right to them. But just then, he needed to remember that they'd had more than conflict between them. No matter how they'd snarled at one another, they still loved each other.

"Come in," Kara's voice said through the door that kept him separated from her. She didn't sound irritated, which was a good sign. Nick wouldn't share a room with her, though he allowed himself to hold Kara at night because he and his wolf could barely stay away. It was especially difficult when they knew she was across the hall, mere feet away, curled up in a bed all by herself. He could feel her need for him through the bond, and sometimes it drove him crazy. Tonight was one of those nights.

Nick turned the knob and pushed the door open. He stopped in his tracks as his eyes landed on the woman he craved like a drug. She wore a tank top that revealed a hint of cleavage and shorts that were so small they should be illegal for any unbonded female. Kara was stretched out on her stomach on the bed. Her legs, bent at the knee, swung up and down behind her, her heels bouncing off her delectable backside. Do not look at her delectable backside, Nick berated himself. She propped herself up on her elbows, a book laid open in front of her. Kara's eyes were fixed on the pages as if whatever they contained was the most intriguing thing she'd ever seen. His wolf growled. He didn't want to share her attention with anything, not even a book. His wolf was ridiculous. But then again, Nick wasn't really any better.

"Whatcha doing?" he asked and wanted to smack himself because it was obvious what she was doing.

"Planning my next vacation. It's been so long since I've been on one. Like"—she tapped her chin—"never. Because I've never been on one." She glanced at him, a smirk on her face. "I'm reading a book, dork. What does it look like I'm doing?"

"Smartass." He walked across the room toward her. He told himself he would keep his eyes focused on her face. He lied. His eyes roamed over her body, and he knew if he didn't stop, he would end up panting just like his wolf.

"To what do I owe the honor of your presence?" She closed the book and looked up at him, resting her chin in her hands.

Nick sat down beside her and took a deep breath. Her scent filled his lungs, and he couldn't stop the rumble that rose in his chest.

Kara grinned at him. "I love that sound."

Nick lifted his hand and slipped his fingers into her hair, running them through the brown locks that held streaks of blonde, which weren't entirely natural. He hated the smell of the chemicals that lasted a few days after her dye jobs, but he liked the way it looked. After the Volcan crap, Peri had noticed that Kara's hair had grown, and the brown roots showed where the blonde had grown out. She gave Kara a permanent hair dye job with the streaks, and Nick strongly suspected the fae, too, didn't care for the chemical odors.

"You okay?" Kara asked, her grin fading as she stared up at him.

The answer was "no," he was not okay. But he couldn't tell her that. "Just miss you," he said softly. Nick picked up the book and tossed it to the bedside table then rolled his mate to her back. He typically slept in nothing but shorts, but once he'd given in to the need to see her, he'd slipped on a shirt. He immediately regretted it as he stretched out beside her, and her palms laid against his chest. He wanted her skin on his.

"Nick?" Her lips turned down in a frown.

"Have I told you how much I love you?" Nick asked. He traced her lips with his forefinger. "You're a miracle."

Her hands flexed against his chest. Her frown fell away, and the lips he touched turned up in a small smile. "I love you, too," she said, her words filled with the same fierceness that her voice held. "No matter the battles we seem to have, I love you, Nick. I hope I haven't made you doubt that."

Nick's eyes took in every detail of her face—every contour, nuance, and tiny detail. It wasn't just her outside beauty that drew him. Though Nick wouldn't lie and say that if he saw her on the street, he wouldn't take a second look ... or a third. But it was Kara's inner beauty that called to him. It called to his beast, who constantly fought the darkness. "I don't doubt it, sweetheart," he told her, sliding his finger out of the way and replacing it with his mouth against her lips. He allowed himself few things as intimate as kissing. Though he held her and touched her as often as he could, kissing her was a massive test of his self-control, especially when she broadcast so loudly, both verbally and through their bond, that she welcomed his advances.

"Stop thinking for a minute and just feel," Kara said through their bond. "Just be here in this moment with me."

Nick ran his tongue along the seam of her lips, and she opened her mouth for him. Her taste flooded his mouth. His chest rumbled as desire rose like a fire doused in gasoline. He felt her chest rise and fall against his own, and her breathing increased. Kara's hands slid slowly up his chest. He could feel every indentation of the pads of her fingers as she pressed them into his muscles. She briefly stopped at his shoulders and gave them a gentle squeeze before continuing her exploration until her hands wrapped around his neck. The heat of her skin met his own, and he felt his wolf pushing to take control. He wanted to be closer. He wanted more. Both he and his wolf wanted to taste the skin on her neck. The salt he knew he would find there. His wolf could smell the perspiration coming off her. He wanted her supple flesh between his teeth, and then he wanted the tang of her blood in his mouth. He needed her.

"Mine," Nick said into her mind, unable to curb his possessiveness as she pressed closer to him. One of his hands ran down her side, across her ribs, her waist, and her hip until it rested against her thigh. She was so small compared to him. His palm spanned her entire thigh, and he wrapped her tightly in his hand as he hiked her leg up and over his hip. She gasped at his boldness, and Nick chuckled. She nipped his bottom lip, tugging on it before releasing it. He pulled back so he could look down at her.

"Do you feel that?" Kara asked him. "Your heart against mine."

"The same rhythm," he said, his voice gruff with desire. "Our souls are united. Our hearts beat as one."

Tears filled her eyes, and she brought a hand up to cup his face. Her bottom lip trembled, but it wasn't with sadness or anger. Nick could feel through their true mate bond that the intensity came from the knowledge that she was not alone and never would be again.

"I'm yours, Kara," Nick told her, his forehead pressing against hers. Her warm breath fanned over his face. She seemed to struggle to draw air into her lungs. "I am yours and yours alone, and you will always have me."

Tears fell as her body shook. Nick felt her emotions flow through her like a violent storm. He wrapped his arms around her and rolled them over until they were on their sides, chest to chest, face to face. Their legs tangled, binding them together as *tightly as the surest knot. Nick's hand slipped up the inside of her shirt, his palm sliding against her silky skin until it wrapped around the back of her neck. He could feel the heat of her all the way up the inside of his forearm which was pressed tightly against her.*

It wasn't the first time she'd fallen apart to the point that she seemed to need him to keep her together. He would gladly hold her in his arms for eternity. Nick could lay in this bed, just like this, and never tire of her being there. "I've got you," he whispered as he buried his face in her neck and breathed her in deeply, filling his lungs with her precious scent. "I've always got you, and I will never let you go."

He felt her head nod even as she sucked in a quavering breath through her tears. "I know," she responded. "I know."

Nick held her as she cried. He held her even as her tears subsided and her lips pressed sweetly to his neck. He held her as she drifted off to sleep, exhausted from her own emotions. He held her all night, and he relished it. It was a memory he would tuck away for the lonely nights that would remain until the day he could complete the blood rites with her and become one with her in every way. Then he could hold her every night.

He wasn't there for the first seventeen years of her life. He hadn't been able to protect her from all the ugly in the world. He couldn't make sure she had good experiences or memories in her previous life, but he promised himself that when they bonded—when he marked her with his teeth and his body—that it would be a memory she could treasure. A moment in her life that she would forever look back on and know that she'd meant so much to him that he had been willing to wait until she was ready in every way: mind, body, and soul.

"Soon, baby," he whispered as she slept. "Soon, I will make you mine in every way."

• • •

NICK WAS JARRED from his thoughts as his feet pounded against the ground. An arm bumped him, and he was reminded that he wasn't running alone. Today, Drayden joined him. Nick knew his alpha was worried about his mental state. Without the bond, the darkness in Nick would grow. With Kara in danger, the darkness would grow faster. The longer he was unable to get to her, the more feral his wolf would become. Soon, he would no longer only be a danger to his enemies. *How long until I'm a danger to those I count as friends, a danger to my pack?*

Suddenly, Nick stumbled. The world around him disappeared, and his wolf senses took over. Nick felt his wolf seeking Kara through their bond, even though it seemed the bond was no longer attached to their mate. But then it *was* there, snapping taut back into place. *She* was there. The sensation of his mate was faint, but she was there. And then, through his wolf's eyes, he saw her materialize. Nick had no control over any part of himself. His beast had simply taken the reins and was in full control. All the man could do was watch. Nick didn't know how long he was lost in the moment. His mind was in one place and his body in another. But as quickly as it had happened, it was over. Nick was thrown back into reality, and he could once again see his alpha and the pack grounds around him.

"I felt her." Nick's breathing was rapid from more than just the jogging. His wolf was growing frantic inside of him. "My wolf saw her." His feet froze as he stood outside the Canadian pack mansion.

They'd searched for a month. First, they'd tried to determine if perhaps Ludcarab and Alston might have decided to stay close to their previous compound. Nick thought it was a long shot, but perhaps their enemies thought it would be the last place the wolves would consider. The only thing they'd encountered were some newly made vampires. Nick and the others had happily dispatched them. His wolf had felt a miniscule amount of pleasure at having ended the lives of such despicable beings.

They'd also searched every hidden supernatural establishment in the human realm but had likewise discovered nothing. If anyone had known anything, the fear of facing Fane would have made them squeal like a cornered pig. So far, they had come up empty and had no leads to go on. Drayden had decided they needed to go back to their pack headquarters and regroup. Nick also knew he'd suggested it because Kara's scent lingered there. Though the smell wasn't as strong as it had been a month ago when he stepped into her room, it had brought him some semblance of peace. The feeling only lasted a moment, but it was a moment he treasured.

"What do you mean?" Drayden asked. "You felt her just now, but only your wolf saw her?"

Nick realized that didn't make much sense. He shook his head and started pacing. "I mean, the bond has felt completely severed until now. But for an instant, it was there. We were connected again. And then my wolf showed her to me." He closed his eyes and pictured what his wolf had seen. "I was in a forest just looking out into the trees. I could feel the bond. Then, my wolf's attention was suddenly alert, his focus somewhere else entirely. His gaze searched for what we both felt. And then he heard footsteps." Nick took a deep breath, afraid to believe that it was true. Maybe it was simply a figment of his imagination because he missed her so deeply. Maybe the memories he'd allowed to play out so vividly in his mind had begun to drive him mad. Half of him was missing. He was incomplete without his Kara. "When my wolf turned, she was there. At first, the beast didn't trust what he was seeing, but then he smelled her. That's when he let me in. He let me smell her and hear her voice. I phased. I tried to move toward her, but my feet wouldn't budge."

"Did she say anything?" Drayden asked, his voice urgent.

"She asked if she knew me," Nick answered. "She looked confused, but there was something else. Something like hope, longing. I could see my own emotions echoed in her eyes. I know every nuance of her beautiful face as well as I know my own reflection in a mirror. Her brow was drawn low, and her mouth tight, as if trying to figure out who I was and it caused her pain." Nick stopped pacing and turned to his alpha. His voice trembled. He clenched his jaw to keep from howling. Finally, he spoke. "She didn't know me." He wished he was stronger, that his voice didn't waver. But not only was she lost to him, she also didn't know who he was. He was a stranger to his mate. "My female doesn't know who I am."

Drayden walked over to Nick and pulled him into a hug. Nick didn't care that others might not understand the need for him to have the touch of his alpha, the comfort of someone who loved him like a brother. "See this for what it is, Beta," Drayden growled. "She is *not* lost to you, not if the bond between you is strong enough to break through whatever magic the Order is using to keep you apart. This is hope."

"*He's right,*" his wolf rumbled. "*She's alive. Some part of her remembers us. Her soul sought out its other half. If she didn't remember us, there would have been no reason for her to do so.*"

Nick considered the words of his alpha and the wolf. They were both correct. Kara still felt a link between them.

Now, he just needed to figure out how to get through to *her*. The bond was still there. He just needed to access it.

"What were you thinking about when it happened?" Drayden asked. He pulled back from Nick, giving his shoulders one final squeeze.

Nick didn't want to answer. He didn't want to share his private thoughts or moments about his mate with anyone, not even his alpha.

"I don't need details," Drayden huffed, seeming to understand Nick's feelings on the matter.

"I remembered one of our worst fights and one of the nights I allowed myself to hold her while she slept. The emotions the memories evoked were"—he paused and swallowed—"intense."

"Emotions make the bond stronger," Drayden pointed out. "I, obviously, haven't experienced the bond, but I've learned a lot about it over the course of my existence, and mated males have told me that when they or their mate experience intense emotions, the feelings cannot be blocked. Maybe that is why the bond was able to reconnect, though briefly."

Nick considered it and had to admit that it was as good a guess as any.

"So, try focusing on more of those memories. Even if they're painful," Drayden added quickly. "Pain can be an overpowering, even crippling, emotion. Mix that with the fact that she has the other half of your soul. I would guess that combination would create one hell of a response."

Nick looked out over the empty field and finally nodded. "I need to be alone. And being surrounded by her scent will help." He turned back toward the mansion without another word. He didn't bother to stop for a shower, a drink, or food. Nick marched straight to his mate's room. He shut the door behind him and closed his eyes as he slid to the floor. His head leaned back against the wood, and he whispered. "Come back to me, Kara." He let his memories of her assault his mind. "I'm here. Help me find you."

TEN

"The only thing certain in life is death and taxes, or so I've heard. And at the time, my young, uneducated mind didn't fully understand the saying. Now, experience, and, well, *more* experience has shown me that the saying is bullshit. It is *certain* in life that you will experience many things so much worse than either of those aforementioned crapfests. It is certain in life that you will endure heartache, torture of various kinds, be it physical or emotional, shock, disbelief, and rage to the point of possibly committing murder. It is also a certainty that you will experience joy until your heart might burst from the sheer radiance of it. You will experience love of many kinds —some you might expect and some that might knock you right off your feet and onto your possibly too-big backside. So, are there certainties in life? Absolutely. Can anyone predict how *you* will encounter those certainties? Nope. They can only tell you to try and prepare yourself for them. How do we do that? I haven't figured that out yet. Maybe saying *yes* to drugs.

Okay, not really. Therapy? Definitely. Being open to learning, change, offering forgiveness, grace, and accepting that you will not always be in control. This is a start, I think." ~Jen

"Iwant it known that I am not okay with being left behind." Sally stomped, maturely, back and forth from one end of the room to the other. She, Costin, Gavril, Rachel, Bethany, Titus, Slate, and Thia were all battened down in an enormous suite within the sprite's great hall. Sally hadn't figured out exactly how big the great hall was, but it was vast, and the number of rooms within seemed endless. She wondered if the building was like the Harry Potter tents that appeared tiny on the outside but were basically entire houses within. She shook her head at her meandering thoughts. Jen had mentioned several times lately during one of Sally's ever-increasing zoned-out sessions that she must have pregnancy brain. If that meant that Sally had the attention span of a two-year-old on Mountain Dew capped off with a side of speed, then her friend was not wrong.

"I thought you were upset about being left behind," Costin's humor-laced voice filled her mind. *"How did you go from being upset to Mountain Dew-drugged toddlers? Wait. Are you thinking of filling Thia up with some caffeinated concoction and then giving her back to Jen when they return? Because I'm totally on board with that."*

Sally stopped and turned to look at her mate, who was draped across one of three large couches filling the living area. One leg was slung over the end of the armrest, and his back leaned against the pillows as his left arm laid across the back of the couch. He looked more like a lazy jungle cat than a wolf.

"Want me to purr for you?" He winked and smiled, flashing her one of his dimples.

Sally rolled her eyes at him. *"Flirting with me is not going to un-tick me off."*

"That's not a word."

"Don't care."

"It's worked before."

"Not this time."

She continued her pointless walking and found herself rubbing her small, rounded stomach. It was barely a bump, but she could definitely tell it was no longer flat. Sally knew for the safety of their child that she couldn't go with Jacque, Jen, and the others to help deal with Peri, but that didn't mean she liked it. The fae held a special place in Sally's heart, and she always would. No matter what the woman had said and done, Peri would always be family to Sally.

"It's going to be all right, brown eyes," Costin said. Though his voice was in her mind, his arms were very much touching her physical body as he wrapped them around her from behind, forcing her to stop pacing. He laid his hands over her stomach and gently flexed his fingers. "They're going to bring her home. And when they do, you will be here safe and well rested so you can lay on the pregnancy guilt trip about how she shouldn't have worried you while you're in such a state, and so on and so forth like you females do so well."

"Are you trying to tick off all women everywhere just to distract your mate?" Bethany asked from where she sat holding Hope. The two-month-old girl was currently being taught all about werewolves, courtesy of Titus. Although she couldn't understand a word Titus said, the little girl stared at him with rapt attention while she gripped Bethany's finger tightly in her small grasp. Sally's son rarely left Hope's side. He'd taken on the role as her protector, and he took his job very seriously.

"Considering only the females in this room can hear me," Costin said, his breath warming Sally's neck, distracting her in other ways, "I'm apparently only trying to tick off you all. It's a small price to pay for her peace of mind."

"Hmm, I can't even begrudge you that." Bethany glanced down at Hope. "I'd think less of you if you simply let her fret in order to keep from offending us." Bethany looked up and met Sally's eyes. "He is right," she told her. "They will bring Peri back. She's hit rock bottom."

"The only place left to go is up," Sally finished for her.

Bethany smiled. "Exactly."

The door opened, and all of them turned to see Sally's mother walk in, pushing a tray loaded with food. Cindy walked toward a large table and looked at Sally. "I was hungry, which made me think that maybe you all were hungry. I just brought an assortment, courtesy of some help from the sprites, considering I didn't really know what anyone wanted."

Sally smiled. "Thanks, Mom, that was really thoughtful."

"*She misses you,*" Costin said through their bond. "*You haven't spent much time with her since we found out about the baby.*"

"*There's been a lot going on,*" Sally argued. But he was right. She *had* been avoiding her mom and dad. The irritating thing was Sally didn't know why. Truth be told, she hadn't wanted to be around anyone other than her mate, Jacque, and Jen since Peri had lost her crap. Maybe it was because she felt safe being vulnerable in front of them. Her parents had never made her feel weak or judged her for how she'd handled her struggles. They hadn't said anything when she'd shut down after finding out about Peri. But she *did* feel weak. After learning everything she had about her mom, Sally realized just how incredibly strong Cindy Morgan was. There was a part of her that didn't feel worthy of being her daughter.

"Okay, now you're just being silly," Costin told her. *"You are amazing."*

"You're my mate, so you have to say that," Sally whispered.

Costin chuckled. *"You're right. I have to tell you the truth, because that's what mates do."*

"Sally?" Cindy held out a sandwich to her. "Peanut butter and jelly?"

Her mouth watered. Thank goodness she hadn't developed any weird cravings so far, nor had she discovered any aversions to foods that she loved before her pregnancy. Sally nodded and stepped out of Costin's arms, walked over to her mom, and took the offered food.

Cindy stepped closer and laid a hand on Sally's arm. "Your dad and I"—she paused and bit her bottom lip—"we love you. You know that, right?"

Sally's lips turned up. "I do, Mom."

"I'm here if you need anything or want to talk. But I also understand if you don't."

Sally frowned. "You do?"

Her mom nodded and glanced over Sally's shoulder. "Once upon a time, I would have been the first person you came to when you were dealing with stuff. But our circumstances change as we grow. You have a mate now. He should be the first person you turn to. That doesn't mean I will ever stop being here. Neither will I be offended if you *don't* seek me out. I want you to know that. I'm okay, and so is your dad."

Sally let out a deep breath. How did moms always know what to say? Was it a superpower they developed during pregnancy or something that evolved over time during motherhood? Sally glanced at Titus as her free hand rested on her stomach. However it happened, she hoped it was a skill she would obtain. "Thank you, Mom. I needed to hear that."

Cindy gave her a quick hug and then started offering food to the rest of the room. Costin carried Titus over to the table and sat him down, then gathered up Thia and Slate and sat them in highchairs. As he prepared each of the kids their own plates of food, Sally watched him. He caught her and winked. *"I'm totally getting you all hot and bothered with my mad-dad skills, aren't I?"* he asked her without so much as a pause in dealing out the food.

Sally snorted as she took a bite of her sandwich. *"Totally."*

"You say that like I can't sense your emotions or smell your—"

"Costin," Sally mentally cut him off, feeling the heat of her blush on her skin. Her mate still loved to tease her mercilessly.

"Gotta keep things interesting, Sally-mine," he purred through the bond. *"Wouldn't want you to get bored."*

Sally couldn't help but laugh out loud. "I doubt our lives will ever be boring," she told him before popping the last bite of her sandwich into her mouth.

Titus climbed into one of the empty chairs at the table and smiled up at her. "Nope," her son agreed. "We will never be bored, especially once Torion gets here."

Sally frowned. "Who's Torion?"

Titus grinned, and despite the fact that he wasn't Costin's birth son, he managed to look just as cheeky as her mate. "Sorry, Mommy, I can't tell you that. But I can tell you he's awesome. And Thia is going to love him."

Sally's eyes widened and then snapped to Costin's. "Oh dear."

ALSTON STOOD at the entrance to the enormous mountain. It reminded him a bit of the warlock stronghold. Outside, a perfectly formed geologic feature, but inside, a fortress fit for a king. He'd used his power to mold and shape the earth into rooms, halls, and spaces that would be useful for his army. As he worked on the new Order headquarters, he'd reached out to some of his long-time spies amongst the ranks of the pixies and trolls, sending them out to gather information and new warriors. That had been a month ago. Now the fortress teamed with supernatural followers: trolls, pixies, warlocks, fae, and vampires. No elves had joined, but he wasn't concerned. Ludcarab could handle those warriors. He was likely keeping them close for the time being. Cain had not arrived either, though Alston had sent out a few vampires to let the vampire king know their new compound was ready. Alston could only assume Cain was busy rebuilding the vampire community as quickly as possible.

"You've done well." Shehan, the warlock leader for the Order, walked up beside him. Thus far, she was the only leader that had made herself known after Peri's destruction. Shehan hadn't been at the compound when it had gone down. Thankfully, she'd been out recruiting more of her people.

"It's not the first time we've had to rebuild, Shehan," Alston reminded her.

"True."

"Still no word from the other supernatural representatives?" Alston asked.

She shook her head. "It's time to appoint new representatives. We have to assume they went down with the compound."

Alston agreed. Now that they had a place to continue to work on their plan, there was no reason to wait. They needed to move forward.

"What about Ludcarab?" the warlock leader asked.

Alston clenched his teeth as he thought of the elf king he so despised. "He will be here when it is time."

"That's quite cryptic." Shehan narrowed her eyes on him.

Alston shrugged. "We're all evil masterminds, Shehan. 'Sharing is caring' is not our motto."

The warlock snorted. "Despite all we've lost since Perizada's stunt, I think you gained a sense of humor." She nodded at him and walked further into the mountain. "It looks good on you. But evil masterminds or not, sharing *is* caring because it keeps our evil mastermind asses from being blown up. Maybe think about that a little."

Alston watched the warlock representative walk away, her words rubbing against the inside of his skull like wool against his skin. There were definitely secrets among the Order representatives. Could it have been some of those very secrets that had allowed Perizada her way in? Maybe. But transparency required trust. And Alston didn't trust anyone.

"There's still no sign of Tenia, my lord." A small voice came from behind him.

Alston turned and looked down. One of his pixie spies, a little over a foot tall, stood staring up at him.

"I've searched everywhere, even the warlock mountain," the pixie hurried on. "I found the fae you'd assigned to accompany her and the djinn."

Alston titled his head as he waited for the pixie to continue.

"He'd been killed. Stabbed with a fae blade."

"The blade had been left behind?" Alston asked, his brow drawing low.

"N-n-oo," the pixie stuttered. "I could feel the magic residue left from the blade in the wound. He'd been dead for a while. But a fae blade leaves quite a significant amount of power."

Alston took a slow, deep breath and waved the pixie off. If Tenia was alive, but her son, who had been in the compound at the time of the cold fire, was dead, then he no longer had any leverage over her. It wouldn't be surprising if she'd killed the fae male who'd accompanied her to the warlock stronghold. It also wouldn't be surprising if she joined with his enemies now that she didn't have a child to protect. "That would be most unfortunate," he muttered to himself. Most unfortunate indeed. Tenia was entirely too powerful to have as an enemy. The uniqueness of her power made her especially dangerous. The fae would have to be removed at the first available opportunity.

Turning his back to the interior of the mountain, Alston looked out over the vast range of peaks arrayed before him. Most of it was bare, as winter still held the plants in its grips, but here and there, tiny buds of new life began to emerge. The promise of spring. Soon the mountain range would be covered from top to bottom in all different shades of green. He took a deep breath, the cold air filling his lungs. A new season was coming, and, with it, a new Order.

CAIN WRAPPED the darkness around him as he stood on the far side of the Wyoming mountain range, staring in the direction of Alston's new construction. The high fae had been busy. Cain had been busy as well, searching high and low, contacting old covens, reestablishing his ranks. So many had been destroyed by those accursed wolves. But he would rebuild. That was the great thing about being a vampire. As long as there were humans to turn, he had a potential army just waiting to be built.

The problem was, while Cain had been away from the high fae and Ludcarab, he'd discovered, or rediscovered, how very much he disliked both males. He found the idea of working with them again, even as a charade, downright nauseating.

His time away from the other two leaders had given him some perspective. He now realized with Sincaro gone that *he* was the new vampire king. And it was *his* decision if he continued working with the current Order leaders or ventured out on his own.

What Sincaro had failed to realize was that the vampires were by far the most important race among the Order's ranks. No other species could reproduce themselves so quickly, effectively raising an entire army in weeks. Of course, he'd need to have his lieutenants share the workload. He couldn't have a vast swath of warriors taken out in a single blow if he lost a sire that had created too many new vampires. But that was no big deal. Cain still had many of the powerful elder vamps under his control, and they were stronger than Ludcarab and Alston knew. With such power, Cain should be leading the Order, not that pompous high fae.

Cain raised a hand, resting his elbow on the arm still folded across him and tapped his chin with his finger. "Perhaps it *is* time for the vampires to rise up," he said to the surrounding forest. "You other supernaturals have ruled long enough."

LUCIAN HADN'T MOVED from where he sat against the tree. His eyes were closed, his face turned up toward the winter sun. The weak rays couldn't penetrate the chill of the cold air. Three days had passed since Disir had left him sitting in front of the draheim veil. He'd gone hunting a couple of times, taking just enough sustenance to keep himself alive. Other than that, he hadn't left his vigil. For a fleeting moment, he'd felt her. Her presence had been faint, but he knew it was her, and the bond was intact.

Over and over, Lucian replayed in his mind their last argument. Sometimes, he regretted the words he'd spoken in anger. Other times, he knew they needed to be said. He loved his mate with a fierceness he'd never thought possible. And it was because of that love that he refused to simply sit by and watch her destroy herself and every relationship she'd built over the years. Then he had lost her. When he'd walked away, Lucian had thought that they would have plenty of time to sort things out. He hadn't considered that his three-thousand-year-old mate would be gone for good. And now... He wasn't sure what was going on. Was she back? Even though he'd felt her for a moment, she was still out of his reach. But not for long. He would find her. And when he did, there would be no walking away. This time, he would make her listen. He would fight for her, for them. He would fight, and he would win, even if it was his own mate he had to fight.

"Have you been sitting there since Disir left you?"

He'd smelled the group before Jen spoke, but he still didn't open his eyes. With his eyes closed, he could see his mate. She lived in his mind's eye, and he didn't want to lose sight of her for even a second.

"Gotta admit," Jen continued, "that's some serious devotion. Not even a phone to distract yourself with. And the bladder control, that's even more impressive. I mean, as a mom—"

"Jen," Jacque's voice cut her off. "Lay off."

Jen huffed but didn't continue her monologue.

"I'm sorry it took so long," Disir's voice spoke next.

Lucian did open his eyes now. His gaze roamed over the group gathered before him until they landed on the high fae.

"I did some digging in our archives first, then I went back to the sprite realm," Disir explained.

"And the answer you came up with was to bring back a support group?" Lucian asked, unsure why there were so many supernaturals standing in front of him. And a human. Apparently, Chris Morgan, Sally's dad, was as much a warrior as the supernaturals in their group. Otherwise, they wouldn't have brought him along.

"You're not the only one who wants Peri back," Myanin said. She was adorned with weapons, as if she was about to charge into a serious battle. Perhaps she thought if they got through the veil, they would have to fight the draheim.

Lucian did not think that would be the case, not if his mate had taken sanctuary in their realm.

"I'm aware of that," Lucian said. "I guess I just didn't expect so much help."

"How many times do I have to tell you that what happened is water under the bridge?" Heather asked from where she stood next to her mate. "Tell him, Kale."

Lucian met Kale's eyes. After several heartbeats, the great white wolf dropped his eyes. Not because Lucian wasn't as dominant as the Ireland beta, but out of respect for the male and humility for what Lucian had done. It impressed Lucian that Kale hadn't tried to kill him. It was what he deserved, and Lucian would have let him do it.

Heather elbowed her mate, causing him to grunt. "We talked about this, Iceberg."

There was a snicker from several of the healers as they glanced at the couple.

"Iceberg?" Jen asked, and then her face lit up. "Shut up! Kale. Like the lettuce? So you"—she pointed at Heather and then at Kale —"call him different types of green veggies. Damn, that is awesome! How did I not come up with that?"

"Try not to be too hard on yourself," Heather told her as she patted her male's chest. "You've had a lot on your mind. You haven't had time to think about how to make fun of his name yet."

"I'm standing right here," Kale muttered dryly.

"That you are, Romaine," Jen said and slapped her thigh as if it was the funniest thing she'd heard in a while.

Kale sighed and looked up as if trying to get a hold of his irritation. Lucian understood the feeling well.

"Look," the Ireland beta said and then dropped his eyes to look at Lucian. "Am I still pissed over what you did to my mate? Yes. But"—he paused and clenched his teeth—"I know all too well that we make mistakes. Our beasts can be unpredictable. Especially when we're dealing with painful issues concerning our females. So I'm choosing to let it go. I might have done the same thing had I been in your shoes."

Lucian's brow rose in surprise. He'd expected it might be years before Kale would be able to even be in the same space as Lucian without wanting to shred him to pieces. Instead, the male looked at Lucian with understanding and even empathy. Lucian pushed up from the ground and stood. He bowed his head to the beta. "Thank you. Though, just like my apology is not adequate, neither is my thanks. But it's all I have to offer at the moment. I can promise to protect your mate if ever there is a time that she needs it."

Kale gave a sharp nod but said nothing more.

Lucian turned his attention to Jacque, who'd been watching him the entire time. He'd felt her eyes on him, as if she was attempting to assess his emotional state. Maybe she'd even spoken with her mate through the bond, reporting what she saw as she watched him. Her bright green eyes held compassion that reminded him of Alina. They also held intelligence and perception that would serve her well in her new role. "You are good?" He inclined his head in the alpha's direction.

"I am." She gave a small smile. "How about you?"

Lucian's eyes darted to the trees behind the group where the veil was located. He clenched his jaw in frustration then looked back at Jacque. "I need to see her. Until then, I cannot pretend to be all right."

"Nobody expects that of you, Lucian," she said. "We also don't expect you to go through this alone. You and Peri belong to us. We will get through this together."

Lucian could practically feel the anticipation of the group, waiting to see how he would respond to her words.

Would he shut them down, or would he embrace what they offered? There was only one answer. "Thank you. I need my pack."

There was an audible sigh from several of the group, mostly females, Lucian noted. Yet many of the males relaxed their rigid stances as well. He looked over the group and noted that Costin and his mate were absent, which wasn't alarming, considering she was with child. He was surprised to see the Springfield and Coldspring pack alphas. They both gave him silent nods when his eyes met theirs.

"We're waiting on three more people," Jacque told him. "Then we—"

"Are getting through this veil even if we have to die trying," Myanin interrupted the alpha.

"I'd prefer the not-dying method," Wadim said as he pulled his mate closer to his side. "I've got plans, not to mention, we still have a riddle to work out, which might actually help us with this." He motioned to the veil.

The djinn didn't look impressed. "Your plans can wait, and we can figure out the riddle once we get Perizada back by just asking her what it meant. So put away your pen and get out your sword."

"Myanin," Lilly said. "Maybe save the intensity for once we actually start working on the veil?"

"CT's just getting pumped up, Ms. P," Jen said, bouncing on the balls of her feet. She pulled a knife from either side of her cargo pants and spun them in her hands. "Some of us need to psych ourselves up."

"I know we don't know each other that well," Dalton's mate, Jewel said to Jen, "but I can just look at you and tell that you *stay* psyched up. I don't think any pumping is necessary."

"Truth," Jacque and Lilly said at the same time.

"Oh, the things I could do with that sentence." Jen looked almost forlorn. She shook it off and said, "I don't want others to feel bad about themselves if they don't stay in kick-ass mode all the time."

"Ahh," Jewel said with a slow nod. "That's … gracious of you."

Jen smiled, her eyes lighting up mischievously. "It is. It really is. Jen's my name, and giving is my game."

Wadim coughed, and Lucian was sure it sounded like he said, "bullshit." Zara slapped his arm, but she was trying not to smile.

"Wow." Jeff, the Coldspring alpha, breathed out, shaking his head at Decebel's mate.

"No, no." Jen shook a knife at Jeff. "No more admiring how awesome I am. You're officially on my mate's kill list."

Jeff's eyes widened. "What?" He took a step back, his hands raising. "What did I do? And he has a kill list?"

Jen frowned. "Don't you?" Then she looked around at the rest of the group. "I thought that was just a given for *Canis lupus* males."

Myanin raised her hand, looking sheepish. "Not just *Canis lupus*. I have one. But I've taken a few names off recently, those whose demise isn't entirely necessary."

"Understandable." Jen nodded. "Considering the whole 'killed an innocent person' thing. Makes your kill list a little more subject to scrutiny."

"Your list needs serious scrutiny as well." Jacque narrowed her eyes at Jen. "And I thought we agreed you'd burn it."

"That was before." Jen tossed one knife and caught it effortlessly by the handle.

After several seconds, Heather cleared her throat and

asked, "Before what? And dude, you can't answer so obscurely and expect us to just let it slide by."

"I agree with Helen." Stella, the healer mated to Ciro, pointed at the blind healer. "That's not how we roll. Spill it, Stabby."

Jen's lips turned up slowly. "Is that my road name?"

Lucian almost cracked a smile when every female in the group groaned. Peri would have gotten a kick out of the entire situation. He'd have to remember to share it with her once she was back at his side. "Do I want to know what she means by road name?" Lucian asked Jacque.

The alpha female shook her head. "It just encourages her."

"Sure, it's your road name," Stella answered Jen. "Considering you're tossing around blades like they're hacky sacks that couldn't impale you or someone standing close to you. Forget that. Finish your story. What happened that lets you get to keep your list?" she repeated Heather's question.

"I agreed to burn my kill list before my hellion was taken by the Order, before my alphas were killed, before Peri fell apart, before Jacque nearly lost her heart, and before Kara got snatched. Now, the list will not be burned, and it has actually gotten longer."

"No disrespect, Jacque, but I think she can totally have a kill list," Heather said. "Lots of people need to die."

"Agreed," Jewel, Stella and Anna, the one healer who hadn't said a word so far, said in unison.

"Gah." Jen grinned. "They're so bloodthirsty. I love it. We're totally keeping them."

"I'm not even going to ask what she means by that," Myanin said. "What's taking Nissa so long?"

"I'm here," the high fae in question said as the group

parted. Beside her stood Thadrick, the djinn, and his mate, Jezebel.

"Thank you, Nissa," Jacque told the fae. "I appreciate your willingness to help get them here. And thank you Thad and Jezebel for coming."

"I also have these." Nissa held out her hands to show five fae stones.

"Those fancy rocks are busy lately," Jen said.

Jacque nodded. "It's a good sign that they're here with us."

Lucian's attention was drawn back to Thadrick as the djinn started moving toward him.

"Nissa has explained about the draheim veil," Thadrick said, his eyes holding Lucian's. "I will use what power I can to see if we can open it. But I cannot use too much or the destruction I will cause—"

"Will make Peri's cold fire look like child's play," interrupted Jen. "We get it."

"Understood," Lucian said and then waited to see what the djinn would instruct.

"Form a circle, please." Thadrick motioned to the group to spread out. Lucian appreciated the djinn getting right down to business. The wolf's skin crawled with the need to see his mate, and though the earlier chatter distracted him, that's all it was—a fleeting distraction.

When everyone had created a circle, Thadrick walked over to the veil and motioned for Nissa and Disir, who stood in front of it, to spread apart and make an opening. "This is not an exact science," the djinn told the group, his back to them as he looked at the space between the two large trees. "Considering the amount of mixed power in this group—sprite, wolf, witch, warlock and fae—I think holding hands to combine the power will be useful. Jezebel will hold my hand, as well as Nissa's, and she will funnel the power from you all into me. I will attempt to blend it with my own, hopefully reducing the amount of my magic I will need to use."

Lucian looked beside him and saw Jacque on his right and Jen on his left. He took their hands and ignored the way his wolf growled, disliking the touch of any other female besides their own. *If this is what it takes to get her back, then we will hold their hands,* Lucian told his beast. The wolf didn't respond.

"Considering my lack of magic," Myanin stepped up beside the veil, "I'm just going to stand here and be ready to cut something once the veil comes down."

"Myanin," Gerick, the warlock general, called. Lucian noted the intensity with which the man fixed the female djinn and saw the same possessiveness in Gerick's eyes that he saw in the eyes of other true mates.

"I won't do anything stupid," Myanin assured him, her eyes softening a bit.

"Liar," Jen mumbled.

"It would be good to have someone ready in case there is draheim waiting on the other side," Thadrick said. "Thank you, Myanin. Magic or not, your fighting skills are unparalleled."

Myanin looked at the male djinn, and Lucian saw something pass between them, but he didn't recognize what. "Thank you, Thadrick." Weariness, maybe, but also respect.

"Focus," Thadrick said, his voice deepening. He reached for his female's hand. "Picture the magic that lives inside of you as something that flows like water. It starts in the center of your chest and runs throughout your body," Thadrick continued. "Now focus on pushing it down through your arms and into your hands. See it flowing into the person next to you. Jacque, pull on the pack bonds. Your mate will answer you, as will your pack."

Lucian did as the djinn instructed. He saw the magic that made him the supernatural being he'd been created to be. But that wasn't the only thing he saw. He also saw a current of blue power running through him. Confusion filled his mind. He'd never seen that power inside of him when he looked at his bond or his pack magic. This was new. He reached out with his hand in his mind's eye and let his fingers run over the current. Lucian sucked in a sharp breath when he felt his mate's magic fill him. Then he felt her. All of her.

Lucian dropped to his knees, but Jacque and Jen didn't release his hands. His head fell forward. So many emotions, memories, and thoughts filled his mind.

"Thad, we've got an issue." Jen's voice sounded like it was coming from somewhere far away.

"Don't stop," Thadrick called back. "Whatever it is, we will deal with it after the veil is open."

"We've got you, Lucian." Jacque's voice was soft but strong next to his ear. "We won't let go."

Lucian got the strange feeling that Jacque knew what was happening, or she at least had an idea. He could feel her empathy through the pack bonds that were currently wide open. As more of his mate's magic slammed into him, he realized he had no choice but to trust Jacque, because he was lost to all that happened inside of him. His wolf attempted to take over, but Lucian kept control of the beast and just let himself sink into the moment. What more could he do? He didn't want to fight it. He wanted her, needed her close, and this was the closest he'd felt to her in far too long.

"My mate," Lucian said through the true mate bond that currently wrapped itself around the blue magic, threading itself in and out until the gold and blue were a single cord. *"Come back to me."*

Another pulse of power hit him, so strong that it knocked the wind from his chest. He felt himself tip back, and he would've been knocked down if Jacque and Jen hadn't held him upright. Lucian clenched his teeth against the onslaught, trying to breathe air in through his nose. His lungs burned with the need of the precious oxygen. *"PER-IZADA."* Lucian's wolf roared in his mind, reaching to her through the now joined cord.

His heart beat painfully in his chest, and he was sure at any moment it would simply stop from the amount of power flowing through him. Then, like all the air being sucked from a room, the magic whooshed out of him. It went through his hands and into the females on either side of him. He heard Jen curse, and Jacque joined her a second later.

Lucian started to ask them if they were okay, but then his mouth slammed shut as his mate's presence filled his mind. *"Lucian."* Her voice caressed his soul, tentative and gentle.

"I'm here, beloved," he told her.

"You have to go." She sounded as if she was in pain, and he had to fight the need to rip his hands from Jen and Jacque and throw himself at the veil.

"No. Never again," he argued. *"I will never leave you again."*

"I have nothing left to give."

"I will take you as you are, no matter what that means. If you are a wraith left to wander the earth, then I will wander with you. If you are a shell, empty from the pain, then my love

will fill you. If you are broken beyond repair, then I will hold your pieces until we pass from this life into the next. All I need is you, Peri. Nothing more."

He felt her fear, torment, and anger. But beneath that, he also felt a small sliver of hope. *"That's not fair,"* she said.

"Life isn't fair, beloved. And to expect it to be fair is setting ourselves up for constant disappointment. Instead, we do the best with what we have, and we find joy in every circumstance. I find joy in you. You do not have to doubt me. You can feel the truth through our bond and see my thoughts. You are the other half of my soul, Perizada. No matter what happens, that will never change. I will forever need and want you. You are mine. I'm sorry I didn't handle my anger in a better way." Lucian reached further down the bond, pictured her face in his mind, and ran his fingers across her cheek. He heard her quick, indrawn breath and knew she'd felt him. A moment later, the heat of her palm on his own cheek warmed his skin. Lucian let himself soak up her touch. Though it was only through the bond, he grasped on to the feeling like a drowning man clinging to the only floating object in a vast ocean. He sensed her slipping away from him, though her magic was still there, inside of him, a part of him.

"I'm not going anywhere, Perizada. I sat in the Dark Forest for centuries. I can just as easily sit in this one."

There was a final caress as her voice whispered in his mind, *"You will be wasting your time, my love."*

"All I've got is time."

Jacque held tightly to Lucian's hand on her left side and Jewel's on her right. She wasn't completely sure what happened when Lucian collapsed to the ground, nearly taking her and Jen with him, but she could feel something more than just his power coming through the pack bond. She could feel a cold magic intermingled with his power. When she closed her eyes and searched for it, she found the thread that connected Lucian to the pack. Then she saw that there was a blue flame wrapped around his cord. Cold fire, she realized. Then, as more of the power flowed into her, she recognized Peri's magic. Perhaps because she'd become a part of their pack by being mated to Lucian, or by proxy simply because they'd claimed her as pack, Peri's magic seemed as familiar to Jacque as any of her other pack members.

As the coldness filtered into her, Jacque wondered how on earth Lucian could withstand it. She was receiving it secondhand, and still the sensation was so strong she thought it might knock her unconscious.

"I've got you, Luna." Fane's voice filled her mind. *"I've always got you."*

Jacque did not know how much time passed as they stood in the circle, hands joined, power flowing from one person to the next, but she grew tired, and her legs ached. Her eyes roamed over the group, and she saw others struggling to stay on their feet as well.

"Thadrick," she called out to the djinn. "We need a break."

The djinn lowered the hand held out in front of him. His shoulders rose and fell with his breaths, and he slowly turned around. He looked straight at her. His eyes swirled with a rainbow of different colors, but then gradually faded and returned to normal.

"You can let go," he told the group.

The current that had flowed through Jacque abruptly stopped, and she stumbled. She slowly released Lucian's hand and looked down at him. He was on his knees, his shoulders hunched forward and his head hung low. When she and Jen let go, he rolled forward onto his hands and knees and phased. The huge, white wolf shook as if his fur was coated in water. Then he threw his head back and let out a soul-shattering howl. The sound died off and then he bolted away, disappearing into the trees.

"Is he gonna be okay?" Stella asked, her voice wobbly, and her hands on her knees. "Because he did not look like a man who was in control of himself, or his wolf for that matter."

"He'll be back," Jacque said, instead of answering the healer's question.

"So, I guess this will be nothing like last time." Jacque heard Elle's voice before the fae stepped from the forest.

"I thought you were with the hunting party," Jacque said, her breathing labored.

"Fane asked me to pop in and see how things are going." She ran her eyes over the group. "And I have to say, it's not looking too good. No judgment." She held up her hands. "But this is not at all how it went down with the pixie veil."

Jacque looked toward the veil and saw Myanin pressing her hand against the invisible wall, which was as solid as if it were made of bricks.

"Not even the slightest give," the djinn said.

"It will take time," Thadrick said. "The draheim magic is powerful."

"Are you saying we're going to be here awhile?" Stella asked. "Because this is starting to feel way too familiar."

"At least Jewel isn't talking about resorting to drinking our own urine yet," Heather said as Kale helped her sit on the ground.

"I wasn't stuck with y'all in the pixie realm. It was the

Dark Forest," Jewel corrected. "And it's still early. We've got a few days before we will need to resort to urine hydration."

"Or"—Jen said, drawing the word out— "we could ask our friendly high fae friends to get us food and water."

"Winner, winner, chicken dinner." Heather held up her hand. "Oh, come on, don't leave me hanging. Someone give me a damn high five."

Jacque couldn't help but laugh at the blind healer. She was a breath of fresh air. People like Heather who helped others continue to see the light in dark places.

Anna walked over and slapped Heather's hand. "There ya go. Don't say I never gave you anything."

"Thatta girl, Gypsy, way to have your wheeler's back." Heather grinned.

"New road name!" Jen hollered as she collapsed to the ground. "I *knew* you guys would be all over it."

Jacque eased to the ground, her shaky legs no longer able to hold herself up. "I'm shocked you don't already have a notebook with everyone's road names preassigned."

"Who says I don't?" Jen asked. "But I'm open to suggestions."

Jacque shook her head at her best friend and then looked at Thadrick. "How long should we take a break?"

Thad examined the group, who almost all now sat on the ground. Lilly, Myanin, and Kale were the only ones left standing. "We shall rest an hour and measure our strength at that point."

Nissa stood back up and held out her hand. In it appeared a large loaf of bread. "This will help." She tore off a piece and then passed the rest to Jeff. He did the same and then handed it to Tyler. This continued until everyone had taken their own piece of fae bread. The moment Jacque swallowed it, she felt the magical properties of the food begin to restore her energy. A bottle of water appeared in front of her. She picked it up and looked over at Nissa. "Thank you."

The high fae bowed her head and then tipped her own bottle up to her mouth.

"So, we're sitting around in a circle in a forest... man, just like old times." Heather spoke up again. "Me and my girls have experience with this. Have no fear, friends, this will not be boring. We can do this for days, weeks, months, even. Jewel is an overflowing well of knowledge. Some useful, some scary, and a lot ridiculous. But we love her anyway. In a pinch, Stella can teach us all to pole dance using the closest skinny tree. And Anna can tell us all about her past because, hello, her mom is a witch related to a dark witch that you guys killed. How can that not be an awesome fireside story? "

"Can we knock her out?" Anna glanced around the group. "I mean, we've got a fae here. Surely she can make it painless. We can wake Heather back up when we need her again."

Myanin sighed and sat down beside Anna. "Perhaps you and I aren't *supposed* to be friends because of the history I have with your mother." Myanin glanced at Jezebel and inclined her head. Jezebel returned the gesture, her face blank of any anger or judgment. "But I think I like you."

"Knocking people out is your thing, isn't it?" Anna pulled her knees up and rested her arms on them.

"Definitely," Myanin said, mimicking the healer's pose and glancing at Heather.

"She's looking at me, isn't she?" Heather asked dryly.

Jacque leaned over toward Jen and whispered, "I think they're just as bad as you, me, and Sally."

Jen's eyes roamed over the girls, and she nodded slowly. "I keep telling you we have to keep them."

Jacque threw back her head and laughed. She took a moment to thank the Great Luna. Though they were in the midst of terrible circumstances, for this brief moment, there was also joy and goodness. Who knew how many attempts it would take to get into the draheim realm? Regardless of how long it took, she knew they wouldn't give up. And she was glad she belonged to such a strong pack that would lift each other up when necessary, even if that lifting came in the form of threats to knock one another unconscious.

"While we're recovering," Wadim spoke up from where he sat on the ground with Zara propped up against him, "let's see if we can make any progress on this riddle. She obviously told it to us for a reason."

"I doubt it has the answer to why she's locked herself up with a bunch of dragons." Jen huffed. "Or how to get her out because she obviously DOESN'T WANT TO COME OUT!" Jen's head turned toward the veil, and the last sentence increased with volume as she spoke, as if Peri could hear her and the irritation lacing her tone.

"But Wadim's right," Zara said. "She didn't just pop in and toss some stones at us because she was suddenly feeling nostalgic. It's obviously important."

"The stones helped us heal Jacque," Lilly pointed out.

Jacque nodded. "That is true, so that knocks out the first part of the riddle." She waved her hand at Wadim. "Tell us the words again. Let's see what we can come up with."

Wadim pulled out a folded piece of paper from a pocket of his cargo pants and read.

"They go where they are needed most. The power of the

stones is a mystery. They heal, and they reveal. And so they've brought me here. I bid you listen and do not speak. Now is not the time for questions."

"She's bossy even while delivering a riddle … or prophecy … or whatever it is," Jen muttered.

"The prodigal is returning," Wadim continued, "and a new son will join your ranks. Evil will think it has prevailed, but hope will be born from the supposed triumph."

Jacque considered the second half of the riddle and then looked at Jen. "It does sound like a *prophecy*, not a riddle. She's *foretelling* something that is going to happen. Prophecies aren't necessarily meant to be 'figured out.' The stones appeared when we needed them in order to help you all heal me. I think even if they'd been left there on the floor and we hadn't realized that's what they were there for, they'd still have generated magic for the healing."

"So you don't think we need to work out who the prodigal is," Heather asked, "or this new son thing, or even about the triumph? Which I might add, we really could use the morale boost of a triumph right about now."

"Totally could use a triumph," Stella agreed.

Jacque shook her head. "I don't think we need to figure it out. I think we need to be paying attention so that when these things come to pass, we will know how to react. We will be prepared for it."

Jen's face scrunched up as she groaned. "Ugh, prodigal son. As in a member of the family that has strayed away, done stupid stuff, and then wants to come back. Please, for the love of pixie butts, don't let that mean Alston. Because that isn't happening."

"That seems a bit farfetched. Alston would be the prodigal of all prodigals. But it could mean Boain," Wadim offered. "He has been gone, and then he came back at the challenges."

"Yes, but then he left again," Jacque said. "He wasn't among those who surrendered."

"Was he among the dead?" Jen asked.

Wadim sighed. "No. Unless he crawled off somewhere, died, and wasn't found, which I doubt. Most likely, he's gone."

"*Wadim is right,*" Fane's voice said through the bond. "*Boain left at some point during the challenges. We found no trace of him.*"

"Why would he come back, only to then leave again?" Jacque asked.

"*Perhaps he was not a part of the coup and didn't want to be lumped in with them,*" Fane suggested. "*But I don't think he is the prodigal son in Peri's prophecy.*"

She sat up straighter. "*Why? Do you know who it is?*"

"*I don't,*" he said, and she felt the truth in his answer. "*But I feel like the answer is on the edge of my mind, and I can't seem to reach it no matter how much I think about it.*"

"*I hate that feeling. Like when you have something on the tip of your tongue, but your brain just won't spit it out.*" Jacque mentally sighed. "*We're taking a break from our B and E efforts. Whatever magic is keeping this veil closed is powerful.*"

"*Just be careful,*" Fane said softly. "*The draheim probably aren't going to be pleased with you busting down the veil to their realm. But I understand why you all must try.*"

"*Peri needs to know that we haven't written her off,*" Jacque said. "*She needs to remember what pack means. That she's not alone and that we will be here no matter what she's going through. Our willingness to face the draheim to get her back, hopefully, will make that very apparent.*"

She felt the gentle caress of his fingers on her cheek.

"She knows," Fane assured her. *"But she definitely needs to be reminded. Just be safe, Luna."*

"I will. Oh, I've been so caught up in what we're doing that I haven't even checked in on your end. How is the hunt? How's Nick? Any progress?"

She heard his chuckle and felt the warmth of his love flowing through their bond. *"Any other questions before I answer those? I don't want you to forget anything."*

"Shut up," she teased. *"I've got to spit them out while they're on my mind or they fall off into the abyss of 'holy draheim balls, we have to save the world, a healer, a high fae, and somehow keep it all a secret from the human race.'"*

"One thing at a time, Jacquelyn. To answer your questions," he continued, *"we might have made some progress. Kara managed to contact Nick through their bond. Though from what Drayden said, I don't think she was aware that she was doing it. She didn't know who Nick was."*

"So it was her soul reaching out to him." Jacque shifted into a more comfortable sitting position.

"It would seem so. Drayden mentioned Nick was feeling very emotional at the time it happened, reflecting on intense memories with Kara."

"Ahh." Jacque nodded. *"Because intense emotions can't be blocked from the bond."*

"Exactly."

"Well, I'm praying to the Great Luna that it works. If he can connect with her again, maybe she can tell him where she is." Jacque was already sending up prayers to their Creator, as she had been since Kara was taken. She didn't understand why it happened, just like she still didn't understand why Sally had endured what she'd gone through. But Jacque believed that the Great Luna loved her creation and would

always work things out, even the most horrible of situations, for their good.

"My dad believed the same thing," Fane said, having heard her thoughts. *"And I do, too. We will get through this, Luna. And we will be stronger for it."*

"I know," Jacque said, her voice strong with the conviction she felt. *"I love you."*

"And I you."

CHAPTER
ELEVEN

"I want to run to you. I know that in your arms I will find safety, acceptance, protection, and love. I want to hear my name on your lips. I long to be near you. But I fear I have lost my right to ask for such things. Sometimes the consequences of our actions are just too terrible. They take us past a boundary from which we cannot return." ~Perizada

Peri bowed her head. Lucian's words filled every empty place inside her. She let her mate's warmth invade her. His pain had hit her out of nowhere and sucked the oxygen from her lungs. Once she'd caught her breath, she realized it was the fae bond that had forced them to connect. She'd kept that bond closed to Lucian because of how vulnerable it would make her to him. She'd been a fool to think he wouldn't one day find out about it.

Peri allowed herself several minutes of solace that came from the brief contact with her mate. She didn't deserve his comfort, but she took it anyway. Since traveling to the sprite realm and delivering the message given to her in a dream, all she wanted to do was go back there. For a few seconds, she'd been in the presence of her pack, her family. She'd felt her mate through the bond and had fought the need to reach out to him. If she'd stayed even a second longer, Peri knew she wouldn't have been able to leave. Instead, she flashed back to the draheim realm and wandered aimlessly while her thoughts continually jumped back to her conversation with Serapha.

When in my long past was I saved? Why?

What could have possibly been happening to cause Peri to be in need of help from another? Why couldn't she have saved herself? Question after question filled the high fae's mind, and she couldn't ask the damn draheim. Serapha was nowhere to be found.

With the risk of her own thoughts potentially driving her mad, Peri returned to the cave and to the three supernaturals now in her care. Perhaps she could find a way not to screw this up. *Don't hold your breath.* Pushing away thoughts of Lucian that would weaken her resolve to stay away, she turned her attention instead to Skender.

"Does anyone else know of your history?" Peri sat in the cave they'd claimed as their temporary sanctuary. Tenia was still unconscious, and Peri used her magic to keep the woman clean and nourished. But she didn't know what else she could do for the female fae. So Peri sat against the wall on the other side of the cave and watched as Skender did the best he could to care for her. He and Torion took turns brushing her hair, washing her face with warm water from a spring nearby, and even moving her limbs. Though Peri told him none of this was necessary, the wolf seemed to *need* to do something for Tenia.

Upon hearing the question, Skender's eyes grew large and darted to where Torion sat. It was obvious the wolf was worried about the boy realizing Skender's story was about himself. But Peri didn't care. She would shield no one from the truth, and she would not pretend for Skender's benefit. Torion seemed absorbed in a one-sided conversation he was having with his mother. Skender's eyes left the child and met Peri's. "If my history was yours, would you go around sharing it?"

Peri shrugged. Maybe he had a point. The wolf had a checkered past: convoluted, painful, and embarrassing. "Probably not."

"So forgive me if I do not broadcast my failures to the world."

"But some of this you didn't know or didn't remember," Peri told him. She thought back to the sound of Skender's voice as he'd spoken, the inflection and pauses, as if Skender seemed to be learning his story as much as Torion was. It had been very apparent to Peri that the wolf was shocked by the revelations coming from his own mouth.

"That doesn't change that it happened. It doesn't change what I did." Skender's voice was thick with regret.

Peri never thought she'd see a day that she could relate to the wolf who'd caused such pain to Sally, but here they were. Both of them looking back at the terrible pain they'd caused, unable to change it and drowning in the aftermath. "You might as well get it all out." Peri motioned to Torion. "And give up the pretense that this story is about anyone but you. The boy is smart and resilient. He can handle it."

Skender's face darkened as he stared back at her. Clearly Peri's interference was not appreciated. He'd get over it.

"I already know the story is about you, Skender," Torion

said. He shifted his body and faced them. "You've slipped up a couple of times."

Skender pinched the bridge of his nose and let out a defeated sigh. "I wish you were wrong, but I want you to know the truth, and I don't want you to find out from anyone but me."

"Okay," Torion said simply.

Peri settled back against the wall and focused all her attention on the wolf across from her. She would let the new information about Skender's story distract her from another wolf. At least for now.

SKENDER CLENCHED his jaw and considered all the ways he could slant his story to make himself look less like a dirtbag. None existed. Everything he'd done was just as it appeared—horrible. "When I arrived back at the Order," he began, picking the story up where he'd left off, "I helped Alston do something vile." He waited to see what Torion's reaction would be. The boy simply sat there listening, his eyes soft. Skender saw no judgment lurking in their depths, so he continued.

"I helped him capture a healer that is a member of the Romanian wolf pack. Alston took her memories, her life, and erased it. He gave her a new life, one without her true mate, her friends, and her family."

"Why?" Torion asked, his face screwed up in confusion.

"Because he wanted to gain her magic for the Order. He thought if he removed all her knowledge of the supernatural world and then reintroduced it to her from the Order's viewpoint, she'd be willing to join them." Skender felt disgusted as he remembered watching Alston work his power on Sally. How the hell had he let himself be a part of that?

"What happened to the healer? Is she okay?"

Skender grimaced. "She is now. But her experience, I'm sure, has left scars, the kind you can't see. Scars on the inside." He ran his hand down Tenia's arm, gathering his thoughts. Then he forged on. "I lied to my pack. I purposely tried to mislead them in order to get what Alston wanted. I helped him steal the children of pack members. I fought against my own family. Even once I realized what I was doing was a mistake, I couldn't leave. By that point, I'd felt the pull of my mate. It was the realization that I had a mate, and that she was so close, that seemed to snap me out of the trance I'd been in. I didn't even realize that's what it was until the fog lifted.

"I'm not making excuses for what I did, Torion," he added quickly. "No matter how or why it happened, I hurt people, and I can never take it back."

"Not going to lie, wolf," Peri said. "Hearing it out loud from the mouth of the guilty is making me a little zappy."

Skender cast his eyes to the ground. "I wouldn't blame you if you killed me where I sit, Peri. Though I would ask you to wait until I know with complete certainty that Torion and Tenia are safe."

"Don't kill him." Torion's eyes were glassy with unshed tears. "Please, Perizada. Skender made mistakes. I make them all the time." His small voice wavered as he spoke.

"Some mistakes are bigger than others," Peri said. "They have more serious consequences. Therefore, the punishment is more severe."

"What if someone says they're sorry?" Torion asked. "And what if they really mean it? My mom says when I apologize, I must actually be sorry and not just because I got caught. What about then?"

Skender kept his eyes on the ground, unable to meet the high fae's gaze. He knew what Peri would say. Sometimes sorry just wasn't good enough, no matter how sincere.

"Do you think Skender is sorry because of what he did or because he got caught?" Peri asked Torion. It wasn't what he expected her to say.

"I think he's sorry because he never wanted to hurt anyone, and then he did. And somehow that's even more painful than doing something bad that you actually *wanted* to do."

Skender heard Peri let out a low whistle. "What are they feeding you kids these days? I swear each one is smarter than the last." She cleared her throat and then added. "I think you're right, kid. And I never thought I'd say this. In fact, I'm pretty sure at some point I believed hell would freeze over before I would ever extend an olive branch to Skender. But here we are."

Skender looked up and saw that she held her hands out, palms up, as if to punctuate their current circumstance.

"I've killed hundreds, possibly thousands, because I let my anger control me. Am I any better than Skender?" She met his eyes. "The self-righteous bitch in me wants to say yes, just so you know."

Skender's lips kicked up slightly, but not into a full-blown smile. There was too much pain, like nerves being exposed all over his body.

"The reality is none of us are good. We all have the capacity to do horrendous things. And we all have the capacity to feel genuine remorse. After all that I have done, I know I have no room to judge you, Skender. I also know that we don't get to pick and choose who deserves grace and mercy. If you and I don't, then who does?"

Skender felt a warm palm on his face, and his eyes dropped to meet green eyes staring back at him. "*Soarele meu*," he whispered as he leaned closer to Tenia and pressed his hand over hers, tight against his flesh.

"The answer to your question, Peri," the fae said, her voice thin and weak from lack of use, "is none of us. But because the Great Luna loves us, she offers it freely. And we have the choice to offer it as well."

Skender shook his head. "I wouldn't expect that of you," he said. "You don't know all that I've—"

"I heard you, Skender," she cut him off. "I heard everything."

Skender felt nausea build in his stomach at her words. "It doesn't change anything, Tenia. I don't deserve you."

She shook her head at him. "That's not your choice. It's mine. And I'm choosing you. I'm choosing us." Then she turned and her face lit up when she saw her son. "Torion," she gasped, reaching for him with her free hand.

The boy didn't hesitate. He threw himself at her, wrapping his small arms around her and burying his face against her neck. Skender heard the boy's sobs and watched as Torion's body shook with the emotions that he'd seemed to have kept hidden.

"I've got you," Tenia whispered. "You're okay."

Skender couldn't help himself. The wolf had to touch his mate. He ran a hand across her hair, over and over, knowing that her scent would be on him and his on her. He waited while mother and son reunited and felt his heart swell with love for both of them. They were both alive, unharmed, and for the moment, safe.

Several minutes passed before Torion pulled back and sat on his heels. "You heard us?" he asked her.

She nodded. "Every word. It's what kept me here." She looked at Skender. "Can you help me sit up? I've got a few questions for that fae who tried to barbeque us."

Skender smirked. He slid an arm under her lower back and lifted until she was in a sitting position. To his surprise, Tenia shifted her body so that she leaned against his side and then took his hand in hers and entwined their fingers. Tenia motioned for Torion to come to her. He scuttled over and smiled as he pressed against her other side. The joy on his face was contagious, regardless of any ugliness Skender had just confessed. Torion's exhilaration at his mother's waking was enough to push the darkness aside, for now.

When she was settled, Tenia's gaze landed on the high fae across from them. Skender looked at Peri as well. She didn't appear the least bit unsettled. She simply watched them.

"How the hell are we still alive?" Tenia said, her voice a sharp slap, which actually caused Peri to flinch. Before the high fae could answer, Tenia barreled on. "Why on earth did you think it was a good idea to use cold fire on the Order compound? Have you lost your ever-loving mind? Did you consider there might be a different way to take down that scum? Did anyone else know you were going to jump off the ledge of sanity and into the abyss of madness? And if so, did they try to talk you out of it?" Skender felt her quick breaths against his body when she finished her questions.

"I see where he gets it from." Peri's voice was cool, almost bored.

"What?" Tenia bit out. "What does that mean?"

"I see where your son gets his inability to wait for a

response after asking a question," Peri explained. "It's taxing."

"She doesn't like it when I do that," Torion said, sounding as if he enjoyed the revelation a little too much.

Tenia pointed to her face. "Do I look like I care if you're taxed?"

Peri tilted her head slightly and pursed her lips. "No. You look a little, well, crazy. Just being honest."

"Fantastic. Honesty. That's a good place to start." Tenia motioned with her hand. "Let's go with that theme. What happened, Peri? You're a three-thousand-year-old high fae. You can remember every question I just asked, in order, no doubt. So continue being honest and answer the damn questions."

"Remind me never to tick you off," Skender said through their bond without bothering to wonder if it would work. Communicating with his mate was instinctual, and he felt his wolf's relief that the bond was once again open between them.

"Who says I'm not ticked off with you already?" she asked. And even though she used the bond, her attention stayed focused on Peri.

"Fine," Peri sighed. "Let's get this over with."

TENIA HELD TIGHTLY to both Skender's and Torion's hands and listened to Peri's account of how she'd come to the compound, intent on destroying it. Mission accomplished. But she hadn't expected Torion to show up or Tenia to be there. But by then, it was too late for her to stop what was already in motion. Perhaps the biggest surprise of all was the giant dragon appearing amid the chaos to spirit them away.

"I've never been so happy to see one of the massive beasts in my life." Peri's eyes and voice filled with relief. "I just wanted you and Torion out of there. And I knew there was no way I could save you."

Tenia remembered the way her body had burned, how painful it had been. Skender growled next to her. She looked up at him and saw pain etched across his face. "It's over now," she told him, knowing how the memories of her injury affected him.

"I should have been there with you," he said softly. His free hand lifted and brushed softly across her face. Tenia leaned into his touch. She'd never known that she could crave someone so much. But she craved Skender like a drug.

Peri cleared her throat, pulling Tenia from the private moment with Skender, and she turned back to the fae. "So the captured draheim saved us and then what?"

"I told him where Skender was," Torion piped up with a grin on his face.

"We picked him up, and then the draheim brought us here, to his realm," said Peri.

"Didn't you worry he might have been bringing us back as a snack for his family, considering we were part of the group that held him captive?" Tenia asked.

"I wasn't really concerned with being eaten," Peri answered dryly. "I was too busy hoping you weren't already dead or that Torion might die from his exposure to my power. And once I figured out that you both were alive and staying that way, at least for the moment, I had to decide whether to kill Skender, considering... you know..."

Tenia narrowed her eyes at the high fae. "No one is killing my mate."

"I'm not the one you need to be worried about. I may have changed my mind regarding him, but you need to be prepared for the reaction of those he has wronged. They will not be so understanding." Peri crossed one leg over the other and leaned forward, resting her elbow on her knee. "You've been out of commission for a month, Tenia. I imagine Myanin and Lilly are worried sick. And from what I know of Myanin, it isn't a stretch to say that she might go on a killing spree just to find out what's happened to you and Torion."

Tenia's lips twitched at the thought of the female djinn. "You're not wrong, especially if she hasn't had any stress-relieving cotton candy." Then she frowned. "An entire month?" Tenia felt Skender's lips against her hair, then heard him breathe in her scent. His wolf reached out to her through the bond and shared the comfort she brought him just by being close to her.

"Do you have any more questions?" Peri asked. "Because I have a feeling you and Skender have much to discuss. I can take the kid out to see Galan."

Tenia squeezed Torion's hand tighter. "Who?"

"Galan," Peri answered. "He's the draheim who saved us. The beast has taken a shine to Torion, probably because, despite his size, Galan is still very young."

A grimace passed over Tenia's face. She and Skender certainly had things that must be addressed, but she didn't like the idea of her son anywhere but right next to her side.

Peri seemed to read the apprehension on her face. "I know after what I've done, I have no right to ask for your trust, Tenia. But I give you my word. I will protect your son with my life."

"Galan is great, Mom. He lets me ride on his back," Torion pulled his hand from hers and then gave her a hug.

"He *what*?" Tenia pulled him closer and squeezed him tighter.

"Remind me to talk to you about things you should and shouldn't say to your parents when you're trying to go do something fun," Peri said. "Now, come on. Let's give them some privacy so your mom can properly put her wolf in his place."

Tenia snorted and released Torion. "Please don't fall off."

"Mom," Torion grinned. "I'm a fae. I can just flash to the ground."

"The kid is smarter than the adults. We'd all just fall to our deaths like idiots." Peri held her hand out, and Torion took it.

He looked back at Tenia, and she had to swallow down the emotions threatening to explode from her gut. Her son was alive. He was alive, unharmed, and free from the Order's clutches. And he was about to ride on a draheim. *What the hell?*

"Quit worrying, Mom," he told her. "The Great Luna saved us. Oh…" He held up one hand. "Please don't make Skender leave. I know he messed up, but he belongs with us."

"I'll take that into consideration when making my deci-sion." She smiled at him. "I love you, Torion. More than anything."

"I know. See ya soon."

"Don't you dare fla—" Peri started, but then they were gone.

"She hates it when he flashes them instead of letting her do it." Skender's voice rumbled against Tenia.

Tenia shifted, trying to gather all the thoughts that had been whirling around in her head while she'd been in her weird coma. At the time, she thought she knew exactly what she would say. But now that Tenia was in his presence, feeling him against her, breathing in his scent, all she could think about was how badly she missed him and how scared she'd been that she would never have this with him.

"Tenia?" Skender's voice was tentative.

She moved, shifting forward and then turning so she faced him. Then Tenia crawled forward and swung a leg over his lap, sitting down on his thighs. Her hands rested on his chest, her fingers flexing and relaxing as she touched him. Her mate. Never in all of her existence would she have thought that she'd be given a mate. Once upon a time, Tenia's heart had beat for one reason only—Torion. Now, two people were the cause for the rhythm in her chest. No matter what Skender had done, she could feel his remorse. Tenia understood those emotions all too well because they also lived inside of her. Tenia's inability to protect her child, to keep him from the evil that was the Order, still plagued her.

His eyes softened as Skender stared at her. His gaze roamed over her face as if trying to memorize every inch, every nuance of her expressions. Tenia opened her end of the bond completely. She didn't want there to be any secrets between them. She pictured what she saw when Peri ignited the compound in the cold fire. Tenia remembered the burning against her skin and her sheer terror when Torion appeared and she'd known there was nothing she could do to save him. She let him see every thought that ran through her mind when she'd been sure her life would end.

Skender's hand rose, and the pads of his fingers ran across her forehead and down her temple to her cheek. Her face wasn't the only place she felt his hand. Skender used the bond to let her feel his touch in her hair, down her back, and up her calves to her thighs. He overwhelmed her senses. Her nerves felt exposed as he pushed his own emotions through their open bond. "If I could turn back time, I would give anything to keep you and Torion safe. Even if it meant tying you both to my side. I would *do* anything to keep you from going through what you did," he whispered. The reverence in his voice only punctuated the longing Tenia felt from him.

"When we first met, I was so angry." She bit her lip as she recalled the first time she'd seen him. Her eagerness to get Torion away from the Order had been her only focus ... until suddenly she saw Skender. He'd been standing right in front of the door that kept her son captive but also safe from the ugliness that had become their lives. "I wanted to kill you, but in equal measure, I wanted to be with you. I was so confused."

His lips turned up in a small, crooked smile. "I was pretty sure you were going to follow through with your threat to slit my throat."

Tenia winced as she remembered the words she'd spat at him. She'd said a lot of things out of terror and rage—things she didn't mean. She lifted one of her hands and ran her finger across the flesh of his neck where she'd threatened to plunge her blade. Now she'd protect his throat with her own life.

"No." He shook his head, having picked up on her thoughts. "My life is not worth sacrificing yours. Don't you ever consider it. *I* protect you. That's how this works."

She shook her head in return. "I don't think so. If that was how it worked, then there would be no mate bond that tied our lives together. Our souls are two halves, remember? One cannot exist without the other."

"That's only if the bond is complete," Skender said. "As

long as that doesn't happen, I can die and you will continue this life with Torion."

"And if I died?" she challenged. "The darkness would destroy you. Your wolf would become feral. And you would have to be killed anyway." He opened his mouth to speak, but she pressed a finger over his lips. "And even if we both live, without the bond complete, the darkness will still continue to grow inside of you."

Skender leaned forward and pressed his forehead to hers. "But not as fast. Having you near would be enough to slow it down."

Tenia's anger flared as she realized what he was saying. "You still don't want to complete the bond with me?" Just saying the words out loud felt like a blade being shoved into her heart. "Even after we nearly lost one another? Even after I've told you I don't care what has happened in your past? You're mine now. You're Torion's now." Tenia gripped his shirt in her hands, fisting it so tightly her knuckles turned white.

"I have lived for centuries on my own, Skender. I accepted the reality that I would always be alone. That Torion would be the only love in my life. And until you, I *was* content with that. Or at least I thought I was. And then you and your damn patient, protective, selfless ass had to go and ruin my contentedness." She pulled her hands back, his shirt still gripped within them, and slammed her knuckles against his chest. "*You* gave me something I didn't have. You gave me hope. You made me realize I didn't want to be alone anymore. But not only that I didn't want to be alone, but that I didn't want to be without *you*. YOU!" She snapped her mouth closed, trying to contain everything that had built inside of her, threatening to erupt. If she wasn't careful, Tenia might just hit her mate with a bolt of her magic in order to knock some sense into him. "You told me once that you were made for me and I for you. Are you telling me now that is no longer what you believe?"

He growled. "Of course not. I told you when we were in the compound that I would never complete the bond because I wouldn't allow you to tie yourself to the likes of me." He pulled his head back from hers. Then as if he couldn't help himself, Skender pressed a tender kiss to each of her cheeks. He ran his hands through her hair and gently pulled as if to punctuate his words, "You shine brightness into the dark parts of me, my own personal sun. I will not bite you only for you to bear *my shame* as your own, simply because you wear my mark."

Tenia gritted her teeth and tried to rein in her temper. "That is not your decision to make. How many times do I have to tell you that?"

"But it is, my sweet Tenia. I have the right to choose whether I bite *you*."

She couldn't help it. Before she even realized what she was doing, Tenia opened her palms, releasing his shirt and slammed her hands into his chest, shooting a bolt of her magic. She didn't hit him with enough power to cause any damage, but the jolt got his attention.

"Dammit, female." Skender barked and grabbed her wrists, pulling them away. He pushed them down and pressed them against the side of her thighs, effectively shackling her. "Was that really necessary?"

Her eyes narrowed. "Have you changed your mind about completing the bond?"

His lips drew taunt across his face. "No," Skender bit out.

"Then yes, it was necessary." With his hands wrapped around her wrists, Tenia's fingers were still free to zap him again, this time in his leg. He snarled and gripped her tighter. She probably shouldn't have smiled, but Tenia couldn't help it. She smiled even bigger when she thought of how Myanin would totally approve of her friend's persuasion tactics.

"Zapping me will not change my mind. Can't you see you deserve better than me?" he practically shouted. "If you take me as your true mate, you will also bear my shame, Tenia. Don't you get it? It's not just about me not being worthy. It's about the fact that you aren't just mating me. You take on all of my sins as your own. You will not have a pack, because I don't have a pack. You will face the rage of others, simply because you are mine and I am yours. Torion will be affected as well. He will not be able to be with the other kids because we won't be welcomed. He will live with the stigma of a father who did horrible things and he will never be able to get out from under it."

"You're a bigger fool than I thought." She gave him one more pulse of power, this time hard enough that he released her. She leaped to her feet and took several steps away from him. Skender slowly stood, his eyes never leaving hers. "Being a pair, sharing a soul, choosing to love one another comes with all of that, no matter who we mate, Skender. The person's baggage doesn't determine their worth, and it shouldn't determine our ability to love them and be with them, despite what we might endure. That's what love does, it endures."

"Love isn't always enough." He sounded utterly defeated, which just pissed her off more.

"Are you saying that the Great Luna got it wrong?" She motioned between them. "What? Was she having an off day when she matched two souls that couldn't be together? Did the creator of all supernatural beings fall asleep on the job and then just say, 'To hell with it. Let's just see how they do together?'"

Skender frowned. "Of course not. She's a goddess. She doesn't make mistakes."

"You sure about that, wolf?" Tenia asked, her voice a hoarse whisper. "Because you're telling me I deserve better than the true mate the Great Luna gave me, the one she created to be the other half of my soul. It sounds a lot like you are accusing our goddess of screwing up."

His eyes widened, and it looked as if he was finally catching on to what she was saying. Tenia didn't look through the bond at his thoughts. She didn't know if she could handle hearing anything more about how he didn't want her.

"I never said I didn't want you, *soarele meu*." Apparently, *he* was not staying out of her head.

"It feels like that's what you're saying, Skender." Tenia shook her head and closed her eyes. It hurt to look at the man who'd broken through her defenses and made her see that her life hadn't been complete. Tenia swallowed hard. She realized that if she didn't have Torion, she might have actually wished that the cold fire had taken her life. It was a hell of a lot less painful than what she was enduring at the moment.

"Don't *ever* think something like that again," Skender snapped, his hands suddenly wrapped around her shoulders, giving her a small shake. "I cannot imagine a world where you don't exist."

Tenia lifted her head and opened her eyes. She felt tears gathering and hated that she couldn't keep them at bay. She opened her mouth to respond, but a bright light caused her to clamp it shut. Warmth filled the cave, and then the aforementioned goddess stood before them.

Tenia immediately fell to her knees, and Skender did the same. His shoulder pressed against hers as they bowed their heads before their Creator.

"The questions from your mate are valid, Skender," the Great Luna said, her voice the sweetest music to Tenia's ears. "You have shown remorse for your transgressions. Your heart is no longer the same. I know of your intentions to atone to those you've wronged in an effort to make peace. Are these the actions of a man not worthy of love?"

Tenia heard Skender suck in a breath and felt his body tremble against hers.

"Do you think that my grace is insufficient to cover your wrongs?"

He breathed out quickly. "No."

"I have blessed you both with a true-mate bond," the goddess continued. "I was not distracted, or asleep, or having an off day when I created either of you. I bound your souls, and then each of you was born when I deemed it your time to be here. I knew all that you would endure. I knew every step your feet would make even before you could walk. I knew every ounce of pain your hands would deliver and also every act of love they would give.

"I made you, as you told Tenia, to be her mate. And she is yours. Nothing I join can be separated, not even by you. You have the choice to follow the path set before you, the one you veered from recently, or you can step off of it again and leave behind what I have for you. I have loved you, Skender, with an everlasting love, and I will continue to love you, but there are consequences when you stray. Think about those consequences before you deny the mate I've entrusted to you. Think about all who will be affected if you do this." The light intensified in the room, and Tenia had to close her eyes against the glow.

"I stand before you," the Great Luna said, her voice echoing off of the walls, "as your creator. I bless this union. Even if you put the past behind you, the way forward will not be easy. You may share a soul, but you are still two distinct personalities with your own wants and desires. They will clash, often. But it will be in those moments of conflict that you have the opportunity to show one another the grace I have shown you. Skender." Her voice was sharp as she said his name. "Stand."

Skender obeyed immediately.

"This is the woman who is the light to your darkness. Will you take her as your mate? Will you love her, love her son, and take him as your own? Will you obey the commands I have given true mates regarding one another? Will you stand beside her when she needs to lean on you, behind her when she is too weak to stand on her own, and in front of her when she needs to be shielded from the dangers in this world?"

Tenia couldn't breathe. The Great Luna was throwing down an ultimatum to her mate, and Tenia was terrified Skender's guilt would keep him from embracing the gift their creator had given them.

When he didn't answer right away, Tenia tilted her head back slightly so she could look up at him. His eyes were closed, and tears ran down his face. She reached up and took one of his hands. He threaded his fingers through hers and held on tight. Tenia felt his love pouring through their bond. She felt his apprehension and worry that he couldn't be what she needed. She also felt his yearning to have what the Great Luna offered.

"Please," Tenia whispered into his mind. *"Don't leave me only half a soul. Don't doom us both to such misery when we*

have been offered such an amazing blessing. I love you, Skender."

Skender sucked in a sharp breath. His mate's confession was the final push that shoved him off the edge of indecision. Regardless of the many excuses he'd given, no matter how valid, Skender wanted Tenia with an intensity he barely understood. It was unlike anything he'd ever experienced, but he was beginning to understand the many things he'd heard from other males about how they felt when it came to their mates. Earth shattering, humbling, and life changing were just a few ways he could describe it.

Yes, he'd made some heinous mistakes in his past. And there would be consequences for those mistakes for many years, if not decades, to come. But, here and now, his Creator offered him grace. She wouldn't take his true mate from him, or him from her. She'd blessed their union and called him to be the man Tenia and Torion needed. Would he really throw that back in her face because he refused to accept the forgiveness she offered? No. He knew he wasn't worthy, would never be worthy, but the love of the Great Luna gave him the opportunity to work toward being a better person, a better wolf.

He finally raised his head, though his eyes remained on the floor. "I take her as my mate," he said, nearly stumbling over the words because of the overwhelming peace that covered him simply by taking that first step. "I love her, and I love Torion as my own. I will obey the commands you have given me as her true mate. I will st—" Skender's words faltered. He swallowed several times, trying to get himself under control. "I will stand with her in whatever capacity that she needs."

"Then do what she deserves." the Great Luna's voice filled his mind. He thought of the Blood Rites that his race had performed for centuries.

The light faded from the room, and Skender didn't hesitate. He pulled Tenia up to stand beside him. He turned to face her and dropped to one knee. "On this day, I kneel before you, as a servant to my mate, to ask if you will make me whole. Will you give yourself to me? Finally calming the beast inside, bringing order to chaos, shining light where there has been only darkness? Will you bind your life to mine, your fate to mine, and your soul to mine? In so doing, will you complete the mate bond?" He looked up at her, hoping she could feel the sincerity in his voice. He needed her to know she would never have reason to doubt his love for her.

Tenia's cheeks were wet with tears as she nodded her head. She pulled him up and pressed her body against his.

"Can you say it out loud?" he asked, wanting to hear it from her lips.

"Yes, Skender," she said, her voice soft. Her eyes held his own with a determination he'd come to respect, though at times, it drove him crazy. "I will give myself to you. I have been yours from the minute I saw you, even if I didn't want to admit it."

Their faces were inches apart, and Skender could feel her warm breath against his skin. He lowered his head slowly, giving her the opportunity to stop him if this wasn't what she wanted. His heart pounded painfully in his chest, and his breathing quickened. Skender released her hands and lifted his to cup her face. Lightning shot through his fingers, through his arms, and radiated throughout the rest of his body from the simple contact with her. He leaned closer and tilted her face up. Her eyes softened and desire filled them. Desire for *him*. "You have my heart," he whispered, expressing the thought he knew was already reaching out to her through the bond. "You are my everything." Tenia's skin warmed beneath his hands and took on a slight glow. "*Soarele meu*. My sun." Skender sighed in awe of the female he'd been given.

He closed the distance between them and nipped her bottom lip, holding it briefly before releasing the plump flesh and then softly pressing his lips to hers. Tenia moaned, an incredibly sexy sound of which Skender's wolf approved wholeheartedly. He ran his tongue along the seam of her mouth, and she obeyed his silent request, opening her lips. Her taste rushed into him, and he knew he would never get enough of it.

Skender dropped his hands and wrapped his arms around her waist, picking her up and carrying her over to the bedding where she'd laid unconscious for so long that he'd been sure he'd lose her. He eased down to one knee and then the other, never breaking the kiss, and then lowered her onto her back. Skender released her waist so he could brace himself over her with his hands. Only then did he pull his lips from hers. He smiled when she raised her head, attempting to follow his mouth. He took pride in the fact his mate's skin flushed with want for him. Her chest rose and fell as she tried to catch her breath. *I did that.*

"Are you sure?" he asked, lowering his head to nuzzle his nose against hers while breathing in her scent. "We can wait if you want to make sure this is really what you want."

Tenia turned her head, bearing her neck to him. "*This is what I want. I want to be yours in every way.*"

Skender's wolf rumbled as he watched his mate submit to them. He felt no hesitation through their bond, and he wasn't going to disrespect her by questioning her again.

Tenia was a grown woman. She knew what it meant to be his mate, and she accepted all that came with it.

He lowered himself until their bodies touched from legs to chest and rested his weight on a forearm so he didn't crush her smaller form. Then he slipped his other hand under her head and wrapped his fingers around her delicate neck. Skender lifted her slightly so her head dropped even further to the side. He roamed his eyes over the skin that ran from behind her ear, down her neck to her collarbone. His mouth watered, and he felt his teeth sharpen. The wolf rose to the surface, instinct taking over. His lips skimmed down her flesh until her shirt impeded his progress. His beast growled and took the fabric in his mouth. With a quick jerk of his head, Skender tore the shirt from her shoulder, exposing her flesh down her arm and collarbone.

Tenia gasped, but he smelled no fear. "We could have just taken it off," she said.

"Mine," he growled, so lost to his wolf that he couldn't even form a sentence. With nothing between them now, Skender licked her skin, starting at her shoulder, over to her collarbone and then up to the spot on her neck where she'd wear his mark. His heart beat so hard in his chest he could feel his blood pulsing through his veins. With every breath, her body pressed closer to his. The desire that he'd tried so hard to keep trapped burst forth like a broken dam. His lips closed over her flesh, and his teeth pierced her silky skin. Tenia's blood filled his mouth, and he pulled deeply on the wound. She was a decadent feast to all his senses. Her taste, her scent, her touch, the beauty of not only her body but of her soul. The sounds coming from deep within her encouraged both man and beast to take what belonged to them. Skender only allowed himself two more swallows of the precious liquid and then pulled his teeth from her.

"Don't stop," she said, her voice husky as she tried to tug his head back to her neck.

"It is enough, *soarele meu*." Skender turned her head so he could see her face. "Look at me, Tenia." She opened her eyes with languid blinks. "It's your turn."

A small smile graced her face. She ran her hands down his neck to his shoulders and tugged at his shirt. "I'm pretty sure we're both overdressed for this whole mating thing."

Skender chuckled. He pushed back and braced himself on his knees, then reached over his back, pulling his shirt up and over his head. He turned to toss it to the side and heard Tenia suck in a sharp breath.

"Your markings," she whispered and sat up, her legs still between his.

"They're on my back, but they've moved up to my neck since meeting you," he explained. His wolf perked up from the lust filled stupor at the mention of their markings. *I want to see her markings*, his beast demanded. Skender needed to see his claim on her just as badly as his wolf, but he tried to be a little more tactful about it.

"As my true mate, you will have matching markings on you," he told her and knew his eyes were glowing as his wolf tried to take over.

Tenia looked down at her still fully clothed body. "I haven't seen any."

He chuckled. "Then perhaps you need a second pair of eyes to check you over." A grin spread across her face, and it sucked the air from his lungs. "By the goddess, you are beautiful." He leaned forward and gripped the bottom of her shirt. He met her eyes, raising his brow in question.

She nodded. It was all the permission he needed. He peeled the torn shirt from Tenia's body. His eyes drank her in, but Skender forced himself to be patient. It wasn't easy.

He wanted to rip the rest of the clothes from her body. "No markings here," he said, his voice gruff with his need to make her his.

Tenia reached behind her back, and Skender held his breath as the straps of her bra loosened and fell down her shoulders. Tenia's eyes didn't leave his as she took the garment off and tossed it aside. He was frozen, unable to move for fear that if he did, he'd wake up from a dream.

"I think your neck is going to need to be a little closer to my mouth." She held out her hand to him.

Skender moved without thought, his body covering hers, skin against skin, warmth mingling as he wrapped himself around her. With his hand behind her head, he guided her mouth downward. "Don't think," he rumbled. "Just bite. Hard."

Her lips placed a gentle kiss, and then he felt her teeth. Tenia didn't hesitate; she did exactly as he told her. She bit him so hard he grunted at the pain. But as quickly as the pain came, it was gone. In its place was a pleasure he hadn't known could exist.

He rolled onto his back, taking her with him so that she laid on him. His hands roamed, petting, tugging at clothes, memorizing his mate. Skender paid attention to every sound she made when he touched her, noting particularly sensitive areas and filing that information away for later. "Enough, love." He breathed and pushed her gently from his neck. When she finally pulled back enough that he could see her face, she looked euphoric, lost in a high that he now completely understood.

Skender finished undressing both of them, his lips trailing over every piece of flesh as it was exposed. When he pulled off her pants and she shifted her hips, he finally saw his markings on her skin. In the blink of an eye, he flipped her over, placing Tenia on her stomach. His left hand ran up the back of her left leg, starting at the bend of her knee and moving up her thigh. She sucked in a breath as he continued caressing her buttocks and on until he reached her waist where the mark ended.

"Skender?" she asked, sounding breathless.

"They're beautiful." He let his fingers trace the markings again. "My mate, my love." He leaned forward and pressed his lips to the top of the mark on her waist and then began trailing them down her flesh.

"Skender," she said again, her voice higher and louder.

"Hush," he commanded gently. "Let me love you," he said before going quiet and taking control of her body. She submitted to him, moving with him and whispering encouragement when he pleased her. Skender let himself soak her in. He grew drunk on her as they made love and knew that he could never walk away from her, no matter if he wasn't worthy of her. The bond snapped into place, tight and strong as their bodies became one. "Mine," he whispered again before sinking his teeth into her once more.

Pressing his head closer to her and holding tight as if she'd never let him go, she agreed, "Always."

CHAPTER

TWELVE

"Sometimes I think we make things so complicated when they should be simple. Over the course of my existence, it has become pretty obvious that the answer to any problem is love. That's what it always comes back to. Who do you love more? Yourself or someone else? What do you love more? Things or people? What are you willing to do for love? I didn't say that following through is easy. Just that the answer is always right there in front of us." ~Nick

Peri sat on a rock watching Torion and Galan chasing each other in the forest clearing. Maybe she should have been concerned that the adolescent dragon might accidentally stomp on the kid or knock him over with his tail. But so far, Galan had managed not to kill Torion, so Peri figured worrying was a waste of time. Peri wondered how long the boy's mother and Skender would need to handle their private business. She couldn't deny that she was envious of the couple. Though they would have tremendous obstacles to overcome, they would overcome them together. That's what true mates were meant for, to have someone to lean on, someone who would stand by your side no matter what. And Peri had thrown that away. Not because she didn't love Lucian. Quite the opposite, in fact. She'd pushed him away because she loved him, and she'd already known that she was going to be the one to destroy the Order. Knowing that her death would also mean his was more than she could stand. Lucian had suffered so much while being trapped in the Dark Forest for all that time. And if that wasn't enough, she had his nephew to think of. Fane had lost plenty already; he didn't need to lose his uncle as well.

"True mates are not meant to exist without one another," her subconscious whispered. No, that was a lie. It wasn't her subconscious that was speaking. It was her soul. Ever since the bond between her and Lucian had been momentarily opened, her soul, the other half of his, had relentlessly nagged her. *"Did you have the right to decide for him whether he would live without you?"*

She didn't have to answer the annoying voice because her attention was suddenly grabbed by Torion's high-pitched giggles. She watched him trying to climb Galan's leg. The draheim stuck out his snout and lifted the boy until Torion was perched atop Galan's back. Peri growled and stood, holding out a hand. She pushed an invisible barrier around the young draheim. When he tried to unfurl his wings, they bumped into the barrier with a thud.

He looked in her direction and gave a growl.

"Free my wings, fae."

"What are you doing?" Peri asked, ignoring his command.

"The boy wants to fly and so do I."

"Not gonna happen," she replied.

"I will not let the child fall," Galan said. He shifted his enormous feet and tried to stretch his wings again, but Peri's magic kept them still.

"The child's mother doesn't want him going on a joyride," Peri said. "And though I would normally be fine with disregarding the parents' wishes, especially if they're wolves, I promised no harm would come to him. I can only assure that if he is within my reach."

"You could come with us, Peri," Torion suggested, his voice full of excitement as if it was the greatest idea in the history of ideas.

She planted her hands on her hips, tilted her head, and stared at the two troublemakers. Peri assumed it would be some time before she could take Torion back to his parents. What else did she have to do but sit around and listen to her soul pining after Lucian until it drove her crazy?

"What the hell?" Peri threw her hands in the air. At the same time, she removed the magic that kept Galan grounded. She took a few steps and then bounded up onto the draheim's back, just behind Torion. Peri wrapped an arm around the boy and pulled him tightly against her. "Have your takeoffs gotten any bett—" Her words were cut off when the young draheim launched them into the air, his powerful wings beating rapidly to help him climb up into the sky. His body rocked from side to side, and Peri used her power to keep her and Torion still so they wouldn't roll off the side of the beast. "Guess that answers that question," she muttered.

After several minutes, Galan finally stopped climbing and leveled out. His wings spread out on either side, allowing them to glide, using the wind currents to float through the air. Every now and then, he would give a lazy flap of the giant wings to keep them in the airstream.

Torion threw his hands in the air. "WHOOOOP!" Laughter bubbled out of him. "Isn't this awesome?"

Peri opened her mouth to answer, but Torion shook his head and said, "Never mind. Don't answer that. You'll ruin the awesomeness."

Her brow rose. She leaned closer so she wouldn't have to shout. "Believe it or not, there used to be a time when I was awesome."

Torion turned slightly and narrowed his eyes. "Prove it," he challenged. Then he turned back around and continued to howl with glee.

"I cannot believe I'm letting a child manipulate me," she said under her breath as she lifted her hands. Gathering the power inside of her, she shot pulses of light upward in varying colors from her hands, one after another. The pulses exploded in dazzling starbursts of color above them. Humans would have called them fireworks, but Peri didn't need fire in order to create a light show in the draheim realm's sky.

"Yes!" Torion threw his fists up in the air as if he'd won some glorious victory. "Is that all you got, the mighty Perizada?" he asked.

"Bloody hell." She groaned but then continued to throw out huge balls of fire that exploded, one after another. Soon there were so many that Galan was dipping and dodging the falling sparks from the explosions. The acrobatic flying only made Torion shout louder as his excitement grew. Apparently, the fae boy was an adrenaline junkie.

They flew for a half hour before Galan slowly started making his descent. Peri looked down and saw that the draheim was heading for a clearing where his mother, along with several other of the beasts, gathered. Thankfully, his landings were much smoother than his takeoffs.

As they landed, Peri flashed herself and Torion from the dragon's back to the ground. The fae boy turned around and wrapped his arms around her and squeezed. "Thank you so much," he said. He released her and ran to Galan. The hug was so quick it caught her off guard. Peri was still processing it when Serapha sidled up next to her. Peri noticed again how the draheim moved with eerie quietness for such an immense beast.

"You've finally decided to grace me with your presence?" Peri asked the elusive draheim.

"I don't know why you have such a hard time finding me. It's not like I can hide behind a tree," Serapha goaded.

The image of the huge female dragon attempting to conceal herself by a mere tree nearly made Peri laugh. She felt a little carefree after the flight with Galan and Torion, and a little more alive. She wasn't sure if that was a good thing or not, considering Peri hadn't fully decided that being alive was what she wanted. *Then it's a good thing it doesn't matter what you want,* her pesky soul whispered through her consciousness. Peri ignored the inner voice. Perhaps if she stopped acknowledging it the voice would go away. *"I'm your soul, moron, not a stray dog."* "Good grief, am I really that obnoxious?" Peri asked out loud despite the fact that Serapha wouldn't have a clue what she was talking about.

"Do you really want an answer to that question?" the female draheim asked.

Peri held up her hand. "I already know the answer. I don't need confirmation."

Serapha settled next to Peri, her colossal form resting gracefully on the ground.

"Are you going to tell me what you meant when you said I had been saved by a draheim?" Peri asked. She wasn't hopeful Serapha would give her an answer.

"When it is time for you to know, then the knowledge will be revealed."

Peri rolled her eyes. "That's a non-answer. Non-answers suck."

"You seem to be more yourself as of late," the beast noted. "It has been good for you to be here."

"How would you know how I've been? You've been off gallivanting around while I'm trying to figure out the meaning of my life and how I will go on now that I've made a right mess of things back in the human realm." Peri was whining. She heard it in her voice and wanted to kick her own ass for it. Maybe she *was* beginning to reclaim a little of her old self.

"What do you think that will look like?" Serapha asked. "You walked away from those you cared about because you were afraid to lose them. So, you essentially made your own fear come to pass."

"Are you striving for the Captain Obvious award?" Peri muttered.

"You've now realized," Serapha continued, not bothering to acknowledge Peri's comment, "that your rash decision led to rash behavior, and none of it was what you wanted. You let your emotions control your actions. So how do you correct it?"

Peri clenched her jaw. She seemed to have a permanent headache since she'd released the cold fire, as if she needed the reminder that what she'd done had been the wrong course of action. "I just take the next step in the *right* direction," she finally said after several minutes. "I walked for a very long time in the *wrong* direction, and the only way I know how to start over is to turn around and walk away from the path I am on back toward the path I should never have stepped off."

Serapha's large eyes bore into Peri. The high fae wondered what the draheim female saw. "I think that's a very good understanding of where you are and where you're going."

"I need to make amends." Talking it out seemed to help Peri feel grounded and less like a lost child with no one to guide her. "I need to show with my actions, not just my words, that I will put them first. My mate, my friends, my family, and pack. Basically, I'm going to be shoveling in very large quantities of humble pie."

"I've heard of all the pies you could possibly eat, it's much better than the consequences of the others."

"True. Humble pie won't give me an ass the size of Jen's or cause me to have a sugar high and run around like a cracked-out Thia." Peri smiled at her description. She missed her friend and even her weird child.

"What's a cracked-out Thia?" Serapha asked.

Peri scrunched up her face and shook her head. "It's really better if we don't talk about it. It's kind of like speaking of the devil. Say her name too many times, and she just might show up."

"I'll take your word for it," the draheim said and then turned her attention back to Torion and her offspring. "Galan has asked if the fae child can stay here with us," Serapha said. They watched as Torion patted the young draheim's snout. Peri sensed Serapha was attempting to distract her from her thoughts, and for that, Peri was grateful. It was very easy for her to get lost in her own mind and chase rabbits that would offer no answers or comfort.

"He realizes the child is not a pet, right?" Peri asked at the same time that Galan told Torion to sit and stay.

Serapha chuckled, her voice rumbling deep in her chest. "Yes, he understands that. But he has come to think of Torion as his charge. Galan believes he is the boy's protector."

"Galan will have to take that up with his mother. She's awake."

"Why don't you sound happy about that?" Serapha asked, showing more astuteness than Peri expected.

She stood quietly watching Galan and Torion play, carefree and safe without the threat of vampires, evil fae, or corrupt elf kings chasing them. "Because time is running out."

"Even if she hadn't woken, your mate and his mismatched pack are knocking on our proverbial door," Serapha pointed out.

"Is that what you call it when a group of powerful supernaturals attempt to tear your veil open? A knock?" Peri smirked.

"They don't mean me or mine harm," Serapha said. "They want *you*. Your mate discovered your location because a soul cannot hide from its other half for long. And he is going to do anything to get to you. The question is—"

"There are no questions," Peri interrupted. "You've said enough."

"Why don't you want to be found?" the draheim continued, showing no offense at Peri's interruption.

She sighed. "What part of 'there are no questions' did you not understand?"

"The part where you forgot I could squash you like a bug if you get on my nerves by not answering my questions."

Peri laughed. It was something she would have said to one of her own annoying friends, some of whom were currently attempting to help her mate get into the draheim realm. *Damn, I miss them.* The part of Peri that had been cold, shielded in ice by her fear and anger, was thawing. And now the anguish of being separated from her family, her pack, settled into her bones and ached.

"I'm just not ready," Peri finally said. "Besides, Tenia, Skender, and Torion are safe here."

"I understand Tenia and Torion need to be protected from the Order. Tenia's power is unique, which makes her valuable. But the wolf?" Serapha asked.

Peri snatched the opportunity to change the subject. She began to relay to Serapha the story of Skender and his past. More than two hours later, the draheim up to speed, and Peri found herself wishing the wolf had done more stupid things so the story was longer. Night had fallen, and when she glanced over at Galan, she saw Torion was furled up against the adolescent draheim's chest.

"So you want Skender to stay here so that the people on the other side of our veil don't kill him," Serapha said.

"Exactly." Peri snapped her fingers at the draheim.

"Do you think he should die for his crimes?"

"Six months ago, I would have said absolutely," Peri admitted. "But now"—she tilted her head back and looked up at the star-covered night sky—"I need to believe that even someone who's made Skender's choices can be shown mercy."

"We all make mistakes, Peri. That is simply the nature of an imperfect being. Some mistakes are greater than others. And the consequences are more dire. That does not mean that mercy can't be granted. But you aren't giving your family a chance to show you love and grace by hiding from them."

The draheim was right. Peri knew she had to face her mate and the rest of her pack. She took a deep breath and nodded. "One more day," she said. "Just to let me gather myself and plan a way to keep Jen from killing Skender the minute she sees him."

"This Jen is a fierce warrior?" Serapha asked.

Peri shrugged. "You could call her that. But those of us who know her call her batshit crazy. Most of the time, the two are indistinguishable."

Serapha's gigantic head pulled back as she frowned. "I do not understand the human sayings. How can the droppings of an animal be mentally unstable?"

"It's better not to overthink anything the humans say." Peri walked over to Torion and rested her hand on his shoulder. "It will start killing brain cells." She flashed her and the boy to just outside the cave. Torion didn't stir. He laid at her feet in the same position he'd been sleeping in when curled against Galan. "I hope you two are dressed," she called out. "If I have to alter my memories to forget the sight of you two groping one another, I will be very put out."

A few seconds later, Tenia emerged from the rear of the cave. *Thank the Great Luna she has clothes on.*

Tenia's eyes dropped to her son. "I see that you've worn him out."

"Surprisingly, you are not worn out. Skender must be a lazy lover." Peri clucked her tongue. "Strong intimacy is the backbone of any healthy relationship, Tenia. Don't let him start out with mediocrity beneath the sheets. It will be all downhill from here."

Tenia's eyes widened. "I don't even know what to say to that."

"Sometimes ignoring her is the best response." Skender marched past his mate and straight to Torion. He scooped the boy up and turned before walking briskly back the way he'd come.

Tenia turned to follow Skender and glanced back over her shoulder. "Are you coming? Surely you need some sleep before we have a talk about our next move."

"I will be in shortly. Tomorrow we will have that talk, but tonight, we rest."

Tenia's eyes softened. "By rest, you mean avoid the inevitable hell that's going to break loose once we leave this realm?"

Peri nodded. "Astute as ever, Tenia."

"I'll agree to that," Tenia said, surprising Peri. She was sure the fae would argue with her. "For Torion's sake, we'll have one more night."

Peri watched Tenia until the woman disappeared to the rear of the cave after her mate and child. Then Peri stood there for a good twenty minutes, arguing with her mate-starved soul. Her subconscious was giving voice to the part of her that was scared to move forward. Though Peri hated to admit it, she was frozen with fear—unable to go back and do things differently, yet unable to move forward and face the consequences of her actions.

"Dammit." She huffed and then flashed from the cave opening, reappearing in front of the draheim veil. She stared out at the group of supernaturals currently resting on the ground in various states of repose. Some sat. Some lay on their backs or their sides, but all looked exhausted.

The image brought back so many memories of times

she'd been in some forest or another with these very people, fighting the good fight, protecting those who need protecting, and yes, even attempting to break into closed veils. "My, how the mighty have fallen," she whispered and snapped her fingers. A chair appeared next to her. Peri tucked her robes under her and took a seat, crossing one leg over the other. She leaned forward and rested her elbow on her knee. As her eyes ran over the group again, she realized Lucian was not among them. Peri's heart clenched painfully in her chest. Her eyes were hungry for the sight of him, and yet he was nowhere to be seen. Had he tired of waiting? Had he given up on her?

"Is this what the great Perizada has been reduced to?" Peri said to the empty forest around her. "Pining pitifully after friendships that I damaged and a mate that I pushed away?" She shook her head and closed her eyes. "Why am I so afraid?" The words stumbled from her lips, then she snorted. "And I'm talking to myself." When she opened her eyes and looked at the veil again, Peri was startled to find Elle standing just on the other side, looking straight at the gateway. The fae's brow drew into a deep V on her forehead. She appeared to be concentrating intensely. Peri knew Elle couldn't see her. The ward she'd set on the veil was too strong for the younger fae to penetrate, not to mention Serapha had lent Peri some of the draheim realm's magic to reinforce her own power. But her comrade still stood staring as if she could will her eyes to see beyond the magic.

Movement behind Elle caused Peri's eyes to shift. Jen stood up, her mouth moving as she walked toward Elle. She took up a place next to Peri's longtime comrade and looked from Elle to the veil. Jacque was up next. She took a place on Elle's other side. Jewel and Stella joined the women next. Then Peri watched as Anna took Heather's hand and pulled her up from where she'd been sitting with her mate. They walked her over to the line of women standing in front of the veil.

Peri gingerly pushed up from the chair, her movement hesitant. She watched the other women continue forward. Next came Myanin, Lilly, Jezebel, and, finally, Nissa. Eleven in all, standing mere inches from her, yet she felt as if a great chasm separated them. Each of these women held a special place in her heart. They'd been through the fire with her in one way or another. They'd forged unbreakable bonds because of the trials they'd faced together. Had she really thought about throwing that away? Before Vasile had sought her out several years ago, Peri had simply been an ambassador. She'd followed the Great Luna's commands to keep communication open between the other supernatural races, though she specifically represented the wolves more often than not. She'd taken on the role, like the rest of her race, as the supernatural police. In some ways, both positions had set her apart and kept her from having any sort of deep friendships. But then something happened to change all that. The prince of the Romanian pack found his true mate. Their relationship seemed to be the catalyst for all that had followed in Peri's life. Since then, Peri had been pulled into the fold of their pack, and they'd held onto her just as tightly as she'd held onto them.

The ice that Peri had wrapped around her heart before she set the world on fire was gone. She was no longer protected from the painful emotions that came from caring for someone else. Seeing Elle, remembering the last words she'd said to the female fae, gutted Peri. And she deserved to feel every ounce of the pain because of the hurt she'd caused Elle and the others. Peri knew it had to happen. Like a physical wound needed to be debrided, washed, and bandaged, emotional wounds had to be purified through the process of confession, humility, and a willingness to accept one's responsibility for the injury. Before this instant, she hadn't been ready to let the process begin. Fear ruled her heart and kept her from being what the Great Luna called her to be. Now, standing before people she'd willingly die for, and who she knew would die for her in return... Maybe she *was* ready. She'd wasted enough time. Though the fear still held on tightly, her need to restore the broken relationships was stronger.

"I can feel you, just on the other side. Either your shields are dropping, or you're just getting old and tired." Elle's voice filled her mind through the unique bond that Peri had with each of the fae she'd commanded over the centuries.

Peri's throat threatened to close when she heard the familiar voice filled with worry. *"You wish. I age like a fine wine. I get more delectable with time,"* she said, easily falling back into the familiar banter they'd always shared.

"Why are you over there?" Elle asked. *"You can't get on anyone's nerves from the draheim realm. And as you can see, we desperately need entertainment."*

Peri *almost* smiled.

Elle turned her head slightly when Jen started speaking to her, though Peri couldn't hear the blonde's words. Elle nodded, and then Jen placed her hands on her hips and slowly turned her head back toward the veil. Apparently, Elle had shared the fact Peri was there. Jacque's mouth moved next while she stared straight at the veil. One by one, each of their eyes widened at the revelation that Peri was just on the other side of the veil. Peri looked down the line again and frowned.

"I'm sure Sally is safe with her mate in the sprite realm. But where is Kara?" Peri looked around the girls at the males

behind them. *"And where are the rest of the mates to these females? Where is Fane?"* What had she missed? When Peri had delivered the message to the sprite realm, she'd hadn't known why she was delivering the message, just that the Great Luna had commanded her to do it because her friends needed help. She'd seen Jacque lying in a bed, not looking her best, but she did not know what had happened to the female alpha, and she hadn't allowed herself to dwell on it. Mostly because she'd been having her own pity party.

Considering Jacque stood just feet away and looked healthy enough now, Peri assumed the fae stones had done whatever it was they'd been sent to do. But that didn't explain Kara's absence.

Elle's face darkened, and she folded her arms in front of her. *"Kara has been taken by the Order. Fane is with Nick and some of the others as they hunt for her. I've been with them but came here after Fane asked me to check in on the group."*

Peri's stomach crashed to the ground. *"Was she at the compound when I ... when I destroyed it?"*

The high fae could actually read the profanity spewing from Elle's lips. *"We do not know. No one is exactly sure when she went missing."* It looked as if an idea struck Elle. She dropped her arms and took a step closer. *"What about the message you delivered in the sprite realm? Wadim and Zara have been working on it constantly, trying to figure out what it means."*

Peri's mind pulled up the words that the Great Luna had given to her. *"The fae stones heal, and they reveal,"* she said to Elle. *"When I showed up, there was something wrong with Jacque, right?"*

Elle nodded.

"And the fae stones helped her heal?"

Another nod.

"And they traveled with me in order for me to reveal how they were needed."

"But what about the rest?" Elle asked. *"The prodigal is returning, and a new son will join your ranks. Evil will think it has prevailed, but hope will be born from the supposed triumph."*

Peri knew exactly who the prodigal was, but she wasn't sure now was the best time to mention Skender's name. As for the "new son," there was only one son that she could think of that now had ties to their pack: Torion.

"Peri?" Elle's voice interrupted her thoughts.

"I have some theories, but I don't want to throw them out there just yet. I think I need to right some wrongs before we can move forward."

Elle's eyes softened, and she bowed her head to Peri.

"I will return in the morning," Peri told her. *"Then I will open the veil."* Peri's head snapped to the side just as Lilly suddenly dropped to the ground. Peri raised her hand, but before she could utter a word, Elle spoke again, her words issuing with an urgency Peri could practically feel.

"Lilly says do not open the veil. She said it's not time."

"Not time for what?" Peri's hands itched to remove the boundary between her and the warlock queen who was currently in Jacque's arms on the ground.

"You know it doesn't work like that." Elle sounded weary. *"She can only tell you what is permitted, and she might not even know why she's giving you the message, only that she's been prompted to do so."*

Peri took a step back and crossed her arms in front of her chest, hoping it would keep her from denying Lilly's order. If the warlock queen said it wasn't time, then it *wasn't* time. She watched as they raised Lilly back to her feet. The warlock queen took several deep breaths. Her mouth moved as she spoke to Elle, and then the fae turned back to Peri.

"She said all she knows is that if you come out too soon, the knowledge will be lost. Timing is everything. There will be beauty from ashes. It must happen this way."

Peri wouldn't lie and say she understood or that she was okay with waiting. Mostly, waiting sucked. But she'd been alive long enough to know that *not* waiting until the right time for the Great Luna's plan had dire consequences. Hence the position she found herself in currently.

"How long do I need to wait?"

Elle turned back to Lilly, presumably to ask the queen Peri's question.

"Lilly says you will know when it's time."

"Fabulous," she muttered under her breath. She glanced around the group one more time, but still didn't see her wolf. *"I will check back in tomorrow,"* Peri told Elle.

"Stay safe, Perizada. I love you. But don't think that doesn't mean I'm not going to kick your ass for being a butthead."

Peri did smile that time. *"I look forward to it."* She glanced one more time at the people who'd shown up to get her back. They'd come because they cared. Despite what she'd done and the mistakes she'd made, her friends had shown up. Peri sent her thanks to the Great Luna for such an amazing family and then flashed back to the cave.

When she rounded the rocky outcropping that gave the group privacy from the entrance, she found Tenia and Torion curled up together on the pallet bed, sound asleep. Skender sat next to them, staring at the dancing flames of the fire, his expression forlorn.

"You've found your true mate. She's forgiven you for all your crap. You've completed the Blood Rites. And you've inherited an amazing fae son." Peri took a seat across from him. "So, why, pray tell, do you look like someone just drowned your favorite kitten?"

Skender continued to stare at the fire. His legs were drawn up close to his chest, and his forearms rested on his knees. Peri noticed his shoulders were coiled with tension, as if he might need to jump up at any moment to protect his mate and child. After several moments, he finally answered. "I wasn't going to allow myself to claim her," he said, his voice deep but soft, as if to keep from waking Tenia and Torion. "She deserves better than the likes of me. But she wouldn't take no for an answer."

"Tenia is no spring maiden. She's a grown woman who has lived a very long time." Peri leaned back against the cave wall. "She's capable of making her own choices. Not to mention, considering it affects both of you, she should have a say in the decision."

Skender's eyes left the fire and met hers. "Are you seriously lecturing me about my relationship with *my* mate?" There was humor in his voice, not condescension. "Considering you're here and not with your mate, where you *should* be."

Peri smirked. "Ironic, isn't it?"

"It just goes to show that no matter how 'put together' someone's relationship looks on the outside, that doesn't mean it isn't a complete mess on the inside." Skender sighed and glanced over at his mate and child. "I thought you and Lucian were solid."

"And how would you know?" Peri asked. "You were too busy betraying us. It's not like you had ample time to sit around and chat with us over coffee."

"True. I suppose I just thought that true mates always just worked, no matter what."

"Nothing *just works*, Skender. Everything *takes* work. No

matter the type of relationship, soul mates or not, any union takes two individuals willing to put aside their own wants and needs for the other. It takes sacrifice, and that sacrifice makes you very vulnerable. I don't think any being, human or supernatural, wants to feel vulnerable." Peri's words weren't just for Skender's ears. They were for her own as well. "Vulnerability opens you up to the possibility of pain, and pain is something most people avoid at all costs, regardless of whether it's emotional or physical."

"Is that what happened to you?"

Peri found her mouth suddenly dry, and it was difficult to swallow. She cleared her throat. "In my long existence, I have never experienced the kind of pain I felt when Vasile and Alina died. And for a time, all I wanted was to make sure I never felt that kind of pain again." As the agonizing memories emerged, Peri didn't try to stop them. Instead, she let them play like a movie in her head, a horrible, tragic, gut-wrenching movie. She knew that if she didn't let them out, healing would never begin.

"I was just so angry," she said. "I didn't understand what purpose their deaths served. How did it help anyone or anything to lose two strong, steadfast leaders while we are in the midst of a battle against the worst kind of evil?" She sighed. "So, yes, I guess that's what happened to me. I attempted to avoid any further pain." Peri realized she'd been too proud to lay her pain at her Creator's feet and ask for help in bearing the burden of the alphas' deaths. "I took the lives of so many, so I don't have the right to judge." Her voice strained against the shame she was trying to swallow.

"We all—"

"If you say, 'We all make mistakes,'" Peri cut him off, "I will turn you into—"

"A turd," he interrupted. "Yes, I'm well aware. You need

to get some new material, Peri." He chuckled and then added, "What I was going to say before you made your assumption was that we have all judged people unfairly. Whether it's because we compare ourselves to them and come up lacking or because we take relief in seeing that their transgressions are worse than our own."

"Is this a pep talk?" Peri asked. She rubbed her hands together and held them out to the fire. Not because she was cold but simply because the warmth against her skin was pleasant. "If it is, you really need to take a class. Or watch one of those movies full of epic battles where the leader spurs his warriors on to run headlong to their deaths and feel good about doing it."

Skender pinched the bridge of his nose. "It's not a pep talk. It's just two people who've made some really crappy decisions having a conversation. I'm lending a listening ear."

Peri scrunched up her face. "Do you mean bonding? We're bonding?" She could hear the disgust in her voice and tried to tone it down. "It's not that I don't want to bond with you because of your past. It's just, bonding with you or anyone else is not on my to-do list. I mean"—she waved a hand at him and blew out her cheeks with a breath—"if you could see my to-do list and all the repairing I have to do, you'd understand why I cannot add another relationship to the list of already jacked-up friendships."

"While I'm glad to see you becoming yourself again"— Skender lowered his legs and picked up a couple of pebbles, rolling them around in his hand—"I kind of liked the stoic, didn't talk so much, version of Peri."

"You're just giving me another reason for *not* being that version," Peri said. "Okay, enough about me. I made a mess of things, ruined some relationships, killed some people, and now I have to do something about it. Let's move on." She tapped her chin and looked at Skender. "What we need to talk about is your history, considering I agree with Torion regarding your childhood. Someone had to have altered your memories and used magic on you.

"Skender, you were essentially a plant by the Order, waiting for decades to be activated when they were ready for you. Your future had been mapped out beforehand, and you didn't have a clue. You betrayed those you love. You hurt—"

Skender held up his hand, his eyes glowing, and Peri heard a low growl. "Your pep talks suck, too."

"Touché." Peri nodded. "But what I'm trying to say is that everything you did wasn't totally your fault. Magic is powerful, Skender. It can make people do things they would normally never do."

"That doesn't change my actions," Skender argued. "Regardless of why I did those things, they still hurt people, and I am still the one responsible for their pain."

"Damn." Peri huffed. "It's so annoying when a person you want to dislike has likable qualities." She tilted her head as if to see him from a different perspective. "Truth be told, the only reason I wanted to dislike you so much was because of how you helped the Order. But now, it's just because you're a wolf. It's not nearly as bad, but it's still annoying."

"For someone who despises my race so much, you sure are quick to offer your help," Skender pointed out.

Peri sniffed and settled the robe draped around her. "It would be boring if I liked everyone. And wolves have thick skin. They can handle my snide remarks and not run off with their tails tucked between their legs. Sometimes they even fight back, and that's when things get really fun."

"I don't think you have to worry about boredom in this world, ever," Skender said. "There's too much evil that needs to be dismantled and burned to ash. Speaking of which"—he shifted forward—"now that Tenia's awake, and you're, well, not suicidal anymore, it's time to connect with Fane, Jacque, and the other supernatural leaders. They need to know what's happened."

"I agree, but I've been instructed by the warlock queen slash seer sprite that we are not to open the veil of the draheim yet."

"Why?"

Peri rolled her eyes. "If I knew the answer to that question, I would have included it in my statement."

"So we're just supposed to sit here and wait?" Skender's wolf had risen to the surface again, and his eyes glowed at her.

"Yes." Peri nodded. "We wait."

"That feels so anticlimactic." Skender's shoulders rolled forward as he dropped pebbles carelessly on the ground.

"Perhaps you should enjoy the anticlimactic reprieve for now," Peri suggested. "I've been to the draheim veil. Jen is on the other side looking way too stabby. Not to mention Jacque, Elle—"

"I get it, Peri," Skender snapped. "If I walked through the veil to the human realm right now, I might end up skewered like a pig."

Peri pursed her lips. "Hmm, that's putting it mildly. They really do not like you. And Jen will be first in line to take her retribution out of your hide."

"Titus said we wouldn't let her kill Skender," Torion said, his voice rough with sleep.

"How do you know Titus?" Skender turned to look at the fae boy.

"The angel took me to him." Torion paused. "Well, she's actually the creator of the supernaturals, but she looked like an angel."

Skender looked back at Peri. "Did you know about this?"

Peri shrugged. "He might have mentioned it to me, but he didn't tell me any more than what he just told you. He did basically tell me to stay out of his business."

Skender looked back at the boy he claimed as his own. "Was it in a dream that you met him?"

"It felt like a dream, but it also felt real." Torion pushed himself up into a sitting position.

"Why does Titus think you two can keep Jen from killing me?" Skender asked.

"Because I'm her future son-in-law."

And just like that, Peri's world shifted on its axis, nearly toppling her sideways even though she sat flat on the ground. Her mouth opened and closed several times before she finally shook her head and looked at Torion. "All I can do is give you my condolences."

"Peri." Skender snarled.

"What?" She blinked innocently. "Someone ought to tell the boy what he's in for. He's going to need decades to prepare himself for what he's facing. And then he's going to need years of counseling—wait, no." She pointed at Torion. "He's going to need a lifetime of counseling because Jen is, well, Jen. And her offspring should have trouble tattooed on her forehead."

Tenia stirred, and Skender shot Torion and then Peri a warning look. "Let's keep this between us for now."

"She's going to find out eventually," Peri said.

"I'm well aware of that." Skender sighed. "But she has

enough on her plate. There's no reason to add more to it until absolutely necessary."

A few minutes after Skender finished speaking, Tenia sat up, rubbing the sleep from her eyes. She blinked as if trying to get the room to come into focus. "Is it morning already?" She looked between Peri and Skender.

"Not quite," Peri answered. "When I returned from my errand, Skender was sitting here staring at the fire as if it held the secrets of the universe. Then Torion woke up. We've just been having a chat."

"About what?" Tenia scooted closer to Skender until her shoulder pressed against his arm. Torion crawled over his mom, passing in front of the fire, so that he was on the other side of Skender. He leaned against the wolf, just as Tenia did.

"We can't leave the draheim realm," Peri answered. Might as well rip the proverbial Band-Aid off quickly, she thought. "The warlock queen warned we had to remain here. Apparently, if we leave before we're supposed to, the sky will fall."

Tenia arched her brow. "The sky? Will fall?" she said slowly, turning the four words into two questions.

"Something along those lines," Peri said, "As much as it pains me to sit around and do nothing. I've also learned that when we move before we're supposed to and take matters into our own hands without considering the consequences, others get hurt." She dropped her eyes as shame rushed through her veins like boiling water. "I've got enough blood on my hands to last an eternity."

"Okay," Tenia said after several tense moments. "I trust Lilly. If she says we need to wait, then we wait. No matter how long that is."

Peri didn't open her eyes. Her body was suddenly tired, and her mind wanted to check out for a bit.

"Rest, beloved." She heard Lucian's voice in her mind. Again, he used the bond that was unique to them because of her fae blood instead of the mate bond. It took a ton of effort to keep him blocked from her mind through the fae bond. And apparently she was too tired to even try. *"You are safe. You are loved. I am waiting for you."*

Peri let his words wash over her and found herself reaching for him through their bond. In her mind's eye, she pictured his arms wrapped around her and her face buried in his neck. He could protect her from the darkness in the world. Lucian could bear her burden on his strong shoulders. He could walk with her through the fire if only she would let him. *"I'm sorry, Lucian."*

"I know. We're going to be okay, Perizada. No matter what doubts you're facing, do not doubt me. You were created for me, and I for you."

Peri let sleep take her as she clung to her mate's words.

CHAPTER

THIRTEEN

"I'm beginning to realize that the soul is not simply the whole of a person. The soul is an amalgamation of pieces. As the body has many parts, so does the soul. And just like parts of the body can die, so can parts of the soul. I am biding my time, waiting for the right moment. But while I wait, small pieces of my soul are dying." ~Kara

"I lived with a girl named Bree in one of my foster homes. She used to burn herself," Kara told Dyna who was twining Kara's hair into a long braid.

"Why did she burn herself?" Reena asked, pausing on her way to the bathroom. The elf was preparing the ritualistic cleansing Kara had undergone every night for the past month. Ludcarab insisted she come to him spotless. The fool didn't realize he was the one who made her dirty. *He* was the reason she needed cleansing in the first place.

"Because the physical pain distracts from the pain

inside," Kara explained, her eyes unfocused. Though there was a mirror in front of her, she didn't see herself. "It hurts less. Although, one time when we talked about it, Bree told me she also did it because it made her feel clean. I didn't understand at the time. She explained she'd done a project about metals in her science class. During the project, she spoke to a silversmith. One of the things she'd learned was that fire purifies silver. The purification only happened when the silver was plunged into the hottest part of the flame and held for just the right amount of time. Too long in the fire and the silver ruined. Too short and the impurities weren't removed."

"How did the silversmith know when to take the silver out of the fire?" Coya asked.

"I asked the same question," Kara replied, remembering Bree's face. "She said the silversmith told her he knew to take the silver out when he could see his own image in it."

"Then how did Bree know when to stop burning herself? She wasn't metal. She was human flesh." Coya laid out Kara's required clothes for the evening.

Dyna stepped away, finally finished with Kara's hair. She stood and looked at Coya. "I don't know. I left the foster home and never saw Bree again." With a blank expression, Kara walked to the bathroom. She swallowed down the familiar bile that rose in her throat every night during her preparations.

Reena helped Kara out of her robe and then took the girl's hand to steady her while Kara stepped into the tub. Once settled, Kara sat motionless as granite while the female elves began their ritualistic chanting. Kara started when she felt a hand on her arm. She turned to see Dyna crouched down next to her. The elf's eyes were filled with worry, and her voice quavered. "You do not need the fire, Kara," Dyna said softly. "You are not impure."

Kara silently held the elf female's gaze. What could she say? Dyna wasn't the one being forced to be with a man she didn't want. What did she know of purity? How could she possibly understand a single touch of Ludcarab's hand made Kara feel as if she'd been forcibly submerged into a river of sewage. She could smell the stench on her flesh. It never left her, regardless of all the soap, scrubbing, oils, or anything else the elves used to try and "clean" her. Bree had been on to something. Being bathed in flames seemed like the only viable choice.

Dyna's eyes filled with tears. "Can you hold on just a little longer?" she whispered. "Just a *little* longer."

The words triggered a memory–a strawberry blonde girl with more knowledge in her tiny pinky than most people had in their whole brain. "Jewel." She said the girl's name out loud. Jewel was her friend—her brave friend who had taught Kara what it meant to hold on. As she thought about Jewel, other faces popped into her mind. "Stella, Anna, and Heather," Kara said quietly, her heart suddenly feeling lighter. She hadn't forgotten them, but her mind seemed to have tucked them away somewhere, and it took a trigger to bring them to the forefront.

"Hold on a little longer, Kara," Dyna said again. "For yourself and for the people you just mentioned. Hold on."

The elf's voice brought her back to the present and reminded her why she'd thought of Jewel in the first place. Jewel had once told her one of the ways she'd survived Volcan. She'd told Kara, "The difference between a hero and an ordinary person is five minutes. A hero endures and fights five minutes longer." That was how Jewel survived. And it would be how Kara would survive as well.

"Okay," Kara said, her voice barely audible. "A little longer." She had no idea what she was promising. Not to burn herself? Not to kill herself? Had those things really been what Dyna had seen in Kara's eyes? Maybe, Kara thought, then shook her head. No. There was no way she would leave this life without taking Ludcarab with her. If she died, then that bastard did, too.

Kara let her mind slip into the trancelike state she'd mastered over the past month while the elf females continued their ministrations. She could still hear things going on around her and even smell the scents of the oils. But her consciousness, her soul, went somewhere else, somewhere safe where Ludcarab couldn't touch her.

As she was led to Ludcarab's room, her physical feet touched the cold stone floor. But in her mind, her bare feet were tickled by soft grass underneath. The castle walls were gone. Instead, a forest surrounded her. She hurried forward, knowing she would break through the trees any second and *he* would be waiting in the clearing for her. For a brief second, her breath caught in her lungs. What if he wasn't there? What if he didn't want to see her?

"Kara." The deep voice she'd grown to love filled her mind. *"I'm here."*

Three steps later, she saw Nick sitting in the same place he always did, staring out over the valley below the hill that was her sanctuary. Kara stopped and took in his features. He kept his hair trimmed so short he was nearly bald. The hairstyle didn't detract from his good looks; it only added to the mysterious air about him. He had a strong jaw, sensual lips, and eyes so dark it was almost impossible to see the edge of his pupil where the color began. His shoulders were broad and looked as if they could carry the weight of the world without bowing. Everything about

Nick radiated masculine dominance. Which translated to *safe* in her mind. A male this strong could protect her.

"Are you just going to stand there and stare at me?" he asked, his deep voice playful. His lips didn't move, yet she still heard him. When she'd asked him how that was possible, he'd told her it was because their souls were one. Kara still wasn't sure if she believed him.

"Come sit by me." Nick patted the grass beside him.

She walked over and sat down. Kara drew her legs up until her knees were bent, and she wrapped her arms around them. She could feel Nick's eyes on her, but she didn't turn to face him. For some reason, when she looked at him, Kara felt like a blubbering schoolgirl attempting to talk to her childhood crush. She found it easier to speak if her eyes focused on something else. *"Are you real?"* It wasn't the first time she'd asked him the question. She asked him every time she escaped into her mind.

"Yes." He gave the same answer each time. *"One day soon, we will meet outside of this place."*

"You mean outside of my mind?" Kara shivered, and Nick immediately pressed his side against her. The warmth of his body seeped into hers, and the sensation felt so incredibly real that she nearly cried. Her desperation for *this* reality to be her life, instead of what was happening outside of her mind, was the only thing that gave her any hope.

"Yes, sweetheart. We will meet again in the real world. Our bond is growing stronger every time you come back to me here. I will be able to find you soon." Though his words were gentle, she could hear the frustration that filled his voice. He truly cared for her. *More* than cared for her. Nick loved her. He told her every time she said goodbye before she was sucked back to reality.

"I wish I could remember you," she whispered into his mind.

"Can I ask you something?" Nick plucked a piece of grass from the ground and began to twist it. When it broke, he plucked another piece and did the same.

"Of course," Kara answered as she watched his hands.

"When we meet like this"—he motioned between them —*"our souls are seeking one another. That is because we are true mates. But we shouldn't be able to because some powerful magic is blocking our bond. The only way to overcome that barrier is if one of us is experiencing something that causes profound emotion."* He paused and took a deep breath as if he needed to gather his courage to continue. *"I am under extreme strain being apart from you. That is giving my soul the emotional fuel to seek you out. But you must be experiencing something terribly emotional as well or you wouldn't be here. What is happening when your soul reaches for mine? What is the intense emotional experience that gives you the power over the magic separating us?"*

Kara shifted so they were no longer touching shoulder to shoulder. The warmth from his nearness fled as though ice water was being injected into her veins. Kara's lungs tightened, and it became difficult to draw in air. Her mind rebelled against the idea of bringing the outside world into their safe place. "Nick," she started, speaking out loud instead of through the more intimate mind-to-mind bond. Her voice sounded scratchy as she attempted to force sound past strained vocal cords.

He turned his body so that he was facing her. Kara didn't want to look at him. She didn't want him to see the answer in her eyes. After all, the eyes were the windows to the soul, right? She had no doubt he would see what her soul was defending her from during her escapes to this reality.

"Kara, look at me, sweetheart," he said gently. When she didn't move, he leaned forward so he could grip her hips in both hands, and then he turned her body until she faced him. He lifted her chin. She kept her eyes closed. "You can tell me anything," he assured her.

She nearly blurted out, "Not this," but then clamped her lips shut. Kara shook her head, or tried to, but Nick's hand still held her chin, forcing her head to remain still.

"Do you want to know why I'm able to meet you, despite the bond being weakened?" His voice was soft, coaxing, as he ran his thumb just under her bottom lip. She still didn't respond, but she did find herself leaning into his touch. "You are my world. From the moment I laid eyes on you, everything else disappeared and you became the air that I breathe, the food that I eat, the drink for which I thirst. Without you, half of me is missing. There's no reason to laugh, no reason to enjoy life, no reason to live if you aren't there. I am slowly going out of my mind, and the only thing holding me together is these moments we have like this. The only thing keeping me from going feral is this." He cupped her cheek, and she finally opened her eyes. Kara needed to see the truth in his dark orbs. "Seeing you, touching you, smelling your scent, even only through the bond, is all that keeps me from killing anything and anyone around me."

Tears ran down her cheeks. She looked at his handsome face and saw raw emotion there. Nick's body trembled as if his nerves were exposed to the elements and the sensation was too much for him to handle. Kara clenched her hands into fists and reached for the strength that had kept her from losing her mind while in foster care. This would not break her. She wouldn't let it. And if Nick was real, then she wouldn't allow Ludcarab to take away the possibility of being reunited with him. This man claimed to be her true mate and unabashedly admitted his feelings for her. If he really was who he said he was, then this terrible truth wouldn't break either of them.

Letting out a quick breath, she finally spoke. "Every night, I have to escape into my mind because the reality of what is happening is not something I can face. At least, not right now. Maybe if it was only once..." She shook her head. "No, not even once. I created this place in my mind the very first time. But since then, every night for a month, I return here and leave my body with him." Kara shuddered at her words. The mere idea of Ludcarab touching her made bile rise in her throat. Giving voice to the thought was almost too much even in this reality.

Nick's eyes began to glow, and a low rumble filled the quiet space around them. Kara watched his arms sprout fur and claws erupt from his fingertips. He took several very deep breaths, and the changes stopped. A second later, he was once again just a man.

"Are you all right?" Kara wanted to reach for his hand and clasp it tightly in hers. But she didn't know if her touch would be welcome after what she'd just revealed.

Nick moved as fast as lightning. He grabbed her around the waist and hoisted Kara up, settling her sideways on his lap. He wrapped an arm around her body until his hand rested on her hip, his fingers stretching all the way to her stomach. She marveled at how much bigger he was than her. "You—and only you—can touch me anytime," he said, having heard her thoughts. "Don't ever hesitate."

He buried his face in her neck, and she felt his warm breath on her skin. She heard a hitch in his breathing. His shoulders shook, and Kara realized he was crying. She wrapped her arms around his neck, pulling him tighter, as if this incredibly strong male needed her to hold him together.

"I'm so sorry," he whispered so softly she barely heard him. "This is my fault."

Kara shook her head. "No, Nick. The blame falls on the Order."

"They wouldn't have gotten to you if we hadn't been fighting," he said. "You needed to get away from me because I drove you crazy with my refusal to complete the bond. You were in a vulnerable position because I refused to compromise. It *is* my fault."

Kara wished she could understand what he was talking about, but the memories weren't there. No matter how she searched her mind, there was only an empty space where her recollections should be. "I was aware that the Order was a threat, and yet I chose to put myself in a situation that compromised my safety. Doesn't that make me to blame?"

He pulled his head up and looked at her, his brow drew down in a deep V. "No. You didn't purposely put yourself in a vulnerable position. You were just trying to keep from strangling me, which I assure you I deserved."

"Regardless of how I ended up here, it doesn't matter. The past is the past. We can't get stuck there because then we will never move forward. We will never figure a way out of this," she told him. Kara was still cold as she sat in his lap, resting in his arms and firmly pressed against his chest. "I need to get out of here, Nick." She held his eyes as she spoke. "One way or another, I cannot stay here. My sanity hinges on these moments with you. I don't remember what we are to each other, but I know that there is something powerful between us. Somehow I am going to get free of the elf king's clutches."

It didn't take him long to figure out what she implied. "No." He shook his head, his jaw clenched tightly. "It's selfish of me to ask this of you, but if you're implying death, I cannot accept that. This life has no meaning without you."

Kara pressed her hand to his cheek. His eyes were glassy from the tears he'd shed while he held her close. "I will not let Ludcarab win," she told him gently. "Even if I die, I will kill him first. I cannot keep doing this, Nick." Her voice trembled as the tightly controlled emotions began to unravel. "I cannot keep allowing him to have pieces of my soul, because that's what happens every time he takes my unwilling body." Kara's hand dropped from Nick's face and curled into a fist. She slammed it into his chest. Then she shook her head as a sob wrenched from deep in her gut. "I can't." She punched him again. Nick simply held her and let her beat his chest. Over and over, her knuckles connected with his hard body. She didn't know why she unleashed her anger on him, but Nick didn't attempt to stop her. He didn't placate her with false hope or attempt to soothe her. And for that, she was grateful. Kara didn't want empty words. She wanted permission to lose her shit. She needed to unleash her rage into something other than an empty bathroom with scalding hot water and soap that would never wash away the filth that permeated her skin. Kara needed to express every feeling that threatened to suffocate her. Every morning as her eyes opened, she knew that eventually the sun would set, and her torture would start all over again. Shame radiated from deep within her chest, and it felt like her heart would split in two. Logically, she knew this wasn't her fault. She'd done nothing to deserve Ludcarab's actions, and yet the humiliation wouldn't leave.

Like a disgusting oil that clung to her skin, coating every inch of her, the shame left her unclean. The thought forced her face into Nick's unyielding chest as she let out a scream so violent it terrified her. She thought the sound must be coming from some terribly wounded beast rather than her own throat.

As the echoes of the scream died away, Kara felt Nick's hand run down the back of her hair. Over and over, he petted her, though he still didn't speak. She felt comfort flowing through the bond that connected them, but she also felt his deep sense of desolation because he'd been unable to protect her.

Kara clutched his shirt in her hands, her face still pressed against him as her tears soaked the fabric. No matter how many times she told herself to pull it together, she only cried harder. She'd been so alone, even in the presence of the three female elves who tended to her. They weren't her family, her pack. *Pack?* The word resonated inside of her. It felt right, even though she wasn't entirely sure why. Just like she wasn't entirely sure why she felt comfortable enough with Nick that she allowed herself to fall apart in front of him.

Her breathing began to calm as Kara started to regain dominance of the torrential tsunami that had been her loss of control. The tears subsided, and her tense muscles relaxed. She turned her head until her cheek rested against Nick's shoulder. If it was up to her, she'd never leave this position. She'd happily stay in his protective embrace forever.

"I would give anything to hold you for eternity," he told her. Kara felt his lips against the top of her head.

She leaned back and tilted her head up. The passion in his glowing eyes burrowed deep into her and chased away the cold with its warmth. She didn't have to ask him for what she wanted. Kara knew he could pick it straight out of her mind.

He leaned down, without hesitation, and pressed his lips to hers. Electricity ran through her body, starting at the point where their mouths connected. It flashed down her neck, chest, hips, and all the way to her toes. Nick's hand tightened on her waist, his fingers squeezing hard enough that if they hadn't been in some alternate mind reality, he'd probably leave bruises. They'd be worth it, just to have a single kiss from this passionate man who claimed her as his. His hand held the back of her head, keeping her close to him.

Kara continued to fist his shirt in her hands, afraid to loosen her grasp for fear that he might disappear. She could feel his heartbeat against her chest and realized her own heart beat in rhythm with his. As butterflies danced in her stomach and her flesh grew more sensitive with every touch, Kara realized this was how it should be. This is what intimacy, shared and freely given, felt like. And she wanted more. She wanted the opportunity to replace every disgusting touch from Ludcarab with Nick's soul-quenching love. And she would do whatever it took to make that her future. Some magic prevented her from knowing this man who held her so tightly yet tenderly. She would find out what that magic was and break it.

Suddenly, Kara felt a violent pull, as if a string wrapped around her heart had jerked her backward. She broke away from the kiss, her eyes wide with fear. A tidal wave of panic built in her gut. Nick clutched her face, and she could tell he saw the terror in her face. "Kara?" he growled. "Stay with me, dammit."

"I can't," she whispered. She felt the pull again, a

reminder that her body wasn't in this place, only her mind. And now, the torment her physical body was experiencing was coming to an end. The protection was no longer needed, and she had to go back. She had to let her mind return so she could take care of herself. But Kara would do more than take care of herself. She would plan. She could try to fight the pull back to reality. But if she didn't go back, then things wouldn't change. *"Nick,"* she said through the bond, hoping he could hear every ounce of pain it caused her to leave him. She looked at her hands and saw they were fading out of existence. She looked up, and her eyes met his. She saw that the usually dark orbs glowed a soft silver. His jaw clenched as he narrowed them on her.

"I'm coming for you, sweet Kara. And I'm going to kill the one who has taken you from me."

She didn't have time to respond. Kara was suddenly back in Ludcarab's room. Her body was folded into a fetal position on the cold floor. Her skin was pressed to the cool stone, and air ran across her back and shoulder. The dawning realization that she was naked, lying like a dog on Ludcarab's bedroom floor, chased the chill away and caused her blood to boil with fury.

"I know what you've been doing, Kara," Ludcarab's voice slithered across her skin like a snake, and she had to fight the urge to swipe at him. But she refused to give him the pleasure of seeing her unnerved. "What if I told you that though your mind is not present when you're with me, your body is all too willing to be mine?" He practically purred the words.

Kara bit the inside of her cheek until she tasted blood. She wanted to scream "liar," but she was too afraid that he wasn't. What if his words were the truth? How could she ever look at herself in the mirror again and not see a weak female who couldn't even keep herself from being a willing participant in a monster's bed? Was that what she was? Could she even call it rape if her body did indeed respond to him? Kara's stomach roiled, and she came dangerously close to puking on his floor again. She slowly pushed herself up until she sat facing her tormentor. Without a word, Kara stood and grabbed the robe from the end of the bed where Ludcarab lay languidly, looking exactly like the snake she reminded her of.

She slipped it on and tied it closed, never taking her eyes from his. If looks could scream "I'm going to slit your throat and bathe myself in your blood," that's what hers would say. She began to back toward the door. She wasn't about to turn around, given that he looked at her like he was starving and she was his last meal.

"Nothing to say?" A sly smile stretched across his handsome face. The good looks were only skin deep. Everything beneath it was a festering, infected wound that stunk of evil.

Kara still didn't say a word. She put her hand behind her and moved it around until she found the doorknob, then she pulled the door open. As she continued to walk backward, she began to close the door, but before she could get it shut, his words slipped through the small crack. "I'll see you tomorrow, my queen. It shouldn't be long now before you carry the first half-elf, half-gypsy healer child."

As soon as the door clicked closed, Kara turned and ran. She reached the bathroom in her room—her prison—just as her stomach's contents erupted. She felt a cool rag against her neck, and then a cup with water appeared on the counter next to where she stood hunched over the toilet.

"I'm sorry, child," Reena said. Kara could hear the

sincerity in her voice. None of the three females forced her to Ludcarab's chambers, but neither had they offered her any chance of escape. They did what was expected of them, but she didn't know why. She didn't get the feeling they were loyal to Ludcarab, which meant he had some sort of leverage over them.

"S'not your fault." Kara coughed out the words. Her stomach tried to expel more vomit, but it was empty. After several minutes, Kara shakily stood. She grabbed the cup of water and took a sip, swishing the liquid around in her mouth before spitting it into the sink.

Dyna stepped into the bathroom, and Reena moved aside so the other female could hand Kara clothes. Kara looked down and saw a note sitting on top of the folded clothes. The message said "after your shower, we need to talk." Kara looked back at Dyna who gave her a sharp nod.

The two elves left her to tend herself, shutting the door quietly behind them. Kara wasted no time getting into the shower and turning the hot water to scalding. Fifteen minutes later, her skin looked as if she'd sat out in the sun for an entire day. She'd soaped every inch of herself, twice, and still she felt sullied. Ludcarab's words reverberated in her mind, and Kara started the process of scrubbing her flesh all over again. Never in her life had she ever wanted to remove any and every part of her that made her a female. Not because she didn't want to be a girl, but because those were the parts of her he claimed responded to him. "No way in hell," she bit out. Her nails dug into the tops of her breasts so hard that when she looked down, she realized she'd drawn blood.

The rivulets of red running down her skin seemed to snap her out of her momentary insanity. His words were meant to take power away from her, but she wasn't about to let him take anything else. She rinsed off the soap and blood and focused on the time she'd shared with Nick in her sanctuary. It gave her the strength to finish bathing, drying, and dressing.

Before leaving the safety of the bathroom, she brushed her teeth, the roof of her mouth, and her tongue. If she'd had some rubbing alcohol, she'd have gladly swished some of it in her mouth like she did the water, just to kill any Ludcarab germs that might have remained. She shuddered and pushed that image far from her mind.

When she finally emerged to the bedroom, Dyna and Reena sat on the couch in the small seating area. Coya was nowhere to be seen, which was odd because all three females were always together. Dyna patted the chair next to them. Kara walked over and sat down. She started to open her mouth, but Reena shook her head. Kara snapped her lips closed.

A minute later, the door opened and Coya walked in. She didn't say anything. Instead, the elf came over and sat on the couch with the other two. Kara lifted her brow and looked at each of them. Coya held up a hand and slanted her head to the side, as if to say, "Wait for it." Less than twenty seconds later, a woman suddenly appeared in her room. Kara jumped, though she managed not to squeal like a scared pig.

The woman, who Kara knew must be fae since she'd flashed in, lifted her hand and turned in a slow circle. Her lips moved, though no sound came from them. When she'd made a full rotation, she lowered her hand and then took the last empty seat. Kara frowned and stared at the woman. Something about her was familiar, but she couldn't figure out why.

"We can speak freely now," the woman said.

"Ember," Dyna said. The warmth in her voice made it clear she knew the fae well. "Thank you so much for coming."

Ember nodded. "We agreed that if we ever needed one another's help, we'd be there. We can't survive against the Order on our own."

"You've managed to stay out of their clutches," Coya said.

The fae shrugged. "I've been in hiding for a long time. I've learned some tricks along the way."

Kara stared hard at the fae trying to figure out why she felt as if she knew her. *Ember.* She hoped the name might trigger a memory. But there was nothing.

Ember looked at Kara. Her intense gaze was unnerving. After several heartbeats, the fae said, "I remember you, child, from Perizada's house last year. When Volcan was still alive."

"Peri?" Kara said the name. It sounded foreign on her lips, but at the same time it resonated with something inside, as if this person was somehow important to her.

"Ludcarab has altered her memories." Dyna motioned toward Kara's wrists. The markings of the bracelets on her skin were still there, a constant, silent reminder that the elf king held power over her.

"What do you remember?" Ember asked. The fae's body was slim. She carried her shoulders pulled back, and her spine was so straight it made Kara want to stop slouching.

"What do you mean?" Kara asked.

"Before he put on those." She pointed to the markings encircling Kara's wrists. "How much do you remember of your life before?"

Kara bit her lip. She focused on what she could recall of her life before she was taken by the Order. She frowned when she realized she couldn't even remember what she'd been doing when she'd been kidnapped. When she'd seen Nick in her mind, he'd said something about her needing some space from him. Had she gone somewhere?

"You obviously remember some things about the supernatural world," Ember pointed out. "You didn't scream. And you know that Ludcarab is the elf king, or at least he was at one time."

Kara nodded.

"Do you know what you are?"

"A gypsy healer," she answered.

Ember nodded. "And what about the other gypsy healers? Do you remember them?"

Kara's mind immediately pictured the faces of the four girls she'd thought of earlier. "Stella, Anna, Heather, and Jewel," she said. "Yes, I remember them. We went through hell together. We fought a psycho high fae and lived to tell about it."

"There seems to be a common thread with you fae," Coya said, "going crazy and attempting to take over the world."

Ember shrugged. "Why do you think I live in the human world, away from the supernaturals? People in power, no matter how pure their intentions might start out, always grow to want more power. It is the nature of any race."

"The prince of our race has been on the throne for a very long time, and he has not become a tyrant," Dyna said.

Ember shrugged. "Maybe he will be the exception to the rule." Then she looked back at Kara. "Those markings on your wrists." She motioned to Kara's lap where her hands rested. "Alston put them there using a pair of bracelets?"

"Yes," Kara answered, lifting one hand to rub the other

wrist. She glanced at the three female elves. "They have them as well."

"Ours are different," Dyna said.

"They haven't caused us to forget," Coya added.

"Their purpose is so we *don't* forget," Reena said, seeming to finish the thought of her two comrades.

"Alston, as you have figured out, is very powerful. He uses dark magic and blood magic. No doubt, he has figured out that using the blood of an ancient power such as Ludcarab could create things like those bracelets." Ember looked up and around the room, as if seeing something the rest of them couldn't. "If this was Alston's castle, I wouldn't have been able to ward this room. And if Ludcarab returns while it is warded, he will sense the magic. So we need to get on with this."

She reached down, slipped her hand into her knee-high boot, and pulled out a dagger. The blade gleamed and then glowed a soft blue light as Ember spoke again in a language that Kara had heard before. It was the language of the fae, she presumed, considering Ember was fae. Why was it familiar? *Peri*, she thought, as the name she'd spoken earlier floated through her mind. Kara felt in her gut that this is where she'd heard the fae language spoken before, even though she still couldn't place the woman thanks to her altered memories.

As Kara watched the blade's light grow, she saw engravings begin to etch themselves into the blade, as if an invisible pen were writing on it. When Ember finished speaking, the light faded, but the etchings remained.

"This is a fae blade," Ember began.

Kara raised a brow. "Not to point out the obvious, but you're a fae and you just pulled it from your boot."

Ember's lips raised slightly. "So he hasn't broken you."

didn't understand what it was that Ludcarab held over them to keep them from attempting to escape, but it must have been important. They could have been cruel to her while they performed their duties on Ludcarab's behalf, but they were kind.

She turned back to Ember and forced her feet to keep from moving. "What do I need to do?"

"You will drink the poison. It will not hurt you. It is a plant from the fae realm that has properties that affect the magic of an elf. He will be rendered powerless, unable to access his magic. His strength will be even less than that of a human male.

"The poison will saturate your cells. The mucosa in your mouth, the pores of your skin, any place where your body produces any kind of moisture."

Kara held up a hand as she swallowed down the urge to retch. "I get the picture."

"The hard part will be waiting for it to fully take effect," Ember continued. "He's powerful. You will have to remain in the moment, Kara. If you don't stay alert, you could do something to give yourself away and not even realize it until it was too late. You cannot escape to your sanctuary, no matter how badly you want to. Do you understand?"

Kara's hands tapped the sides of her legs, and she bit the inside of her cheek. "I do." She had to force the words out of her mouth. It had become a habit to run away as soon as her body hit the elf king's bed. She knew this would probably be the hardest thing she'd ever done in her life. She looked at the blade in Ember's hand. "I assume that is the weapon I will use to kill him?"

The fae nodded. "But it is also to remove those," she pointed at Kara's wrists. "Once they're gone, your forgotten memories will return. That might give you the strength to do what you need to do. You will remember what you're fighting for.

"I am not a wolf," Ember continued. "I do not have a true mate, but I've been around a long time, and those of us in the supernatural world know just how special that bond is. Many of us envy what the wolves have. A life partner who will always stand at their side. Your mate will *never* stop looking for you. He will destroy the world to find you. He will kill anyone, friend or foe, in order to have you back at his side." She paused as her eyes took on a lost quality, as if she was thinking of another place and time. "Many would give up anything to have what true mates have. When you remember that—remember who he is to you and the emotions that bind you to him—then you will be able to survive Ludcarab. I do not ask this lightly, Kara. And if there was another way, I would not ask that you allow him to touch you ever again. But this might be the only chance we have to get close enough to kill him before he, Alston, and the vampire king are once again together, combining their power."

Kara knew Ember was right. They had a unique opportunity, and they couldn't squander it, no matter how sick it made her feel. Kara had learned in foster care that there wouldn't always be someone there to fight for you. No matter if you were only a child, you were your own advocate. You were the one who had to choose to fight or lay down and accept your circumstances. Kara never laid down, even if it appeared that way. She was simply biding her time. She always chose to fight. And she would fight now. "What do I need to do?" She walked over to Ember and stared at the blade.

Ember looked at the three she-elves. "You're going to have to hold her. I could use magic to keep her still, but I don't want to leave a magical fingerprint on her that could alert Ludcarab." Ember looked back at Kara. "I can remove the power of the bracelets, but I will have to leave the markings on your skin so he won't be aware they no longer hold any control over you."

Kara hated the idea of keeping the bracelets on, but she'd deal with that later. "Do it."

"This is going to hurt," Ember warned.

"Physical pain is a welcome reprieve," Kara told the fae. "Do your worst."

Dyna stood and walked behind Kara. She wrapped her arms around Kara's waist and pulled her tightly to her chest. Then, Coya and Reena each took one of Kara's arms and held them tight. They were much stronger than they looked.

Ember took Kara's left hand and wrapped her fingers around it until Kara's fingers were scrunched tightly together. Kara attempted a slight tug to test the fae's strength. The woman's hand didn't even flex, and her arm didn't budge.

The fae took the flat of the blade and laid it on Kara's wrist. Then Ember closed her eyes. Instead of speaking softly, the fae's voice came out strong as she spoke in her language. There was a lyrical quality to her words, and Kara felt her heart picking up the rhythm of it. Several minutes passed. Kara was beginning to think the spell wasn't going to work; she hadn't felt the slightest discomfort. All of a sudden, her mouth clamped shut on its own as pain seared her skin. It felt like the blade was burning through every layer of her dermis, through her blood vessels, and straight into her bones. The heat radiated up her arm, through her shoulder and into her neck, and then up into her skull. She was sure Ember was attempting to cook her brain. The heat intensified, and Kara wanted to tell the fae to stop, but she couldn't. Even though the urge to roar from the torture boiled up inside her, no sound could escape her vocal cords. Perhaps Ember had melted them.

Kara tried to put up walls in her mind to keep the pain away.

"Leave your thoughts open," Ember snapped. "I have to remove all the magic from your mind. That's why your memories are blocked."

Kara wanted to tell the fae that it wouldn't matter if her memories were blocked if her brain melted out of her ears.

"I'm not melting your brain, healer," Ember said, somehow picking up her thoughts. "I'm killing the magic that Alston allowed to take root, like a parasite, in your mind. You get through this, and you're one step closer to getting your life back."

The fae's words were enough to make Kara accept the pain and drop the walls. Scalding waves of fire licked across her skull, down the right side of her neck, shoulder, arm, and straight into her right wrist. Kara instinctively wanted to pull away, but she didn't fight the elves holding her. She simply gritted her teeth and mentally cursed Alston and Ludcarab to the deepest level of hell, praying that they would endure an eternity of unimaginable torment. The only thing that might make it even better is if she could have a front row seat and some popcorn to watch the show.

"Keep those emotions at the forefront tomorrow night," Ember said. "Keep the rage, the retribution owed to you for all they've done, Kara. They do not deserve mercy."

Finally, the burning subsided, and the elves released her. Ember also let go of her hand. Kara looked down at her wrists. The marks were still there, but something was different. She hadn't realized that they'd felt heavy before, like she'd been wearing shackles. Now, there was no weight. The burning in her head was replaced with a tidal wave of memories so intense it drove her to her knees.

Kara sucked in a harsh breath when Nick's image filled her mind. No longer unfamiliar was his shaved head, handsome face, and black eyes. She remembered the first time she'd laid eyes on him. Every part of her had responded to him in a way she'd never done with anyone. He'd held her captive before he'd ever said a word to her. "Nick," she whispered as the memories assailed her.

She remembered being in the fae realm, lying in a field with him. He was in his wolf form, unable to speak with her because of Lucian's punishment. Kara had poured out her heart to him. She'd been brave enough to do it because, at the time, he'd been unable to say a word to her. Not to mention, speaking to him while he was in his wolf form seemed easier. It had made her feel less vulnerable.

"I don't trust easily, Nick. No one has ever given me a reason to trust until I met Peri and her group of crazy supernaturals. I never believed there were men out there like Costin and Lucian. Men who would die for the woman they love but, even more impressive, will live sacrificially for her. Dying is easy. Giving up your own wants and needs for another, that's the hard stuff. Can you give me that?"

Kara couldn't believe she'd been bold enough to say those things to him. But then she remembered how desperately she'd wanted what she'd seen in the other true-mate couples. And she still wanted it. Maybe even more so now.

Her mind continued to play out her memories like a movie—memories Alston had stolen from her. One memory in particular made her smile. She realized the gesture was foreign to her lips. She couldn't remember the last time she'd smiled. Nick had asked her if she was disappointed that he was her true mate. She'd been unable to keep from word vomiting all over him.

"Disappointed? I'm a lot of things right now: shocked, excited, worried, flummoxed—is that a word? Whatever. I'm curious, overwhelmed, and, yea, even, ah, um, a little, well, aroused. Yeah, I went there. But disappointed? Of you? Have you seen yourself?

"You're tall and muscular, with these brooding good looks and devouring obsidian eyes. You walk around with this devil-may-care attitude. But you're also kind and gentle. And really, really strong."

"Is that important?" he asked.

"Maybe, yes. I can't say that if I was out hunting for a werewolf mate that I would be like, 'Hey, who's the weakest of the bunch? Yeah, I want you.'"

Kara chuckled and shook her head as she remembered the way he'd laughed. She'd been unable to take her eyes off him. He was beautiful. He'd taken her breath away. The memory of that same day continued, and she had no power to stop it, not that she wanted to.

"If I kiss you, I won't be able to let you go. My wolf is already attached, as am I. But if you let me get even a small taste of you, my mate, I will follow you to the ends of the earth and attack any male who comes near you."

Kara waited, holding his eyes with her own.

He let out a growl. "I'm going to hell." His hand slid through her hair, tugging gently, forcing her head back as his lips crashed down onto hers.

Kneeling on the floor in the cage that was her room in Ludcarab's castle, she reached up and ran her fingers across her lips. She could practically feel that first kiss they'd shared. He was supposed to have been the last male she'd ever kiss. He'd made that perfectly clear. *"There will be none after me."* The words reverberated so hard in her mind that she felt it in her soul. Her lips had touched another's and would again.

"Shit." She gasped and fell forward, barely catching herself before she face-planted. While the memories were a blessing, they also felt like a curse. Nick might not have been her first kiss, but he was supposed to be her first *everything else*. Ludcarab had stolen that from her. She slammed her hand against the floor so hard it rattled her bones up her arm and into her jaw. The pain felt so good she did it again and again. When Kara was sure she'd gotten herself under control, she pushed herself back up into a kneeling position and then stood. When she raised her head and opened her eyes, setting aside the precious memories that she never wanted to lose again, she looked at Ember. The fae female took a step back, and her eyes narrowed.

"You still have Volcan's power in you," she said, her voice steady, but everything else about her spoke of fear. "The bracelets must have been suppressing that part of you as well."

"Volcan?" Dyna asked. The tone of her voice made it clear she knew exactly who Ember was speaking about.

Ember nodded. "Volcan managed to get his hands on the new healers in Peri's charge. He made them witches."

"But I don't feel any evil on her," Coya said. Instead of taking a step away from Kara, she moved closer. The elf studied her, as if she'd be able to see the magic on Kara that made her something more than just a healer.

"I'm not evil," Kara said. "Peri helped us change the magic that Volcan used. We have some of the powers that witches had, but not dark magic."

Ember shook her head. "Everyone has the potential to

have dark magic, Kara, especially when it has been passed on from someone like Volcan."

Kara considered the last couple of months that she'd spent as Ludcarab's captive. She thought about all that he'd taken from her. And then she looked at Ember. "Perhaps you're right. After what Ludcarab has done, what he's taken from me, I will do anything to destroy him. Even if that means using dark magic."

"You won't need it." Ember held the blade out, handle first. "This will kill him. Like any being, he cannot live without a heartbeat."

Kara took the dagger. It seemed small and insignificant considering what task lay ahead of her.

"Use the blade to cut your hand. The blade will use your blood to bind itself to you. You cannot carry the weapon with you ... for obvious reasons. But when it becomes linked to you, all you will need to do is mentally call it, and the blade will come to you. It will also strike true when you wield it, even if you have to throw it. Once it is bound to you, it will carry out any intention you have," Ember explained.

Kara didn't hesitate. She ran the blade across her palm, and it sliced through her skin as easily as a knife across warm butter. She expected more pain, but she only felt a slight sting. A few seconds later, the wound closed completely.

"Fae blades hold a lot of power," Ember said. "Now, you must drink this."

Kara looked up to see the fae holding out a small vial of silver liquid. She reached out and took it. Kara tilted the vial this way and that, watching the thick poison coat the bottle. "How long will the effects last?"

"The poison will stay in your body until it has carried out its purpose," Ember answered.

Kara pulled the cork out of the bottle. Without considering all the ways the plan could go to hell, she poured the liquid into her mouth and swallowed. She waited to see if she felt anything, but other than a slight warm flushing of her skin, which dissipated in a matter of seconds, she felt fine.

"IT's DONE." Ember looked at each of the elf females. "Once Ludcarab dies, I will remove the bracelets from your arms."

Kara frowned. "Why can't you do it now?"

Dyna took a deep breath and let it out slowly. "If for some reason you fail—"

"I won't," Kara bit out.

The elf pressed her lips tightly together and then continued. "But *if* you do. We can't look as if we had anything to do with it. Our bracelets do not do the same thing yours did. He would know if they were no longer imbued with his power."

"There was a time when I loved supernatural books and movies," Kara said, thinking back to a period before she'd known of the world she was now a part of. "I thought magic was so cool. To have the power to fight off those who would hurt you." She shook her head. "But now"—she huffed out a laugh that had no humor—"I think it sucks."

"Any power can be abused," Ember said. "But power can also be used for good. That is what we must remind ourselves when we are tempted to abuse the power the Great Luna has given us."

Kara handed the empty bottle back to the fae and then took the blade over to her bed and placed it under her pillow. She suddenly felt very tired. The adrenaline from all that had just happened seemed to have seeped from her body, and now she was just weary.

"I think we should let Kara get some sleep," Dyna said.

Kara looked over at her and tried to smile, but she could tell by the sorrow in the elf's eyes that the attempt hadn't been convincing. "Thank you. All of you."

"Be strong," Ember said. "Your eyes are haunted for one so young. I will leave you this, and I hope it encourages you. Your name has many meanings in different tongues. But my favorite, and the one that I think rings truest for you, is 'beloved.' For that is what you are. To have a true mate is to be beloved. That alone is reason enough to fight, even when you just want to give up and escape the horrors you are facing. But tonight, you are more than just beloved. You have become a warrior, preparing to enter battle. I so name you, Kara Luisa, beloved, renowned warrior. For if you kill the elf king, you will indeed be renowned in every realm by every race." Ember bowed to Kara, the fae's eyes never leaving hers. "Until I see you again." Then she flashed.

Dyna, Reena, and Coya each bowed to her as well. Without a word, they filed out of the room.

"No pressure, Kara Luisa," she muttered to herself. The weariness that had come over her settled even further into her bones, and she found herself lying on her side, her legs pulled up to her chest with her arms wrapped around them. Her thoughts immediately jumped to Nick: her true mate, the other half of her soul. She acknowledged the deep longing inside, and she wished for all the world to be back at Peri's home again, sitting with him, talking to him, seeing the adoration in his eyes as he looked at her. "Nick." She whispered his name like a prayer.

"KARA!" His voice filled her mind like a boom of thunder, so powerful she actually flinched.

"Nick?" she asked, her own voice trembling. She wasn't sure if this was another escapist fantasy, but Kara hoped it wasn't. She wanted this to be real, needed it to be real—Nick speaking to her through their bond. Kara felt a flood of love straight into her heart and soul. Like nourishment for a starved body, she allowed him to invade every cell.

"My Kara, my heart," he said, his voice full of reverence that she could feel through their bond. *"I'm losing my mind. Please tell me this is real. Tell me where you are. I have to find you."*

"I can feel you," she told him. *"I remember you. I remember who you are to me."*

"Thank the Great Luna." He breathed out and his relief enveloped her. *"Where are you? I can feel you, but I can't locate you. Something is still blocking part of the bond. Do you know where they're keeping you?"*

Kara started to tell him, but then bit her tongue. She quickly threw up a mental wall to the thoughts that Nick didn't need to know. Not yet. He couldn't come for her yet. She had to complete her mission. She *had* to kill Ludcarab.

"Sweetheart," he said, using the endearment that he knew she loved. *"Do you know?"*

"I can't tell you yet." Kara could have told Nick she didn't know where she was, but she didn't want to lie to him. There were going to be many painful truths that she would have to share with him soon. Confessing that she lied to him would not be one of them. *"There's something I must do first. I have to do this. The plan is already in place, and I cannot veer from my path."* She didn't allow him to see the details of that plan. Perhaps now she was a hypocrite, because a lie of omission was still a lie. But she knew if Nick found out she

was going to attempt to kill the elf king, he would likely go crazy.

"You do not have to do anything without me by your side," he told her, his voice so full of anguish that she almost gave in. Because she knew Nick wouldn't hesitate to kill Ludcarab. And if she was being honest with herself, Kara was terrified she might hesitate for half a second too long and lose the chance to kill her tormentor. *"Let me protect you. I failed you once. I will not do it again."*

"You didn't fail me, Nick. Don't ever think that. You gave me something I have never had before, somewhere I belonged. You gave me a family." Tears streamed down her face. She tucked her knees closer to her chest and buried her face in them. Kara felt as if she might shatter from the inside out. The ache of needing her mate, being separated from him for so long, and feeling all of his pain from their separation was something she never wanted to go through again. Just five minutes more. She reminded herself of Jewel's persistent chant. And she knew she would say it all night long, throughout the next day, and up until the moment when she would plunge the dagger into Ludcarab's black heart.

"I love you, Nick. One more day, then we will be together, and I will never leave your side again. Even if you ask me to wait a decade to complete the bond. I will happily do it, as long as you never let me go."

"Ka—"

She didn't let him finish the words before doing the hardest thing she'd ever done in her life. Kara closed the bond between them, cutting off the first contact they'd had in months, knowing it might push her mate over the edge. She had to trust that those who loved him, their pack, would take care of him until he could be with her again. In her gut, she knew this was what she had to do. The Great

Luna had told her when she'd arrived that it wasn't time to fight back, but now Kara knew with complete certainty that it was.

"*I am with you, beloved, renowned warrior.*" The Great Luna's voice filled not only her mind but the surrounding room. "*I will steady your hand, I will shore up your weaknesses, and I will be your strength when you think you cannot finish the task before you. Now rest, Kara. For tomorrow your arm will deliver my wrath.*"

FOURTEEN

"I never thought I would be thankful for foolish gypsy healers, determined to run headlong into situations that will most likely end in their deaths. But I am. And that's the first step to repairing a part of my life I've completely and utterly destroyed. A reality filled with self-destructive healers is familiar and oddly comforting, as silly as that might sound. I will have to thank Kara for carrying on the longstanding gypsy tradition of 'watch me get my ass handed to me.'" ~Peri

"Are you just going to let him throw another piece of furniture out the window?"

Nick heard Fane's voice but not Drayden's reply, and he didn't really care what it was. Nick had *felt* her. He'd *spoken* to her. For a few brief moments, his beloved was within his reach. Now she was gone. The beta picked up the next closest thing to him: a massive television.

"I could stop him without injuring the wolf," Adam said.

Nick roared, and the TV went flying, crashing through a window. The shattering sound of the glass satisfied him for... perhaps a second. Would there be consequences for the damage he was causing to their pack home? His wolf didn't care. The beast raged at their inability to find their mate. The restoration of the mate bond had made things worse, not better. Before, he only knew mentally that his Kara was held captive somewhere, hurting and alone. Now, he felt it with every fiber of his being. And worst of all, after having been reconnected with her for such a short time, she'd shut him out. This time, she'd *chosen* to close the bond.

"WHY?" He reached for a lamp he knew would shatter into a thousand pieces, a fitting symbol for what had happened to his soul when Kara re-closed the bond.

"Not the lamp, Nick," Drayden growled, forcing a bit of his alpha power into the command.

Nick turned and looked at Drayden.

"You were okay with him throwing out a television worth thousands of dollars, but you're worried about a lamp?" Adam asked.

"I like that lamp." Drayden shrugged his large shoulders. He met Nick's eyes, and they began to glow. "Put it down. And talk to me." It was a full-fledged alpha command. Surprisingly, Nick was able to fight off the command for nearly a minute as his wolf grappled against the need to submit to their alpha and the need to find their mate. Finally, Nick set the lamp down and rolled his shoulders. His teeth, which had phased into his wolf's canines without him realizing it, bit into his bottom lip.

"The bond is back," Nick finally said after he leashed his

wolf. "I spoke to her. I felt her." Just saying the words out loud made the gnawing need inside of him grow tenfold.

"Did she tell you where she is?" Drayden asked and took a step toward him.

"Based on his current behavior," Dillon, the Colorado pack alpha, said, "I'm going to go out on a limb and say no."

Nick's wolf pushed forward, and he couldn't hold the beast. It was the wolf who responded to their alpha. "My mate refused to tell me. She claims she has something she must do before we can be together. And then she closed down the bond. Tight." He snarled the last word. Nick wanted to throw something again, and Drayden must have seen it in his eyes.

"Destroy nothing else," his alpha commanded. "Think of the positive things. You know she's alive. The bond is back. And you will be with her again. These things should quiet your wolf."

"Her task is dangerous, Alpha," Nick said. "I could practically smell her fear. She will not let me come to her."

"That's because she's a gypsy healer," Crina said. "We've learned over the past few years that the healers have some kind of weird hero complex. They're not actually seeking glory. The girls are trying to be selfless. The healers truly think they are saving those they love and that they're the only ones who can do it. Unfortunately, it rarely works out how they planned. "

Nick's fists clenched at his sides, and he felt claws sink into his palms.

"Judging by the blood dripping onto the beautiful hardwood floor, I don't think that's helping, babe," Adam said to his mate.

"My bad." Crina took a seat on the arm of the only remaining couch in the living room.

"Are you sure you detected nothing in her thoughts that might give you a clue as to where she is or what she is doing?" Fane stood against the wall directly beside one of the shattered windows. The alpha hadn't even flinched when an end table had sailed past him through the window, causing glass to rain over his body. He'd simply brushed it away and then resumed his relaxed stance.

Nick tried to think through the haze of fury and grief that clouded his mind. He tried to remember anything that his wolf might have picked up on in her thoughts that the man might have missed while he'd been speaking to her. For a split second, he saw the face of a female. Her ears were pointed, much more than that of a fae. "A female elf," he said quickly. "She thought briefly of a female elf."

"Does that mean she's in the elf realm?" Crina looked at Thalion. He and his mate, Cyn, stood off in a corner of the room, watching. Neither of them ever said much, but they had offered any help they could in rescuing Nick's mate. Nick looked at them now, hoping they knew the answer to the she-wolf's question.

"Not necessarily," Thalion said. "Supernaturals from all races work with the Order. Many different types of supernaturals were at the compound in Arizona," he reminded them. "Is there anything else? Anything about her location, maybe? The walls, the lighting? Anything that might give us a hint as to the type of structure. It could help us rule out a realm."

Nick concentrated but found nothing. He shook his head. "Then we search every damn realm!" Nick bellowed as his wolf snapped, grabbing the lamp he'd previously set down. He launched it across the room. Decebel ducked, and the lamp whizzed by, shattering against the wall where the beta's head had just been.

Decebel's eyes glowed as he looked behind him at the mess on the floor and then back at Nick. "I've been where you are," he said, his thick accent making his words sound menacing. "In fact, all the men in this room who have true mates have been in this situation. We understand your control is slipping. But we must wait until we have more information. Running off without a plan is not the answer." Decebel took a step toward Nick while rolling his neck and cracking his knuckles.

"And standing here doing nothing is?" Nick shot back. "What good are any of you if you're just going to sit here and talk? If you aren't willing to take action to find my mate, why the hell are you here?" In the back of his mind, a tiny voice told him he was being unreasonable, but the wolf crushed the tiny voice, and Nick continued his tirade. "My mate is alive, in the hands of a sadistic elf king, and you expect me to just sit here twiddling my thumbs?"

"I expect you to be smart." Decebel snarled. "But your wolf is feral, and that means you're going to make some *very* dumb decisions. We will not let you do that. In order to leave this compound, you will have to fight and defeat all of us."

"Wait, what?" Adam said, but Nick paid the fae no attention.

"You think you can take me?" Nick's wolf chuckled. Decebel wasn't wrong. Nick's wolf *was* feral. If he didn't get himself under control, Drayden might be forced to put him down. But that wasn't going to happen because if Nick was dead, then he couldn't help Kara. "When has a feral wolf ever been bested without being killed?"

"You're looking at one." Decebel pointed to himself, then he pointed to Fane. "And that one. And Costin. And I could name more. Something we've learned over the years about feral wolves whose mates are still alive is that there is always hope. We will beat you to within an inch of your life if that's what it takes. But we will keep you alive until we can get your mate back."

"I'm pretty sure I did not volunteer for this. So why exactly are you tossing me in with the wolves, literally?" Adam asked.

"Because that's what pack does," Decebel rumbled. "We do whatever is necessary to meet the needs of those who can't help themselves. Punches or hugs, whatever it takes. We were there for you when you needed us. Now our brother Nick needs us."

Fane pushed off from the wall, his casual stance nowhere to be found. Nick glanced at the alpha and saw that his bright blue eyes glowed with his wolf. "Let's take this outside. There's no reason to destroy any more of Drayden's home."

Fane headed for the door, and Decebel followed, calling out over his shoulder, "We'll understand if you decide to stay inside. No one will think less of you if you're afraid to face us."

"Bloody hell." Adam groaned and stood up before following the other two males. "Crina, I want you to know I love you. And I love our pack. But our beta has finally been driven mad by his psycho mate."

Crina laughed. "Probably. Quit whining and go impress me with your fighting prowess."

He waved a hand at her and exited out the open door.

Nick looked around the room and watched as Dillon, Ciro, Gustavo, Thalion, and Sorin followed the others out the door. Then Cyn and Crina went as well, though he was pretty sure the females wouldn't join in the fight. *Would they?* Elle, Sorin's mate, had not yet returned from checking on the other group that was dealing with the Peri business, which might be a good thing. She seemed a little more blood hungry than Adam. He'd hate to have to kill her. Maybe the thought that he'd even consider that should have concerned him. It didn't. All he was concerned with was his mate.

When he turned to his alpha, Drayden raised a brow at him. "Is your wolf under control?"

Nick shook his head. There was no point in lying. He wouldn't be able to keep his wolf from destroying the rest of the house and then anything else in his path.

Drayden let out a sigh. Then, without so much as a twitch to betray his thoughts, the alpha ran straight at Nick. His shoulder plunged into Nick's solar plexus, knocking the breath out of the beta. The attack was so fast Nick didn't even have time to plant his feet. Drayden pushed him back, propelling him through the open front door and out of the mansion. Nick stumbled but he managed to gain his feet and jump backward into the air, turning before he tripped down the stairs. Instead, he flipped in the air like a cat, rotated, and landed on his feet in a crouch. His wolf took over, shoving the man aside. Nick phased, shedding the human skin and giving himself over to the feral beast that could think of only one thing: kill anything between him and his mate. At that moment, he considered every male in the surrounding circle his enemy. If they would not help him search for her, then they were in the way. *"They will all die,"* his beast said with a cold, detached voice that should have worried Nick. As his sanity slipped away, he gave over his humanity to the wolf and let his instincts dictate his actions.

Fane was the first of his foe to phase. The alpha shook out his fur and then turned those glowing eyes on Nick. His wolf was massive. Fane pulled his lips back in a menacing snarl and took a step toward Nick. The beta was acutely aware of the fact that Fane, of all the wolves, fae, and elves present, could kill him the easiest. And maybe that's what needed to happen. But Nick would make sure the alpha of alphas had to work for his pelt.

Nick lunged, but at the last second, he dropped his head and chest to the ground and snapped his jaws out toward the alpha. Nick's teeth latched onto Fane's front leg. He bit down with all of his might and felt the bone snap beneath his jaw. The alpha didn't so much as whimper. Nick released him and rolled back onto his feet, keeping the others in view out of the corner of his eyes. When another wolf started toward him, Fane snapped his jaws at the wolf, a clear order to back off.

Fane and Nick circled one another. Nick dodged forward, but Fane was fast. He darted to the side before Nick could get his teeth on him again. He noticed Fane didn't limp, although Nick had felt the alpha's bone snap. The Great Luna's blessing must have included some incredibly quick healing. It didn't worry Nick. Just hearing the bone crunch between his teeth had satisfied his wolf's bloodlust, at least temporarily.

He took a step to the right and settled back on his haunches, ready to launch himself forward again, but Fane beat him to it. The massive black wolf pushed off the ground without even getting a head start. He flew through the air and landed right on Nick's back, flattening him to the ground and knocking the wind out of him. Fane's teeth sank into the scruff of Nick's neck. He snapped his head back and forth, shaking Nick as easily as if he'd been a pup. Nick immediately stopped fighting and let his body go limp.

Deadweight was much harder to manipulate. But Fane didn't seem bothered by the load.

Just as quickly as the alpha had attacked, he jumped off Nick and once again stood across from him, his head lowered and ears pressed back against his head. Saliva dripped from his snarling lips. Fane's teeth were coated red with Nick's blood.

Nick pushed up from the ground. Then he heard his alpha's voice in his mind. *"Stay down, dammit."* Nick shook his head. He could not submit, not while his mate needed him. They would have to kill him if they didn't want him to search for her. He would torture every supernatural he came across until he found someone who knew something about her whereabouts. Someone somewhere was left alive after Peri's attack. They had to know something.

He shook himself and saw flecks of blood hit the ground. He didn't know how bad his wound was, but he still felt strong enough to fight. He threw his head back and howled. Then he ran at Fane, barreling his head into the alpha's ribs. Again, Nick heard the snapping of bones. He kept moving, forcing Fane over onto his side. Fane continued to roll, coming full circle and springing back up to his feet. The alpha whipped around, at the same time slinging his head, smashing his skull into Nick's.

Nick stumbled but didn't go down. He backed up and forced himself to push away the stars that danced across his vision. When he could again see clearly, Nick saw Fane had stepped back into the circle, and another wolf had stepped forward in the alpha's place. Nick recognized the wolf as Ciro, the Italian alpha. Nick could feel the old wolf's power. It wasn't as strong as Fane's, but he was definitely a formidable fighter. Nick felt his wolf smile as more of his sanity slipped away.

"Wow," Adam said from beside Fane. "I don't think I've ever seen any of you lose it like this."

Nick turned his head to the fae and snarled.

Adam held up his hands. "Just making an observation. By all means, carry on with your suicide plan."

Before Nick could turn back to his opponent, teeth latched onto his back leg. His front legs collapsed to the ground as he was dragged backward and then whipped around like a rag doll. Ciro released him, and Nick crashed into a tree, hitting the ground with a bone-rattling thud. He struggled to his feet, stumbling.

"Bloody hell, Nick," Drayden practically yelled. "Submit." He didn't give an alpha command, either because he wanted Nick to get his ass kicked, hoping it would snap him out of the feral state, or because Nick was too far gone to be affected by the order.

Nick paid no attention to his alpha and turned back to Ciro. He took a deep breath and tried to inventory his injuries. He definitely had a broken rib or two. His leg, where the Italian alpha had grabbed him, wasn't broken. So Ciro had just used the appendage to throw Nick, not to make him lame.

He ignored the pain in his side and walked toward Ciro. He would not submit. He would not turn belly-up while Kara needed him. Rational or not, they *would* have to kill him if they believed he wouldn't hunt his mate. He would search for her until his body gave out, or he'd turned every realm inside out to find her, whichever came first.

"IT'S BEEN A DAMN MONTH, PERI." Tenia ran a hand through her hair. Peri had noticed a stir-crazy look come into the fae's eyes a couple of weeks ago. Since then, Peri had been doing her damndest to keep Skender's mate from doing something stupid like leaving the draheim realm before Lilly said it was time.

Peri understood Tenia's frustration, but she also understood that if they acted at the wrong time, they could wind up getting people killed. There was clearly a reason Lilly had been blessed with the gift of foresight. They would be foolish not to use that gift to their advantage. Though Peri kept repeating this to the fae, Tenia continued to grow restless.

"Do not mistake my lack of inaction for lack of concern, Tenia." Peri's voice was cool with her own anger. "You have seen what I am capable of if I allow myself to take action without considering if that action is part of the Great Luna's plan. It is a lesson I never want to relearn. My impatience cost many people their lives, and I will not be pushed against a wall because of your anxiety."

Skender stepped forward, placing his body in between them. "Arguing is not productive." He looked at Peri and then at his mate. "I know you're desperate to see Myanin and Lilly. But we have to do this the right way."

Tenia threw her hands up and turned away. "I know. I know," she said again, finally sounding reasonable. "It's just, I feel useless. Myanin is my friend. And I imagine she's not dealing with any of this very well. She's not exactly the most stable person, even on a good day."

Peri laughed. "That's putting it mildly, though she seems to have more control than you give her credit for. Every time I go to the veil to check on things, everyone is still alive. She has been sparring with those who are dumb enough to agree, but she hasn't mortally injured anyone. The djinn is a skillful fighter, even without her magic."

"Is Gerick with her?" Tenia asked, though Peri assumed the fae already knew the answer.

"Yes," Peri replied, trying and probably failing to sound patient. "He hasn't made a run for the hills yet. And I'm sure by now he's realized his mate is a borderline psychopath. You will be happy to know Myanin has formed a bond with Jen."

Skender frowned. "And why would that be a good thing? Jen is way past the borderline of psychosis. She is the last person Myanin needs to befriend."

Peri clucked her tongue at him. "Jen has grown over the years. Matured even. Well, maybe matured is a bit too strong of a word. Nonetheless, she is keeping Myanin distracted. Mostly because Jen needs to get rid of her own pent-up energy." Peri sat on a chair she had magicked to their little abode. "Nissa has been taking the females with children back to the Sprite realm so they may care for their younglings. This appears to help curb Jen's thirst for blood momentarily. But Myanin helps even more." It also helped that she and the other females were taking turns getting to see their mates, courtesy of the fae flashing them to their males. Peri knew first hand how difficult it was to be separated from your true mate, and she was glad that Nissa and the others were able to take the females, especially the healers who were all newly mated, to see their mates.

Tenia took the seat across from Peri. "That's something, at least. You mentioned Thad is there with Jezebel. Does Myanin seem bothered by that?"

Peri shook her head. "The amazing thing about mates, as you should know, is everyone else ceases to exist in any way other than an acquaintance or friend. Nothing more."

Tenia looked at Skender, her eyes softening as she met her mate's gaze. "Yea." She nodded. "I get that."

Skender grinned at her, and Peri thought of her own mate. He was always in the forefront of her mind, even as she waited to hear from Lilly for approval to make their next move. Thoughts of Lucian created a constant pang in her chest. The need to see him, touch him, beg him to forgive her, choked her up and made breathing hard.

"You are already forgiven, my love. How many times do I have to say it?" Lucian asked through their bond.

"Why are you never at the veil?" Peri went every single day, not only to find out if there was any change in their circumstances but also with the hope of seeing him. But he'd yet to be there.

"My wolf is restless. Moving, hunting, distracting him until we can touch you keeps him from running headlong into the impenetrable veil that stands between us. I was a fool to walk away from you, Perizada."

"No," she said quickly, *"It is I who am the fool. I should have turned to you, not away from you. I should have trusted you to stick with me even while I was a complete mess. But instead of allowing myself to be vulnerable, I destroyed the bond we'd built. Though it wasn't as strong as it could have been because of my own insecurities."* Peri shook her head. *"Thousands of years old, and yet I acted like an adolescent human."*

"We will get through this, beloved. And we will be stronger because of it. Please believe that." She felt his hand on her cheek and fought back the tears that always seemed to be on the verge of spilling.

"I do believe it. I will never doubt you again."

"MOM!" Torion's bellow jerked Peri's attention from her mate. She jumped up and followed Tenia and Skender to the opening of the cave. She watched as Torion jumped off the draheim, Galan, who'd become his constant companion. The boy hit the ground at a run and sprinted to them. In his hand, he clutched several pieces of paper. Tenia made sure her son had pencils and paper at all times because of his own gift, just in case he saw something Lilly did not.

"I'm here, Peri. Do what you need to do." She felt Lucian recede to a far corner of her mind, where he could watch without distracting her.

She knelt down where Torion was spreading out three pieces of paper. He put them side by side, and Peri saw the drawings on them connected perfectly, flowing into one large picture. As she stared at them, the drawing came to life, and the figures on the pages began to move.

"Who is that?" Tenia pointed at the female in the picture.

Peri recognized the healer immediately. "Kara." She breathed out as she watched the drawn form of Nick's mate walk into a room. "She's the gypsy healer the Order has abducted."

"That's Ludcarab," Skender said. He pointed to a male form that stood in front of an oversized bed. The figure held out his hand to Kara, beckoning him to her.

"Torion, come with me," Skender said quickly. He grabbed the boy's hand and pulled him up away from the picture. It wasn't difficult to figure out what was happening on the page, and Skender was right to get his son away from it. Peri didn't want to watch it, but she had to.

The robe that Kara wore slipped off her shoulders and dropped to the floor. She placed her hand into the elf king's. Peri's eyes traveled to the next piece of paper when it started moving. Now, the two figures on the page lay on the bed. Kara's body shook as she straddled Ludcarab. He wrapped his hand around her head and pulled her face down to his. Their lips touched, and Peri swallowed down bile that rose in her throat. She felt her power growing in lockstep with her rage and knew her skin must be glowing with it.

"No." Tenia breathed out, her voice shaking with horror as they watched the elf king take what wasn't his. Peri knew Kara would not be doing this of her own volition.

Movement on the next page drew Peri's attention. Now Ludcarab lay still, his eyes wide with shock and horror. Kara sat up. She lifted her hand, and a blade suddenly appeared in it. The healer didn't hesitate. She drove the dagger down into the elf king's chest, straight into his heart.

"It is time."

Peri's head snapped up as the Great Luna's voice filled the cave. The high fae bowed her head and saw Tenia out of the corner of her eye do the same.

"Judgment has come to the fallen king who has dared to touch one of mine," the goddess said, her voice so powerful and full of rage that it rattled Peri's bones. "It is time to gather the scattered pack and find your lost healer. It is time for the prodigal to be reunited to those he hurt and atonement to be paid. It is time for the pack to welcome a new son. Soon, hope born from this evil act will be revealed. Everything happens for a reason in its appointed time. And everything works toward the good of those who love me."

Peri felt peace beyond any understanding fill her, regardless of the horror she'd just witnessed in Torion's drawing. She felt the Great Luna's love and knew it would be that love that drove her to fight for her pack, rather than the hatred of the Order. She felt a righteous anger, not one born of her own need for revenge.

The power faded from the room, and Tenia quickly

gathered the papers as soon as they realized the Great Luna had gone.

"I think I'm going to be sick." Tenia's hands shook as she tried to stack the papers.

"There will be time for that later." Peri stood. "Right now, we need to get to the veil and share what we've learned. Then we haul ass to the hunting party."

A minute later, Skender returned with Torion. He took Tenia's other hand, the one that didn't hold the pages that revealed the horrible prophecy Torion had drawn. It made Peri sick to realize that the child had seen it even though Skender had taken him away. The boy had been the one to draw it, after all.

Movement caught Peri's eye, and she turned to see Galan still hovering at the opening. Next to him, his mother beat her wings, which held her bobbing in the air outside the cave. "We are here when you need us," Serapha said. "You have our allegiance, Perizada of the fae."

Peri bowed her head to the draheim and then looked back at Tenia. "Let's go."

They flashed and reappeared in front of the veil. Peri didn't waste a second placing her hand against the invisible barrier. It dropped in a heartbeat, and she stepped through. Tenia, Skender, and Torion were right next to her.

The group, most of which had been sitting down, jumped to their feet. Some had taken on attack stances, while others simply stood with wide eyes. It didn't surprise Peri in the least when Jen was the first one to get over the shock.

"Finally," the blonde growled. "Someone to kill. Elle," Jen yelled to the fae and held out an open hand. Elle threw a blade, and the she-wolf caught it without looking.

"What the heck is going on?" Heather asked.

Peri didn't take her eyes off Jen. She tried to decide if she should just let this play out so Jen could exorcize a little of the crazy Peri could plainly see in the blonde's eyes, or if she needed to stop it and force the beta female to comply.

"Jen," Jacque called out.

"Not now, Red. And if you give me an alpha command, I will make your life a living hell, alpha or not." She broke into a sprint. When she was a few feet away, Jen leaped toward Skender, the blade swinging.

Skender shoved Tenia and Torion to the side, and Peri grabbed them both, pulling them behind her.

"Peri," Tenia shouted. "Stop her!"

"I'm sorry, Tenia, but this has to happen." Peri snapped her fingers, binding Tenia and Torion where they stood.

Skender didn't move an inch as Jen's blade slashed across his chest, ripping through his shirt and the flesh beneath it. Neither did he cry out or even wince.

"Skender!" Tenia yelled. The anguish in Tenia's voice nearly cracked Peri's resolve.

Jen whipped around and dropped to the ground, sticking out her foot and sweeping Skender's legs from beneath him. He hit the ground with a thud. Jen was on him a second later, her hand on his throat and the dagger held over her head. The image was eerily similar to the one Peri had just seen on the paper that Torion drew. Peri flung out a hand and the blade flew out of Jen's grasp. It sailed away and embedded itself into a tree.

A second later, Myanin stood behind Jen with her own blade to the blonde's throat.

"I've grown to like you, Jen," Myanin said, her voice soft but threatening. "But killing Skender would hurt Tenia and her offspring. And no one gets to hurt them, no matter what reason you have to justify his death."

Jen didn't appear fazed at the loss of her weapon or the knife held against her flesh. The crazy she-wolf actually leaned into the blade, causing it to cut her skin. A trickle of red ran down her throat, and she smiled as if she enjoyed the pain. Peri mentally rolled her eyes. The nutjob probably *did* enjoy it.

"Myanin." Gerick walked toward his mate. "This isn't your fight. This is wolf business."

"If it involves Tenia, then it *is* my business," she said coolly.

"Myanin, Jacque won't let Jen kill him," Lilly said. She looked over at Tenia, and Peri saw the affection the warlock queen had for the fae. "It's good to see you, Tenia. And I can't wait to get to talk to your son."

"I'm sure the feeling will be mutual once—" Tenia's words froze, and then she cursed. "Really? Another one? How many crazy ass wolves do you have in this pack?"

Peri turned back to Skender, Jen, and Myanin to see that Zara had joined the fray. The girl was too short to reach the djinn's throat, so Zara held a dagger against Myanin's chest, directly over her heart.

Peri looked around until she found Wadim. "Seriously?" Peri asked him. "I'm gone for a couple of months and your mate goes from sweet, but sassy, to stabby twin of Jen?"

"That should totally go on a shirt," Heather said. "I've heard that Wadim likes to wear hilarious shirts. That would be perfect for him."

"Maybe not the best time for fashion advice," Anna told Heather.

Heather snorted. "Dude, I have no clue what's going on, so I get to pass out fashion advice like it's candy. Granted, you will all look like idiots if you take it because, you know"—she pointed at her eyes and then sang—"blind."

Peri shook her head. Things were going to hell in a handbasket, and yet the healers still found time to verbally spar. Some things never change.

"Zara," Wadim called to his mate. "That dagger was for emergency use only, remember?"

"I think this qualifies as an emergency. I love you, history-boy, but nobody gets to kill Jen. She provides too much entertainment and makes all the rest of us seem normal." Zara didn't move an inch.

"She's not wrong," Jacque agreed.

Peri shot her a look. "Not helping."

The alpha female shrugged. "What? You know we've all wanted to kill her at one point or another, but for some reason, we don't. Zara has a sound argument for why, like a cockroach, Jen manages to survive."

Peri pinched the bridge of her nose and forced herself to refrain from simply flashing to the Canadian pack mansion with Tenia and Torion and leaving the rest of them to sort it out on their own.

"Even if Myanin manages to cut my throat," Jen said, "I will have Skender's throat torn out before I'm dead. So in my demise, he finds his as well." She leaned down closer to Skender, causing Myanin's knife to dig even deeper. "Give me one reason I shouldn't rip out your throat where you lay," the beta female snarled.

Skender's eyes flicked over to his mate and his son. Peri saw a glassy sheen of tears. He looked back at Jen and said, "I can't."

"Right answer." Jen's nails phased to wolf claws.

Bloody hell! Jen really *was* going to kill him. Peri was about to bind the three women when a small voice yelled.

"WAIT!"

Peri turned to look down at Torion. Tears streamed down his small face. He must have been terrified.

Peri looked back at Jen. The female's head turned to see where the voice came from. Her eyes widened when they landed on Torion. Myanin's eyes were still locked on Jen, and Zara still held her dagger on the djinn.

"Who are you?" Jen asked, her voice menacing.

Peri released her magical hold on Torion, though she kept Tenia bound. She had no doubt Skender's mate would attempt to kill Jen the second she was free. This fight didn't need another participant.

Torion, the brave boy he'd proven himself to be since Peri had known him, walked forward until he stood a foot from Jen and his adoptive father.

"I am Torion," he said, his voice slightly shaky. He held his head high and pulled his shoulders back before continuing. "I am Skender's son. Tenia, my mother"—he turned and pointed to her—"is Skender's true mate."

Jen's eyes narrowed. A casual observer might have thought the child's words didn't affect her. But Peri saw the slightest hint of shock in her eyes. "Why should I care, Terrance? Your mother is no one to me. You are a child with another T name, and already you get on my nerves. And your so-called father is a backstabbing turncoat whose crimes are punishable by death."

"Jen, you remember that a not-quite-sane djinn is holding a sharp object at your throat, right?" Jacque asked. The alpha female had moved closer and now stood only a few feet from the bizarre kill-or-be-killed pack of women.

"I expect you to avenge me, Jacque. You know I'll haunt you for the rest of your existence if you don't. Now, quit distracting me."

"I know who he is," Torion said, pointing at Skender. "And I know what he's done."

"Are you sure about that?" Jen challenged.

Torion nodded, then gave a very abbreviated version of the story Skender had told him. When he finished speaking, everyone was completely still.

Jen sat back, but she didn't get off Skender. Neither did she remove her hand from his throat. Myanin's blade shifted with the she-wolf, staying connected to her skin. Jen didn't seem the least bit troubled by it. "You still haven't given me a reason not to kill him," Jen challenged.

"The Great Luna took me to meet Titus," Torion said. This finally drew a visible reaction from the female beta.

"You have *got* to be kidding me." Jen gritted her teeth, then sighed as she continued to stare at the boy. "Titus hasn't mentioned you. Which is odd, because the boy never shuts his trap."

"It wasn't time for you to know," Torion said. "Now it is."

"Know what?"

"I'm not just Skender's son. I will be yours." He paused and tilted his head to the side and shrugged. "Well, not your son like I am my mother's son. The Great Luna told Titus I will be your son-*in-law*. But I don't think that will happen for a long time."

Jen eased to her feet. Myanin stepped back but kept her dagger up, and Zara shifted as well, her own blade still pointed at the djinn. At least they're no longer touching one another, Peri thought. That's progress. Jen lifted her leg as she turned. When she took a step, she used Skender's stomach as a makeshift step as she walked over him and closer to Torion. Myanin followed behind Jen, her eyes narrowed as if ready to pounce in a split second.

Zara started to follow, but Wadim snatched her wrist and pulled her back. She quickly turned, holding the blade at the ready, but her mate had obviously expected the movement and caught her wrist in his hand. He grinned down at her and darted in for a quick kiss. "I think you can stand down, killer," he teased. "No one is going to die."

He pried the blade from her hand, and she growled. "I expect to get that back," Zara warned him.

"You know how sexy I think it is when you threaten to cut people. Do you think I'd deprive myself of such a sight?"

"This is the weirdest pack I've ever seen," Tyler, the Springfield alpha, who Peri hadn't even noticed, muttered.

Jen took another step toward Torion, and Peri focused on the unpredictable she-wolf.

"Touch him and I will turn you into a puppet to do my bidding for all of eternity," Tenia said with such vehemence Peri didn't doubt for a second that she meant it.

Jen glanced at Tenia. "I don't hurt children," she growled.

"Hurting Skender *would* hurt me," Torion pointed out.

The Romania female beta sighed. "Just what I need, another rational male stomping on my killing parade."

Torion's head tilted in the other direction as he seemed to study Jen. "Titus mentioned you're a little crazy." His voice no longer shook. Apparently he'd decided the threat to his father had passed. Peri hoped he was right.

Jen looked back at Skender.

"Jen," Jacque said again. This time, Peri felt her power. "Fane is the one who decides his fate. Not you. Accept your place and stand down. Now."

"Regardless of what my alpha decides," Jen continued to glare daggers at Skender, "I will never forgive you. You will never be welcomed back into our pack. You're a disgrace."

Skender climbed to his feet. He didn't cower or hang his head. Instead, he walked over to Torion and picked him up. Then he walked over to Tenia. "I have not asked for your forgiveness, nor would I ever expect it. I live every day with the shame of my actions."

"Good." Jen spat and gave him a wicked smile.

"Jen," Torion said, his small arm wrapped around Skender's neck. "Can I ask you a question?"

Jen sighed. "Why do kids always say that when they're going to ask the bloody question, even if you say no?"

"Have you ever made a mistake?"

"Oh, snap." Zara's voice was soft.

"I have made many mistakes, Tommy. How about you?" Torion nodded.

Jen's brow rose. "Is that all? Nothing to add?"

"Nope."

Peri forced herself not to smile. The child's point might not have much effect on Jen now, but he'd planted a seed. It would grow inside of Jen, especially once their world wasn't crumbling down on top of them. With the threat to Skender's life momentarily passed, Peri glanced over Jen's shoulder and looked at Myanin. "I think you can put that away now."

Myanin didn't move for several seconds, but then she finally flipped the blade around and slid it into a sheath on her thigh.

One more death averted. Peri looked around the group, noting who was present. "We didn't come through the veil to watch Jen lose her crap and start a ripple effect through an ever-growing population of mentally unstable females in this pack," Peri said. "Jacque, you might want to get the water tested to see what's making your females psycho."

"You have to add your name to that list, Peri-fairy," Jen said slyly. She walked over to stand next to Jacque, folding her arms across her chest. "From my point of view, you're not just a member of the crazy chick tribe. You're the leader. Congratulations. We will throw you a celebration after we've got Ludcarab's head on a stake in our front yard."

"I told you not to let her watch that movie about Vlad the Impaler," Zara told Wadim. "Now we're going to have staked heads all over the grounds."

"I concede your point, Jennifer," said Peri. "And as the leader of the CCT, I am beseeching you to listen up."

"Dammit," Jen muttered. "How am I supposed to stay mad at her if she's making up acronyms?"

Peri ignored her and continued to address the group. "It's time for us to act. The Great Luna has made that clear." Peri looked at Lilly. "Do you feel any differently?"

"I no longer feel the need to tell you to stay put," she said.

Peri released Tenia from her hold and motioned for the female to step beside her. "This is Tenia, as her son pointed out. She is a fae that Alston controlled by keeping her son a prisoner. Torion has a very special ability. Tenia..." Peri motioned for the female to take over, but before Tenia could open her mouth, a blade suddenly stuck in the ground at Tenia's feet, a mere inch from the female's toes.

Tenia glanced at it and then looked up. "You don't have to be so dramatic, Myanin," she said dryly. "I just watched my mate get mauled by a crazy she-wolf and found out my son is to be the son-in-law of the same crazy female. And I've been stuck in the draheim realm, unable to do anything but sit around and wait. There is no cotton candy in the draheim realm, so I don't have a peace offering."

Myanin, who hadn't said a word since she'd threatened Jen, closed the distance between them until she stood in front of Tenia. "You're a freaking fae. Magic me some cotton candy, and I might forgive you."

Tenia rolled her eyes. "Forgive me? For what?"

"For making me like you. It's annoying as hell to like someone who gets themself killed."

"Not dead." Tenia pointed at herself.

Myanin raised a brow. "We can argue about it later. Cotton candy." The djinn held out her hand.

"I think I liked the draheim realm better," Peri muttered as she held out her hand, and a bag of the sugary treat appeared.

Myanin plucked it from her hand, though her eyes stayed on Tenia. She opened the bag and then tore off a piece and put it in her mouth.

"Better?" Tenia asked.

"For now," the djinn said, mollified. She stepped to the side so the rest of the group could once again see Tenia.

"She makes me look normal," Jen mumbled.

"Can someone *please* tell me what in the blazes is going on? I've only got bits and pieces. Throw me a damn bone," Heather shouted, drawing everyone's attention.

"Nobody has died," Jewel quickly supplied. "And, most importantly, Myanin has finally gotten the cotton candy that Nissa or Elle could have magicked her at any point. But I think watching her suffer amused them too much to give in."

"You mean we've listened to her mutter under her breath about cotton candy all this time and it could have been dealt with?" Heather asked.

"You must not have kids," Tenia said. "If you give a child something because they complain enough, they will just do it more in the future."

"Are you comparing me to an offspring?" Myanin asked around her mouthful of cotton candy.

"It sounds like she's comparing you to a spoiled brat." Heather shrugged. "If the djinn shoe fits."

Peri was sure at any moment she would have to stop a flying blade from hitting Heather in the forehead, but Myanin just rolled her eyes at Heather and continued eating.

"Okay," Heather sighed. "I'm just throwing this out there, but I think someone should volunteer to be my walking commentator. I'll start taking applications ASAP. Please proceed. *But* if anyone starts killing anyone else, I expect a play-by-play."

"Glad to see you're as high maintenance as ever, Helen," Peri said, genuinely happy to see each of the healers. And to see that they were still thick as thieves. Though there was a vast hole where Kara should have been.

Peri looked back at Tenia, waiting for her to continue. The fae glanced at Myanin one more time, but the djinn just kept eating her cotton candy. "My son prophesies the future through his drawings," Tenia began. "We don't know when the scenes he draws will occur. We just know that they *will*."

"He draws it?" Jacque asked. "Can you clarify that?"

Tenia nodded. "He draws with incredible artistic skill, *supernatural* skill. Every detail is perfect. Then the drawing comes to life. What will happen plays out like a movie on the paper."

"He drew what I did at the Order compound," Peri said and watched their jaws drop open.

"How long after he drew it did Peri show up?" Nissa asked.

"Less than an hour," Tenia answered.

Gerrick motioned to the paper in Tenia's hands. "And what has he drawn this time?"

Tenia looked at Peri. And though Tenia didn't know Kara, she could see the pain for the healer in her eyes.

"He's drawn Kara."

Stella, Anna, Jewel, and Heather all stepped forward simultaneously, their combined voices overriding the muttering from the others. But it wasn't their words that froze everyone in place.

Wind whipped around the four healers. Their clothes ruffled, and power radiated from them—Volcan's residual power.

"Where is she?" Anna asked, her voice so dark it was almost unrecognizable.

"Okay, that escalated quickly," Zara whispered.

"We know she's with Ludcarab," Peri explained, "But not the exact location." She had already been thinking about Kara's whereabouts as she'd watched the horrific scene play out. "But I'm hoping Thalion might be able to help. You four need to calm down ... now."

The wind slowly calmed, as the four healers seemed to gain control of the fears that had stirred their magic.

"What exactly did he draw?" Stella asked, much calmer now.

"We don't need to wind up explaining it twice," Peri said. "Thalion needs to look at it." She hated having to repeat herself. They'd already wasted enough time.

"You think he's in the elf realm?" Nissa asked.

"Honestly," Peri huffed, her own frustration growing, "I don't have a clue. But it's a starting point."

"Then we go to the Canadian pack," Jacque said. "That's where the hunting party is."

Peri nodded. "Nissa, Elle, Tenia, myself, and"—Peri glanced around, having felt his power even though she hadn't seen him—"Disir." She motioned for the high fae to step forward. "We'll take as many at a time as we can. We may need to make two trips. Jen, you're with me." Peri had noticed the blonde eyeballing Tenia. She would have to closely monitor the dagger-happy she-wolf.

Everyone began shuffling about, each trying to get hold of a fae. Just before Peri flashed, she felt a hand touch her back. She looked over her shoulder and into the piercing silver eyes of her mate. Relief flooded through her as he leaned down and took a deep breath.

"We will get her back," he said through their bond. *"You will not lose anyone you love today."*

"But I might in the future," she said, knowing she had to come to terms with the fact that everyone had an appointed time to leave this life.

"Yes. But I will be with you always, through every loss, until we are called home to our Creator." He pressed a kiss to her forehead and then nodded, telling her without words it was time to go.

"Flash to the front steps of the Canadian pack mansion," Peri told the other fae. She only hoped this next reunion would go better than her last, which wasn't a terribly high standard. As long as no one got stabbed, then mission accomplished.

CHAPTER

FIFTEEN

"You never know what you are truly capable of until you are put in a position to prove how far you will actually go. Whether the situation requires you to save a life, take a life, give up your own life, or stand and do nothing—you cannot predict your actions until you find yourself in that moment. What you can do is pray that moment never comes. Because regardless of what decision you make when the crap hits the fan, that decision leaves you forever changed." ~Kara

"Is he dead?" Anna asked, just as Jacque felt the ground beneath her feet once again. She released Nissa and looked in the direction Anna was pointing.

"Oh man," Stella breathed out. "Please tell me he's not dead."

"Is who dead?" Heather asked.

"The human brain can go three to six minutes without

oxygen before permanent damage begins," Jewel said. "Maybe werewolf brains can go even longer. We could still have time to help him."

"I know it's annoying for me to constantly point this out, but I am seeing impaired. So who the heck is dead?" Heather asked as she and her mate stepped up beside Jacque.

"Nick." Jacque stared at the bloody mess of a man lying in the center of a circle of wolves. "I'm pretty sure he's not dead. Fane wouldn't allow it."

"'Pretty sure' is not the same as 'sure,'" Anna pointed out.

Jacque didn't acknowledge the healer. Instead she kept her eyes on Kara's mate. *"What happened?"* Jacque asked Fane through their bond. She saw her mate, in his wolf form, sitting on his haunches across from her on the farthest side of the circle.

"He's feral," Fane answered.

She could feel his anguish over what they'd had to do in order to subdue Nick, but she also felt his conviction that it was necessary. *"Is he alive?"* The words sounded as if she was begging him for the answer she wanted rather than asking a question. For the moment, they knew Kara lived. If they got her back and Kara returned to find out her mate had been killed, well, Jacque didn't know if that could be considered an actual rescue. The other half of her soul would be gone forever. That was a condemnation to a half-life or torment, not a rescue.

"He lives, but only just," Fane answered.

"Why is he in his human form? Didn't his wolf take over?"

"His wolf is out of control. I forced him to phase back to his human form in hopes that, perhaps, the soul of the man might think instead of simply acting on instinct," he explained.

Jacque continued to stare at Nick, attempting to see if his back rose and fell with life. *"By the looks of it, I'm guessing it didn't work."*

Fane chuckled. *"As always, Luna, you have a penchant for pointing out the obvious."*

Finally, she saw the prone man take a breath. It seemed to shake his entire body. *"Peri has new information about Kara,"* she told Fane and turned to look for the high fae. *"We need Thalion's help."* She opened her mind to Fane so he could see the memory of everything Peri and Tenia had shared. *"And Skender is here. Tenia is his mate and Torion is her son, which Skender is claiming as his own."*

Jacque felt Fane's weariness and dread at having to deal with that particular mess—*after* they'd gotten themselves out of the current one, of course.

"That will have to wait until after Kara is returned to her mate's side where she belongs," he told her. Then he phased, clothes covering him the second his human form took shape. It was good to have fae friends, Jacque thought as the rest of the wolves followed Fane's lead. "Drayden," Fane said, looking at the Canadian alpha, "Jacque informs me that Peri has news of Nick's mate. Let's get him cleaned up. And if you agree, we will allow the fae to subdue him if need be, so he may listen to what Peri has to say."

"Agreed," Drayden answered. He moved to Nick's battered form. Decebel joined him and helped Drayden lift the injured beta. Apparently the man wasn't as subdued as everyone thought. With lightning quickness, Nick's head snapped up. He turned, lunging with human teeth at his alpha. A bolt of energy hit Nick in the chest, and his body went limp. His head drooped, and if Decebel hadn't been holding him, the beta would have fallen back to the ground.

Jacque turned to see where the magic had emanated from. Adam lowered his hand, then looked around at everyone staring at him. He shrugged. "What? You all have beat the crap out of him for the better part of three hours. I'm just doing my part."

"Well done, Adam." Jen gave him a slow clap.

Adam glanced at Jacque's blonde BFF and grinned. "Psycho or not, Jen, at least *you* always appreciate my contribution."

"Is that seriously where you try to find your approval?" Peri asked the male fae. "Because I thought I taught you to set your standards higher."

Adam's smile vanished, and he looked at the high fae. He rarely frowned, but he did now. Jacque could see the weariness and hurt in his eyes as he looked at his longtime leader. "Are you okay? We thought the cold fire—"

"Killed me?" Peri finished for him. With Lucian at her side, Peri approached her comrade and stopped a foot away. "There is no apology adequate for my behavior. But that is all I can offer. And time to hopefully heal the pain I caused."

Jacque bit her lip. She felt Adam and Peri's hurt flowing from both of them through the pack bond. But she could also feel the deep love they shared for one another, the same way she loved Jen and Sally. It was rooted in years and years of shared experience, standing together through thick and thin. Unfortunately, the downside of having that kind of bond meant the pain caused by a friend hurt much worse than that of an enemy.

Adam held out his hand. Peri looked at it and then back to Adam's eyes. Finally, she reached out and clasped his forearm. "We are far too long-lived to hold grudges," the younger fae said. "Not to mention, I'm sure over the centuries I've driven you crazy enough that you owed me a little grief." Then he pulled her to him and wrapped her in a hug.

"While I totally agree that Peri needs to make amends to many of us, we don't have the luxury of the time that will take," Anna spoke up. "Kara needs us."

"I agree." Heather raised her hand. "We can all kick Peri in the shin later. Now, we rescue Kara."

Peri pulled away from Adam and marched toward the mansion's entrance. "You'll have to find my shins first, Helen," she called out to the blind healer.

"I love a good challenge," Heather countered as her mate led her along with the rest of the group.

Jacque waited for Fane to reach her before moving to go inside.

Fane took her hand, lifted it to his mouth, and pressed a kiss to it. "I missed you," he said softly.

Did she melt a little inside? Yes, yes, she did. And she knew she would continue to melt every time he looked at her with those beautiful blue eyes that filled with adoration when they met her own. "And I you, wolf-man."

He blew out a breath. "Let's do this."

Jacque's eyes widened when she stepped into the living room of the pack mansion. It looked like a place where broken objects came to die.

"This is a familiar sight." Jen glanced around the room. "I think your man did something similar to a hospital waiting room if memory serves me correct, Red." She gave Fane a cheeky wink.

"Have I ever mentioned that since I joined up with this merry band of supernatural nutjobs, I've seriously begun to loathe my lack of eyesight?" Heather said. Kale pulled her to his side, and Jacque watched as he leaned down and whispered in her ear. Heather reached up and patted his cheek.

He grabbed her hand and pressed a kiss to her palm before lowering their joined hands and turning his attention back to the room.

"The information we have is time sensitive." Peri ignored the commentary and got straight to business.

"How much time?" Fane asked.

"That's the million-dollar question." Peri shrugged. "The odds are not in our favor. But then again, it's not the first time we've been in this position."

Nissa and Disir flashed in with the last of the group from the forest. Jacque took stock of everyone and found all were present, including Thad and Jezebel. She'd wondered if they would come, since his purpose had been to help get the veil open and that was no longer an issue. Jacque had assumed he and Jezebel would return to the djinn realm.

"Kara is important to Anna," Fane said, keeping his voice soft. "And Anna is important to Jezebel. I imagine they will stick around until Kara is safe."

Jacque hadn't considered that. Sometimes it was easy to forget who belonged to who, because they'd all become a pack in many convoluted ways. Through all the trials they'd faced together, and although some of them were on completely different continents, they were still pack.

"My father would be proud to see this," Fane said, having picked up on her thoughts.

She nodded. "He would. This is his legacy, Fane. He's gone, but he's still with us."

A minute later, Nick stepped into the room from where he'd been deposited to rest in a spare room. Drayden stood at his side, his eyes glowing with his wolf.

"I apologize for the lack of seating," Drayden began but stopped when new furniture suddenly appeared.

"No offense, Alpha," Peri said, "but we don't have time

for an explanation of the obvious. If Nick can control his wolf, then we need to get started."

Nick's head snapped up, and his obsidian eyes narrowed on the high fae. Jacque sucked in a sharp breath when she realized the blackness in them wasn't because of their color. Without his mate, the darkness in Nick had taken over.

"Can he be saved?" Jacque asked. "Even if we do get her back?"

"If Kara is brought back alive, then Nick will heal," said Fane. "If we are too late, I will put him out of his misery myself, unless Drayden claims the right. Regardless, Nick will be too dangerous to be allowed to live."

Jacque prayed to the Great Luna they wouldn't be too late. She hoped that whatever information Peri had would allow them to save Kara and, by doing so, save Nick, as well.

Nɪᴄᴋ's ᴇʏᴇs bore into the high fae. His wolf wanted to rip the female apart. She had information about Kara, and she wasn't speaking fast enough. But if they killed her now, then he and his wolf wouldn't get the information they needed to find his beloved. So he forced himself to stand still. "What do you know?" he asked, his voice sounding like a fifty-fifty mix between wolf and man.

"Sorry about this, wolf," Peri said, "but you will need to be restrained before watching this."

"I don't think everyone needs to see it, Peri," a female fae that Nick didn't recognize said.

Peri looked around the room and then back at Nick. He'd spent a lot of time with the high fae when they'd been up against Volcan, and he'd only ever seen that look in her eyes one other time: when they thought Jewel had died.

"She's right," Peri said. "This is sensitive information. To protect Kara's"—she paused and cleared her throat —"dignity, we should limit those who see this. When we've decided how to move forward, Nick can determine how much you all need to know."

"You can use my study," Drayden offered. "Who needs to be present?"

Nick's heart pounded so hard in his chest he could barely hear Peri's words. She walked closer to him and said, "This will not be easy, Nick. Pick those you trust to lean on. Myself, Tenia, and Thalion need to be present. I would counsel you to include only enough males to help keep you under control."

If Peri didn't think other males should be involved, then whatever he was about to learn about his mate must concern intimate details that no mate should ever have to share with anyone else. He stumbled, but Fane and Drayden caught him. Both were strong enough to bear his weight, both willing to do whatever had been necessary to keep him from harming anyone in his feral state. "My alpha and Fane," he said. Then he looked past Peri to the four healers huddled together on the other side of the room. Each of their mates stood at their backs, looking ready to kill anyone who moved too close. "And Kara's sisters." He motioned toward the girls.

Nick didn't miss the flinch in Peri's face at his request. But she waved them over despite whatever reservations she held. "Jewel, Stella, Heather, and Anna, please come with us."

The four girls started forward, and their mates followed, but Peri shook her head. "Not you," she told the males. "Trust me, please."

"Not to be rude," Ciro spoke up, "but your track record is not great right now, Perizada."

"Your own mate isn't going to allow you to walk into the room without being at your side. Why should we have to wait here without our mates?" Dalton asked, his voice dark as he stared daggers at her. They had a rough history, and apparently her recent behavior hadn't done them any favors.

"I understand your protests," Peri said. "But your mates will be safe. And this is about preserving Nick's mate's dignity. I promise you, if it was one of your females, you would not want a room full of males bearing witness to what he is going to have to see."

Nick felt bile rise in his throat at the high fae's words. What the hell was he about to see?

Dalton, Ciro, Kale, and Gustavo didn't look happy, but after a tense couple of minutes, they each finally nodded and took a step back, watching as their females followed Drayden and Peri. Nick turned and walked after them with Fane at his back. As he walked down the hall toward Drayden's study, he felt as if he was walking to his death, which was probably easier than what awaited him.

When they were all assembled in the room, he watched the female fae called Tenia lay out three pieces of paper on a table. She lined them up so that they touched one another side by side.

"Tenia's son has a gift of prophecy through his drawings," Peri explained. "He drew this earlier today. We don't know the location, but this is the elf king in the drawing. I thought Thalion might know the place."

At the mention of Ludcarab, Nick stepped closer to the table, as did Thalion and the rest of the group. His eyes locked on to the first piece of paper and watched it come to life. He heard gasps around him, and even sobs, but he couldn't look away. Like passing a car wreck that has left mangled bodies littering the street, he couldn't force himself to look away. His mind would not save him from the horror that held him captive. With each movement on the page, Nick felt himself getting sicker. He fell forward and had to brace himself with his hands on the table in order to keep from crashing to his knees.

"What is it?" Heather asked, her voice shaking despite not knowing what everyone had seen.

"Later," Stella told her. "Trust me, please."

Nick's knees almost gave out again as his eyes moved to the next piece of paper. Drayden was at his side in a second. His hand wrapped around Nick's neck, skin on skin, as he felt his alpha's power giving him strength and comfort. Fane, the most powerful alpha he'd ever felt, rested a hand on Nick's shoulder and bowed his head. Fane's voice was soft, but Nick heard bits and pieces of what he said. And he realized Fane was praying. Fane, alpha of alphas, prayed to the Great Luna for Nick and for Kara.

"You said your son draws prophecy," Anna said. "That means this is the future. It hasn't happened, right?" Her voice shook, and Nick could smell the healer's anguish.

Though he waited for Tenia's answer, Nick still didn't look away from the papers. His eyes moved to each of them as the story unfolded. As his eyes landed on the third sheet of paper, he saw his naked mate on top of the elf king and a dagger raised above her head. It gleamed, and for a split second, Nick saw markings on the blade. But then, it was arcing down. Wielded by Kara's hand, she plunged it into Ludcarab's chest. The elf king's eyes barely widened before she yanked the dagger out, only to drive it back down, this time into his throat.

"We do not know," said Tenia. "The picture could be drawn days before the actual occurrence, or mere minutes. We only know that Torion's drawings have yet to be wrong."

"I know this place," the elf prince said.

Tenia quickly gathered the papers, stacked them, and then turned them over so they could no longer be seen. Then she laid her hand on top of them and, with a bolt of power, reduced them to ash. She glanced up at Nick and gave him a small nod. She'd made sure no one else would see the drawings. He gave her a nod of thanks in return. It was all he could manage, considering he barely held himself together.

"Where is it?" Nick's wolf asked. His beast had taken over as they'd watched their mate be raped and then kill her captor.

"There is an old castle in the elf realm, long abandoned," Thalion said. "I recognize the pictures and tapestries on the walls that Tenia's son drew."

"You're sure?" Peri asked, her hands resting on the table as if she, too, had to hold herself up.

"Yes, unless someone has removed those decorations and taken them to a different location, and I cannot imagine why they would," the elf prince answered.

"It's the only lead we have." Drayden turned to Nick. His alpha's eyes glowed with his wolf as he looked at him. "Can you do this? Without killing your allies?"

Nick pictured the images he'd just seen and nodded. He just wanted her back. If he could spare her the agonizing experience he saw depicted in the drawings, then he and his wolf would do whatever it took to get to her, even control the feral rage inside of him. Or at least they would try.

"I haven't been back to the elf realm in the past month," Thalion said. He shifted on his feet and crossed his arms in front of his chest. "If my father is there, he will have probably tried to lock the entrance. And if he has been unable to do that, he will have warded the castle."

Fane slipped his hand in his pocket and pulled out his phone. Nick watched as the alpha tapped the screen and then put the phone to his ear. "Thad, we need you and Jareth. Peri will gather the high fae. Wait for us outside the front doors." He ended the call and turned to Peri.

"The high fae are aware of the situation." Peri slipped her own phone back into some pocket in her robes. "As well as the sprite queen and Lilly. The healers"—she pointed at the four women—"have a ton of power as well."

"Thalion," Fane said, looking at the elf prince, "Can you let the fae know what veil is the closest to the castle?"

He nodded. "You need to be aware, if the veil isn't locked, then he will have certainly done something to protect the castle. Wards, traps, any manner of magic he could use to keep foe away. My father is dangerous. How many are you willing to risk for this healer?"

Nick growled, but Fane held tight to his shoulder, keeping him from moving. "I will risk the same number I would if it was your mate we were rescuing, the same number of people as if it was any one of our allies. We do not measure the value of someone's life. Their value is given by the Great Luna, and if she created them, their value is limitless."

The elf prince bowed low to Fane and then said, "Then you are exactly the alpha we all need you to be. Forgive my need to test you."

Fane nodded to Thalion and then seemed to put the matter to rest as he turned to Nick. The alpha gripped either side of Nick's neck and leaned close. "We have our individual packs, but we are also one pack. You are one of mine, Nick, mate of Kara, beta of the Canadian pack. I will do anything, use every resource we have, to bring your mate home. I give you my word."

As they filed out of the room, Nick heard Peri giving directions and saw people moving out of the corner of his eyes, but the only thing his mind could focus on was the image of his mate standing in a doorway, wearing nothing but a robe. And though she stood straight, her chin boldly lifted, her eyes told a very different story. He knew he would never forget the determination *and* defeat that filled them. Such an odd combination to bear at one time.

His legs were on autopilot as he followed Drayden out of the mansion. His hand rested on Peri's shoulder, then darkness engulfed him. An instant later, he and the rest of the hunting party stood on an enormous cliff. He turned and saw a wooden bridge held together by rope, suspended across the gorge between their precipice and the one on the other side. Far below them, at least a hundred feet down, a turbulent river roared across mammoth boulders.

"I assume the veil is across that rickety bridge," Anna said.

"How rickety are we talking?" Heather asked.

"Let's just say I hope the wind doesn't pick up while we're crossing," Stella said. "We're using the term bridge loosely. Frayed tightrope would be much closer to the truth."

"I wish it were that simple," Thalion said. "The veil is down there." He pointed to the raging water below.

Everyone except Heather cautiously peered over the edge. "Um, down where? What exactly are we looking at?" Jen asked. "I don't see anything but a very pissed-off river."

"The veil is somewhere between here and the water. It rests horizontally in the chasm. There is but one way to enter it," Thalion replied.

Heather groaned. "Don't tell me."

"Jump," the elf prince said.

"Um, and just how will we know if the veil is open? You know, *before* we hit it?" asked Jewel.

"We don't," Thalion said.

"And if it's closed?" Anna asked with raised eyebrows.

"We bounce," Peri offered.

"And bounce right onto one of what I'm sure are very soft boulders, or fall into the peaceful, tranquil waters, which I'm equally sure will float us quietly downstream," Jen said.

"That water doesn't sound a bit peaceful," said Heather.

"And if you could see the boulders, you'd know they don't look a bit soft," said Stella.

Thalion shrugged. "We have no other choice. I guess the fae could magic us some kind of rope, and we could hoist one another down. But we don't know exactly where the veil is between us and the water. It will take some dangerous exploring just to find it. And I believe time is of the essence."

Once again, the voices around him faded into background noise as Nick walked to the cliff's edge. He saw neither river nor rocks. The man only saw Kara's beautiful face, her teasing smile, and her haunted eyes from a past that made her grow up much too fast. He was supposed to have ensured she never endured such ugliness again. As her mate, it was his job to protect, provide, and love her. He closed his eyes and felt a tug in his chest—the bond.

"*Kara,*" he said, reaching for her. And then, there she was, standing in front of a mirror. She looked down, and he saw a dagger in her hands. The etchings on the blade were the same ones he'd seen in the drawing. It was already beginning. *"KARA!"* He tried again, using all of his power to break through the walls she'd put up between them. Her head snapped up to look in the mirror, and he knew the instant she saw him through their bond. A tear slipped down her cheek as she mouthed the words, "I love you." And then he felt not only her healer magic but the witch power as well as she shoved him from her mind and rebuilt the wall between them.

"NO!" His wolf roared as pain seared his chest.

"Go after her, Nick." The Great Luna's voice penetrated his mind. *"I made her for you. I will not deliver her from this trial, but I will make you both stronger because of it. Even in the most painful experience, joy can be found. Trust me, and go after her."*

Nick saw again the image of the blade in her hand and Kara's eyes staring at him through the mirror. He sucked in a huge breath and jumped.

CHAPTER
SIXTEEN

"Once upon a time, there was a girl. She had no home. She had no parents to hold her when she was scared or to cheer her on when she achieved a victory. This girl was alone in the world, fighting to protect herself from monsters who preyed on the vulnerable. What the girl didn't know was all the monsters she faced had prepared her to face the darkest monster of them all. Not only to face him but defeat him." ~The Great Luna

Kara looked down at her shaking hands and saw they were covered in blood. Her breathing hitched, and she felt her pulse pounding in her neck. A chill ran down her spine as fear like she'd never felt threatened to choke her.

"Kara?" Dyna said, her voice soft but still loud enough for Kara to hear her.

She turned and looked down the hall to see the three she-elves watching her, each with tears running down their cheeks. Kara looked back down at her hands, and the blood was gone. She took a deep breath, pulling her shoulders back and lifting her chin. Kara stood a foot away from Ludcarab's door. She'd been standing there for at least a couple of minutes. Kara knew she needed to go inside. She had to go through with the plan, but feeling Nick through their bond had shaken her resolve. She was terrified he'd seen her intentions. It was nauseating enough for her to actually go through with her plan, but she didn't think she could handle Nick knowing she was fully intending to... She couldn't even form the thoughts.

"You can do this," she whispered under her breath. "Think of all the people he can never hurt again, Kara. He will never touch you again." Regardless of all the reasons Ludcarab needed to die, Kara was afraid. She'd never been more afraid in her life. Not when she was a child in foster care at the mercy of exploitative adults, not when she was pulled into a supernatural world she didn't understand, not when she faced a crazy high fae who turned her into a witch, not even when she'd made the sacrifice to never bear children. The fear she felt now froze her. It robbed her of her breath and assaulted her mind with all the ways this could go wrong. This fear was like a living entity. It wrapped itself around her, whispering into her ear that she would fail, that she would die, and so would Nick, and so would all of her friends when Ludcarab unleashed his wrath on them for her actions.

"You are not alone, Kara." The goddess's voice spoke into her mind. Warmth enveloped her, chasing away the fear that had imprisoned her. *"I know you don't understand why this is happening. Or why it is you that must walk this path. What happens today will have a ripple effect through more lives*

than you can ever imagine. Good things can come from tragic circumstances."

"Why me?" Kara asked. *"Why must I be the one to do this?"*

"Because I have chosen you. Because there is nothing you will endure that I have not already felt. Because I love you enough not to cripple you by removing every challenge you might one day face. Because I created you for such a time as this."

The Great Luna's words took root in her mind. And though she *didn't* understand it, she knew she wouldn't ask someone else to take her place. And that meant Kara had to do it. She took a steadying breath and then wrapped her hand around the doorknob and turned it. With one last look at the three women who'd become her friends, Kara pushed the door open and stepped inside.

The room, as usual, was lit only by candlelight. With a different male, it would have been romantic, but because it was Ludcarab, the dancing flames felt sinister.

"You look lovely as ever," the elf king said, drawing her attention from the room to where he stood in front of the bed. He held his hand out to her, and she knew there was only one option.

Kara commanded her feet to move and placed her hand in his. His other hand pulled at the belt to her robe, untying it with ease. He dropped her hand and then used both of his to push the fabric from her shoulders until it slipped down her arms to the floor.

She was unable to look at his eyes while his hands grazed her skin, so she focused on his throat. Her mind began its usual routine of slipping away, but Kara bit her cheek hard to keep herself present. She tasted blood on her tongue and swallowed the metallic flavor.

His hands on her hips turned her until she was against

the bed, then he pushed her back, his body coming down over hers. *Don't fight.* Even though she felt like she was now a willing participant, staying in the moment yet not pushing him away, she knew it was still rape. Plain and simple. She didn't want his touch, didn't want to give him any part of her. He knew this, but he took it anyway.

Kara mentally cataloged all the places he touched her. She counted the number of minutes that his body was against hers. Her brain worked overtime, tallying every single breath of air on her skin as Kara let him manipulate her like a puppet. Bile rose in her throat, but she forced it down with monumental control. The air was stifling as the elf king ran his mouth across her throat. She nearly cried out when he suddenly rolled and she sat astride him.

Ludcarab held her wrists in one hand while his other hand ran up her calf, over her knee, and up her thigh. His eyes roamed her body as if he had a right to look at her. As if she'd been made for him.

"Look at me." His voice rumbled.

Kara did as he commanded. His eyes narrowed. "You're different tonight, little healer. What has changed? What has made you decide to not only give me your body but your mind as well?"

Every cell in her body wanted to scream, "I've never given you my body," but Kara had to play the part. *Five more minutes. Just hold on five minutes more.* Instead of answering him, she leaned down, shuddering in revulsion, though she hoped he thought it was desire, as her chest touched his. She needed to kiss him. And she needed to do it now because she was losing her composure fast.

"My queen," he whispered and released her wrists, pressing his hand to the back of her head. "You're mine. I will own you. I'm glad you finally understand." The rage that had been growing inside of her for the past month began to heat like volcanic lava preparing to erupt. She felt not only her healer magic but the magic Volcan had imbued into her as well. But this time the witch magic they'd managed to turn to light was again dark. Her anger fueled it, and Kara didn't try to stop the transformation.

She realized that the bracelets Alston had placed on her had not only made her forget, but they'd also blocked her from accessing her power. The scary part was that she'd never even *thought* to try to use her magic. She'd laid in this bed while Ludcarab molested her, running away in her mind when she could have at least tried to use the power she'd been given.

He pulled her down until their lips met. Kara allowed him to open her mouth, allowed him to taste what was never meant for him. His claim meant nothing, and she sure as hell hadn't had some sudden epiphany that made her understand his delusional thinking. Kara heard him groan as he bit her lip hard enough that he drew blood. This seemed to excite him because his movements became more fevered. She couldn't even focus on all the places he touched her because his hands moved so fast. Tugging and pushing, pulling, and grabbing. It was too much. Kara's wrath filled every part of her. She could feel it running through her veins, dancing along her nerves and clouding her mind in a black shroud. She was just about to push him away when he suddenly went slack. His hands released her, and his arms dropped helplessly to the bed.

She froze, waiting to see if this was a trick. But then she felt him stir. He was trying to move, but he couldn't. She pushed up from him, her rage so all-consuming that she didn't even care she was naked.

"Wha—" He tried to speak, but his lips couldn't move enough for him to get out a word.

Kara lifted her hand in the air and mentally called to the blade that was bonded to her blood. In a single heartbeat, she felt the hilt in her palm, and she wrapped her fingers around it. There was no second thought, no speech to give, no satisfied look. Kara screamed with everything inside of her and swung the blade down as hard as she could. All her power, dark and light, gave strength to her arm as it moved. The dagger slid easily through muscle, tendons, and bone, but *not* into his heart. *No, he will remain alive and aware to pay for what he's done.*

Ludcarab bellowed as she pulled the dagger from his chest. Apparently the adrenaline from the shock and pain had given his body the strength to at least make that sound. A second later, the sound was cut off as Kara brought the blade across his face. The lips he'd only moments ago pressed to her body were ripped away, leaving only gore behind. "That's for putting your mouth where it didn't belong." She hissed at him. His eyes stared up at her, wide with fear. She reveled in it. Next, Kara dropped the blade to one side of his head. He tried to jerk away, but his head barely moved. With a quick flick of the wrist, Kara removed an ear. She brought the blade to the other side of his head and took the other. She leaned down and whispered, "That's for the lies you made me listen to."

Kara felt wind blowing around the room. Her hair swirled. The candles guttered, but remained lit, as if they were the audience to the great Ludcarab's downfall.

"This is for touching what only my mate should ever touch." Kara leaned across him and brought the dagger down on his wrist. She funneled her power into the blow and cut his hand clean from his arm. The sound that escaped from the elf king fed the tempest inside of her, and she severed his other hand. Still, it wasn't enough.

She gazed down at the bloody mess. For the past two months, she'd never felt so helpless and violated in her life. He'd made her doubt her own innocence. He'd looked upon her with coveted, lust-filled eyes and taken everything he wanted.

"YOU HAD NO RIGHT," she screamed. Kara dropped the knife and grabbed his head, shoving her thumbs into his treacherous eyes. This time, Ludcarab managed to move, but not enough to buck her off. Kara pulled with her thumbs and ripped his eyes from the sockets with a sickening wet squelch. She flung the orbs away, the optic nerves trailing behind. His body shook as blood poured from his wounds. The surrounding sheets were saturated. Red had never looked so good.

Kara took stock of her work. She had removed his lying lips, cut off his stealing hands, and gouged out his covetous eyes. But still he drew breath, in and out. His heart still beat despite the amount of blood he'd lost. Kara picked up the dagger and ran the tip slowly up his stomach. She spoke, not entirely sure he could still hear her. "You tried to break me," she said, her voice sounding eerily calm even to her own ears. "You thought I would give myself to you. You honestly believed you would be the victor in this battle. I'm going to tell you a secret, fallen elf king. I break for no one." Kara wrapped her fingers around the dagger and slammed it down into his heart, then ripped it out, only to turn it and plunge it straight under his chin, up into his skull. The heart that kept his despicable body alive ceased to beat. The mind that birthed his horrendous schemes was silenced.

Kara fell back until she sat at the end of the bed. She couldn't take her eyes from the man who'd tormented her.

She knew he couldn't hurt her anymore, but she still didn't want to look away. The swirling wind picked up speed, and the night beyond the windows lit up with a crash of lightning. Tears welled in her eyes. At the same time, the sky opened and rain poured out over the elfin realm. Deafening thunder boomed, and Kara threw back her head and howled a lament in tune with the elements.

She cried for what she'd lost, and she screamed for the pain that still rested in her soul. She knew it might never go away, but her task was done. Ludcarab was dead, though she'd purchased his destruction for a very high price. And now, she had to live with it.

NICK FELT as if he had been falling for hours. Finally, he hit the ground with a bone-jarring thud. He wasn't wet or smashed against the rocks, which meant the veil hadn't been locked, and he was now in the elf realm. Lightning arced across the dark sky. As if someone had flipped a switch, rain suddenly fell in sheets. The lightning flashed again, and Nick saw the large castle sitting less than a mile away. As he started moving, thunder rolled through the air above him so loudly Nick thought his eardrums might burst. But it wasn't the thunder that quickened his pace. It was a sound *inside* the thunder—a howl so full of pain he felt it in his soul. "Kara." He used his wolf's speed and ran.

He'd only made it twenty yards when a hand grabbed his arm. "My way is faster," Adam said. Nick noticed Thalion on the other side of the male fae, his hand resting on Adam's shoulder.

"Take us to the hall outside of the door I've shown you," Thalion said to Adam.

The fae flashed, and suddenly they were standing in a stone corridor. He turned until his eyes landed on a large door. Nick felt her. His mate. She was on the other side of that door. The sorrow that flowed from her through their bond made it clear he'd been too late.

Nick grabbed the knob and turned, but the door wouldn't budge. His wolf howled. Nick gripped either side of the frame and kicked with all of his might. The door flew inward and clattered to the ground.

The room was dark. Smoke from the newly extinguished candles wafted through the air. The lightning struck again, illuminating his mate's form. She sat on the bed he'd seen in the drawing. She threw her head back and screamed again. The sound shattered a part of him.

"Adam," Nick yelled and flung out his hand. A coat appeared in it, and Nick hurried to his mate. "Kara, sweetheart," he said as gently as he could with his wolf pushing so hard against him. He briefly noticed the mutilated body of the elf king lying on the bed next to her. Then he focused back on Kara. She'd stopped screaming, and she was staring at him vacantly. Nick glanced over her clinically, making sure there were no wounds. It was difficult to tell because she was covered in blood. He draped the coat over her shoulders and pulled it closed in front of her. He pushed her hair away from her face and gently cupped her cheek.

"Nick," she said, her voice rough.

"I'm sorry I was too late." He leaned down and pressed his forehead to hers.

"Nick, I did it," Kara said, her voice growing stronger. "I killed him."

Nick pulled back, his hands framing her precious face. He searched through the bond, trying to figure out what she felt, but her emotions were a maelstrom.

"I didn't think I could do it, but I did." She reached up and touched his face as if she couldn't believe he was actually real. "It's horrible and wonderful at the same time. Why?" Her body shook. "How can I feel both disgusted and triumphant? He deserved what I did."

Nick wrapped his arms around her and pulled her close. She immediately rested her head against his chest and gripped his shirt in her small fist. "Because death is always those things," he whispered. "Sometimes one feeling outweighs the other. But in my experience, the taking of a life is never simple."

"Let's go home." She breathed. The storm outside settled. Though the rain still fell, the thunder and lightning ceased. Nick realized as her breathing slowed that Kara had fallen asleep.

He turned to see more people had arrived, though not the entire group that had stood on the edge of the cliff to the elf veil, for which he was grateful. Peri stepped into the room with Elle beside her. She lifted her hand and then asked, "May I?"

Nick appreciated the fae asked instead of just touching his mate. He wasn't sure what his wolf would have done if Peri had simply taken the liberty. "Yes."

Peri laid her hand on Kara's head, and Nick watched as the blood that had coated her hair and her face disappeared as if it had never been. "The rest of her is clean as well. She deserves to leave this place with as few reminders as possible."

Nissa stepped forward and held out her arm. "If you're ready?"

Nick moved so that the fae's hand rested on his shoulder. Then they flashed. They arrived in the living room of the Canadian pack mansion. Without a word, Nick carried his mate to his room, which would now be *their* room because he was never letting her leave his side again.

"I've got you, Kara," he said against her forehead as he pushed the door open and then closed it behind them, shutting the world out. "I've got you, and I'll never let you go."

~

PERI LOOKED across the blood-covered room. *Damn.* It looked as if an entire army had been massacred instead of only one man. Everyone was silent. Only the rain falling outside could be heard. She walked over to where Ludcarab's body lay. Despite the gruesome scene, Peri felt nothing for the fallen elf king. The man had done abhorrent things in his long life. But the acts he'd committed in this room were the worst, and they'd sealed his fate. Peri was glad Kara had been the one to bring his evil reign to an end.

"Peri." Anna's voice came from just behind her.

"Anna, maybe you should wait outside," Gustavo said gently, no doubt wanting to protect his mate from the grisly display.

"Wait, Gustavo," Anna said. "Peri, do you feel it?

"I feel it." Peri's voice was low.

"What?" Gustavo asked.

"Kara's magic. It wasn't just her healer magic she used. I feel the witch magic, and it feels like Volcan's."

Peri tuned out everything around her and focused on the remnant of power still floating in the air. Anna was right. Dark power coated the place, and it wasn't Ludcarab's. "I cannot blame her for using it," Peri said.

"No," Anna agreed. "I would have done the same."

Peri stepped closer to Ludcarab's body. Though she

didn't want to touch it, she needed to remove any magic that might linger. She had plans for his remains.

"Beloved?" Lucian stood beside her.

"We're going to send a message," she told him and shared her thoughts through the bond.

Peri touched the elf king's torso, using her power to disintegrate any magic left inside. She did the same to each severed body part. Once it was done, she turned to Thalion. "I think he will make a fitting gift for any who want to side with the Order," she said. "Send pieces of him to every dark hovel where the supernatural scum attempt to hide. News of this will get back to Cain and Alston wherever they've taken refuge. They will know that we are aware that they did not die in the cold fire. And after seeing Ludcarab's fate, they will wish that they had."

Jareth, the djinn, stepped forward. "I will take care of it. I can finish what the little healer started so that he fits nicely in smaller packages."

"Thank you. I know it is a distasteful task." Peri stepped away from the bloody bed.

"But you are correct," Jareth responded. "It will send a message. It will make them nervous. And nervous prey make mistakes."

Peri turned to the elf prince. "When he's done, Thalion, do we have your leave to burn this prison to the ground?"

Thalion nodded. "We need to cleanse my realm of his evil. Taking down this castle will be a start."

"Will Nick be okay?" Anna asked Drayden, her eyes glassy and red. The Canadian pack alpha stood just inside the door, his eyes focused on the bed. He was a strong alpha, but it was apparent to Peri that this incident had shaken him.

He took his eyes from the bed and looked at Anna.

"They will both have a long road ahead of them," he told her. "But we are all here if they need us."

Anna wiped the tears from her cheeks. "After everything we faced with Volcan, she shouldn't have had to bear this."

"No one should, sweet Anna." Gustavo pulled her into the shelter of his arms. "Drayden is right. We will ensure that Kara and Nick heal. But it will take time."

"If you will allow it, Thalion"—Andora, the sprite queen, spoke for the first time since they'd arrived—"I can send some of the luminous sprites to come and help cleanse the land around this place."

Thalion nodded. "That would be much appreciated."

"Peri." Elle's voice came from the hallway just before she stepped into the room with three elf females in toe. "Kara wasn't Ludcarab's only prisoner."

"Dyna?" Thalion said, his voice unusually soft. "Reena, Coya. We thought you'd left, that you'd gone to serve my father."

The one he'd called Dyna shook her head. "We tried to leave, but not with him." Her voice shook as she wrung her hands. "He captured my sister and my son. Reena and Coya were with us when we attempted to flee the castle, your castle, when he first returned. He—" She swallowed and shook her head as if she couldn't say the words.

Reena, the elf standing next to her, took over. "He used her sister and son for dark spells. And made us watch as he took them apart piece by piece."

"Bloody hell." Peri breathed out. Lucian's hand wrapped around hers, and she felt his strength flow through their bond into her.

"He and Alston fashioned bracelets that bound our magic and also made us relive every moment of what we'd seen anytime we even thought to escape. We'd been ready to try, regardless of our fear, but then he showed up with Kara. We couldn't leave her here with him. He charged us to take care of her, to prepare her to be his queen."

"We hated every minute of it," Coya said, grabbing Reena's hand and then Dyna's. "But we were working on a plan. It took longer than we hoped, but we were finally able to get a message to a friend, an ally who'd promised to help us in our time of need."

"Who is this friend?" Peri asked.

"Ember," Coya answered. "She came while Ludcarab was away. She broke the spell on Kara's bracelets," she held out her arm, and Peri saw the markings on the elf's wrists. "Kara's memories, her bond, and her magic were no longer blocked. Kara was the only one who could get close enough to kill him."

"Why didn't Ember remove your binds?" Fane stepped out of the shadows from where he'd stood. He'd been hidden, in case there'd been any surprise threats within the castle.

"Because we didn't want Ludcarab to sense that his magic no longer resided in us. If we happened to be around him before tonight, we couldn't risk him knowing." Coya covered her mouth as a sob broke through. "We didn't want this for her. But we didn't know what else to do. She had to get away. Every day, we saw more light fade from her eyes. Every day, he took a little more of her soul. She's so young, with so much life left to live."

Dyna, who'd seemed to have composed herself, said, "We knew we might die, that he might have figured it out. But it was a chance we were willing to take. Our priorities shifted once she showed up. We have lived long lives, but Kara, she's just a child compared to us."

"Thank you." Drayden bowed his head to the three

elves. "For taking care of one of mine. She is the mate to my beta."

"Has Ember returned?" Peri asked.

Dyna shook her head. "She is planning to return tomorrow."

Elle reached out and took Dyna's wrists. She held them in her hands and used her power to remove the evil that Ludcarab and Alston had tainted her with. Then she repeated the process on Coya and Reena.

All three of the women rubbed at their wrists as the marks faded. Then Reena looked at Peri. "Ember left the markings, though void of power, on Kara's wrists because Ludcarab would have noticed them missing."

"I cleansed Kara before she left this hellhole," Peri said, looking around the room in disgust. "The markings will no longer be present."

"Good," Dyna said. Her eyes conveyed a wealth of relief.

Power suddenly filled the room, and even Peri stumbled under the weight of it. She turned to see Fane's eyes glowing as he glanced at the bed. "Let's get this done and then get our people back to the sprite realm. Though this is a victory in one form, it is also a great tragedy. We need rest, time with our loved ones and pack. And then we need to prepare for the retaliation that will come." He looked at Drayden. "What do you think is best for your beta and his mate? To remain at your pack headquarters or to come to the sprite realm?"

Drayden ran a hand down his face. Peri could practically feel the weariness weighing down the Canadian alpha. "For now, Nick will definitely need what's familiar and to remain in his own territory. We will just have to wait and see."

Fane nodded. "We will strengthen the wards around your compound, as well as the other packs."

"I will speak with Disir," Peri offered.

"And I will speak with our council as well," Jareth said from where he stood by the bed, his back to the room. Peri noticed he was using some sort of magic to blur the space around him so that nothing could be seen of what he was doing. *Smart djinn.*

"Let me take Drayden, Anna, and Gustavo to their respective places, Peri," Elle said. "Disir will have made sure the group on the cliff has been taken back to the sprite realm. But I'll double check just in case. Then I will return to help clean up."

Peri nodded. "Fane?"

"I will stay until it is done."

"Very well," Peri said. "Let's burn this bitch to the ground."

Adam rubbed his hands together, his bloodthirsty side in full view as he smiled. "Best pep talk ever."

SEVENTEEN

"Where you lead, I will follow. Where you stand, I will remain. Where you rest, I will stay. When you cry, I will weep. When you smile, I will capture it and hold the memory of it in my mind. You are mine, and I am yours. It's as simple as that."
~Nick

Kara closed her eyes as Nick traced the contours of her face with the pad of his finger. She'd lost track of time since he'd brought her home. She'd woken up laying in his bed, and he'd only left her side long enough to retrieve food that had been delivered to them on a regular schedule, tend to his bathroom needs, and give her the privacy to tend to her own. The rest of the time, they simply laid in his bed, both on their sides, facing one another. Sometimes they slept. Sometimes he slept, and she watched him. But her favorite times were when they were both awake and simply staring into each other's eyes.

Any time her thoughts started to veer toward the past couple of months, Nick would kiss her until all she could think about was him. Though, the first time, he'd asked her permission. "You never have to ask to kiss me, Nick," she told him. That had been all the words he'd needed to hear because she knew he felt the truth in them through their bond. And kiss her, he did, often.

"I love you, yeah?" he said. He always finished the words with a question, as if to ask if she understood. She couldn't decide if it was a Canadian thing or a Nick thing.

Kara nodded. "Yeah, you do."

He chuckled. She opened her eyes because she loved to watch him laugh. It wasn't something he did easily, especially lately. Then his face grew serious as his fingers threaded through her hair. Nick leaned closer and touched his forehead to hers. He took deep breaths, and she knew he took in her scent.

"It calms my wolf," he said.

Kara lifted her hand and wrapped it around the back of his neck, letting the warmth of her skin seep into his. "I don't have a wolf, but your scent calms me, too." She could feel his need through their bond. Nick wanted to talk. He was desperate for her to open up to him. She felt his fear, his worry, and even the residual pain from their separation.

"I don't know if I can say any of it out loud, Nick," she told him honestly. "I'm not trying to keep anything from you. I never want there to be any secrets between us."

"I will give you whatever you need, sweetheart," he said, his warm breath brushing her skin. "If you never want to speak of it, then we won't."

She shook her head. "No. That's not what I want. I literally mean, I don't think my mouth can form the words to describe what happened. But"—she moved her hand from his neck until it rested against his cheek and her fingers on his temple—"I can show you. But only if that's what you really need. I don't want to make this any harder on you than it has already been."

He leaned back enough that he could look into her eyes. "Harder on me?" he asked. "Kara, I wasn't the one at the mercy of a sociopath. You don't need to worry about me."

"We belong to one another, yeah?" she said, ending her sentence just as he always did, which drew a small smile from him.

"Yeah," he agreed.

"Then we will worry about one another equally. This isn't about me or you. It's about us."

His eyes jumped back and forth between hers as if searching for anything that might prove her words to be untrue. Then he nodded and bent his head to press a chaste kiss to her lips. Nick slipped an arm under her waist and wrapped the other around the top of her, pulling her close to him. Then he buried his face in her neck. *"Show me."* His voice whispered softly into her mind.

Kara took a deep breath and reminded herself that the ordeal was over. She'd lived through hell. She'd faced the devil and won. Kara opened her mind to the memories that she'd pushed into a box the moment she'd woken up in Nick's room. They flowed out, beginning with the moment when Alston, Ludcarab, and Cain showed up at the pack compound. She kept her breathing even as the past two months played out like a movie. Kara realized as she showed the scenes to Nick that she was watching the story unfold as if it was happening to someone else. She removed her emotions from the equation and held her mate as he endured all that she went through. She knew the bond between them would let him feel every emotion, just as she had.

Kara wrapped her arms tightly around him as his body shook. His breathing hitched against her neck, and she felt wetness on her skin, running down her collarbone. Kara felt her own tears welling up as her strong mate broke beneath the weight of her memories. But then, maybe he wasn't the only one falling apart. Maybe she wasn't as separated from the memories as she thought, because as he saw the moment she walked into Ludcarab's bedroom for the last time, Kara, despite having told the elf king that she broke for no one, felt like she was breaking now.

She remembered the moment the poison took effect and the momentary relief that filled her. Quickly on the heels of that relief had been her vengeance. As soon as she'd felt the dagger in her hand, Kara had turned off any semblance of humanity that might have given him mercy and released every ounce of rage that had built in her since she'd become his captive.

"I never knew there was so much blood in a person," she said and then wished she could take the words back.

Nick lifted one of his hands and ran it down her hair. "Say anything you need to say, my mate. There is nothing you can't tell me."

She swallowed hard and felt her heart squeeze tightly in her chest. She hoped his words were true, because Kara knew once she started talking, she wouldn't be able to shut up. Maybe that was why she thought she couldn't describe what happened. Because if she did, the darkest parts of herself would be revealed, parts of her she didn't even want to acknowledge.

"It's okay, Kara." Nick pulled back. Tears streaked his

face. His eyes glowed with his wolf, and she could feel his anger, but it wasn't directed at her. "Tell me."

"When Ludcarab told me the elixir he gave me would restore my ability to conceive... I wanted..." She choked as the tears came harder. "I wanted it to be true." She tried to push away from him, shame filling her as she felt her skin flush.

"Don't," Nick growled. "Don't push me away." He took her chin in his hand and turned her head to look at him. "There is no shame in wanting a child."

"I thought you'd get to me before..." She shook her head. "I'm not blaming you. Please don't think that. But I thought if I drank it and you got to me before he could touch me, then maybe we could..." Kara bit her lip to keep it from trembling. "But then he came for me, and it was too late."

Nick LOCKED down his emotions tight as his precious mate finally let go of everything she'd been holding inside. He'd been willing to wait as long as it took, but he knew that with all that she'd suffered, she had to get it out. If not with him, then with someone she trusted. He had promised himself that if she chose to share her experience with him, he would not lose control. That wasn't what Kara needed. She needed his strength, but she also needed to know that he hurt *with* her.

"It was too late," she said again as the gates of grief burst open, and her sobs filled the room that had been so quiet for the past week. She shook and pounded her fist against his chest. At times, she pushed at him, only to then quickly grab him back as if she was scared he would leave her to weep alone. But he wasn't going anywhere. He would hold her for as long as she needed. He had no answers. She whimpered when there was a momentary reprieve from her uncontrolled emotions, but the respite never lasted long. The flood of tears started again, and the anguish that pulsed through their mate bond robbed him of his breath. Nick wondered if it was possible for a mate to suffocate because of his female's grief and his inability to do anything to ease it.

At some point, he heard a knock on the door, but he ignored it as he continued to hold Kara, rocking her gently, attempting to calm her because he feared she would make herself sick. Time passed slowly until the sobs slowed to whimpers and then to soft shudders as she sucked air into her starved lungs. When her body finally stilled and her voice was quiet, Nick pressed a kiss to her head and thanked the Great Luna that Kara had worn herself out and fallen asleep. Maybe there she would find a semblance of peace.

The room darkened as the sun set outside the windows, and the moon rose high into the night sky. Still, his mate slept. Nick whispered to her. He spoke of promises of the future they would have. He told her how her soul had called to him and had kept him sane for a time. Mostly, he just told her he loved her and that she would never fight alone again.

"Nick."

He startled at the sound of his name and raised his head to see the Great Luna at the foot of their bed.

"Goddess," he said, bowing his head as he pulled Kara closer.

"It is time for you and your Kara Luisa to see the joy that came from tragedy."

"Kara Luisa?" he asked, confused by what the goddess called his mate.

"It means renowned warrior, for that is what she is," the Great Luna explained as she looked at Kara. "It is time to wake Kara."

Nick shifted as his mate moved. She lifted her hand to push her hair from her face, glancing first at him and then turning to look at the goddess.

"You have been through much," the Great Luna said. She walked around the bed to Kara. "And you have sacrificed greatly. Are you ready to see the gift of that sacrifice?"

Kara pushed herself up, so she was sitting, and Nick did the same. He kept an arm around her, tucking her against his side. "I think so," Kara answered, her voice much calmer than the last time he'd heard it.

The Great Luna nodded and then looked at Nick. "Focus your wolf's senses and then tell me what you hear."

Nick frowned but did as the goddess asked. He pulled on his wolf's power. His eyesight sharpened in the dark room, his sense of smell picked up even the slightest scent, and his hearing honed in on the tiniest of noise. He kept still and told his wolf to pay attention to the sounds. Nick closed his eyes and slowed his breathing. Then he heard it. A small whooshing sound, fast and strong.

His eyes snapped open, and he looked at the Great Luna. She nodded and then looked at his mate.

Nick glanced down at Kara's stomach, and the sound grew stronger now that he focused on it. He reached over and placed his hand on her.

"Nick?" Kara asked. She looked from his hand to the Great Luna.

"This," the goddess opened her palm and suddenly an image, as real and tangible as he and Kara were, floated just above her hand. It was a womb with a child growing inside. "This is what he hears." She pointed to the child's chest, where they could see the flutter of the heart.

"What?" Kara's word rushed out in a breath as she rose from the bed. She stepped up to the goddess, directly in front of the image.

"This is your child, Kara. Yours and Nicks. The child you said you would give up when the sacrifice needed to be made. She did not come into being in the way you expected. But she is not a mistake. Nor is she evil because of the conception that was beyond her control. She, like you and your mate, is my creation. And I have known her since before she was even a single cell. Come closer."

Kara's eyes were glued to the small baby, snuggled warmly in the womb held by the Great Luna. She placed her hand on her stomach, where Nick's had been moments ago.

"See here." The Great Luna pointed to the feet. "You can count her tiny toes. And here"—she motioned to the child's face—"you can see she already has a penchant for sucking her thumb. See her tiny ears that will hear your voice as she grows inside of you. Look at her small legs that will one day carry her across the floor as she runs into her father's arms. And this"—the Great Luna pointed to the little girl's neck—"is where her laughter will bubble up out of her as she discovers the world around her, safely protected by her parents. You and your mate."

The image faded and Kara reached for it, wanting to hold her, but then Nick was there, turning her to face him. He dropped to his knees and his hands framed her stomach as he pressed his ear against her.

"You will complete the Blood Rites," the goddess said.

"And your mate's blood will flow through her veins because of that. She is both of yours. A blessing, a reminder that there is no evil that I cannot turn for good. Your daughter will be a living example for others who suffer as you have suffered. A sign that there is life after death, no matter what kind of death it might be. Love her with the love you never had as a child. Protect her as the precious gift that she is. And know that she means more to me than your finite mind can ever grasp. All of you do."

Kara looked down at her mate who was now kissing her stomach and speaking so softly that she couldn't hear his words. When she looked back up, she saw the goddess was gone, but the warmth she'd brought with her remained.

Nick stood and rested his hands on either side of her neck. His eyes shone with unshed tears. Kara felt through the bond that these were tears of wonder and radiance. "We have a child," he whispered.

Kara nodded, still unable to believe it.

"I know this isn't how—" he began, but Kara placed a finger over his mouth.

"*I* was the product of such a union, Nick," she said, sharing something she'd never shared with another soul. "I was born and left to die in an alley. Does that make me any less valuable or special than a child conceived another way?"

"Absolutely not," he answered without hesitation.

She nodded as she felt tears once again run down her cheeks, but these were different from the ones she'd cried earlier. These were tears of gladness, jubilation, elation, and even relief. "We're going to have a baby," she said, repeating his words.

His smile grew, and she knew hers matched his. "Yes,

we are. And she will be every bit the renowned warrior that her mother is."

"I love you, Nick." The words slipped out, and she heard the desperation in them. She wasn't sure what she was desperate for.

He wiped her tears away with his thumbs and leaned down, his lips a hair's breadth away. "And I love you." His lips touched hers, tentatively at first, but as she stood up on her tiptoes to get closer, he drew her in and pressed his mouth more firmly to hers.

"The Blood Rites," she said through the bond, realizing what had brought the desperation into her voice.

"If you're ready. But nothing more, not yet."

Kara leaned back from the kiss and looked into his obsidian eyes. She nodded. "Okay."

Nick carefully picked her up and sat on the bed, settling his back against the headboard with her on his lap. He gathered her hair and brushed it around her shoulder, revealing the left side of her neck. She could feel her pulse as he pressed his lips into the bend just below her ear.

As she felt his mouth open against her flesh and his teeth press in, breaking her skin as he bit, she heard his voice in her mind. *"On this day, I hold you close, as your humble servant, to ask if you will make me whole. Will you give yourself to me? Finally calming the beast inside, bringing order to chaos, shining light where there has been only darkness? Will you bind your life to mine, your fate to mine, and your soul to mine and, in doing so, complete the mate bond?"*

Kara would have answered if she could have, but after the quick stab of pain, pleasure had quickly followed. She gripped his head, holding him against her. It was over much too quickly as he released her. Kara's eyes fluttered open as she felt the warmth of his palm on her face. He turned her to look at him, and the love she saw there took her breath away. "Ready?" he asked, his voice deep and rough with the desire she could feel pulsing through the mate bond.

Kara nodded and let him guide her head to his neck. Like most of the things that she'd encountered in the supernatural world since being introduced to it, instinct seemed to kick in. Kara felt an overwhelming need to mark him, to bite him and take his essence into her body, which would then flow into their child. She felt Nick tense as she placed her teeth on his flesh and then bit. Warmth permeated her mouth as his blood flowed. Then words flowed into her mind and through the bond. *"On this day, I will make you whole as you make me whole. I will give myself to you, calming the beast, bringing order to chaos, and shining light where there has been darkness. I will bind my life to yours, my fate to yours, and my soul to yours and complete our mate bond. I will take you for my own, forsaking all others."*

Nick let her linger a little longer than necessary as she drank his blood, enjoying the feel of how their souls joined and how complete he felt with her against him. But then he knew it was enough. She would carry his scent, as would his child that grew safe and warm inside of her. "It's enough, sweetheart," he told her and smiled as he felt her disappointment.

When she sat up and looked at him, all the pain he'd seen earlier was gone. In its place was trust, love, and hope. "It's done?"

He grinned as he ran a finger over the fresh bite mark on her skin, his mark. "Almost."

Kara blushed as she let out a small laugh. "Almost," she agreed.

Nick knew that despite the overwhelming joy they both felt now, there would still be times when the past might haunt them. But it would not win. It would not rule their lives or dictate their future. Nothing can dim the light love sheds. He pressed his hand to his mate's stomach and felt love like he'd never experienced before.

"*I am yours,*" he told her. "*And you are both mine. I will love both of my females until my dying breath.*"

"And even after," she said into the quiet room.

"Yes, my Kara, even after."

EPILOGUE

"We don't know what tomorrow holds. We might not even wake up and see another day. So we have to be thankful for every second we draw breath. We have to rejoice in even the smallest of victories. We may shed tears. We may suffer hurts that threaten to rip us in two, but that's when we hold tight to the ones we love and give thanks we have someone to bear our burdens with us. We have each been given a purpose in this life, and we will help each other stay on our path. That is friendship, that is family, and that is pack. Don't be like me and learn that lesson the hard way." ~Peri

Peri stood with Lucian in the large room given by Andora to the Romanian pack to use as a home base. Lucian stood beside her, his arm around her waist. For the first time in months, she felt whole. She knew they had a long way to go. The road to healing and forgiveness between Peri and her mate would not be easy. And the healing she must do with the others would take time. But she was finally back where she belonged, and that was a start.

"All will be well, beloved. The beauty of choosing to love is that people are also willing to choose to forgive."

She laid her head on his shoulder and nodded against him. Words were too hard to speak at the moment.

"I'm not going to lie..." Jen said. Apparently, words were *not* too hard for her. Ever.

"I'm going to call BS on that before you even finish that sentence," Jacque said from where she sat on Fane's lap. The alpha held his mate close to him, while his other hand rested on the back of his son, who slept on a blanket on the couch beside them.

"Nobody asked you," Jen said and then continued before Jacque could respond. "I miss these little powwows being at home in Vasile's office."

"Agreed," Jacque said. And Peri silently agreed as well.

Jen snorted. "I thought you called BS."

"I spoke too soon. But to be fair, there was at least a seventy-five percent chance BS was about to fly out of your mouth."

"She's not wrong," Sally said. She sat on the floor with her back against a couch in between her mate's legs. Costin sat on the couch behind her, looking as content as a fat cat, running his fingers through her hair. Titus had his head in Sally's lap, and, like the other kids, he was sleeping soundly.

"Are we going to address all the elephants in the room?" Adam asked. "Or just do our usual character-bashing banter?"

Crina sighed and pinched the bridge of her nose. "Really, dude. You had to go there?"

"It's my job to rock the boat, babe." Adam winked at her.

"I've spoken to Drayden." Fane spoke up, and the mood of the room changed abruptly. Peri tensed as she waited for him to continue. "He said Nick and Kara are good. But they need some time before seeing people."

"Understandable," Peri said. "They've been through hell."

Nods went around the room. Peri's eyes fell on Sally, who wiped a tear from her eye. She hadn't taken the news well when Jacque had explained what had happened. Jen had, predictably, requested to go vamp hunting so she could decapitate something. Peri was beginning to wonder if they might need to consider an intervention. Jen's fascination with decapitations was getting out of hand. That or they could just get her a T-shirt deeming her the queen of hearts.

"What about Skender?" Jen asked, her voice filled with venom.

"Jennifer," Decebel rumbled as he patted Thia's bottom. She was slung over his shoulder, gripping a sippy cup but sound asleep.

"What? Adam asked about the elephants in the room. He is one big ass elephant. Let's discuss."

Peri saw Fane's eyes meet Costin, and his third in charge gave the alpha a sharp nod. "He and his mate and son will stay with Lilly at the warlock mountain. For now," Fane said with a finality that made it clear there would be no further discussion concerning the prodigal pack member.

"Oookay," Jen said, drawing the word out. "Onto the next big-eared, long-trunked being. Peri-fairy."

"Bloody hell." Zara sighed. "For you, Jen, I threatened to

gut a djinn warrior, who, by the way, could kill me with her pinky. Could we just let the elephants lie for now?"

Peri smothered the grin that threatened to stretch across her face. It seemed Zara had grown into herself and her place while Peri had been gone. It looked good on her.

"You better be glad I like you, Z," Jen grumbled. "You're getting as mouthy as I am." She sighed. "Who am I kidding? I'm dang proud of you. So threaten away, my little protégé."

"Peri." Fane turned to look at her over Jacque's shoulder. "How are the healers?"

Peri thought back to the conversation she'd had with the four girls after they'd burned Ludcarab's castle to the ground. Sharing what their sister had been through was one of the most difficult things she'd ever done. They wanted to see Kara so badly, but it wasn't her choice to make. "They're hurting. Those girls are as close as these three musketeers." She motioned to Jen, Jacque, and Sally. "It's going to take time."

"On a cheerful note," Jen said, "Bethany and Titus's future baby momma are doing great."

Sally raised a brow at her blonde friend. "You really want to go there, Virginia? Because from what I hear, your daughter's baby daddy is T-eerrific."

Jen laughed. "That was a terrible comeback. But also kind of genius with the whole T thing. What is with the T names? But seriously"—her smile fell, and she pointed a finger at Sally—"do not bring up he-who-must-not-be-named."

"I have to agree with my mate," Decebel spoke up, looking thoroughly annoyed. "She wasn't supposed to meet her mate for a couple of centuries."

Chuckles broke out around the room. Peri had to admit it was hilarious to see how much Decebel was bothered by the news of Torion and the prophecy that the boy would one day be his son-in-law. Peri had already decided she would be Torion's ally. He was going to need it to deal with his future in-laws. And it was going to be a blast to teach him the many varied ways to annoy Jen.

The room grew quiet as everyone seemed to sink into their own thoughts. None of them appeared ready to call it a night. Maybe, like Peri, they needed the comfort of just being in the same room. Words weren't needed. Just the mere presence of the people she loved was enough to help Peri cope with all they'd been through.

The silence was broken by a knock on the door.

"Don't answer it," Jen said. "Let's just pretend all is right in the world and we're a normal group of couples with normal problems, like who's going to be DD for the night."

Lucian released Peri's waist and walked over to the door. He glanced at Fane, and their alpha nodded. Her mate pulled the door open, and everyone suddenly became alert.

She saw Fane stand and set Jacque down on the couch next to Slate. "Boain?" He stepped toward the male who'd been missing for a very long time. Though she'd heard he'd shown up at the challenges for Fane's position, their former pack mate had then disappeared again.

"Where have you been?" Fane asked.

"I found my mate." Boain dropped his eyes. "She was among the rogues. But that's not why I'm here."

Fane crossed his arms in front of his chest and tilted his head.

"After the challenges, I left with my mate."

"Why?" Fane's eyes narrowed.

"Because Vasile sent me out as a scout after he found out the vampires were rising again. But while I was on that mission, I found Lorna, my female. She didn't want to remain with the rogues. Her parents had forced her to stay. Even if she had left, as a lone female wolf, unmated, without a pack, she wouldn't have been safe. But once we bonded, she had a choice. She chose me, and we've been tracking Order members, mostly vampires." He paused and shifted on his feet. Peri imagined if his mate wasn't here with him, then she was somewhere close, and he was antsy to get back to her. "We tracked one to Wyoming. We found Alston."

"I told you not to answer the door," Jen sang out. "But I'll forgive you." She rolled off the love seat onto her feet and stealthily pulled two daggers from sheaths on both legs. She spun them expertly in her hands and grinned. "Because now it's my turn to chop someone up."

"Decebel," Fane said, not taking his eyes off Boain. "Take the knives from your mate."

"On it," Decebel answered.

"You're not staying, are you?" Fane asked.

Boain shook his head. "I'm a good hunter, Fane. And Lorna, she's not had the best experience when it comes to a pack. I think we can still help, but we need to be on our own."

Fane held out his hand to the other wolf, and Boain clasped the alpha's forearm. "If you need us, you call."

Boain nodded. "I offer the same. Look for Alston in the Black Hills mountain range." Then he turned and left, shutting the door behind him.

Peri felt her power rising as the information Boain had just delivered sank in. They knew where Alston was. The hunt was back on. "I say let her keep her blades." Peri snapped her fingers and her robes disappeared, replaced by black cargo pants and a black shirt. She pulled her long hair up and tied it into a ponytail. Then she smiled at Jen. "I figure we can do a lot of bonding on a road trip."

Jen's lips pursed. "I'm with you on letting me keep my blades. But you can flash. We don't need a road trip."

"I didn't say it would be a long road trip. Consider it like speed dating. But speed reconciliation instead."

"If it means I get to take out some Order members, consider us good. You messed up. You know you acted like a jackass. We'll pretend you've groveled and, boom, all is right in the realm of the vaginas."

"Raise your hand if you knew that somewhere in that statement she was bound to work that word in," Jacque said as she raised her hand.

Jen gave it a high five. "Don't be jealous, Red. Even if you have to be all responsible and proper as the she-alpha, your membership in The Vagina Society hasn't been revoked."

"Make her stop." Wadim buried his face in Zara's neck, though laughter filled his voice.

"For tonight," Fane said, grabbing everyone's attention, "we will set the blades aside, sheath the claws, and be thankful that we have another day to fight. Tonight is for the pack. Tonight is to celebrate those who were lost and have been found. Tonight is to lift up Kara for her bravery and what she endured. One more of our enemies has fallen. Tonight we offer thanks to the Great Luna."

Their collective voices agreed with their alpha as Peri used her magic to put a drink in everyone's hand. Fane lifted his glass, and they joined him. "For Nick, for Kara, and for Peri. For Tenia, Torion, and even Skender. And as always, for the pack," Fane called.

"For the pack," they said as one.

Peri watched as the mood of the room returned to its former lighthearted state. Fane sat back down, and Jacque resumed her spot in his lap. Jen draped herself on the love seat, her head lying on the side closest to Decebel, who stared down at her with ridiculous adoration. She saw Sally rub her stomach with one hand and lay her other on Titus's back. Costin leaned over to lay his hand on hers. Wadim's fingers ran absently through Zara's long hair as he talked with Adam, and Crina leaned against Adam with a contented look in her eyes as she, too, seemed to soak in the momentary respite.

There was still so much to do and figure out. Peri still didn't know what Serapha meant with her veiled information about how the draheim was connected to Peri's life. They didn't know if Cain was with Alston, or if he'd gone off on his own to build a vampire army, or even how many Order members were still left. They didn't know what would happen with Skender, and Peri had a new perspective after what she'd learned. But she didn't know if it would change anyone else's mind. The other healers were hurting and wouldn't be able to heal until they could see Kara, and Peri didn't know when Nick's mate would be ready for that.

Lucian took her waist and turned her to face him. He lifted her chin to look up at him, and even after all she'd said, he still looked at her as he always had, like she was a miracle he didn't deserve.

"Let it lie for tonight, mate. Be here with me. Be present in the now because we aren't promised more."

So, for once, she listened to her mate and followed his lead. He kissed her and then led her over to an empty seat on one of the couches. Lucian pulled her down into his lap, and she settled against him. Her eyes met Jacque's, who was across from her. Peri felt warmth flow into her and knew it was Jacque sending love through the pack bond. *"You're where you belong,"* the alpha female's voice said quietly in her mind. Peri nodded. *"I'm home."*

To be continued...

Thank you so much for taking time to read The Hunt Begins. I truly hope you enjoyed it. If you did, I would be so appreciative if you took time to leave a review. Thank you again!

Acknowledgments

As with every book I write, I have to give glory to God first and foremost. He has loved me with an everlasting love. He forgives me even though I am not worthy of that forgiveness. And he has blessed me beyond measure, not just with all that I have, but because of the gift he gave me when Christ died on the cross for my sin. He is the ultimate Creator, the author and perfecter of my faith.

Thank you to my soul mate, and best friend. We've been on this journey for 22 years and you have supported me through all of my crazy endeavors. You never once said you didn't think I could do it. You never once discouraged me. Thank you, Bo, for choosing this life with me.

Thank you to my boys. They give me grace when I am snappy because of stress. They hug me when I need it. They tell me I'm a great mom even though I feel like I'm screwing it up all of the time. I love you all so very much.

Thank you to Jessica. I've said it many times over the past 7 years of our friendship, and I'll say it again. You're an invaluable part of my writing process. Thank you for being a sounding board. Thank you for taking your time to read through my books and help me see things that the readers will that I cannot. I am blessed to have you in my life.

Thank you to Lindsey. God knew that we would one day be friends and he knew that we would be kindred spirits. You are such an encouragement to me and I know you don't realize it. Thank you for all the funny texts that get me through tough days. And all the amazing food you feed me.

Thank you to Amy. You're an amazing beta reader, and I am so thankful that you care so much about these characters that you're willing to read through each book multiple times to help me find errors, continuity issues, and character descriptions...that are in fact not anywhere to be found because I forget to describe characters all the time. Thank you for your patience with me.

And thank you to the readers. Thank you to the wolf pack. Thank you to the ladies who constantly encourage me, pray for me and my family, send me cards, letters and gifts. It never ceases to amaze me that you all care so much about my books and about my family. You are the reason Bo and I are able to do what we do. There aren't enough 'thank you's' to say for all you guys have done for me.

About the Author

Quinn Loftis is a multi-award-winning author of over thirty five novels, including the USA Today Bestseller, Fate and Fury. When she isn't creating exciting worlds filled with romantic werewolves, she exercises, reads, and crafts like there's no tomorrow. She is blessed to be married to her best friend for over twenty years and they have three sons, a crazy French bulldog, and a cat that wants to take over the world.

QUINN'S BOOKSHELF

The Grey Wolves Series

The Gypsy Healer Series

The Elfin Series

The Dream Maker Series

The Clan Hakon Series

Nature Hunters Academy

Sign up for Quinn's newsletter here:

You can also find Quinn writing contemporary romances as her alter ego, Alyson Drake.

https://www.quinnloftisbooks.com/alysondrake

9 798446 288199